Wind in the Wires

JANET CHESTER BLY

A TRAILS OF REBA CAHILL NOVEL
Book 1

ACKNOWLEDGEMENTS:

Any other adult fiction I've done has been co-authored with either my late husband, Stephen Bly, or with my three sons--Russell, Michael, and Aaron. We finished Stephen's last novel for him, *Stuart Brannon's Final Shot*, a Selah Award Finalist. *Wind in the Wires* is my first solo adult novel. And yet, that's not entirely true. That is, the solo part. So many people have added input to help me complete this story. I will try to name as many of them as possible. I am so grateful to each and every one. I've listed them in alphabetical order...

Michelle Bly, feedback on cover, Model T details, full manuscript critique

Mike Bly, feedback on cover, Model T details, full manuscript critique

Jan Grueter, full manuscript copyedit

Rachel Hauck, critique and mentoring of synopsis, opening pages, and story concept

Kathy Ide, critique and edit of opening pages

Connie Sue Larson, who encouraged me every step and never doubted I could complete it

Lisa McDonald, Model T owner and advisor

Ken Raney, cover and manuscript design

Lin Thomas, Model T owner and advisor

Many thanks also to those who graciously considered early stage opening pages and provided commentary: Julie Anne Agen, Angela E. Arndt, Edward L. Arrington, Jr., Gail Denham, Tim Dorgan, Richard Fleming, Anna M. Gregory, Ramona (Mona) Lowder, Shannon McNear, Brenda Morgan, Kathleen Roberts-Heppner, Connie Sue Larson, Judith Walston, Pat Wambold

And a huge, heart-felt gratitude to my Heavenly Father, who gave me the spark of a writing gift and the grit and gumption to persevere until completion of this project.

To Him all the glory!

Chapter One

She must find the runaway heifer. And get to Maidie's funeral on time.

Reba Mae Cahill urged her black quarter horse to trudge through the spring green, muddy terrain. Recent rains and snowmelt gummed the pine-dotted, wild flower sprayed high mountain prairie. Puddles and small ponds, tall grass and shadows made search tedious. Johnny Poe stalled.

"Come on, boy, Don said he saw her near here. Got to find that cow before Champ Runcie does. And return home quick."

They rode the moss-covered wood post and barbed wire fence line as she checked the steel stays. A strong whoosh of wind made a ringing sound in the wires. She scanned the long length of Runcie Ranch fencing. Her glance caught at a break in the fence next to stacked tires filled with large rocks supposed to hold the fence in place. Certainly enough space for a moon-eyed, red bovine stray to escape. She peered closer and spied a cut at all five lines, now splayed on the ground. Why would anyone do that?

She slid down from Johnny Poe, pulled on leather gloves from her saddlebag, and eased the wire out of the way. A long strand was missing.

A quick image of a testy Champ flashed before her. Not the first time, she wished the Runcie and Cahill Ranches didn't butt against each other, with so many borders in common. Especially when one side determined not to be too neighborly. "Women, especially Cahill women, don't have what it takes to manage a ranch like theirs on their own," she could hear Champ say.

Reba backed the horse up to get him prepped to ease through the opening. He balked, as she knew he would. She flicked the reins. His ears flayed back. He reared and pawed the air. Reba hit the muddy pasture ground hard on her rear. Pain shot through as she scrambled to her feet and reached for the saddle. She glided on the old leather before he could bolt and cooed at him. "Come on, Johnny Poe, it's going to be alright. Please try. A step at a time."

She imagined what must loom in his mind. Memories of his mother dying, gashed and twisted from withers to poll in a barbed wire fence. Found as a colt by her side. His fear had a firm basis. She patted his neck. "We've got to cross over. We can do this. We *have* to do this. And now."

Johnny Poe snorted and dropped his head as if he'd surrendered to her command, but she knew better. Reba nudged him to a spot a few feet from the fence. "It's okay. Don't be afraid. That wire's not going to hurt you. I'll take care of you."

The horse breathed out, flaring his nostrils, and turned to her like he understood. "Go. Face your fear." He ambled forward. "Good boy."

They crossed a dirt roadway that passed through both pine forest and prairie wheat fields. She heard moos and spied the Cahill Ranch heifer stuck halfway down a Runcie Ranch incline. As they closed in, Reba noticed the cow breathing heavy, head down. Like she was in hard labor.

In May? Surely you wouldn't do this to me.

Not the time of year when Cahill bovine delivered their calves. In October and February, Reba and her grandmother spent most of their days in the stable nursery. Out here she had no disinfectant. No Vaseline. No cozy shed. Only a weedy, scratchy mud hole for a stable. Another reason she couldn't do this ranch by herself.

I can't oversee it all. A first-time, two-year-old mama? An out-of-season pregnancy? The worst kind of birth.

Just like mine?

White circles framed the cow's bulging eyes and dark pools reflected fear and pain. A coyote howled from the draw, heightening the cow's quick, frantic pants as she attempted to raise up. Pain more than fear slit her dark, round eyes. The sound of water rushing over rocks sent Reba's gaze beyond the heifer to Broken Arrow Creek. If the crazed expectant mother charged for that water, she'd drown her newborn the moment it delivered. Poison ivy and a crisscross of debris and brush booby-trapped the slope and creek bank.

How much worse can this situation get? Reba glanced at her watch. "I've got to contact Grandma. I'm not going to get to the funeral on time."

Reba slid off her horse, dropped his reins to the ground, and reached into the saddlebag. She grabbed a walkie-talkie, pulled up the antenna, and pushed the talk button. "Grandma? Reba here. Got some trouble. Over and out." She released the button and stuck the portable radio closer to her ear to detect the hiss of static or her grandmother's voice. She heard neither. She shook the handheld device and tried again. No connection. She slapped it back into the bag and tried hard not to blurt out the words she was thinking.

She scowled at both the frenzied heifer and her skittish horse. She tied a rope to Johnny Poe's saddle horn and worked her way with care through the weeds and mud down to the cow. Times like this, she missed Grandma Pearl something fierce. The past year, she wasn't strong enough to do much of the physical work, what with her knees or hip buckling whenever she overdid. But she could provide advice and a calming influence. They worked the ranch well together. In fact, they had done very well, just the two of them, since they lost Grandpa Cahill.

"The Dynamic Dudettes," half-brother Michael called them.

Reba remembered her grandmother brag, "My granddaughter

can wrangle cows and break horses as good or better than I can."

And Reba loved the freedom and fulfillment of hardy outdoor work. But Reba began to realize the last few months Cahill Ranch may be too much for one woman to work mostly alone. They needed a full-time ranch hand. Or a rancher husband. Someone who would understand the connection to family land and to this lifestyle. That would work.

When Michael Cahill showed up three years before and right after Grandpa Cahill's funeral, claiming to be Reba's younger half-brother, she'd hoped he might take on some ranch duties. But he was more interested in blondes, painting, and drums. He wanted to be an artist. Or a drummer for a rock band.

"Ranching is lonely work. Cows don't have souls. You can see it in their eyes," he told her.

Kneeling in the pungent weeds, Reba stroked the heifer's head and down the magenta coat. She slowly reached inside. One tiny hoof was hung up. The mama's tight muscles fought against her intrusion.

Like last spring.

A calf died before Reba could pull it. She had to cut out the still-born animal, piece by bloody piece.

Please, God, not again.

Clouds covered the sun, graying the landscape, and a breeze kicked up. Reba had sweaty palms and shivered at the same time, as the cow pushed. Reba grabbed the calf's feet, and tugged as hard as she could. The heifer let out a bellow like a long, low train whistle. They both gave a heave and the dazed calf fell into the muck. A black Angus calf born to a white-faced red mama. The unexpected timing made sense. The heifer had been courted by a Runcie Ranch bull. There would be words over this. On both sides.

She heard a rattle up on the road and an engine idle. She jerked around, half-expecting stern Champ Runcie to stand on top, bawling out accusations about the broken fence and trespass. She waited a moment, a hitch in her stomach, trying to think of what to say. Soon a male figure appeared.

Reba shook with relief. "Don! I'm so glad to see you."

"Have you called your grandma?"

"I tried to. No luck."

"Hold on. I'll be right back. There's better reception down the road apiece. I know she'll be frantic to know where you are."

"Thank you so much."

He turned and she heard the pickup drive away.

Widower Don Runcie, Champ's son, telephoned earlier to warn her of the errant heifer on their property. Her heart warmed at his concern that provided a chance to rescue the cow before Champ discovered it. This proved as much as anything his feelings for her. Perhaps their two recent dates had softened him a bit to her side of the Runcie-Cahill feud. However, she wondered what Champ thought of them as a twosome.

Her grandmother certainly hadn't minced her disapproval. "He's old enough to be your father," Pearl chided.

"We went to a movie and danced some at the Grange Hall. That's all." *And he's a rancher.*

"Almost every dance. Everyone in town is talking."

"Is that what you're worried about?"

Grandma pursed her lips tight like she was afraid to say too much. "You can do better than that," she concluded.

Not likely in Road's End, population 400. She'd certainly looked the field of possible contenders over many times from her cowgirl perch. Those rare few bachelors near her age were either divorced and in custody fights or not the ranch work type. Like the McKane brothers who recently moved from California. Jace and Norden bought and ran The Outfitters Shop as a kind of hobby, best she could tell. Jace made his money in software programs and wanted to play at wilderness living. Not her type at all.

"I want a guy to help run our ranch," Reba confided to Pearl and her best friend, Ginny George. Dependable. Faithful. Not with his career focus and dreams elsewhere. "And he cannot be the type to abandon me." *Or our children.* "He will be fully committed and sold out to the rancher lifestyle. Just like Grandpa Cahill." Didn't Don fit that description? A plus on her private Dating Don List.

She thought she had that with Tim Runcie, who was Don's son and her high school sweetheart. At least, she thought so. What a perfect pairing. Everyone seemed to agree. Except, as it turned out, her best friend Sue Anne Whitlow.

She took off her denim jacket, yanked it inside out and wiped herself and the wet clump of calf legs with the wool lining. She stuck a finger in and cleared the newborn's throat and mouth and shoved the baby bundle against the cow's nose. Then the heifer's mothering light flipped on. She mooed and rough-tongued her babe clean.

Reba tensed, mesmerized, as she often did at similar scenes. A hazy picture of her mom popped in her mind. Shaggy, long sable brown and streaked blond hair. Teasing smile. Circling a barrel on a buckskin horse at a rodeo. She'd seen a few photos in a scrapbook and had a framed one tucked face down in her bottom dresser drawer, but couldn't scrounge up live memories of her own. Abandoned at the Cahill Ranch at age three left her with the pain of an "I am not important...I am not of value" message.

She tried hard to avoid the questions that stole in. Did her mother know about Maidie's death? Will she show up at the funeral? Grandma Pearl revealed how her mother Hanna Jo and Maidie grew close over the years. Even Reba spent a lot of time at Maidie's house. Pearl told her stories of the times Hanna Jo tended to Maidie during some of her sick spells. As Reba did with her guitar playing.

"Your mother showed care-giving skills in her early teens," Grandma said. "I thought sure she'd become a nurse."

She sure hadn't cared enough to look after Reba. How could her mom run away from her family and duty? The thought erupted unbidden like a dark, unprotected wound.

And why would she come to the funeral today? She hadn't made an appearance at Grandpa Cahill's service, her own father. She looked again at her watch. "I may not make it to Maidie's either. Where is Don? He arrived like the cavalry and disappeared like Custer."

Reba tried to direct the calf to its mother's udders. But it showed no interest in nursing. "Come on, little one. You've got to eat. Aren't you hungry after all that squeezin' out of your mama?" She tried again and again without success.

The newborn quivered. Reba wrapped her jacket around it, the cleaner side against its skin. Then she stood and faced the mama cow. "Recovery time is over," she hollered. "You have a hill to climb."

The heifer groaned to her feet and took a few steps. Reba grabbed the end of the rope she'd tied onto Johnny Poe's saddle horn and looped it around the new mother's neck. When she jerked on it, Johnny Poe backed up and tugged it taut.

The sound of an engine pierced the mountain air. She peered at the front end of Don's pickup on the ridge above, tires splaying mud, too close to the horse.

"Watch out," Reba yelled.

Johnny Poe reared and raised so high the rope yanked and twitched free. Reba lunged for the cow as she tumbled and scooted into the bulging river. "No!" she screamed, as she bound after her. "You can't drown. Help! Don, please help!" Panic stretched across her chest and froze somewhere in her lungs. "Help!" she rasped again, barely above a whisper. She had to save that mama cow.

She splashed into the creek, boots and all, and reached for the floating rope, the line to life. Everything in her rebelled against the possibility a creature who had just gone through the agony of birth to a sickly, needy babe would now drown without a chance to care for the little one. After a slippery plunge beneath the surface, Reba grabbed traction with her boots on the bottom. The heifer's head burst above water and she bellowed in distress.

Reba raced to the bank, keeping her eyes on the cow's current-drifting pace. She could hear the calf blurt a weak cry. She twisted to see him try to get on his feet. *That's good.*

After another dip, Reba managed to pull the free end of the rope out of the water and tugged as hard as she could. In a flash, strong arms encased her with warmth and comfort and pulled her and the rope to the bank. She didn't resist the protection and assistance offered. With Don at her side and some hefty repeated yanks, the mother lumbered toward them and collapsed a few yards away. Reba trembled both inward and outward in a confusion of emotions. Relief over the heifer. Not wanting to leave the cocoon of Don's arms.

"Thanks so very much." Reba dropped, panting, as her teeth chattered.

"Don't thank me too much. Your horse escaped."

"Why didn't you go after him?"

"He was okay and you weren't. Besides, I don't think that horse likes me much. I've never been able to get near him without the threat of a vicious kick. My dad too. And Tim. He's got a thing against Runcies, I guess."

Is that a sign? The former warm feelings of camaraderie, teamwork, and maybe something more turned to a chill. "Do you know where he's headed?"

"Toward Coyote Canyon, looked like to me."

"I guess I'll chase him later." Reba tried not to show her dismay. She focused on getting to the funeral. "Help me get these two out of here."

He handed her a canteen. "That I can do. Never been a downed cow I couldn't get up." He lifted his head. "Even up a hill."

She filled the canteen at the creek. "I'll carry the calf."

"No, you won't. Get up there and I'll bring him to you."

Reba stiffened at the command. He sounded and looked a lot like Champ in that moment. But when Reba started to protest, her alarm increased for the listless, puny babe splayed on the ground. She gently rubbed drops of water on its mouth as its head drooped.

Don draped the limpid calf across his shoulders and stumped up the incline while Reba followed. A raging war grew inside her. Should she have insisted on carrying the calf herself? Was Don going to claim ownership of the calf, on behalf of Runcie Ranch? She was reminded again how nice it would be to have a capable man on the ranch. She looked ahead and admired his muscular, confident stride.

Don would make someone a good rancher husband, as he already had once with schoolteacher Marge Runcie. *Reba Runcie, that has a ring to it.* She imagined him at her side, plowing the fallow Cahill ground back into wheat fields or buying more cattle at auctions.

Reba cradled the calf and watched from the top as Don below worked to nudge the downed bovine, all one thousand immoveable pounds of her, to get up and go. If they had more time and materials available, they could manufacture a primitive sling to drag and hoist the heifer. "How inconsiderate of your Mama to go down at the bottom of a hill," she told the calf.

"Stop your muttering up there and give me some ideas," Don shouted.

So much for romantic fantasies. "Try to push her."

"She's too fat. What do you feed these cows of yours?"

Road's End pasture, same as you. "Then scare her."

Don stood straight and howled like a coyote. The heifer's eyes got wild, but she didn't move. He kept howling.

Reba didn't know whether to be impressed or amused. She craned around the calf to look at her watch. She began to pray for God and his angels to move that cow, though she knew the heifer would get up when she was good and ready, and not before. "Try yanking her tail. Come on, we've got to go."

Don pinched her ear and pulled back hard on her tail three separate times. Just when they presumed this failed too, she heaved her hulk of a self off the ground as though it were no big deal and moseyed up the hill. Reba set the calf down in hopes he and the mama would connect. He bawled something pitiful and attempted a wobble on three legs. Reba scooped the critter into her arms again and swabbed its lips with water drops. Its eyes closed, legs hung limp, and ears drooped. "This calf is not well. He needs a warm tub bath."

It took both of them to corral the heifer through the barbed fence at the broken line. She and Don pulled back the spliced pieces as best they could.

"You do notice this has been cut," Reba remarked.

"Did you do it? Or your grandmother?"

"Of course not. That's ridiculous. Why did you say that?"

"Because Dad will ask me. This part of the fencing is closest to your ranch."

"But we have no possible motive." Reba shook against the sharp stab of accusation and the discomfort of confusion. *What is going on?*

As the heifer headed into Cahill Ranch pasture, Reba tucked the calf on the front bench seat of Don's pickup and helped him repair the fence. They crawled into the truck with muddy boots, stained jeans, and torn shirts.

"If we go like we are, we'll be only a few minutes late." Reba tried to imagine her grandmother's reaction to her showing up at Maidie's service looking like something the pigs drug to the pen. They might be backwoods ranch folks, but Pearl Cahill insisted on looking cleaned up at social events.

"You look like a drowned fox. A red one, of course. A very cute one."

"Are you flirting with me?"

He grinned, his rugged face relaxed. "Just stating an obvious fact."

Reba scooted the jacket wrapped calf between them. "I had a clean rag in my saddlebag. Have you got anything like that in here?"

"Open the glove compartment."

She pulled out a large, folded piece of white cotton.

"An old t-shirt of Tim's. Do what you can. I'm sure he won't mind."

But I will. She smelled Lava soup and Tide detergent and something else not so clean, but pleasant. She didn't know how she could explain it was impossible to use Tim's shirt, to rub it against her skin. Tim Runcie, a classmate, her first and only real boyfriend. The guy who married her best girlfriend, Sue Anne Whitlow. And a reminder of at least one awkward part of dating Don.

The clouds cleared and a bright sunbeam sprayed through the scattered Douglas fir and ponderosa pines. "Thanks, but that's okay. Just get me home quick. This calf has to be fed."

The truck bumped over the three miles of unpaved road to the Cahill homestead as Reba held on tight to the calf and the truck door. They rolled past charred remnants of a cabin, struck by lightning and burned to the ground. A wooden water tower for an old logging camp at the end of a former railroad spur sagged and leaned so far as though a gentle push would topple it.

A bevy of twenty quails scurried across the road in front of them. They slowed and passed a guy on the roadside in pullover shirt, Bermuda shorts, and deck shoes changing a flat tire on a brand new '91 silver Volvo.

Don rolled down his window.

"Don't stop," Reba said. "We don't have time."

The man turned around and Reba recognized Jace McKane, one of their newest citizens. In his thirties with blond boyish good looks, he looked nothing like his dark and ruddy younger brother, Norden. "Thanks, Mr. Runcie. I'm doing fine. I'm real used to this."

Mr. Runcie? Even Don's dad was called Champ by everyone.

They drove on, in sight of the Cahill driveway turnoff.

"I've seen him tinkering with his car before. Must be a lemon," Don said.

"I hear he's got plenty of money. Why doesn't he just buy a different car that's not a lemon?"

"Must be attached to that one."

As they turned right onto Stroud Ranch Road and another right onto the Cahill driveway, Reba leaned over the calf. "Oh, dear."

"What's the matter?"

Reba checked her charge for signs of revival. At her touch, a muscle moved and he slit open one eye. She dabbed him with water again. "I'm glad we're almost there."

They passed Grandpa Cahill's sprawling mutant Camperdown Elm.

Reba caught sight of a red Jaguar parked behind the bunkhouse. *Who in the world does that belong to?*

Reba hugged the calf close as she slipped out of the cab. Tied to the front porch, Paunch and Aussie, Grandma Pearl's Blue Heelers, eyed them with disinterest. Scat the long-haired calico cat crouched nearby, ever watching, always alert.

Don gestured at her. "I'm going to head home and clean up. If I miss the main service, I'll see you at the graveside later."

"Oh, wait. Here's your canteen."

"Keep it. I'll get it later." He grinned. "Good excuse to see you again." He backed down the driveway.

As Reba eased up the steps in front of the house, Pearl rushed over. Salt-and-pepper hair pulled back in a twist, lips touched with soft pink, dressed in black denim western cut pantsuit and her Sunday best Nochona black leather boots. And eyes squinted in worry. "Reba, you okay?"

"Besides being covered with mud and cow blood, just fine."

Pearl checked the calf. "Get him on a bottle immediately."

"He wouldn't nurse."

"The funeral's running a bit late anyway. I'll do what I can. You get yourself decent." The calf's ears drooped when she picked him up.

Reba knew that look of her grandmother's, steely resignation. "You don't think he's going to make it, do you?"

"The good news is, the vet is here for the funeral. He'll get Dr. Whey's immediate attention." Pearl wheeled around and called out to the first person she saw. "Joe! Joe Bosch, go to the barn and get Olga Whey. Send her here to the house. Emergency calf care needed."

Joe Bosch, Runcie ranch hand, arrived for the service looking stiff and rigid with brown hair slicked down, dressed in navy blue suit, navy striped tie and matching kerchief-stuffed pocket. He tipped his hat at Grandma Pearl and muttered a polite, "Yes, Ma'am."

As he sprinted to the barn, Reba swallowed and tried to smile. "The heifer's safely in our pasture and... Johnny Poe ran away." Reba couldn't interpret her grandmother's response beyond an expected frown. At least she had given her the full report.

She headed for her bedroom and stopped when she heard strains of Bette Midler singing "Wind Beneath My Wings" from the guest room. She stepped closer and wafts of a scent like musk and mulberry misted the hall.

The door from the bathroom at the hall's end opened wide and Pearl appeared. "I forgot to tell you Ginny arrived from California."

"My Ginny? Ginny George Nicoli?"

Pearl nodded.

The music stopped at "I can fly higher than an eagle" when she knocked. With a swish of shoulder-length, corkscrew dark curls and a sweep of black and purple faille, out popped the gal with skin like she'd rubbed it in walnut oil and buffed it to a gloss. She swept up Reba and swung her around. "Surprise! So good to see you, Reba Mae."

"Watch out. I'll mess you all up."

"Don't worry. I brought lots of changes."

"I believe that, but I can't believe you're here." Reba felt as elated as when she'd given up finding elk on a season's last trip she stumbled onto a large herd. "You didn't mention a word about coming to Idaho on our last phone call." Reba thought hard. "Did you?"

"No, it was a last-minute decision. I decided to give myself some time off, the benefits of working for a family business. Good grief, girl, you look like sunburned spit."

"I've been birthing a calf." Reba peered down the hall at the bathroom and closed door. "The red Jaguar. Is that yours?"

"Yep. I drove twenty hours straight."

"You must be beyond exhausted."

"I'll catch up later. I had to be here for Seth and Maidie. And you. And there were other reasons." She squeezed a sad face. "I still can't fathom she's gone. She and Seth have been like fixtures here, like the Hanging Tree, and Champ and your grandma. I can't imagine Road's End without her."

I'd like to see Road's End without Champ. "Yes, they are Road's End. Just like Grandpa was too." A sudden depression gripped Reba. Life and love so fleeting. And all will die.

But Ginny nudged her. "Now, hurry. We've got to get you to the barn on time."

"Too late. We're already fifteen minutes overdue."

"We've been given another fifteen minute extension, by order of Pearl Cahill, the head honcho around here."

"Unless Champ Runcie's on the premises."

"Oh, he is. He and your grandma were exchanging terse words when I arrived. Something to do with his part in the service."

Please, Champ, leave us alone for once. "Grandma suspects he's going to try political posturing at the funeral. She's been firm with him this service is about Maidie and nothing else."

"Like what would he do?"

"Oh, give a stump speech for his re-election as mayor, something like that." Anything to mix it up and mess it up for Pearl and Reba. But, why bother? He had no opponents. He was a shoo-in.

Dr. Olga Whey burst into the house in navy polyester and pumps, carrying a black medical bag, straight brunette hair flowing. Reba pointed her to the bathroom. "I don't think I'm going to get a bath or shower," she informed Ginny as Dr. Whey squeezed by.

"Go out in the backyard and I'll hose you down like we did as kids."

"Okay, but this time with my clothes on."

"And then they come off." She opened a closet door in the guest room. A half dozen outfits hung there that Reba presumed as very expensive. Charcoal gray silky pajamas, a rose pink pantsuit and teal green caftan scattered across the bed.

"You know we don't wear the same size."

"But one of my scarves or jewelry will brighten up whatever little thing you put on."

"And you know I rarely wear jewelry."

Ginny sighed. "How did we ever become best buds?"

Reba snickered as she peered into her bedroom mirror at the tangle of pine needles and cobwebs in her auburn hair. Bloody dung streaked her face. *No wonder you're still single at age twenty-five.*

After a quick backyard hose shower, she changed into a blousy, v-neck black pullover dress and black flats. She blow-dried her straight hair and shook it out.

Pearl Cahill stomped down the hall. "Olga's going to stay with the calf, bless her heart. She gave him electrolytes and Sulpha pills. All we can do is wait and pray. I'm going to the barn."

Reba peeked in on the calf sprawled in the footed tub. At least his eyes were open. "I'm sorry you have to miss the service. Thank you so much."

Dr. Whey shrugged. "It's what I do."

Reba knocked and scooted the guest room door open. Ginny had changed into a brown suede skirt with brown velvet blazer and brown heels with crisscross straps. "The hug stained my black. This will have to do." She looked Reba over and pulled button pearl earrings, a single-strand pearl necklace and a black and cream scarf from her suitcase. "Simple and classy. You'll look great. And it's nothing garish, so don't fuss at me."

Reba smiled. "I wouldn't think of it. Put them on. Dress me up like a doll, just like you used to."

Ginny snapped the necklace and earrings on and draped the

scarf straight without a tie.

Reba touched her ears and the pearls. "I'm so glad you're here."

Ginny admired her touches with a twirl around her. "You're good. Let's go!"

Reba picked up her guitar case as she and Ginny hiked the half-mile to the barn. "You going to sing?"

"Grandma insisted. I often sang for Maidie when she had one of her spells. Seemed to calm her down. Do you ever get a chance to play your harp?"

"Not really. I've got it in storage. Takes up too much room in our apartment. Seth must feel so alone without Maidie, after all these years taking care of her. Such dedication for his special needs niece."

"Grandma and I will look in on him as often as we can. He's going to speak at the service and he's real nervous. I promised to provide him support."

"We still have the toys Seth carved for me and my brothers back when we lived in Road's End."

"Most everyone in town has something Seth made for them." They passed Seth Stroud's Ford Model T., and assorted pickups, SUVs, and motorcycles cluttered around the Cahill Ranch pasture. Reba pushed into the barn and gasped.

Chapter Two

A huge crowd of mourners chatted in hushed, reverent tones. The death of Maidie Fortress crammed hundreds of Road's End residents in the barn that also served as the town's only church sanctuary. Horse flies buzzed the intruders like bombardiers on a mission. High voltage lights overhead shone from naked bulbs. Folding chairs borrowed from homes and businesses crammed into rows of fours with aisles. Instead of the usual collapsible metal music stand for a pulpit, Lloyd Younger stained and varnished a rustic podium and platform made from barn boards. Two large wicker stands of purple and white iris decorated each side of the platform.

Reba waved at brother Michael and did a quick study of his new bleached blonde. Pretty as usual. Good posture. Friendly smile. Reba noticed Ginny eyeing the gal as well and they exchanged a private glance. Where did he find so many different girlfriends in this backwoods region? Reba found the pickings slim.

More than the usual Sunday morning congregation of twenty-five gathered, even though that meant pressed cotton western shirts, polished boots, and stiff Wranglers. And in spite of the fact the past couple decades reclusive Maidie mainly bunkered in her cabin unless she ventured out to her garden. Between Polly Eng and Maidie Fortress, they cultivated spectacular vegetable and flower gardens.

"Road's End could sell tickets for tourists to see them," Cicely Bowers suggested more than once when the city park needed renovation.

Maidie did get out when Seth cranked up his Model T to do their errands and shopping and on occasion he took Maidie for rides in the country. Seth waved at everyone, but shy and withdrawn Maidie rarely did. However, sometimes a flute solo could be heard soaring from her cabin balcony. A number from *Swan Lake* or *Dance of the Sugar Plum Fairy*.

Reba sighted Seth leaning against Pearl, his bent shoulders and wrinkled face confirming his ninety-one years.

Each of the town's folk had his or her way of showing respect for the loss of one of their own, as much for Seth as for Maidie.

Lisl Monte flew the post office flag at half-mast.

Tucker Paddy sobered up for three days in a row.

Beatrice Mathwig, one of the hotel manager widow triplets, took to having one of her cranky fits and got the whole town cleaned with mowed lawns and junk piles hauled away.

And the town kids tied the Hanging Tree with lavender ribbons to contrast with frayed yellow satin bows displayed in honor of Gulf War soldiers, as though they hadn't learned the war was over and the heroes had come home.

But the service still hadn't begun. So Champ running for his tenth term as mayor shook everyone's hand as they entered and again after everyone sat down. Ushers Lloyd Younger and Franklin Fraley scurried around for extra seating for eight members of the Thomas Hawk family of the Nez Perce tribe and guided a few last stragglers like Jace and Norden McKane into random empty chairs.

"I'll go sit next to one of those gentlemen," Ginny whispered. "I know you need to be on the platform with Seth and your grandma."

Before Reba could object, Ginny whisked a folded chair that leaned against a barn wall and set it up in an aisle beside Jace. He had traded his usual Bermuda shorts for tan slacks with an open yellow striped long-sleeved shirt and no tie. Of all the people in this crowded barn she could have chosen to sit by, Reba wondered why that one? He was new in town. She didn't even know him.

Reba worked her way to the platform as she continued to survey the crowd. She brightened at the sight of her grandparents' long-time friend, mine investor and bachelor Vincent Quaid of Boise. He was the grandpa she lost, the dad she never knew. Sometimes they didn't need to talk. They could communicate without words. His puckered smile and nod contained sincere sympathy for their loss.

Next to him, Cicely Bowers from Seattle who ran a bed and breakfast in her home, the only woman wearing a hat and a big, floppy black and yellow one. A woman older than Reba and with redder hair in a black beret leaned into Cicely. Trish, the visiting niece with the bumpy past.

Reba half-expected to see Champ's two eldest sons, Richard and Randall. They and brother Don didn't resemble each other much except for the tendency to reddish highlights in their dark brown hair, like Champ had in his younger years. Prodigals to Champ because they left the ranch, they were successful Coeur d'Alene businessmen to everyone else.

Don who managed to arrive spiffed up in a black sport coat sat next to his grandkids, three-year-old William and Kaitlyn, six, looking like a lost puppy. Grandma Pearl started the barn church soon after his wife's funeral. She imagined Marge beside Don, resolute and resigned, with her thick brunette hair in short waves and ready smile. A Spokane city girl who fit into Road's End as the elementary schoolteacher, her students adored her, including Reba and Ginny back in their elementary days.

How could Reba possibly take her place? How could she bear having Champ for a father-in-law? And Tim as a stepson? *How weird is that?* Reba noted three minuses on her mental Dating Don List.

She stole a peek at Tim. He whispered something in his wife's ear. Sue Ann flinched, scowled, and then smiled. Reba admired her new hairdo. Long blond hair cut in a stylish, mature, chiseled upsweep. Made her look old enough to be a mother.

Reba finally made it to the platform and stepped up. Pearl directed her to sit next to Seth. She hugged the old man and scooted her guitar under her chair. Pearl sat on the other side of her and then Champ.

Spruced up with pine cologne and gelled hair, Tucker Paddy began the service by playing a medley of heaven-as-home hymns with his acoustic guitar. He'd been asked by Seth to do the honors because Maidie considered him one of her few friends. He'd come to visit Seth with his guitar and the three of them would jam together. At the conclusion, he mumbled to Reba, "Is Hanna Jo coming?"

Reba shrugged. Her mom never showed for any event in over twenty years, and folks still thought she should be part of things. Even Don asked the same thing.

Seth joined Tucker's guitar with his fiddle for a duet of "I'll Fly Away." The aging marks of years seemed to melt as the elderly man energized the bow. His arthritic fingers struck and stroked the strings with apparent ease.

Reba affirmed Seth with a nod and smile. Amazing fiddle player at ninety-one. And he made that violin himself from cedar. *I wonder if he'd make me a guitar.* What a treasure that would be.

After Tucker slumped down on the platform, his legs hanging over the edge, the four seated themselves on the one portable pew at front stage: Pearl, Champ, Reba, and Seth. Many in the audience waved paper programs like fans. Reba rubbed Seth's arm as he began to shake.

"Are you okay?" Reba whispered.

"Yeah. I think I forget to eat today. Feelin' a bit weak."

Reba handed him some water.

Pearl marched to the podium. Her tough, leathery skin denoted a woman with strength who'd worked outdoors all her life, yet she wiped tears as she mentioned Maidie's name. Her firm, deep voice carried to every corner of the barn as she read from Psalms and Thessalonians.

Then Champ rose, tugged at his American flag bolo tie, and stomped forward. With cheek lines tight on his grim face, the sort that is stingy with smiles, and his farm-hardened body rigid, he pulled a sheet of paper from a coat pocket. He snapped open a pair of reading glasses to read the following obituary from the Bitterroot County Press:

Maidie Fortress was born November 15, 1912, in Goldfield, Nevada, to Billy Fortress and Molly Stroud Fortress. She died in Road's End, Idaho, on May 1, 1991. She moved with her uncle, Seth Fenton Stroud, and her grandfather, Moses Stroud, to Road's End in 1913. She was preceded in death by her grandparents, Moses and Eve Stroud; by her mother and father; and by her three aunts Lucina, Valmy and Radene Stroud. She is survived by her uncle and cousins Pearl Stroud Cahill and Reba Mae Cahill.

Reba tried to calculate. If Seth and Grandma Pearl were first cousins, what was she to Maidie? Third cousin? Fourth? She was family, though distant. That's all that mattered.

Champ continued, "From my earliest remembrance is a picture of Maidie wearing bright-colored smocks, usually purple, and making up silly rhymes. And at the oddest moments, she'd claim to hear church bells. I'm sure she's hearing them all the time right about now."

Reba envisioned Maidie in the light of beauty and with a whole mind. At the end, it was so sad. Maidie all skin and bones, her eyes wild like a wounded bird.

Champ looked around the barn and took a quick peek behind him. His eyes seemed to avert Pearl's. "First of all, I want to assure everyone I know the Westminster Confession and the Wesley Method, taught me by my parents, Uriah and Roberta Runcie."

"A Calvinistic Arminian?" Pearl whispered to Reba. "That explains a lot."

"I was baptized at three weeks old. But as I've told you often, we've been blessed here in Road's End. For many decades we had no need for a jail and no need for a church."

Reba sat straighter. Where was he going with this? Why was he making it all about him?

Tucker spit on the ground and called out, "Hey, Champ, I remember when you used to say we had no need for mayors either."

As the barn rumbled with laughter, Tucker stood up and twirled on the platform. His wife Ida marched up the aisle and pulled him down to a chair beside her.

One of the smaller Younger girls sitting in the middle of the throng tossed yellow and white silk rose petals from a paper bag, then blew air into it and stomped it with a loud bang. Her mother Ursula yanked her outside as the girl complained, "But, Mommy, it looked like it was time for the party."

Champ cracked a forced grin. "That's right, Tucker, but things change. We go with the demand of the times. And right now Road's End needs ..." He paused and smirked like a cheeky choir boy about to do a first solo. "... a genuine church building. And a real preacher. It's a shame and a sin our one church meets in a smelly barn." He took a deep breath and faked a gag. "More people would attend, including me and my house, if the setting was a bit sweeter."

He waited for the buzz of chatter to subside. "Road's End deserves a place where we can hang a Maidie Fortress memorial bell. And I'm going to see we get it." He stole another glance at Pearl who sat like stone except for her eyes blinking very fast. "And if there's no objection, I'll be glad to take on the duty as chairman of the committee."

A stunned Reba gawked at Champ. Outrage grew inside her. She studied her grandmother's glare and fully expected her to rise and shout a protest. *Champ's not even a church member. What right did he possess to dictate anything about what the folks at the church do? Or don't do. And certainly not at Maidie's funeral. What can he be thinking? He's over the edge.*

When her grandmother remained in her seat, Reba started to jump up to blurt out an objection, but scattered applause broke out and grew louder. Tucker strummed "Peace in the Valley" as Pearl grabbed hold of her hand and gave a tight shake of her head.

Reba had seen Pearl Cahill stand before the state legislature and speak out for tax relief for farmers and home schools. She mediated peace with Nez Perce tribal councils over reservation issues. She debated national representatives about wilderness boundaries. So why didn't she confront this brazen, arrogant, completely out of order man?

Champ shuffled off the podium and sat in the audience next to his wife, Blair. Her steel blue eyes pierced straight ahead, shoulders slumped, as though she suffered one of her migraines. A woman accustomed to coping with pain, she once told Pearl, "I went home to mother so many times, I finally told him I was tired of packing. He could go home to *his* mother."

Tucker finished his song and Pearl strode to the podium again. *What will she say?* Reba's stomach churned with anticipation.

"Thank you, Champ, for your part in this service and your interesting challenge. Most of you know about that first Sunday several years ago when we first met as a church in this barn." Pearl's eyes were wide and alert, her face and stance firm. "You were all invited. I personally made the rounds of the bars, Delbert's Diner, the Steak House, Paddy's Trailer Park, and the Quick Stop on the highway. I even made a special trip to the Runcie Ranch."

Everyone turned to Champ. He gave a quick nod of assent.

"And now, because of Maidie, I'm glad you all were able to come."

Nervous chuckles and sheepish grins flowed through the crowd. Reba held her breath.

Pearl opened her Bible. "This was one of Maidie's favorite verses from Psalm 55: 'He ransoms me unharmed from the battle waged against me, even though many oppose me. God, who is enthroned forever, will hear them and afflict them--men who never change their ways and have no fear of God.'" She panned the crowd before she continued. Some squirmed in their seats. Others frowned. Several had heads bowed and gave the impression of praying. Ginny and Jace had their heads together in fervent conversation. "And now Reba will sing one of Maidie's favorite songs."

She's not going to say a word about Champ's unprompted and out of line suggestions?

Reba fumbled for focus. She felt the sharp barb of disappointment. Her mouth chalky dry, the last thing she wanted to do was sing. Maybe this isn't the time and place. But neither was Champ's announcement. Is a church built by an unbeliever better than no church at all?

Sure wish I had some water.

She fumbled under her chair but couldn't feel the water bottle she'd stashed there. She found a peppermint in her purse and tucked it in her mouth against her cheek. She picked up her guitar, strummed an intro in minor chords, and began in her country western alto voice, "Amazing grace! How sweet the sound--That saved a wretch like me!" As she repeated the last refrain, "We've no less days to sing God's praise than when we'd first begun," Seth trudged to the front.

Stooped by sorrow and age, Seth grabbed the sides of the pulpit with both hands. His face had more lines than Champ's, but fuller, softer. Gray suspenders showed under his black suit coat. A tousle of silver hair flopped over his forehead. His eyes red but dry, he said a few words, firm with purpose, but very low.

Many strained forward to hear. Reba attached a cordless microphone the funeral home loaned them to his white shirt collar. He cleared his throat and began again. "As most of you know, Champ and I go way back. His older brother and I competed for newspaper customers on the streets of Goldfield, Nevada when we were boys." He and Champ locked stares for a moment. "But there's another story. Today I want to tell about two miracles that happened to me, both in the same day. One involved Maidie."

Champ startled everyone by bolting out of his chair. "I didn't know you were going to go there. No need for that."

Seth paid no attention to the interruption. He kept talking, his voice clear and strong. "In 1908, Papa barbered in Goldfield. That's why I took up the trade here in Road's End. A family tradition. But that's not what I'm here to talk about."

Seth waited and Champ finally sat down, but he leaned as far forward as he could. "Mama and my sisters prospected by themselves in a place she called Worthy, on the west side of the Montezuma hills, near Goldfield. Mama discovered an underground spring there. Her name was Eve and she made her own Garden of Eden in the dry, harsh desert."

Chairs scraped and necks craned as everyone scooted for a fuller view of Seth. Ginny stood in the aisle and snapped a few pictures.

Seth moved his hands to the center of the pulpit and clutched them together. "I got worried 'cause Mama hadn't come to town for her provisions, a week overdue. Papa assured me she'd show up soon, but he couldn't leave his shop. So ... on my own, I loaded two burros for Worthy. I waited until dusk, dark enough for the curious not to get my direction. I headed out. Way late into the night, I set camp in the sage cause it got real cold. My ears pained me so much I couldn't hear. Listening is crucial in the desert.

"As soon as a peep of light shined, I led the burros to the trail that veered up the mountain past some prospectors who weren't the friendly sort. All day I watched for the familiar signs. A shaggy head-shaped boulder. A forest of stubby pines and red dirt. A triple crown from the Silver Peak mountain range. Most of all, I listened for the sound of wind wailing in the wires."

Seth sipped from the water bottle Reba handed him. His hand shook, so Reba scooted closer and offered a silent prayer.

"Mama surrounded her place with six-strand barbed wire. The wind produced a low-to- high swirl and whoosh sound. The more gusts, the higher it got. But the air was so still I hardly had oxygen enough to breathe. Already, I was runnin' out of water. The good thing, I knew that was one thing Mama had plenty of in a land where water cost more than liquor." He took another drink.

Tucker whispered loud enough for Reba to hear. "I heard one time about a girl who got strangled with a piece of barbed wire."

"My eyes burned with strainin' to study the cliff sides. My ears rang with tryin' to hear something, anything. Finally, exhausted, I made camp again and tried to sleep. Before sunrise, the wind tore over the mountain. I couldn't walk against the fierce gale. So, I buried my head in my coat to keep the grit out. When it quieted down, I tried to walk, but my legs gave out. I was so weak I sprawled on the ground and didn't move. Then I heard something. A whirring noise, a *whip, whip, whip* kind of tone."

He began to sag and Reba pushed a chair beside the podium. He slumped into it.

"Music it was. I thought God Himself was singin' hymns, it was that sweet."

"Bring me my fiddle." Reba handed it over. "It sounded a bit like this." He hovered over a few strings and made them moan and whine like a squall, up a half scale.

Reba heard a hissing sound and darted her attention back to the vicinity of where Champ sat. He glared at Seth so fierce she wondered if he would stomp to the podium again. *But why is he so agitated?*

He set the instrument on his lap. "I scratched and pulled my arms and legs best I could, till I shimmied to the cliff and scooted down. I near rammed into the barbs, it was so close. I yelled for Mama and my sisters, but my voice croaked so bad.

"Layin' there, helpless, I did something I'd never done before. 'Help, God,' I cried. And He provided. Cain't nobody tell me otherwise. I felt delicious air in my nostrils, punchin' breath back into me. I gathered so much strength, I crawled up the hill for my canteen. I slurped the last swallow of water, as wet and refreshing as I ever tasted. I gave thanks to the Being who'd saved me. That was the first miracle."

Seth leaned back in the chair. Reba held the water to his lips. He trembled as he sipped and waved it away.

"You okay?" Reba whispered.

He nodded and inhaled. "I called for Mama as I ran down the trail, so she'd know not to shoot me, but no one came." He paused for another breath. "I could hardly wait to hug Mama and show her I'd brought her some goods. I stopped at the dugout entrance. The sun blazed on my back and I couldn't see inside the small window slits.

"Then I heard a strange sound, like sobbing. It was much like the wires, but more human and I turned in every direction to search for the source." Seth peered around as though he saw the scene again. "A canvas tent awning flapped open. Weavin' beside it, hands clutched to a pole, was Molly, my oldest sister. Her long hair streamed as she called out somethin', delirious-like.

"'Where's Mama?' I shouted. I scooted past her and squeezed into the tent. When my eyes adjusted, I saw the infant lyin' flat and still, eyes glazed. I thought she was dead. 'Mama!' I screamed and started to massage the hushed chest of the little one, then her stiff arms and legs. I didn't know what else to do. I stroked the bloodless skin till my nerves ached. I prayed again for the second time in my life and in the same day." Sweat beaded on the old man's forehead.

Reba forgot where she was and who else was with her, she was so focused on Seth.

"Again, God had mercy on me. The baby's lashes fluttered and pinkness swirled into the precious cheeks. I snuggled her into my arms and raced to the creek to smooth drops on her lips. She closed her eyes and seemed to drift asleep. I didn't know whether to wake her or not. I kept swipin' her mouth with moisture as I peered around for sight of Mama or my other sisters, Lucina, Valmy, and Radene." Seth's eyes shone with intense light. "All I could think of was, where is Eve and her children?

"After awhile, the baby cried. It was a puny kind of cry, but a welcome sound." Seth let out a deep sigh. "That infant survived and she was my Maidie." After a moment, Seth ended with, "And last week I again saw her flat, still, and glazed. This time she sat in her chair. No amount of stroking could bring her back. She was gone."

He motioned to Reba and began to rise from the chair.

Is that all he's going to say? What happened next? Where were his mother and other sisters? What became of Molly? Reba suspected everyone in the crowd wondered the same thing, but she didn't push Seth to continue. Instead, she helped him back to the pew on the podium.

Pearl stood up. "Thank you, Seth. We all appreciate your sharing your story. Perhaps you can tell us more sometime." She smiled at him and announced, "The graveside service will be held at the Mosquito Ridge Cemetery, as soon as we can get there. Everyone's invited to stay afterward for lunch at the Grange Hall."

She gave the benediction. "Glory be to the Father, and to the Son, and to the Holy Spirit. As it was in the beginning, is now, and ever shall be, world without end. Amen and Amen."

The funeral home director opened the casket and ushers Lloyd and Franklin led people forward, row by row. They walked by the waxen form lying on a silk pillow, resting place.

Reba held Seth's arm as he stepped down from the platform, then they both stared into the casket. She had meant this to be a tender last parting to a woman who meant more to her than she realized. Her world was so small. Maidie's loss would leave a big hole.

But when the moment arrived for her to pause and ponder, nothing seemed natural to say or do. She stared at a gold band with three small diamonds on Maidie's left hand. An engagement ring? What's that doing there?

She wished she'd brought some special token to tuck in the casket. A framed photo of the two of them together. Maybe the heart necklace she and Seth gave her for high school graduation.

Seth whispered something toward the casket. Reba leaned closer. He was saying, "You're okay now, sweet Maidie. Hush, sweet baby, don't you cry. I'll take care of everything."

Pearl from behind placed a firm hand on her shoulder.

"Was Maidie ever engaged?" Reba asked.

"Nearly married Zeke Owens. He died of a broken neck many decades ago. Fell off a roof while chasing birds from a chimney."

Reba reeled back in shock and wondered why she never heard that story before?

Seth nodded at them as though in confirmation, his face grim with grief. And maybe something else. He waved her away when she offered an arm.

"You and Ginny follow Seth in his Model T. I'll ride with Vincent," Pearl said.

Ginny insisted they hop in her red Jaguar. Top down, cool breeze, Reba wished she had on her cowboy hat. She suspected her hair would wimp out of any hint of style. The long line of mourners slowly surged to the canopied hole in Mosquito Ridge Cemetery. Old-timers carried extra jackets, knowing the open cemetery ground could whip up a chilly wind any time of the year. However, today spring sun warmth hugged them.

A determined Don, in silver and turquoise bolo tie and copper-colored western sports coat, edged closer to Reba and Pearl in the reserved-for-family chairs. Reba motioned him to sit down beside her.

"But I'm not family," he said.

"Doesn't matter. They're going to be empty otherwise." She ignored Grandma Pearl's elbow punch.

Ginny had declined reserved family seating and now strolled between Jace and Norden, attentive to something Jace said. She offered him one of her teasing smiles.

Watch it, girl, you're a married woman. "Where's your dad?" Reba asked Don. He shrugged.

"I thought he insisted on starting the service," she said to Pearl.

"It's time and everyone else is here. We'll go on without him."

"Maybe Don could..."

Pearl shot her a warning glance and nodded at Thomas Hawk who offered a brief eulogy. "In her younger days, Maidie Fortress jammed with us. We played our drums. She joined in with her flute. She also participated in several pow wows. She was a good friend and we never forgot." He concluded, "All of us alive on this earth make up a small tribe compared to the numbers who sleep beneath us. They're the majority. Their words and actions while among us should be heeded. Now Maidie has united with them."

His grandson, Elliot Laws, drummed in his desert camouflage uniform from Gulf War duty. Reine Laws, his mother, accompanied with flute for a haunting rendition of "God Be With You Till We Meet Again."

At the end, Pearl asked them to play it again and invited Thomas to sing the song in Nez Perce. "Many of you may not realize that Thomas Hawk is one of less than a hundred people who still speak the Nez Perce language. If you catch on to the words, please join in."

Thomas began with, "Godki pewakunyu hanaka." By the end of the last verse all his family and many in the crowd harmonized the final chorus:

Pewaukunyu, Pewaukunyu,
Jesusnim akthwapa noon.
Pewaukunyu, pewaukunyu,
Godki pewakunyu hanaka.

A whoop and holler rang out from the far end of the cemetery. Riding fast, American flag flying high on a pole and in full rawhide cowboy regalia, Champ charged in with his sandy bay quarter horse. After an abrupt stop, he climbed down and announced, "Sergeant Elliot Laws, will you please come forward?"

Elliot furrowed his brows and took some tentative steps toward Champ.

Champ marched in front of the young Indian man. "As mayor of Road's End, Idaho and as a representative of the city council and citizens, I present you the key to our city, in honor of your service on behalf of our country in peace and in war." He bowed as he handed Elliot a large gold key engraved with *Road's End 1991*. "This key symbolizes that you are a trusted and respected friend of this city's residents, now and forever."

Cheers rose from the crowd as Elliot flushed. "Thank you," he muttered.

"You are welcome to say a few words," Champ urged.

"All I can think to say is thank you again." In an awkward moment, he tried to find a place to tuck the key. Half-hung out of his pant's pocket, his father yanked it out and raised it high. More applause erupted.

Reba peered at Don. He seemed pleased. And why shouldn't he be? His dad rewarded a hero. Nothing wrong with that. But the timing! Champ had this funeral figured out from beginning to end, for his own personal agenda. That was his style. Another reason not to get any closer to his son? One more minus on the Dating Don List. Maybe that counts for extra negative points. Or should she presume the son had his own life and Champ didn't enter into it? After all, she'd never known Marge to complain.

After the graveside service, a long line of rigs led by Seth's Model T, Pearl's green '58 GMC Carryall, Ginny's Jaguar, and Champ's '57 white Cadillac with front steer horns serpentined to the Grange Hall, a country block away. Most stayed outside in groups to reminisce about shenanigans and exploits of early pioneers and caught up on local news. A few sneezed and pulled out inhalers or popped allergy pills.

The churchwomen prepared the food. Ursula Younger covered tables with purple tablecloths and centerpieces of multi-colored pansies in baby food jars. The two large purple and white iris bouquets from the Cahill barn book-ended each side of a chest freezer, over which Reba stretched a cream lace cloth. She arranged a collage of pictures Pearl brought of Maidie and Seth through the years. A pretty girl. A handsome guy. A love story of an entirely different sort.

Lisl Monte kept her eye on Deputy Lomax circling the crowd. "We found a broken window and what looked like forced entry when we came earlier this morning. Brock thinks it might have been a baseball or rock thrown, but I'm not as sure."

Brock? Deputy Lomax? So these two have been getting friendly, like the scuttlebutt claimed.

The Mathwig triplets fluttered around the tables adding silverware and orchid paper napkins. Clones of each other with fading brunette hair and pale eyes, but in different shapes and sizes, they kept busy as they responded.

Adrienne Mathwig opined, "Burglary in Road's End? To steal what? No valuables here. I'll get that window replaced before the next Grange meeting."

Beatrice Mathwig slipped her opal ring in her red-striped broom skirt pocket. "We've got to make more treasures for heaven where thieves and robbers can't break in. Or maybe someone needed a place to stay the night."

Charlotta Mathwig dispensed her usual litany of warnings. "Big city crime has hit Road's End, especially with folks like the McKanes moving in. Better get used to locking your doors, having timed and motion lights, and tucking a gun under your pillow."

Polly Eng and her daughter, Kam, the only ones in town besides Maidie who could grow healthy gardens with the short growing season, bent over steaming woks full of stir-fried vegetables and pork. She steamed the best stir-fry and rainbow trout with Teriyaki sauce, said the citizens of Road's End. Now Polly frowned at her daughter. "A car load of intoxicated juveniles drove around town last week lighting M-80s and scaring our dogs. Fireworks got shot off our deck."

"They thought it was Chinese New Year." Kam blushed a pretty pink.

Ursula, who lived in the big house on the highest knoll reported, "Sure are a lot more dogs roaming around town, even with our leash law. At least one of them is a snarling, foam at the mouth mad dog."

Cicely Bowers, splinter skinny in four-inch black spike heels, bleached white hair swept into a wide-brimmed hat cocked to the side and tied under the chin, and black leggings ending inches above the shoes, added sliced boiled eggs to her huge bowl of famed potato salad with mustard.

She introduced Trish Hocking Stanton. "My niece's daughter from Missouri. She's been staying with me, helping me out. She told me a man failed to pay for his room last week at my B&B. Plus he stole a pillow. Deputy Lomax caught him running our one stop sign. He had false plates and invalid driver's license."

"Tucker left his car parked next to the Trailer Park behind the Pick Me Up Saloon overnight and found two windows smashed," said Ida Paddy. "I keep telling him that's not a good place, especially after 10:00 p.m. We need a curfew."

"I'm sure the bar's a handy draw for your customers," Cicely remarked. "Some of mine complain they have to walk or drive two blocks to get there."

Pearl handed Reba a large tray of sliced meats and assorted cheese to take to the buffet tables, next to Pearl's famed jalapeno and cheddar cheese corn muffins and stacks of potato rolls. "Lawlessness can happen anywhere."

"True, but a combo of high mountain elevation and sparse population tends to weird people out. Present company excepted, of course," Cicely remarked.

Reba headed outside. "Lunch is ready," she shouted.

Women followed children who rushed in. Most of the men lingered on the lawn. Reba opened the door wide for fresh air and to encourage the hungry. She sauntered over to Seth.

"I've had my hand shook and backslapped so often," he told Reba, "I feel beat to cake batter."

"What happened to your mother and sisters?" she blurted out.

A shadow crossed his face. He bowed his head and shut his eyes.

"I'm sorry. I'm guessing you've got painful memories."

"I'll tell you about it. I promise. But not yet."

Her heart beat faster. *Should I be excited or fearful?*

Elliot Laws bumped into her. "My apologies."

"So glad to have you back. We watched you on TV."

"Oh? When was that?"

"The war, I mean. Strange, scary, and exciting to be in the spectator chair for real live battles. We felt like we were watching history happen."

Norden McKane pushed in. "Surgical and quick laser-guided smart bombs. A-10 fighter pilots. F-15 fighters. Tomahawk cruise missiles. Patriot antimissile system. Hey, it was like a video game, only we weren't at the controls."

Elliot turned solemn. "I can assure you, it was quite different from the perspective of those on the ground."

"Why didn't you bring down Hussein while you could?" Norden retorted.

"Following orders." Elliot excused himself and sauntered to the punch table.

Is that a limp? Reba considered going after him. She felt somehow she needed to make amends. He'd had an attitude since he got back. She wondered if he felt uncomfortable playing hero.

Norden turned to Vincent. "How are Idaho opals doing? Should I buy silver or gold?"

"I just purchased a new opal mining claim. That's what I'm into."

"Did you know we've got garnets right here in Road's End? I found some that had washed out of an old roadbed. Interested?"

"I sure am. Let me know where and when I can meet you."

Ginny greeted Vincent, after she pulled away from Jace. "I remember when Reba ran away to try to find her mother after my family moved to California."

"I headed by bus to Boise to his place," Reba said. "Vincent drove me the four hours back to Road's End and promised to look for her himself."

"I sent you regular reports," Vincent said.

"Yeah, she was driving truck with a boyfriend across the southwest. Then she was a lab technician in Thailand. Then a hospital business manager in the Bahamas. I sent cards and letters to the addresses he gave me, but they were all returned. I finally guessed he might be making this up. The last story he told, he claimed she was a nurse's aid in Vegas."

Ginny grinned. "You have quite the imagination, Mr. Quaid."

Michael barged in. "Or maybe it's all true. I know for sure half of it was."

"Why didn't she ever come our way?" Reba asked.

"She wanted to. She wanted to be there for you. She told me that herself."

"Grandma, Grandpa, Vincent, even Seth and Maidie, those were the ones there for me."

Michael plunged his hands into his jeans. "I'm glad you had them. All I had was Mom."

Ginny turned back to Vincent. "Weren't you the one who helped send Reba to UCSB?"

Vincent nodded.

"I'm sorry to say I only lasted one year, as you know."

"We did have two semesters together in the dorm. Then it was you who left me."

"That's because you were such a heavy sleeper. No late night parties with you around," Reba teased.

Vincent hugged Reba's shoulders. "I was proud of you. You aced the whole twenty units."

"But I couldn't stand that cooped up, tied down feeling. I wanted back at the ranch. Don't need a college degree for that."

"I thought you loved watching the ocean waves," Ginny said.

"Uh huh. I still miss that part." Reba punched Michael's arm. "Introduce us to your guest."

He tugged at the arm of the pert blonde behind him and preened like a peacock. "This is Nina Oscar. She's going to be a doctor someday."

Reba held out her hand. "That's quite an introduction. Glad to meet you." *And why are you attracted to Michael?*

"Pediatrician," Nina corrected. "Like my mother."

Nice catch, brother. Is she a keeper?

Chapter Three

A cool noon Spring breeze blew through the open Grange Hall doors as Reba noticed Ginny chatting with Sue Anne Runcie at the food tables. She sashayed toward them and heard Champ discussing his plans for a new church building to a mixed crowd of members and nonmembers. He drew a sketch on a piece of notepaper. "We'll want orange for the upholstery and rugs to go with harvest and Thanksgiving celebrations, since we're a farming community."

Pearl calmly marched over, but Reba noticed fire in her eyes. "Champ, church members will choose their own building, if and when they want one. And they most certainly will decide their own color of carpet. I'm sure the women will have an opinion."

Champ started to speak but Pearl cut him off. "Can we tell the Steak House what color to paint their walls? Do we force the Mathwigs to add on new rooms to the hotel?"

Reba moved closer and silently cheered that her grandmother finally intervened.

Champ's face burned crimson as he scowled like a sea captain whose orders had been defied. "It will be on city property. We can all have a say. A church is different. A church belongs to everyone." He looked around at the skeptical faces and softened his approach. "There's no way your small crew can raise enough funds without a larger support base. Surely you can see that."

"Oh? Where do you propose we put the church?"

"I've already talked to Seth about it. On the Stroud Ranch property on the other side of the Grange."

"But that's Cahill Ranch land."

"Oh no, it isn't."

"Not technically," Pearl retorted, "but we've leased that land from Seth for over fifty years."

"Not anymore. The city is taking part of it over for public use. Eminent domain."

Reba trembled in fury. "How much land do you think it takes for a church?"

"Well, I figure we'll need at least a hundred acres. For parking, playground for the kids, future expansion, possible future public buildings, a well, and other facilities. For the common good."

A hundred acres! Reba and her grandmother needed every acre they had right now to make a viable ranch.

She lashed out at the man in tall tan cowboy hat. "You're powerful in this town, but don't take on God. You're definitely outmatched there."

"Surely your pride isn't so inflated," Champ blustered.

"My pride is not the issue." Pearl raised her five-foot-five-inch frame taller. "It's a matter of relationship."

"But we're all friends. You, me, Seth, Maidie--we go way back. We've pretty much grown up here. Tell me the right words. Anoint me or something. The citizens of Road's End expect their leader to do the honors."

"It's your relationship with the Almighty I had in mind."

A determined glint formed in his eyes. "I'll bring this matter to a vote of the whole town."

"Spiritual commitment is more important than politics."

"But that doesn't require a town vote."

Lloyd Younger tapped Pearl's shoulder. "Some stock of yours got loose on the road. I'll need some help."

"Don and Tim will go," Champ offered.

"I've got my granddaughter," Pearl shot back. "She's all I need."

She and Reba headed toward Pearl's Carryall as Don followed them out. "Can I call you tonight or sometime tomorrow?"

Reba felt like a bull seeing red. Why didn't Don challenge his dad on their behalf? Another huge minus got added to The Dating Don List. "I don't know. I've got some things to work out." With a mix of regret, she watched him hurry back to the Hall. He was an otherwise decent guy, unlike his father.

"Watch out, Reba. Champ is using Don."

"Why would he do that?"

"That man's like a double prong. Always has been. He goads you so you'll kick somebody. Someone he's trying to get at. And in this case, it's no mystery who it is."

"Me? Or you?"

"He's not getting my ranch."

"But Grandma…" If Reba and Don married, they'd have access to more than one ranch. What's wrong with that?

 Pearl frowned her the-subject's-closed face. "I don't know why our cows keep getting out."

"Somebody cut a piece out of the Runcie fence where the heifer got through. You know I check all the fences as often as I can. I suppose I could check more often if there were two of me."

"Maybe…" Pearl began.

"Maybe what?" Reba nudged.

Pearl sped up as they rode down Sourdough Road and turned west toward Coyote Canyon. They stopped by Cahill Ranch barbed wire, lying limp on the ground. "Here's your answer. Someone cut here too."

"It doesn't make sense. Bits and pieces here and there."

"Let's get the cows back in and fix the fence."

"Then take a quick trip to the Canyon. Don said Johnny Poe ran that way."

They herded cows for about half an hour before they coaxed them back on home soil, then another half hour to fix the severed wire. Next came the search for Johnny Poe, which ended in defeat.

When they returned to the house, Reba noticed the Jaguar gone. Dr. Olga Whey met them at the door on her way out. She looked Reba in the eyes. "I'm sorry, but the calf didn't make it. No one to blame. There was something internal wrong with him."

Reba's shoulders drooped in dismay. "Thanks for trying, doc." Not my best day. Not the first lost calf nor the last. But each one stung.

Pearl hugged Reba as they headed inside. Vincent greeted them with "How's Johnny Poe."

Grief over the calf turned to concern for her horse. Reba paced in front of the orange divan with mahogany claw legs. "No sign of him. But we did see remains of campfires, one very recent. Johnny Poe hates fire almost as much as he hates barbed wire." Where is that horse? And where's Ginny? "I sure hope he's not holed up on Runcie land."

"I'm sure he'll show up soon," Vincent encouraged then grinned at Pearl. "Some folks at the service today insisted you would make a better mayor than Champ Runcie."

"I sure hope he never hears that."

"He already did. Tucker argued with him whether men or women's blood vessels narrowed faster with age. Adrienne Mathwig said the blood supply to women's brains was better maintained for longer periods of time. She used to be a doctor, you know."

Pearl frowned. "She was a dentist. But what does that mean?"

"Percentages prove you'd serve in office better and longer than Champ."

Reba stretched her arms to her knees, then her toes. "Grandma's got more influence serving every cause she can think of at the county and state level. Being mayor would slow her down."

"Stop your fidgeting, Reba. You're making me nervous," Pearl said.

Reba spread her arms and stretched her legs. "If I were running for mayor, I'd campaign to move the dumpsters outside the city, limit the issuance of liquor licenses, establish a logging truck parking lot, and advocate for building western decor false fronts for all the businesses."

Vincent and Pearl cheered.

"You got our votes," Pearl said.

Reba sat on the arm of the couch. "Well, I'm trying to stay ahead of our present mayor." Then to ease her frantic mind, she proposed, "I'm going out first thing in the morning and drive every trail on our ranch and on the prairie, if I have to. Johnny Poe's got to be hiding somewhere."

The phone rang. Pearl lifted the receiver from its black cradle.

"You were wrong. He's hurrahing citizens on Main Street," Pearl said when she hung up. "Vincent, help me check on the heifer. Reba, get your rebel horse."

Reba ran to hitch the pickup trailer and looked for heelers Paunch and Blue to help corral her horse. *What's going on Johnny Poe?* He had never run toward people before. If he bolted, he dashed for the wilderness.

She felt a chill. Unruly horses get shot by no-nonsense Road's Enders.

Reba hooked up the trailer to the pickup and sped over gravel roads into town. Shadows crossed the late afternoon route as she turned on the one paved street in Road's End. Reba drove past the Steak House, leather shop, Delbert's Diner and Gifts, the post office, and the apartment complex where Tim, Sue Ann and the kids lived while their house was built on Whitlow property.

She looked down every alley as she drove by Whitlow's Grocery owned by Sue Ann's parents, two of the six saloons in the area, and Jace and Norden's Outfitters across the street.

Some of the same folks who had been at Maidie's funeral just hours before now shouted along the wooden sidewalks while others stood watching in front of the Pick-Me-Up Saloon. Next door the Mathwig triplets and roomers craned for a look from window views from their two-story hotel.

An agitated Johnny Poe cowed before a man with a whip. *Champ! This will not end well.*

Reba yanked open the pickup and rushed over as she tried to talk her horse down. She grabbed the rope hanging from the saddle horn. His coat reamed with sweat, eyes wild, mouth foamed. "Come on, boy, settle down. I've got you. You'll be okay."

A loud crack snapped in her ears as a burning pain lashed across her back. The force and shock of the blow whirled her around and the pain grew intense. Through clenched eyes she saw someone from the sidewalk grapple with Champ and muscle the whip away from him. Hunched over in agony, she couldn't believe she'd been whipped.

Firm hands yanked the rope from her and reached for Johnny Poe. She looked up to see brother Michael talking in a low monotone. He pulled an old navy blue bandanna from his pocket and wiped lather from Johnny Poe's neck. Then he slid the headstall over the horse's ears and dropped the bit out of his mouth. He straightened the saddle and murmured a kind of chant. As he uncoiled one of his own ropes and slipped a makeshift rope halter over the horse's head, he led Johnny Poe by the whispering crowd to the trailer.

Gentle hands eased Reba to her feet, her back seared like a brand. A tube was shoved in her hand. "Rub this on your welt. It's the best stuff we sell." Reba peered into the deep hazel eyes of Jace McKane, a scowl on his face, and Champ's whip tucked under his arm. He rolled up the sleeves on his white on white pin stripe shirt he'd worn to the funeral.

Ginny appeared beside him, concern creased on her full, winsome face. "How are you feeling?"

"I hurt bad and I'm kind of dizzy."

"Come on. I'll drive you home. Jace, you get the Jaguar." She tossed him the keys.

They eased into Reba's pickup with Johnny Poe in the trailer. Michael hopped into his 1980 bronze Mustang Cobra behind the Jaguar. As they made a U-turn, she caught sight of Don opening a truck door for Champ, helping him into the cab.

Why wasn't he helping her instead? Why didn't he take the whip away? Another big minus on the Dating Don List.

Ginny cruised slowly to the Cahill homestead with Reba straight in the seat, back touching nothing but shirt, which Reba wanted to peel off, with great care. "Where have you been?" she managed to say.

"Took a ride around the lake and arrived in town in time to witness your drama."

"Alone?"

Ginny clutched tight on the steering wheel. "No, not alone."

" Jace could pay a big price for wrestling Champ's whip away."

"Someone had to do it."

Ginny parked beside the Camperdown Elm and as Reba gingerly got out of the truck, Michael backed Johnny Poe out of the trailer and led him to the corral. Jace hiked after him and Ginny followed Reba into the house. Reba downed some ibuprofen pills as Ginny applied Jace's salve to the swollen, beet-red welt on her back. "I can't believe what I'm seeing," she said more than once.

Reba shut her eyes and tried mentally to move out of the pain. "How come Jace came with us?"

"Because he drove my car. Because I invited him. Because I'll take him home later."

"What's up with you two?"

"Absolutely nothing. He's an easy guy to talk to and he understands my world."

"That's what you said about Paris...you remember, your husband?"

"Before we got married, you mean. I can't understand why you aren't paying attention to Jace yourself."

"He's not a part of my world. We have nothing in common."

"He used to own horses."

"You mean, played at owning horses. I hear he got bored with starting computer businesses and decided to try the small town lifestyle as a lark."

Ginny scowled. "Are you still pining over Tim so much you've forgotten how to look anywhere except the Runcie Ranch for your men?"

Reba's face burned almost as much as her back. "I don't pine over married men." Not much anyway.

"A heart pines for what it pines. Tim's even cuter now than in fifth grade, in a rustic cowboy kind of way, with that full sweep of chestnut hair under his hat. Are he and Sue Anne happy?"

"I think I'd be the last to hear. And you're giving me reasons to pine, not turn away. What's up with that?"

"That's not my intent. Just an honest analysis." Ginny wiped the cream off her hands and fumbled with her necklace. "I know Jace's father. That's what we mostly talk about. Jace is very concerned about him and he should be. Hugh McKane's a charmer, but he's not a nice man."

"How do you know him?"

"He's a business acquaintance of my grandpa's. And he's in the national news some. He's into the corporate merge-and-purge game. I'm surprised you haven't heard of him."

"I don't read the newspapers much."

"The man's often caught up in some controversy. He seems drawn by new ventures that are, let's say, outside the mainstream."

"Doesn't sound too stable."

"But he's good at making money."

🐎 🐎 🐎 🐎

Ginny insisted on calling Deputy Lomax to file a complaint. He arrived within a half hour. "As a rule, that's a criminal offense," he admitted, upon hearing their version. Clearly, it wasn't the first narrative of the incident he'd heard. He held his breath as though fearing she would pursue.

Oh, sure, she'd like to see him try to arrest Champ and keep his job. "I won't press charges. It was an accident."

"He didn't even apologize," Ginny retorted. "We at least wanted you to know."

The deputy shut his book, heaved a sigh of relief, and quickly changed the subject. "You should know that four prisoners escaped from the minimum security at the Elkville facility yesterday. Used a hacksaw blade to cut cell bars and scaled the wall with a ladder constructed in the prison machine shop by a fellow inmate. But that's a county matter. Unless, of course, they head this way."

"Why should they?" Reba replied. "What were they in for?"

"Petty theft. Scams. Burglary. One of them roughed up a couple girlfriends."

"Well, there's nothing to steal here."

"But how would they know that? They walked away from the minimum-security area and caught a bus or thumbed a ride. Incredible. Still in their prison rags and with ID tags. They were scheduled to go before the review board for parole hearings next month. Never been a discipline problem before. So, go figure. Now they'll be charged with felony escape and could get five years added. Anyway, keep an eye out."

The deputy whisked away with a head nod as Reba and Ginny hiked over to watch Matthew massage Johnny Poe. The horse refused to drink at the free-flowing water source and lapped up shallow rain puddles instead.

"You're good with horses, especially if you can manage Johnny Poe," Reba said.

"He'll let me fuss around, but I'm not going to ride him. You're the only one he'll let do that."

"Seth too. Seth has ridden him before."

Vincent and Pearl met up with them. "The heifer seems to have partial paralysis," Pearl reported. "We'll have to watch her close." Pearl's gazed stopped at Reba's face. "What's wrong? What happened in town?"

When Pearl heard the report of Champ and his whip, she stormed into the house to call the Runcie house. Reba followed, hoping to hear what Champ had to say. She listened in on the extension.

"Champ didn't mean to hit Reba. He's so sorry," Blair Runcie began. "He would say so himself, but he and Don already left for Spokane. They got a call to look at a deal on some new farm equipment. And to order a bell."

"What bell?" Pearl wheezed.

"You know, the memorial bell, for the new church."

Pearl slammed the phone down and waited a moment while she fought for calm. She breathed deep, in and out.

The others slunk in as Reba stepped toward Pearl and forced a pause before she offered, "I'll stay with the heifer tonight."

"No need. Tomorrow should be soon enough." Pearl straightened her blouse and put on her stoic face. "Anybody hungry? There are plenty of leftovers from the service. And we can throw on some steaks too. I'll call Seth to come. Meant to tell him earlier, but things got so hectic."

"Vincent, you going home tonight?" Reba asked.

"No, he is going to stay at the hotel for at least a couple days." Pearl's eyes hugged him.

Ginny winked at Reba who turned to Michael sprawled on the orange couch. "Will you stay? Nina too?"

"She had to get back to study for early exams in the morning. But, sure, I'll stay. You know I'm always hungry."

Ginny turned to Jace. "How about you? Will you eat with us?"

Jace faced Reba full view. He rubbed his close-cropped, butch style dark hair. For the second time that day, she peered into his handsome face with what she detected as sincerity and politeness written all over it. "It's up to Reba Mae and her grandmother."

Reba Mae? Only a few called her by that familiar name. *How dare he.* And she didn't want him staying for dinner. But she had a debt to pay. "I haven't properly thanked you for your intervention on my behalf. And the cream worked wonders on my back." She forced herself to add, "Please do stay."

"And Norden's welcome, too," Pearl called from the kitchen.

"Thank you, Mrs. Cahill, but he told me he'd be busy tonight."

Reba and Ginny excused themselves so Reba could pop some more ibuprofen tablets and Ginny played nurse to her back again. "Interesting group for dinner tonight," Ginny offered.

Reba ignored her and then fed Paunch, Blue, and Scat as Ginny and Jace hiked to the Grange Hall. She shoved a leaf in the dining table and set it for seven.

"Add a few extras," Pearl said. "Just in case."

She prepared several more place settings as Seth drove up in his Model T, followed by Ginny and Jace in his Volvo.

Pearl handed Reba a charcoal drawing of a horse that looked like

Johnny Poe. *For Reba*, it said. *Love, Kaitlyn.* "I believe she drew it during the funeral. She asked me to give it to you right after."

"Tim's daughter," Reba explained to Ginny. "I'm so glad I've gotten to know Tim's kids some. They are sweethearts." Not their fault what their parents did.

"Is Don coming over?" Ginny asked.

"Nope. He and his dad have gone to Spokane."

Dinner ready, they moved into the dining room. Reba sat across from Ginny and Jace who both managed to change into casual clothes. As casual as Ginny ever got, that is. A scatter of rhinestones on a silver silky pullover over jeans. Silver sandals. Jace wore tan khaki shorts and soft yellow pullover shirt. She studied him while he chatted with the others. Slim yet muscular. Green tint to his eyes. Straight white teeth. *I do appreciate the cool balm on my back.*

"Your story today," he was saying to Seth, "it hit a chord. I'm tempted to make fun of things like supposed miracles. But I still feel the tug...well, sometimes I think I could believe."

"It's not hard when you experience it." Seth spooned Waldorf salad on his plate.

Pearl passed steamy mashed potatoes and gravy.

"Did you find your mother and sisters that day?" Ginny asked the question they all wanted to know.

Reba watched Seth's strained face. What she'd suspected she saw there now. Something bad happened. And he avoided talking about it. He looked around the table, complexity in his black eyes.

Pearl cut in. "Jace, if you don't mind me asking, what is your religious background?"

"I had a praying grandmother. But my father worships the almighty dollar. My mother took us to a Presbyterian church."

"Was that Norden's mother too?"

"No, we're half brothers. Different mothers. My parents are divorced."

Ginny gave Jace a saucy look. "How did you make your money?" She ignored Reba's scowl of protest.

"It's a long story. I'll give you the shortened version. It started with McDonnell Douglas in Huntington Beach, which led to Kaiser

Aluminum, which led to Itron, which led to Logue McDonald, then Byte Dynamics, then Kaiser Mead, then Nynex of New York, and then Internet Capital. I mainly designed software and built semiconductor test equipment. Have I bored you yet?"

"No, I'm not bored. Very impressive resume."

"Thank you."

"So why in the world did you move to a place like Road's End?"

"As long as I had small companies scattered around, I could keep a low profile. I stayed pretty much invisible. But as it got bigger, more diverse, I lost the obscurity. Here I've regained it."

"But is this as fulfilling for you?" Reba tried not to sound too nosy. Or too interested.

He wiped his mouth with a paper napkin. "It is. For now. Besides, the industry I started continues and I could probably enter back whenever I wanted."

"You think you'll want to?" Ginny prodded.

"Return to that stress? Not likely."

"You are a strange one," Pearl interjected. "So many young people here try to get out, to see the world."

Like my mom? Reba wondered again what drove her away.

"He traded his Guccis for hip boots," Vincent quipped.

Jace snickered. "That's about right. Working with a computer is a yawn compared to white water rafting on the Salmon River. Or backpacking in the Seven Devils. Or even shooting the breeze with my customers. This is the closest I'll get to being a cowboy." He peered at Reba. "I realize folks here are the real McCoy."

Was that some kind of backhanded compliment? Or a taunt?

"What's Norden's background?" Pearl asked.

"He played football in college. Had to quit when his grades weren't good enough. I'm trying to encourage him to register at the University of Idaho this fall."

"That's where Nina goes," Michael said. "Maybe she can nudge him. On second thought, maybe not."

He's not that confident of her yet?

Vincent pushed away his plate and rubbed his bushy beard. "Elliot Laws got through college on the ROTC program and did quite well until he got action in the Gulf. He seems shaken by the experience. Even popular, short wars can be hell."

Scat took the pause in chitchat as an invitation to jump on Jace's lap. "I overheard you ladies talking about crime in Road's End. What's the biggest problem you face?"

"Yellow thistle," Pearl said.

"Excuse me?"

"Yellow star thistle. A weed that infests our pastures. We hire crop dusters use hand sprayers. It's expensive but thistle's fatal for horses if they eat it."

Reba plunked down her fork. "Our biggest problem? Champ Runcie." She raised out of her chair. "Anybody ready for dessert? We've got Charlotta Mathwig's huckleberry pie. Or Ursula Younger's triple fudge brownies. Or Pam Eng's fortune cookie cake."

"I'd be grateful for one of each," Vincent said.

A chorus replied, "Me too."

Reba balanced a stack of dishes as Pearl cleared some space on the counter. "So, Jace, how do you see Road's End as a community? How would you describe us?" Reba inquired.

He folded his arms and leaned the chair back. "It's a place of reluctant spring thaws with a lot of unpaved roads and few fences in common. That's a quote I remember reading somewhere. It fits this place."

"But what about the people?"

"In the few months I've been here, it seems many folks come to hide from something or someone. Or be left alone."

Quite a speech. And what are you hiding from, Jace?

Vincent leaned forward. "The people endure long, hard winters, and Champ Runcie. Thus, they have to be survivors."

Jace chuckled. "Very well said. Road's End is full of loners and independents who at times succumb to teamwork."

Ginny joined in. "Team. Together Everyone Achieves More. My Grandpa Bony loves reminding constantly of motivational slogans like that."

"Tell me again, what's the name of your family's business?" Vincent inquired.

"George's Marketplace Deli chain. Only in California. Four of them so far. Every time the family grows, Grandpa talks of starting a new store. He wants as many of us as possible to stay with the business. Our headquarters is in Santa Dominga." She looked at Jace. "Also home to kingpin Hugh McKane."

"Is that another brother?" Reba handed out plates of assorted desserts that included Pearl's rhubarb-apple pie.

"No. It's my infamous father."

"That's right. Ginny mentioned him." The way he accented infamous sounded like bad blood between them.

⚞ ⚟ ⚞ ⚟

After dinner, Vincent and Pearl washed dishes. Seth lounged on the orange couch, argyle stocking-feet stretched out on the leather top table. No one commented that they didn't match. Reba spread a Pendleton blanket across him but the motion irritated her back. She gritted against the pain. "You ought to spend the night with us, Seth. No need to go back to that empty cabin alone."

The old man's eyes closed and his chest gently heaved. "I'm okay."

Reba tried to read Seth's response. Worn and weary body. His face furrowed. No mystery there after the long, emotional day. But there was something else. A brooding. She'd never known him to be like that, even during Maidie's long months of illness. He stayed alert to care for her needs. Now, he seemed to mull something over. Did he have a decision to make? A problem to solve? Or was he depressed? Understandable. Almost like losing a mate.

The others pulled up chairs. Reba longed to slather more of Jace's cream on her wounds.

"This house always smells so...horsey," Ginny said.

"No horse has ever been in this house," Reba huffed.

"I think you bring it in with you. But it's nice. I like horse odors. And I like your furniture. Everything you own has feet on it: the couch, the chairs, the Duncan Phyfe dining room table. Even your bathtub. It's charming."

Pearl stuck her head into the room. "You wouldn't think charming if you had to dust all this stuff."

"Grandma, you never dust anything and you know it. I swipe a rag around when I can't breathe any longer." Reba twisted to try to ease the pain.

"Dust protects the wood. It sure never hurt a tree." Pearl returned to the kitchen.

Seth left two heel prints on the table as he slowly repositioned to lay prone on the couch.

"Did you hear about the escaped prisoners?" Ginny asked. "Pretty exciting."

"I shudder to think of criminals anywhere near." Reba winced and tried to grab Ginny's attention as her back throbbed.

"But it's easy to steal things here," Michael replied. "No one ever locks their doors or anything else."

"I'm sorry, Ginny, but I need to pull you away from our guests." Reba grimaced as they excused themselves and scooted to Reba's bedroom.

Ginny grabbed the ointment. "You'd better watch out for Jace. He's hiding something. Beware of men with dark secrets."

"What? Just hours ago you complained about my narrow choice of men. At least he had the guts to challenge Champ. Nobody else around here seems to."

Ginny pressed the ointment a little too hard. "But Jace may be your bigger challenge."

"Jace is nothing to me, barely an acquaintance." Reba stopped, an image of Champ's whip in his hands. "But I do owe him."

When they returned to the living room, Ginny offered to give Jace a ride home.

"I can do that," Michael said.

"Then I'm going to my room. I'm exhausted and I need to call home." She stretched and yawned and headed for the guest room.

Seth set up and pulled on his shoes. "I'm going, too."

"Can I hop a ride?" Vincent called from the kitchen. "My car's at the hotel and I've been wanting to cruise town with that Model T of yours."

"Yes, sir, I'd be glad to have a passenger." He reached over and touched Reba's arm. "But I hoped Reba would come over this evening. I've got something to give you, something that belongs to you."

"Why, sure. I can come over. Did I leave something of mine at your house?"

"Not really. Maidie, uh, left you a present."

Chapter Four

A taupe whitetail doe foraged on twigs of the Cahill's Camperdown Elm. She didn't seem to mind it was a mutant. When she spied intruders Seth and Vincent she flagged her tail and trotted toward the pasture with a fawn behind her.

Vincent stared at the elm as they walked to the Model T. "I remember so well Cole planting that tree on Scottish elm stock, bringing a bit of Dundee, Scotland with him, he said. He was so proud of it. In later years, I heard him several times call it 'a cursed tree, an upside down tree.'"

"A curse came down on us all." Seth thought of the tree with its strange twists and turns. He sank into the slough of despond again. He could feel the intensity of Vincent ogling him.

"Are you talking about Maidie?"

Yes. Maidie. The old man wondered if he should tell Vincent what he suspected. He was a good man. He cared about Maidie. And Reba Mae. And Hanna Jo. But what could he do? What could anyone do? "A curse fell on the whole earth," he finally responded.

"Oh, I see," Vincent said. "You're talking about Adam and Eve in the garden."

"Yes. About Eve." *My Eve.*

"I'll kick the tires. You twist the tail," Vincent teased as he circled the T.

Seth nodded in the evening shadows. He scooted into the driver's seat to turn the switch on at the coil box and retard the spark. He got out and hobbled to the front, pulled the choke wire out and the crank up, pushed the choke wire in, then pried the crank up again. When the car started with a rumble, Scat jumped and banged his head on the fender. Seth scurried around to the driver's side and reached in to advance the spark lever. Scat scrambled off the rolling tire and stiffened in protest. The cat looked all fur ball and teeth, milky eyes aglow.

Seth hobbled around to the passenger door and climbed in, scooting to the driver's side. He made further adjustments to the spark and throttle and waved in Vincent. He set the emergency brake to neutral and touched the low pedal to keep from killing the engine. Automatic movements of a lifetime habit.

"Thanks so much, Seth. This is great." Vincent breathed in deep and stretched out an arm in the fresh evening air.

Seth allowed himself a moment's splurge of relief from the day's grief. He basked in the man's exhilaration of a Model T ride. "I'm surprised this is your first time. Surely Boise has some crankers." He pulled the throttle down slightly and eased the clutch pedal as the car edged forward.

"I have to confess, the oldest car I've ever ridden is a 1935 Ford pickup. But this reminds me that the early cars shrunk the country. And later planes shrunk the world."

"That '35 Ford sounds pretty modern to me." Seth pushed the throttle lever up a bit, let up on the clutch pedal, inched into high gear, and cruised down the road.

"Would sure take a lot of practice to manage this setup. Let's see…brake pedal on the right, clutch and high-low pedal on the left, reverse peddle in the middle…that would mess me up right away."

Seth considered this. "I suppose. If it's not what you're used to.

But it's so easy for me. And if something doesn't work right, I know how to fix it. Most folks just turn a key, shift into drive, and expect to get where they intend to go. They've got no idea the mechanics of the thing. All while listening to loud music on the Hi-Fi." He made a grunting sound. "A driver's got to listen. Feel. Coax. Get in harmony with the machine. Most modern drivers know nothing about that."

"Quite a speech for you, Seth. But all this openness must be tough on the highway. Bugs and all?"

"You do need to learn how to grin with your mouth closed."

Vincent chortled. "So, you increase speed with the rods at the steering wheel?"

"The throttle is the one on the right." Seth squeezed the wheel with his hands and they roared down Cahill Crossing at thirty miles an hour. Then he slowed to take a right at the Steak House on Main Street. He headed to the Road's End Hotel where the lighted lobby revealed the Mathwig triplets and a couple guests huddled around the TV. He applied the brake, put the clutch pedal in neutral, and as the Model T rolled to a stop pulled the hand lever back with his left hand.

"Thanks again, Seth. You take care of yourself. Please let us know if you need anything." Seth nodded and Vincent waved as he entered the hotel.

Seth turned the Model T around in the empty street and turned right on Sourdough Avenue between Whitlow's Grocery and Jace and Norden's Outfitters. Up the hill beyond Lisl Monty's white wood frame house, he passed Polly Eng's gray stone and brick home where daughter Kam pulled clothes off a line. He returned her wave.

Back at home, Maidie's poodle stretched out in the driveway, so fat and old her teeth fell out. She had long forsaken chasing any of Maidie's dozens of cats. Now that the cats had suddenly disappeared, she boldly claimed any part of the property as her napping ground. There at the last, Seth asked Maidie if she had any special requests.

"Yes, I do," she said. "Two requests. One, put all my cats to sleep. We might as well all go out together."

So he did. And now he was about to do the other.

He parked the Model T in the garage.

A weathered chopping block on the cabin's front porch displayed assorted half-finished wooden carvings of cottonwood horses, dogwood owls, and pine howling coyotes. Works in progress. Other carvings looked like slugs or acorns. Red cedar bait plugs for the McKane brothers. A cardboard box held enameled ones with eyes and hooks.

Inside, the coffee table spread with chunks of close-grained cottonwood and dogwood and assorted knives. Comical old men's faces carved out of tree knots crammed around a penknife, a small jackknife with three blades, knives with thin handles and long blades, as well as pieces of copper wire. The tools of Seth's handiwork. His offering of service to God and to the citizens of Road's End.

Various other items sprawled around. A black chest. A pile of elk horns. The large bookcase filled with volumes. And more samples of Seth's carved sculptures on the dining table: sailing ships, a nativity scene, an antlered stag.

And one masterpiece recently completed. In the center of the table spread a chunk of pine formed into faces and abstract limbs joined in a flowing twist of seven people, some adults, but most children. Their open mouths and closed or squinting eyes caught frozen in the midst of a sudden catastrophe.

Seth still slept in the simple, small apartment above the unattached garage. He didn't feel comfortable even now invading Maidie's space in that way. The interior of this home looked like it had been sculpted out of the forest landscape that surrounded them. Seth had crafted most every square of it. He kept the log cabin chinked and varnished. He had always considered it Maidie's home and a display case for his finished work, until he gave most of it away. Or sold it when the receiver insisted on paying. He gently rubbed one of the carved horses.

Two huge pine beds dominated the two bedrooms. A smaller twin size in the living room had been Maidie's hospital bed the past year. She loved looking at the hand carved frames that held pictures on the walls of Road's End and desert landscapes, reminders of the world outside her confined domain. He imagined Maidie lounged in her favorite chair of upholstered purple flowers, long hair braided or up in a bun. Rocking away with sandals or bare feet, eyes closed, intent on listening to every sound as though a blind person.

Seth would often meet Reba at the door with, "Come play your guitar and calm Maidie. She says I've fiddled enough."

Maidie never wasted anything. She even used her gout medicine to kill the cockroaches.

"Best exterminator ever," she insisted.

She kept ants away with mint plants and sniffed cotton balls dipped in peppermint or lavender oil. *I could use some of that right now.*

Though the place was as neat and clean as Maidie left it before she got so ill, he noticed a musty scent and a rotten egg smell. He checked the vents from the furnace.

Please, God, not a gas leak now. He did not need that added hassle, especially with Reba coming to visit at any moment. He wanted the presentation to her to be perfect as possible. Meanwhile, he had to settle things in his mind, how he would do it.

He entered the kitchen and the odor got stronger. He sniffed around the gas stove. Just as he was certain he would have to call someone to come help, he noticed a dozen eggs on the window ledge above the sink. Rotting. The last time he had brought groceries in, how many weeks ago, he forgot to refrigerate them. The sight not only brought relief, but made him chuckle. The sound and feel of it felt foreign, like from a far away country, a distant land.

He held his breath and tossed the egg carton in the back porch garbage can and rolled it out to the backyard. Then he returned to the dining room table. He picked up a four-inch deep antique wooden cigar box which once held cigars imported from the Philippines. He fingered the Pongee and Fine As Silk logos carved on top. He shut his eyes tight. What would he say? How would he explain what's inside? He knew so little himself. But from what he suspected, he sensed a pivotal moment coming. To what, he wasn't sure.

He heard a familiar pickup sound outside and soon a gentle tap at the door. He carefully laid the box on the table and called out, "Come in." His favorite redhead entered, spry and sassy and full of love for him. "You didn't ride Johnny Poe?"

"It's getting dark and I didn't dare ride him down Main Street so soon."

He strolled to the kitchen and brought back sodas, Henry Weinhard Root Beer for him and Mountain Dew for her. He knew she preferred cold from the frig poured over ice and squirted with lemon. However, she guzzled the lukewarm carbonate with zeal. "Sure am thirsty all of a sudden." She tapped her nose as though getting a whiff of the unpleasant odor.

"I had to toss out some rotten eggs." Seth wasn't quite ready to reveal Maidie's treasure. He stalled by showing her a glass bottle with cork, on its side. Inside lurked a large black bug with eight legs, a pair of claws, and narrow, segmented tail.

"What is it?"

"A scorpion. Don't worry. It's long been dead. Part of what I found up in Maidie's attic. Think it was Papa's." He plodded to the dining table and picked up a long pair of tweezers. He pried the cork, poked in the bottle and plucked out two flat yellow bits stuck between the scorpion legs. "I'll bet they're flakes of solid gold." Dropping the morsels on the table, he added, "One way to figure, they resemble cereal flakes in size and weight."

She studied the flakes and scorpion a moment then her attention roved to the wall above the table. "You've hung up some new pictures." She ran a finger around a black and white framed photo of a young man naked to the waist who raced bareback in a herd of wild horses. In another the same male stood barefoot on top two horses, one hand raised, one held the reins. "Is this you?"

He swelled his chest and shoulders. "Yes, and this is my family." He pointed to the faces of five children, pinched heart mouths the same as the stately mother next to them. The woman's neck clustered with pearls, hair set prim. The man had neat beard, mustache curled on the ends, dark suit, dark tie and dark frown. Four of the children wore a single strand of choker pearls, a token of their mother's taste. Their hair bathed in light on the right side with one piled up, one pulled back, the other two flowing free.

"Which one are you?" Reba asked.

He pointed to the youngest, a child about two wearing a dress and hair in ringlets. Seth could feel his face pucker as tears rolled down the crevices of his cheeks. "We lost them. We lost them all." He hadn't meant to break down like this, but the photo brought it all back. The sorrows. The curse against his family.

She patted his back. "Yes, I know. It's so hard. With Maidie's passing, they're all gone now. You're the only one left."

"We lost them," he kept saying. He felt the agitation grow. *I'm losing it. Can't let that happen.*

She placed an arm around his stooped shoulder. "Now I know why you're so good with Johnny Poe." She pointed to the horse pictures. "You've had lots of practice."

Thank you, Reba Mae. His back muscles relaxed. His mouth still twitched, but he leaned his head against her and let out a deep sigh. "I knew him, you know. I met the real Johnny Poe."

"The real one? You mean, he was a real person? I got the name from Grandpa Cole, of course. The way he used the name it was like cussing."

"He claimed to be a cousin of writer Edgar Allan Poe. He played on that connection fierce to get himself in and out of trouble. We were in Goldfield during the rush and he was lookin' for adventure without doin' the work. His luggage was fifty-two pieces: a deck of cards." Seth paused, reliving it. The sights and sounds and smells of Goldfield in his youth returned to him. "But he had his good side. When a customer in one of the saloons ripped an American flag from the wall, Johnny raged till that fella and the saloon was a total wreck."

Seth leaned forward and tried to ignore the remnants of the rotten egg odor. He hoped Reba didn't notice. "His best friends were my Papa and Father Dermody, a big-hearted Irish priest. He said he and the priest got along great since Dermody never tried to talk him into being Catholic and Poe never tried to talk him out of being one. However, he stayed away from Mama. She wanted nothing to do with him. But we went to church a few times. My sisters and I would kick and punch each other during the singing then I fell asleep during the sermon. But not Mama. She stared at the pulpit like it was the throne of God. That gives me some comfort now."

He stopped as two shots rang out close to the house.

Seth and Reba scooted across the carpet and opened the door in time to catch a boy with a .22 taking aim at one of Ursula Younger's Pekingese. Reba shouted and dashed toward him. Seth trailed behind.

The boy aimed at Reba.

Kaboom!

The blast came from behind them. Smoke billowed out the rear of the Stroud cabin. Seth wheeled around, fell, and crawled on his spindly legs. He scrambled toward the cabin as he heard Reba yell at the boy, "Call 911." And then she ordered, "Seth, don't go in there!"

But he wobbled through the front door. He gasped for breath as he plucked photos off the wall. Then he laid them down and grabbed for the cigar box and tried to push the cardboard box under the table with his legs and feet.

"I'll get them," Reba said. "You get out of here."

"The book . . . the box . . . everything," he wheezed.

Reba shoved him toward the door. "I'll carry whatever I can."

He pushed her aside and reached for the table. He heard a man's voice nearby. Someone with firm, strong arms led him away.

The fire spread quickly and smoked spewed the house. Reba pushed boxes out the door and ran back and forth throwing armloads of books and carvings. She finally came out with a tablecloth bundled like a knapsack. She rubbed her eyes and coughed and staggered in a circle. Seth wanted so bad to get up and help her but he couldn't make his legs work. The same man who helped him thrust out his arm and propelled her toward him. She soon sprawled on the lawn beside him.

By the time EMTs Lisl Monte and Polly Eng arrived with volunteer fire chief Buckhead Whitlow and crew, the cabin erupted in full flame. Lisl put Seth on oxygen and took his blood pressure.

"Norden saved us," Reba told Deputy Lomax. "Good thing he was nearby or I'd never have gotten Seth out of there."

The volunteer firemen hosed the garage and perimeter of the burning cabin.

Seth pulled off the oxygen and refused to go to the hospital. Reba tried to talk him into going with Lisl and Polly, but he shook his head as he stared at the blaze.

"I'll take him home with me," she assured them. Reba reached for the treasures he'd risked his life for, but he still clutched them tight. "Seth, you can stay with us for as long as you need to."

"Obliged." He stumbled over to Reba's pickup, piled into the passenger side, and hung his head.

Buck Whitlow scurried over. "We've saved the garage and the apartment on top."

"How about my Model T?"

"We saved it also, but it'll be a bit waterlogged a day or two."

"Who was the boy with the .22?" Reba asked Norden.

"I don't know who you mean." Norden stretched around as though checking to see who was in earshot.

"Well, he saved our lives, whether he meant to or not."

At the Cahill house, Pearl met them at the door. "I heard what happened. Tell me all about it. I'm so thankful you both are okay."

"They think it was a gas leak. I thought I smelled gas the minute I walked in. I should have checked it out."

"But I already had," Seth insisted. So it wasn't the rotten eggs after all.

Reba detailed what else she knew for her grandmother as Seth set several horse carvings and the free flowing wood sculpture of faces and limbs on the mantle, the one with the bald man with clean shaven face and the woman and children with long, tangled, and intertwined hair.

After Seth laid the photos he'd saved on the Cahill coffee table, he balanced the family grouping against the sculpture. The same number of persons in the two settings. Same proportion of adults and children, but no other resemblance. One winsome, expressing unity. The other a caricature of horror. One seemed full of rich history and hope. The other full of death. *The story of my family.*

While Reba stepped out to check on the horses and the heifer, Seth piled his smoke-drenched clothes against Pearl's closed bedroom door. He pulled on some of Cole's old pajamas that Pearl handed him before she went back to bed.

When Reba returned, she scooped up the dirty clothes. "I'll take them to the back porch to wash."

A piece of paper drifted to the floor. Seth picked it up. A torn page from an old Goldfield News, part of an article by W.P. DeWolf with no date showing. His handwritten note at the side: "Mama and her girls, God rest her soul." He rubbed it flat on an end table. Soon he heard the washing machine filling and spinning.

Ginny stirred out of the guest room. "What's going on? Why all the lights? I'm trying to sleep."

"My house blew up." Seth started to tell her more about it.

"Oh. Well, tell me again in the morning." She shut her door.

"She's probably sleepwalking. That girl can sleep through anything," Reba whispered as she tiptoed back in. "I'm headed to bed too. Anything else you need? You can sleep on the couch or out in the bunkhouse."

"I'll stay in here tonight." All of a sudden, he didn't want to be alone. Then a thought crashed over him. *The cigar box!* "Wait. Reba Mae, I almost forgot." He broke out in a cold sweat. This wasn't the way he pictured this presentation. It was all wrong. Awkward. No finesse. But it had to be done.

He stood in front of the two large cardboard boxes, tape-strapped by the EMTs after the fire. He scooted them down the stairs from the attic days before. "These were all Maidie's treasures," he reported. "I need to open them. Now."

Reba scurried to the kitchen and brought back a serrated knife. She sliced them both down the middle and tore back the top.

Seth pulled out the wooden cigar box. "Reba, this is yours. Maidie wanted you to have it." He watched her puzzled look. "Inside. What's inside it."

She took the wooden box and carried it to the dining room table. She slowly lifted the lid, then a piece of parchment paper covering. She tugged at a gold chain.

Seth's heart beat faster as he prepared himself to view this treasure once more. The last time he'd seen it, before bringing down from Maidie's attic, was around his own mother's neck, about eighty years before.

Reba pulled up a long string of attached small turquoise stones as brilliant as robin's eggs. They formed ten ladybug shapes, five on each side, trailed to larger stones on a double-rowed circular center. Delicate multi-strands of gold held them together and encased each setting. "Oh, Seth! How beautiful. I've never seen anything like it."

"It's a squash blossom necklace. Maidie wanted you to have it."

Reba spread it out on the lace tablecloth. "I don't understand. Why would she give it to me?"

Seth almost froze as the moment of decision finally came. Did he tell her the truth? Or skirt around it? "If she got a notion in her head, hard to change it."

"But did she mention any reason?"

Seth felt a chill on his heart. He hesitated and then blurted out, "Because you were so kind to her."

"But so were lots of other people. Grandma too. In fact, I wonder if she's awake. Maybe she is. Unlike Ginny, she's a light sleeper." She slipped to Pearl's door and gently tapped. In a few moments, Pearl peeked out.

"Grandma, look what Seth just gave me. From Maidie."

Pearl's eyes changed from droopy to alert. She admired the necklace with plenty of oohs and ahs. "I'm so glad you were able to save this from the fire. What a treasure."

"I don't mean to be rude," Reba began, "but you both know I don't wear jewelry much. And certainly nothing like this. Doesn't fit with mendin' fence, cuttin' calves, and shovelin' manure."

Pearl helped her clip it around her neck. "Yes, that was rude. Accept the gift. Figure out what to do with it later." She turned to Seth. "Did Zeke give this to Maidie? Or was it her mother's?"

"Zeke Owens? Her fiancé? How romantic." Reba fingered the stones and links.

"Sorry. No to both. It was her grandmother's. I do know my mother had it special made using turquoise and gold from her Worthy, Nevada mine." He looked Reba in the eye. "To tell you the truth, I have no idea how Maidie got it. It was nowhere to be found after mother's death, though she always wore it. My father and I looked everywhere. I sure would like to know how Maidie came by it. I wish

I had asked her before…" *Before she died.* "She told me to fetch the necklace from the attic in the cigar box. She passed before I brought it downstairs. I had no idea…I didn't realize it was *that* one."

"A mystery necklace. How fascinating." Reba scrutinized the design more closely in the mirror over the dining room hutch. "I will wear it and proudly, since it was important to Maidie. In fact, tomorrow at church. That is, if I can find something worthy enough from my cowgirl wardrobe."

"Good. And Ginny will help you," her grandmother reminded her.

Seth pointed to the boxes. "Pearl, I want you to have anything you want in them. All mementos from Maidie."

"Thanks so much. I'm honored. But I don't think I'll look at them right now. Too late tonight and too soon emotionally for me. Besides, we should look at them together. There may be items you'll want to keep."

Reba pressed Seth once more. "In all those years of taking care of Maidie, of living so close to her, you never had a hint she possessed an exquisite gem like this?"

Seth avoided her eyes. A hazy memory hovered over his aging mind. Hanna Jo coming to the cabin to get a high school graduation present. Maidie all *hush-hush* about it. Hanna Jo storming out and running away from home soon after.

"Aha, you know something. Spit it out."

"No, I don't. Well, maybe. I'm not sure, but that's all I have to say." *I've said too much.* Was Maidie trying to give her this necklace? If so, why did she refuse it? And what so bothered her that she had to leave home?

Reba stroked the metal and stones. "I want to know everything. I will know, sooner or later. Don't hold anything back, Seth."

A tense current passed between Seth and Pearl with a quick-shared look of alarm. *What have we stirred up?* Seth regretted more than ever they had never revealed to Reba the whole truth. At least, what they knew of it. Now that Maidie was gone, perhaps this was the time.

Pearl cleared her throat. "It's late. Let's go to bed and talk more tomorrow. It's been a long, tough day."

Pearl closed her door and Reba sauntered to her room, full of wonder. And worry.

Seth lurched and pitched to scrunch his backside into a comfortable position on the lumpy couch, his mind in turmoil with a flood of memories, a tide of speculations. His mother and sisters secluded at a desert plateau garden. Him stalking Goldfield streets seeking newspaper customers. His father plying his trade as a barber. A family split. Connections broken. A mother entrepreneur, ambitious, intelligent, and beautiful. A decent, faithful father, frightened for her safety, scared he'd lost her. Her love. Her life.

He swayed back and forth in agony, mourning once more his mother and sisters. And sweet Maidie, his lifetime charge, a fresh, stark loss. Watching Maidie's life ebb day-by-day reduced him to a helpless youth again.

He squirmed to push his head deep into the cushions, trying to still Molly's pleading voice and baby Maidie's cries. He thrashed the cushions, wishing he had a club to beat the swirl of demons that seemed to surround him. Nothing stopped the image of finding his murdered mother. A gunshot splattered in the middle of her forehead. And no necklace to be found. Anywhere.

Did the murderer take it? If so, how did Maidie get it? And keep it secret for so many years?

Right under Seth's nose?

And did she try years ago to give it to Hanna Jo?

With some effort he wriggled to a sitting position on the couch and attempted to find the switch on the end table light. He bumped his hand on several objects and prayed he wouldn't cause a noise and disturb the house's other residents. Especially cranky Ginny George.

A beam snapped into the dark and he made his way to the cardboard boxes. He rummaged around until he found the leather bound book he determined to avoid reading in his ardent respect for her privacy: Maidie's journal. But he raged with so many pressing questions. More every day. Perhaps she supplied an answer within those pages.

The entries started in 1925 and ended in 1945. The years her mind stayed most steady, sane and clear. Before the craziness began. He read for several hours, suppressing sobs and reliving long ago, but not far away joys. Early days in Road's End. Visits to her grandfather's barber shop. Finding true love with Zeke Owens. Zeke's honorable discharge from the army toward the end of WWII. Coming to Road's End to work for the Runcies. Doing carpentry and odd jobs. He'd forgotten about her working too, as a nanny for Champ and Blair Runcie.

I love little Donnie and his brothers so much. Looking forward to children of my own.

With my wonderful Zeke, of course...

Seth mourned her loss again. And her own tragedy...

Seth flipped the light off as he heard Pearl and Reba stir. He heard them whisper about checking distress noises emanating near the barn. They stole past him and out the front door.

After they left, he turned the page and his heart nearly stopped. He sat up straight. He read the cryptic notes over and over. He conjured every interpretation he could imagine and only one surfaced. Stunned, overwhelmed, he soon righted himself after a lifetime of practice, from thoughts of vengeance to fervent prayers for a righteous-anger kind of solution.

Dear God, should I have given that necklace to Reba? What if she wears it in public? What will happen? Is she in danger?

Trust Me, my son.

"Lord, is that you? Are you talking to me?"

Trust Me.

"I will. I am. Show me, Lord, what to do and I'll act." And soon. By anyone's calculation, his earthly days were numbered. His spine electrified with excitement. With God's help, at least two very cold cases could be solved. But why bother with such ancient history from many decades ago?

Two reasons.

Because every life matters.

And so does justice.

He heard Pearl and Reba's voices and clomps on the front wooden deck and slipped a hand on the light switch. He slunk down on the couch and pretended sleep with a random snore or two. As he devised a plan.

Chapter Five

Reba snuggled under the cozy blankets. Covered all over, thoughts and all. She blessed Him who invented sleep as she sought to sink back into that reset of oblivion.

But soon her mind buzzed with the day before. Birth and death. The loss of another calf. A paralyzed heifer. Maidie's funeral. The whip on her back. The explosion at Seth's house. The shock of the gift of the squash blossom necklace. And another frantic cow alarm last night. At least, this time it happened in the barn. Another late heifer. Another black calf and red mother. However, this one stayed home. No escape to Runcie land.

She burrowed into her pillow and groaned as her back raged. She peeked at the nightstand clock. Five o'clock? What day is it? Not Saturday.

Sunday?

Her eyes popped open as she peeled a cocoon of covering and pulled out of her private shelter. She staggered to her feet to fumble with the arms of her faded blue flannel robe. She slid open the creak-ing bedroom door to see if Ginny or Grandma Pearl had ownership to the bathroom.

Empty.

She grabbed Jace's cream and wondered how she'd dab it on herself. She crept past the closed guest room. No use in bothering Ginny this early.

She grabbed a clean towel and took it to the kitchen, wet it under the sink and stuffed it in a plastic bag. Grandma Pearl claimed a cold pack would work as well as cream. She popped it in the freezer at the top of the frig. *How long? Ten minutes? Twenty?*

She braced herself against the pain, grabbed the ibuprofen bottle, and popped four pills.

"So, you're up?"

Startled, she turned around. Seth stood in the clothes he'd worn yesterday and must have pulled from the dryer. "What are you doing up?"

"I'm going home."

"Right now?"

"Yes, ma'am. It's too noisy here. People up and down, in and out during the night. Snores and moans. A fella can't rest at all."

"Give me a half-hour. I'll take you back."

Reba's attempts to talk Seth into staying failed, so she drove him home, leaving behind all his sculptures, pictures, wood carvings, and Maidie's cardboard boxes.

Reba tried one last plea. "The cabin's burnt to the ground. Your apartment's probably soaked. What are you going to do there?"

"I can sleep outside. Done it plenty of times. And I've got lots of work to do. Might as well get started on it."

"You're a stubborn old man. You know that, don't you?" She gazed at him and her concern turned to alarm. Though he tried to smile, his face sank into grimness. "Seth, if you're depressed, you need to stay with us. You can sleep in the bunkhouse. It's quiet in there and you'll be left alone. I promise. It's just temporary, for a few days."

He reached out and rubbed her arm. "I'm okay. I didn't sleep well last night. I've got an old hammock in the backyard and it does wonders for my aching bones. I'll catch up with a long nap there and be right as rain."

"You want me to come pick you up for church?"

"No, I'll either get there on my own or I won't. I'll make my peace with the Almighty wherever I am."

By a miracle, the hammock had not been touched by the fire. Reba left him there, collapsed and cozy. She also tucked a basket of non-perishables into the Model T. The old touring car had mostly dried and Reba surmised with some polishing would look better than ever.

On the way back to the Cahill Ranch, her rig rattled around a meshed tangle of cottonwoods and aspen trees. A remuda in one of the pastures came on the run. She spotted the black one with silvery right foreleg among the streaks of pulsing horseflesh. Johnny Poe was still her favorite and the only thing besides her truck and trailer she could really call her own. She parked her truck and greeted her horse. After she watched him chew some flakes of hay, she checked the heifers and noticed the one lost-and-found at Runcie's still stiff and not moving well.

Better call the vet.

She prowled around the barn and corrals, shoveled muck, and tried to groom Johnny Poe. Grandma Pearl complained she treated him more like a show horse than a ranch animal, but today she needed to keep her mind off the loss of the newborn and the fire of pain coming from her back. Pain pills and fussing with her horse helped a lot.

After she brushed the thick black mane and set the saddle, she tightened the cinch, climbed up, and made three rounds. She trotted Johnny Poe around the headquarters then reeled him across the north pasture and down to Runcie Road. She avoided pavement and gravel and as many peering eyes as possible. She took the long trails of the detour route to Coyote Hill.

When they reached a certain side trail, Johnny Poe snorted, reared, and yanked his head in the direction of home. She grabbed firm hold of the reins and forced him forward. He took two steps and stopped. No matter what she did, he wouldn't budge.

A bird sang in the pines like the incessant ring of a telephone, but she couldn't answer or turn it off. "Hey, boy, there's no barbed wire here. No wires at all today."

She rubbed his neck and mane and kept talking. Gradually he nudged ahead. As his attention darted from tree to tree, he plodded one slow leg in front of the other. She began winning a victory of sorts, but didn't dare gloat.

Reba did her best thinking perched on a horse. And Johnny Poe rode real nice, when he wasn't stalled. He loved storming the hill, flying with the breeze. He craved speed. At eight-years-old, he was still fleet and agile. Right now he pranced like a hyper kid off his Ritalin. They didn't stop until they reached the top. She reined him in so she could peer around at the farms and city below.

Road's End, a settlement surrounded by dozens of crisscross mountain valley cow trails. A good place, as Jace said, for loners. *Why wasn't it good enough for Hanna Jo Cahill?*

Reba felt free on this mountaintop. But not full. Emptiness gripped her insides. She grieved for Maidie, a lonely old woman who few understood. She mourned a mother who left her and never returned. And she longed for the perfect romance, a kindred spirit, a soul mate that always eluded her.

Johnny Poe pawed the ground.

"I see you're through with meditation time."

His eyes twitched as she ran her hand down his sleek, sweaty back. He faced due south toward the exhilarating downhill gallop back to Road's End. "Be patient. Give me a moment. We'll get back when I'm good and ready. You might as well settle down."

This was the spot her mother brought her before she dumped her at the Cahill Ranch. She tried to see what Hanna Jo viewed that day. What was she thinking? Why did she leave this place? *Why without me?* She kept Michael and raised him. Why not her too? What would her life have been like with her mom?

She patted her horse. "Michael gives me hints. They led some sort of vagabond life, traveling here and there. No connections. No

security. Every stop temporary. No permanent duties or responsibil-
ities. No commitments, except to each other." She sighed. "Not sure
I'd like that. Maybe…" *Maybe I was better off in Road's End?*

She tied Johnny Poe to a ponderosa and scooted under a huge
spider's web glistened with morning dew, strung between two pines.
She hiked to a boulder and eased down against it sideways, avoiding
her back. Her horse neighed in protest as he beat against the ground.
She peeked back and waited until he settled down in the grass, with
several birds landing on top of him. He shook himself until they flew
away.

"Sorry, boy," she whispered. "I need time to myself."

Wildflowers covered the hill in purple thistle and pink and
fuchsia wild rose bushes. She surveyed Road's End again, the rambling village she called home. The layout looked like stray tramps
had claimed squatter's rights long enough to throw up roofs and
walls, then move on. With some exceptions. The businesses on Main
Street. The ranch houses. The sprawling Younger spread above Seth's
still smoldering cabin.

Reba relaxed as she sensed Johnny Poe settle down. She snapped
a sprig of rare mountain elevation rosemary, crushed the leaves, and
inhaled the robust fragrance. She thought about Maidie humming in
her garden. Maidie playing her haunting flute on the balcony. Maidie
over the edge after the tragic death of her fiancé. Maidie pining all
those years, also unlucky at love. Maidie in agonizing pain, prone on
her hospital bed, daily asking to see Reba to bring some relief. Maidie white and angel-like, finally at peace in her casket.

Where would Reba go now, when Grandma Pearl got too bossy?
When she missed her mom real bad? Whose feet would she rub?
Whose shoulders would she massage?

Reba grabbed a stick and dug holes in the dirt to make a mini-
trench around a clump of yellow and orange forest lilies.

Maidie fed the town with garden surplus and stubborn rumors.
Reba noted the irony that she thought more of her now than when
she lived among them. She wondered what Maidie, in her limited
capacity, wanted for her life? And did she get it? She shuddered to
consider the answer.

"I never wanted to be a cowgirl," Reba shouted to the wind. "Not at first anyway."

She was seven-years-old again and Grandma Pearl ordered her to shovel manure in the barn. She missed her mom terrible. She fussed and fumed to no avail and then tossed flakes of hay to the most ungrateful bunch of beasts God ever created. The next day she initiated a sit-down strike in the root cellar. She didn't move a twitch. She never felt such a sense of power as she did down in that hole.

She snickered. *It took Grandma until noon to find me.*

Grandma Pearl took one look at Reba crouched in that tangle of spider webs and rat droppings and said, "All right, you'd rather live down there, that's fine. I'll bring you supper once a day and you can come out once a week for baths. I'll hire someone else to help with our ranchin'." She slammed the door lid and stomped away.

The old rat's den that had seemed a heavenly hideaway moments before soon transformed into a pit of terror. She learned right then it's one thing to choose your own poison, quite another to be force-fed. She scrambled up those rickety stairs so fast she cleared off ten years of serious cobwebs. But Grandma had clamped the cellar door too hard for her fifty pounds to raise even an inch.

She banged until her knuckles bled and her heart nearly burst. Finally Grandma Pearl and sixteen feet square of the sweetest patch of clear Idaho sky appeared overhead.

"That's when I determined to be a cowgirl Grandma's way." She continued her flashback crouched on the hill, tears burned into her dusty eyes. "And that's what I am. So, why am I crying?"

At sixteen Reba broke Johnny Poe before he broke her. He still liked to test her mettle. Her grandfather once told her, "Black beauties steal away innocent girls and urge them to an endless childhood. She felt long past being a child, but still innocent. *Naïve innocent. Ignorant innocent.*

A distant sound like a simple, lilting tune caught her attention. She listened as a full sunrise of burnt orange and gold splayed the sky and heightened visibility. Curious, she stalked behind some high growing wild rose bushes. A light glinted from a far away window and beckoned her through the trees. Drawn to the music as it grew louder, her heart hitched to the rhythm. She began to recognize measures from an old hymn "Joyful, Joyful We Adore Thee." Or was it Beethoven's *Ninth Symphony*?

She crept closer near Bullfrog Meadow, which sheltered a patriot's field of white daisies, blue bachelor buttons, and Indian paintbrush. Random tree stumps scattered the field, some burnt or moss-covered. Reba crossed a private bridge that creaked over a narrow stream with a "Cross At Own Risk!" sign. She plodded over broken top boards and twisted around piles of cut branches, a load of dry, dead logs, and scattered wood chips. Logging residue. Great fodder for a fire.

Sun sparkles shimmered atop the aqua tinted waters of Bottle Lake. A black moose waded in to feed on pondweed and water lilies. A few red cedar trees competed with a blanket of lodge pole pines around the small lake and streamed up the hills. Sage hens purred as she caught a glimpse of a stripe of colored neck feathers. Flies buzzing seemed as loud as an electric saw.

Rough splintered wood formed a crude sign with drippy red painted letters of "NO." No what? No shooting? No hunting? No trespassing? All of the above?

Not far away she spied a man whose hat shadow made a moon shape on his face. His jaw set hard like he tried to keep his teeth together. He pulled out a gun and shot once. He hiked eight steps and lifted a huge striped garter snake. The twitching skin hung straight and witless as a rope.

He turned around. His eyes glowered and seemed to meet hers through the swath of tall grass. She tensed, ready to run. *Champ Runcie?* Was he already back from Spokane?

He pulled out a bowed knife and hacked weeds and pulled down grass. Then he sunk down in silence with occasional glances around. After he hiked away, Reba found the stomped and cleared place next to a stone marker with two short lines: Daniel David, February 23, 1945.

The same day of her mother's birth. *How curious.* Was David his last name? Was the date of his birth or death? *Curiouser and curiouser.* She registered the surprise and amazement of an Alice in Wonderland. She caught her breath and half-expected the morphing of talking animals, singing flowers, and a quarrelsome queen or two. What's going on here? How come she never knew about this place before? She determined to ignore any signs that read, "Eat me!"

In a swale surrounded by high weeds and pines, and down a long corduroy path made with perpendicular stripped branches, she stumbled upon a tiny dilapidated chapel with cross that ministered to a rodent congregation. A piano retired under decades of dust. Smells of mildew and bat dung permeated the building the size of a twelve by fifteen shed. Perhaps some scrubbing and hammering and the strains of old hymns could be heard again through the shabby walls.

Reba lifted the instrument's rusty lid and tried to play on the yellowed ivory keys. She noticed on the bench an imprint in the dust of someone who recently sat there. Was Champ playing this piano? Or did he have some sort of boom box with him? She didn't move as she tried to soak in a moment of wonderment and determine if it was also sacred. It certainly was undisturbed, heavenly calm.

She finally pulled away from the mystical mood, crept out of the building, and hiked up the hill to her antsy steed.

Back at the Cahill corrals, Johnny Poe trotted, laid back his ears, and reared high three times. Reba fell off and smacked hard on her bottom. Her throbbing back wracked with agony.

"I thought you had that beast whooped."

Reba grimaced and strained to get up. "Michael, what are you doing here?"

"It's Sunday morning. Thought I'd come to church for once. Might do me some good, if the barn doesn't cave in."

"Hey, that's great. Glad to have you join us." She popped some pills she tucked in her shirt pocket and reached for her canteen just in time before Johnny Poe kicked his hind legs in fury and jumped the corral fence. "It's your red Polo shirt," Reba yelled. "He doesn't like red."

Michael yanked off his shirt and sauntered forward. As he got closer to the agitated horse, he clamped hard to the reins and nuzzled the bright red cotton into the animal's nose. Johnny Poe took some tentative sniffs, rubbed against it, and visibly settled down. Michael handed her back the reins. "You should have neutered him."

Reba remounted, her back raging, raring for a fight. "You claim to hate ranch work, yet show off like that."

"I never said I hated it." Michael pulled his Polo with striped collar back on, leaving it unbuttoned. "It's just not as easy with this." He shoved his left hand toward her with two short stubs. Blown off in a fireworks accident, he claimed.

"You could learn to adapt, if you really wanted to." Reba felt an easing of the fire as the meds kicked in.

"Which I don't." He softened the response with his easy going grin. "Nina and I would like you to come over to my place for pizza sometime soon. Will you come?"

"I've got Ginny George staying with me. What day works for you?"

"Tonight."

"I suppose you and her will still be going together by then?"

Michael scowled. "I'm really serious this time. I hope she stays."

"Can Ginny tag along?"

"Oh, sure. I like Ginny. So does Jace McKane. Want to invite him too?"

Was her flirting so obvious to everyone? "Sorry. Not a good idea. Ginny's married, you know."

"But you're not. I was thinking of you."

Oh, sure. "Um, I don't think so. It's just me and Ginny, if she's available." *Besides, I'm kinda, sorta dating Don.*

"Never connected with Paris last night or this morning." Ginny's brow furrowed in worry.

"Maybe he's staying with one of your family members. Or a friend," Reba suggested.

"Maybe." She patted her forehead with makeup and powder over the wrinkle of creases. "That squash blossom necklace will go with most anything in your closet, including denim. Wear it with pride and confidence and everyone will think it's the newest style. That's what the professionals do."

Reba wasn't a professional anything, unless it had to be with a rope or saddle. She settled on black denim Wranglers and black round-necked chiffon blouse with her black Noconas.

Ginny adjusted the necklace, exactly centered, all gems in full view. She pulled out some turquoise dot earrings. "These will match perfect. And they aren't too big. In fact, you can keep them. Too small for me." In her teal caftan dress with black beads, she swirled around her burnished auburn friend. "Stunning!" she ruled.

They sauntered down to the barn with the guitar case. Reba almost slung it across her back before the pain stopped her. When she groaned, Ginny grabbed it by the handle and rolled up the strap. "I hope no one challenges me to play this."

"But you could. You know how to play the harp. They both have strings."

"Not the same thing at all. Especially without practice. And it's been so long on the harp."

About a fifty person church service that morning, twice the usual number, including Jace with a familiar looking boy about eight years old. Reba worked her way over to them first and Ginny followed.

Jace began with a soft whistle. "You girls look gorgeous." And followed with, "I'm so sorry about Seth's place."

Reba bristled at the dubious compliment. *He meant Ginny and had to include me.* She looked around for Seth and couldn't find him. "Who is your young friend?"

"I'd like you to meet Abel McKane, my youngest brother. I think."

"Oh!" Reba wondered why Norden seemed puzzled when she'd asked about the lad.

"You think?" sputtered Ginny.

Reba recovered. "Well, he saved me and Seth from certain harm by alerting us with his .22 in time to get away from Seth's exploding cabin."

"Oh!" Jace turned to the boy. "No guns. You leave our weapons alone. Understand?"

Abel scowled. "I hear you." He glared at Reba.

"How long has he been here?" Ginny asked.

"He was at my doorstep when I got home last night. Norden left the place unlocked and he had his run of the place before I arrived." He paused. "And no, I didn't know he was coming. His, uh, parents wanted it to be a surprise."

"Hugh's boy?" Ginny probed.

"Yep." His eyes and brows curled up as if embarrassed.

"Who is the mother?"

"His latest wife." He lowered his voice. "She couldn't keep a nanny and didn't want to be bothered anymore."

"So they sent him to two bachelor men in the wilds of Idaho? And without a warning?"

Jace shrugged. "Not the first time."

Before Reba could ask a question, she stepped out of the way as Tucker Paddy in red suspenders bumped her. Wife Ida with their two sons in tow angled for seats together. The biggest stunner of the morning happened with the arrival of the entire Runcie clan, including their ranch hand Joe Bosch.

Reba greeted Don. "I thought you went to Spokane."

"We looked at the equipment and came right back. Wasn't what we needed."

"Sure glad to see you all here today." She thanked Kaitlyn for the horse picture.

"It was Johnny Poe," she said. "He's my favorite, even if he won't let me ride him."

"Yeah, he's not a kid horse." She hugged the girl.

When she raised up she noticed Champ staring at her. His attention fixed so long, she wondered if he'd seen her that morning at the gravesite. His face flushed crimson. His eyes seemed to puff large, infused with a red rush. He looked like he'd started down a steep hill too fast and couldn't stop.

What is bothering him?

He shoved her in the aisle, away from his family. In an instant his fury reached a near boiling point. "Where did you get that?"

Reba searched around for protectors. The deputy. Grandma Pearl. Even Jace. Or Don? Her supposed romantic interest fussed with his grandkids, tugging off Kaitlyn's sweater, pulling crayons from his pocket. "What are you talking about?"

"That." He punched hard with a finger near her Adam's apple. "That necklace. Who gave it to you?" Champ loomed so close she inhaled minty breath and the ticking of his watch vibrated against her skin. "Or did you steal it?"

Astounded the necklace erupted such a reaction, she took a moment to consider her response. An assortment of retorts spitted around in her mind. She settled on, looking him straight in the eye. "I'll answer you, if you'll tell me who David Daniel is." She immediately realized her mistake.

What shot from his mouth resembled a rattle and hiss. He jerked around, stomping on her toe, and motioned to Don. "All of you. Get up. We're going."

Blair blinked hard. "What?"

"Now. Out of here." He glared down each one of them…Blair, Don, Kaitlyn, William, Tim, Sue Anne, and Joe too. "We're not going to a church full of hypocrites. They are liars and thieves."

A crowd circled around them.

"What's the matter?" Pearl asked.

"Nothing," Don replied as he scooted to the aisle.

Pearl reached out to hug the children. "I don't get the sense that it's nothing."

Don's eyes met Reba's, etched with bewilderment and perhaps shame. "I'm so sorry. Dad's not feeling well. We're going to take him home to rest."

With that, the Runcie crew exited the building.

"It was about my new necklace," Reba said. "He wanted to know where I got it and called me a liar and thief."

Vincent leaned over and studied the jewelry. "Beautiful work. I think you should get it assessed. Looks worth a lot of money."

"Perhaps you shouldn't wear it at all," Jace said. "I suggest you put it in a safety deposit box."

Reba fondled one of the stones. "What's the point in that?"

Pearl directed Reba to the platform to play a chorus or two. Subdued, everyone settled into their seats and Pearl tried to prepare their hearts for worship. She began the service. "Heavenly Father, we thank you for this barn where we can freely meet. Fill this place with Your presence. May all who come and go, arrive and depart with Your peace."

Reba thought of Champ's angry face and the cowed looks of his family as they left. She didn't understand any of it. She wished Seth were here to perhaps explain.

After singing hymns and choruses, Thomas, Floyd, and Franklin took up the offering with leather saddlebags. Pearl shared encouragement and exhortation from Psalm 34:14, "Turn from evil and do good; seek peace and pursue it."

Reba only half-listened, but bits and pieces pierced through.

"Turn from evil. Don't get sucked in. Run from bad influences. Flee temptation."

"Do good. For anyone, anytime, however you can. Good overcomes evil."

"Seek peace. Don't be the one to stir things to chaos. Be a mediator."

"Pursue peace. Even though everyone else around you is in turmoil, stay calm."

Reba felt anything but peaceful. Her insides riled up as she replayed the scene with Champ. Why didn't she tell him how she got the necklace? That's all he wanted to know. That would have steadied him. She should have known the secret place where she spied him that morning was a sore mention for him. A very private spot. And none of her business. Why did she goad him that way? *Forgive me, Lord.* She wasn't open with the simple truth and Champ's whole family plus Joe paid a price. They may never come back to this church again.

After the service, Jace grabbed Reba's arm. "Have you ever had a regular preacher or pastor?"

Reba eased her arm free. "Pastor Kiersey from Elkville fills in on occasion. But he has his own church and youth ministry. Or sometimes a traveling missionary shares with us."

"What did you do before you had the barn church?"

"It was just the three of us. Grandpa did the reading. I led the singing. And Grandma preached. In good weather, we met under Grandpa's Camperdown Elm. In the winter, in our living room." Reba considered whether to say more. "I think Road's End may have had at least one small chapel in use. I think I saw it. This morning, in fact."

"Really? Maybe you can show me sometime."

Reba hesitated. If she showed him the chapel, he'd see the grave too. She didn't want to incur any more of Champ's wrath, if she could help it. On the other hand, she'd like to go back there herself. That would provide an excuse. "Maybe."

Did his face light up? With a maybe?

Pearl tapped her elbow. "I'm going home to prepare lunch for our guests. But don't hurry. We're having more leftovers." She smiled at Jace. "Invite anyone else you want."

Pearl scooted away and Reba turned to Jace. "I think she meant you. Want to come for lunch?"

"How about it, buddy?" he asked Abel. "You hungry?"

Abel nodded and dealt a swift kick to Reba's shin.

Jace popped him on the bottom. Abel kicked him too. Jace grabbed the boy and offered her a chagrined smile. "As you can see, there's lots of work to be done."

Reba felt a trickle of empathy ooze into an unguarded prick of her heart. For the first time, she observed a side of Jace as more than an arrogant playboy. He was willing to patiently mentor his needy brothers, both Norden and Abel. He showed signs he'd make a great father himself. A positive mark already checked on her newly crafted Possible Future Date Jace List.

But she must also enter a negative. A big one. He wasn't a rancher.

With a blush over her private fantasy, she started to respond to Jace, but noticed a determined Don walking toward them. She offered an awkward greeting.

Don nodded at Jace and crossed his arms. "I need to talk to Reba. Alone."

"No problem." Jace turned away, his hand on Abel.

"But you'll come to lunch, won't you?" Reba said.

"We'll be there." Jace sauntered toward Ginny who chatted with Vincent and Elliot Laws.

She realized her mistake. In a bind, having mentioned lunch to Jace, she said, "You're welcome, too, Don. We're having after funeral food."

Don dismissed the invitation with a wave of his hand. "I'm so sorry, but Dad insists that necklace belongs to him. He had it made to give to my mom years ago and it got stolen. He wants it back."

Reba touched the stones and chains. Sure, it was a bit gaudy for her simple style. And she'd only owned it a few hours, so no special attachment, except her love for Seth and Maidie. In addition, she didn't want to turn this into an uglier situation than it already was. But something didn't ring true. "Is he sure, Don? Could there be another necklace like this one?"

"No way. Look at the intricacy. It's not the type made on an assembly line. He's absolutely positive."

"But Seth gave it to me. He told me it belonged to Maidie and she wanted me to have it. Seth said she's had it for over forty years. At first, I presumed she got it as a gift from Zeke Owens, her fiancé."

"Well then, Zeke stole it. He worked for my dad, you know."

Reba's stomach churned. How quick Don accused a dead man unable to defend himself. She took offense on behalf of sweet Maidie. She tried to recall everything Seth told her about the necklace. "No, I was wrong. Seth told me this necklace belonged to his mother, to Maidie's grandmother. It was made special for Eve Stroud using turquoise and gold from her Nevada mine."

Don hung his head. "Unfortunately, that's a lie. It belongs to my dad."

Reba hit an impasse. She didn't know what to do. But she had no doubt who she believed. Seth had been proved many times as honest, faithful, and true, both to Reba and to Maidie. As for Champ, she didn't trust him as far as she could spit him out. And Don toiled as a mere minion for his father. He knew nothing.

Trouble is, as far as she could determine, there was no way to prove legitimate ownership either way. However, Champ held power chips over ordinary citizens like her or Seth. If Champ can have anything he wants, except one thing, that's what he'll go after. With a vengeance. Reba had seen him haggle over prices of groceries. He could get real irate over a can of peaches, especially since he believed he owned part of the leased store, the land underneath.

She took a big breath. "Tell you what. I won't wear the necklace. I'll store it in a safety deposit box until we can figure this all out."

"Dad won't be pleased, not at all."

But it's a peaceful solution. *I'm trying to be a mediator here.* "He wants me to turn it over to him just like that? On his say-so? Without any proof or legal papers or anything?"

Don averted her eyes. "Uh, huh. What do you think? Surely you know my dad well enough to surmise that." He seemed focused anywhere but her face.

Champ finally did it. He provoked a head-to-head with Reba. This was no accidental whiplash as she intervened to tame down Johnny Poe. This was direct hit confrontation. She must decide: fight or turn tail and run, like most did. And here she stood in the stall of the barn church where Grandma Pearl exhorted them just minutes before to seek Christ's way of peace.

She flipped around and noticed the dozen or so who still lingered in the barn, chattering with vigor in small groups. She did a quick study of them all. She walked over to step up on the platform.

"Ginny," she called, "Come help me."

Ginny rushed over and she helped Reba unclasp the necklace.

Then she called everyone else over, including Don. "You all are our witnesses. Champ Runcie claims this necklace belongs to him. Seth Stroud gave it to me last night and told me Maidie Fortress kept it in her attic for decades. Before she died she told him she wanted me to have it. I don't know why she said that. I certainly don't feel I deserve it. But here it is." She held up the beautiful, cascading squash blossom.

"I want you all to witness I'm surrendering the necklace to a mediator. If you're agreeable, Vincent Quaid, I give this to your safekeeping. As most of you know, he is a gem collector and assessor. He's fully capable of this duty. Are you willing, Vincent?"

Vincent hopped up on the platform. "Good idea. I will hold the necklace until an official ruling of some kind can be made as to who this necklace really belongs to."

"Thank you," Reba replied. "Meanwhile, you are free to store it as you see fit."

"We can immediately lock it up in the hotel safe," Adrienne Mathwig announced.

Don rushed the platform and tried to grab it. "I object." He peered around, fire in his eyes that resembled Champ's. "Dad won't agree."

Reba determined to stay cool, to lean on reason. "But if this truly belongs to him, he'll be able to figure a way to prove it. We're a society of laws. That's the way we do things. Nobody can demand he or she owns certain property without a proper claim."

Jace held up his hand. "Possession is nine-tenths of the law. That means the onus is on Champ to make his case."

Don hit the back of his neck and screwed up his face into a frown. "Okay. I'll give you round one. But you know my dad will charge out on the second round."

"But he'll be dealing with me," Vincent said, "Not just Reba Mae."

"And me," Jace said.

"And me," all the others gathered agreed.

"We'll be here to make sure it's done proper and legal," Jace stated.

Jace had yanked another whip from Champ. Her heart soared at the display of the fellowship of community, the power of group support. But she realized she'd alienated Don, perhaps forever, by going for the jugular of his loyalty to his father. She might as well rip up that Dating Don List.

But if there were a smidgeon of evidence the necklace belonged to Champ, she'd turn it over to him. No fuss. No regrets. Whether she got Don back or not.

Don marched out of the barn in a huff, slamming the door shut behind him. Nobody envied his job of reporting the turn of events to Champ. His curt exit dashed Reba's meager hopes she'd ever find a Road's End rancher husband.

Jace snapped together a folding chair. "He knows he's smart and assumes everyone else is less so."

As they cleared chairs, Seth strolled in and peered around. "Am I late for church?"

Chapter Six

Although less than a quarter mile from the house to the barn, Pearl drove the Carryall that morning to cart flower sprays from the funeral, instead of her usual walk. As she drove back home and parked in the garage beside her '53 deep red Willys Jeep, her mind troubled, she replayed the incidents surrounding necklace and the Champ Runcie family walkout. She prayed for each person affected. For salvation. For truth to be revealed.

So intent on this newest Champ controversy, she didn't notice right away something amiss as she entered the house. Then she nearly slipped on utensils scattered on the kitchen floor. "What the blazes…?"

The house looked like a helicopter flew through it. Several holes gaped in the walls. Cracks marred the dining room windows. Cushions, drawers, and papers scattered everywhere. The antique roll-top desk had fallen face front. In her bedroom, mattresses from the high oak bed, made by Polly Eng's local Chinese ancestors before the turn of the century, were slashed and tossed.

How could this happen without anyone at the barn hearing?

And why tear up an old house?

She began to suspect a vengeful Champ when she heard a rustle behind her. Before she could turn, a rough shove toppled her as she flailed to keep her footing. Someone scuffled across the floor, the front door slammed, and she heard yells. She crawled to the door in wincing pain and peered out.

A man in baggy overalls and another in orange prison suit rushed for the bunkhouse. Shouts, glass breaking, and soon Ginny's Jaguar careened like a movie stunt over her lawn, tumbling a barrel of purple petunias. The red car staggered full throttle down her driveway with Paunch and Blue in full chase, barking in fury like hounds after a prey. Scat leaped a foot, hit the grass running, and did a frantic run up the Camperdown Elm.

Pearl managed a shaky rise to her feet, rubbed her shoulders and legs, and limped to the garage. "I may be an old, crippled up woman, but while I still have breath…" She backed out with a squeal of tires though doubts assailed her. She should go for help. It's dumb to take such a risk. "But it will be too late to catch them." She slapped the steering wheel. "They can't get away with this."

Adrenalin high, she booted the floorboard and passed around Paunch and Blue. She raced after the Jaguar and cut them off on the right as they tried to turn down Cahill Crossing. They sideswiped her and she gave it right back. They swerved down Stroud Ranch Road and crossed Runcie Road toward Bottle Lake and Bullfrog Meadow. A dead-end. Nothing but clogged up dead brush and trees.

The Jaguar made a complete U-turn.

One of the men leaped out and tried to get her to stop.

How dumb can he be?

She rushed him and he jumped out of the way. The Jaguar driver rammed a blockade sideways behind her. The other man banged on her window. She throttled the Carryall into reverse. *Oh, no, what am I doing to Ginny's car?*

She slammed into the Jaguar. It flipped around and roared past her. The two cars raced down the road. Then Pearl watched in horror as the Jaguar crashed into a stand of cottonwoods. She braked to a stop and waited. When she saw no movement from the bashed Jaguar, she backed up beside it. She rolled her window down and hollered, "Are you okay?"

An arm reached inside and grabbed for her steering wheel. She shot into reverse and dragged the man until he finally let go, collapsed on the ground.

Paunch and Blue yapped behind them and rushed toward her. She got out, opened the door for them, and they hopped in the Carryall. Before she could close the door, the man who had been the Jaguar driver now with bloodied and bruised face pushed her in the back with the dogs. He crawled into the driver's seat and aimed a revolver at her. Pearl studied the gun's markings. Her late husband Cole's revolver, stolen from her house.

"How did you get out of that wreck?" Pearl thought fast about her options while she tried to calm the dogs.

"Must be the good life I've lived." The man drove one-handed over to his partner and yelled at him. "Poison! Hold this gun on that crazy lady." He motioned him to the front seat.

"You're the one who's crazy. Get her and the dogs out of here and let's go. The gang's waiting for us."

"Not yet. She and I have a score to settle."

When Reba dialed 911, she got a lot more than EMTs or the law. The Cahill ranch exploded with neighbors, strangers, and assorted kids and dogs that flooded the road and converged on the front lawn. They mingled and analyzed and told Reba they wanted to be the first to "sniff around while the tracks are fresh."

Meanwhile, they obliterated the tracks.

Reba refused to let anyone in the house except Ginny and Vincent. Seth guarded the front door in Pearl's hickory rocking chair, his Model T parked under the Camperdown Elm. He hummed a tuneless song and carved a galloping horse from white pine.

"I'm waiting for the deputy," she announced to the growing crowd of spectators.

"Road's Enders are polite to a fault when it comes to private domains," she told Ginny. "But news of a break-in is such a shock."

"I'm so glad I locked my bedroom door," Ginny said. "Big city habit. Found a key in one of the drawers."

"Where is that deputy? Surely not hanging out at Lisl's place." Reba rang Postmistress Lisl Monty.

"The deputy's delayed," Lisl reported, "but he'll be there soon."

"How come you're not here? There's a full-blown tailgate party at Cahill headquarters."

"Someone's got to watch downtown while there are vandals and kidnappers loose. Maybe even murderers. After all, this is a government building."

Even if it is a fourteen by fourteen shack with a flagpole. "Kidnappers? Murderers?"

"Until we know where Pearl is, we've got to leave all options open. By the way, Don Runcie's on his way over too. Be sure to give him coffee. Black. No cream or sugar. But you know that. I'm nervous and just rambling."

Don? Black coffee? She didn't know that much about him yet. Her mind jogged to a flicker of Don and Lisl as a momentary couple, sometime that first year after he lost Marge.

Reba hung up and checked her ransacked bedroom. Chest of drawers pulled out and emptied. Clothes ripped out of the closet. She couldn't find her jewelry box with its store of trinkets and treasures. A silver and diamond cross and chain. An amethyst ring, her February birthstone. A Reba pin in rhinestones. A thick, gold chain with small gold nuggets, a gift from Grandpa Cole. "The only gold in Road's End ever," he liked to tease.

So glad I wore that necklace to church. Or am I? She grimaced at the scenes it evoked. All she wanted now was peace and quiet. Not happening any time soon.

She also found missing a music box that played "Memories," given to her by Tim Runcie.

Reba changed into jeans and a red flannel shirt, sleeves rolled to the elbow. Ginny rushed in, "My Jaguar's gone!" They heard a distant siren and ran to the porch.

The patrol car squeezed as close to the house as it could through the maze of vehicles. Deputy Lomax pushed through the crowd and ignored their questions. "What's missing?" he asked inside.

Reba peered around once more at the clutter. "Some food. Some of Seth's carvings. Some jewelry. Haven't had a chance to check everything. No big stuff."

"How about my Jaguar?" Ginny retorted.

"Yikes! Sorry, I'm kinda flustered right now." Reba offered her a conciliatory shrug.

Ginny scooted to the kitchen.

The deputy scribbled a flurry of notes in a small leather notebook. "Make as complete a list as you can. Check any stashes of cash. Or drugs. Prescriptions."

Ginny burst in the dining room with a tray full of cups, teakettle, and tea bags. "Maybe they were searching for a cache of gold. I recall the legends surrounding Road's End. Your Grandpa Cole told us some of them."

"Maybe the deputy would prefer coffee," Reba said.

"Oh no, he's a full-blown tea sipper. Aren't you, Brock?"

"Yep, when I'm on duty. Too much caffeine gives me the jitters."

Brock? They're on a first-name basis after two days?

The deputy snapped pictures in every trashed room. "No reason to search for tire tracks. The spectators messed up the outside crime scene. Okay, Reba, where have you been today?"

"Besides church? Up on Canyon Hill with Johnny Poe."

"Looking for lost heifers?"

"No, just riding. Grandma, Seth and Ginny were here when I left about 5:30 a.m. I took Seth home and headed up the hill. After I returned, we went to the barn, to church. Grandma came home first and haven't seen her since."

After the deputy left, Reba and Ginny started cleaning.

"Where did all this stuff come from?" Ginny said.

"Hoarding and accumulating proves thrift, in Grandma's mind."

Clusters of trash piled in the corners of the empty dining room. Assorted sizes of boxes, stale cosmetics, fluffs of lint had been tossed out of odds and ends drawers. Reba packed unfamiliar items back into the two boxes Seth brought after his house explosion. "I don't know all that was in here," she muttered. *Will check with Seth.*

She picked up an old scratched leather bound book with worn edges and metal clasp. She opened it slightly and noticed cursive writing. A journal. *Maidie's?* She tamped down the urge to do any more peeking inside. No time. And it wasn't hers to read. *Seth gave these things to Grandma.*

Cash in a tin box from a kitchen cupboard amounted to $27.50. Service-for-eight antique silverware still filled the dark plum velvet lined mahogany chest. Pillow case wrapped costume jewelry tucked at the bottom of Pearl's wardrobe closet.

"What in the world were they looking for?" Reba asked.

"They were in a hurry," Ginny noted. "And they may have been interrupted in the act."

"By Grandma." Reba shivered as she wondered what happened. She said a quick prayer.

"You know what else is missing? The dogs aren't howling at all that company."

"Surely they didn't steal Paunch and Blue. Oh! I've got somewhere else to look." Reba rushed back into Pearl's bedroom. "Grandpa Cole's revolver and shotgun are gone. They're armed."

"Or maybe your grandma grabbed them."

"I sure hope we can find grandma soon. And your Jaguar."

"I noticed the deputy didn't make any inquiries. I've got an idea." Ginny ran out on the porch. "Has anyone seen my car today? Rides like an ocean breeze. Fancy wheels. White convertible top. Pair of white seagulls hanging from the mirror. A Don't Even Think About Smoking sign on the dash. Has anyone seen it?"

"What model?" someone shouted.

"It's a Jaguar."

"Lady, that's all you had to say. Don't need no other detail in these parts," Tucker with the red striped suspenders said.

"Could be I seen it." Jesse Whitlow, Sue Ann's younger brother, displayed a distinct drawl copied from his Georgia native dad. "What's the engine like?"

"Fast," Ginny replied.

Jesse's older brother, Rod, spit out, "5.3 liter V12."

Jesse whistled. "I'd sure like to see it."

The crowd buzzed with possible sighting stories.

"Could of sworn I spied it parked near the McKane cabin last night," Tucker claimed. Several others nodded.

Reba peered at Ginny's crimson face and clamped mouth. Finally, Ginny wrenched back her shoulders. "Where could someone hide a Jaguar around here?"

"If you don't care how banged up the rig gets, there are a dozen cow trails and gully washers that crisscross the sections," Seth told her. "Goat paths once provided the only access in or out of here. But those thieves may be long gone by now."

"The only decent road from our place to anywhere goes straight to Main Street," Reba said. "Or Highway 95."

A six-year-old Younger boy raced past them carrying Scat and wearing an *Earth First!ers Not Welcome* t-shirt.

At least the cat's not missing.

Reba and Ginny slipped back inside the house. Reba peered out the kitchen window as Ginny scouted the kitchen for more coffee, tea, chocolate and cider, enough for a mob. Norden edged through the crowd in a Harley-Davidson motorcycle, a bright burnt orange skull cap on his head. Abel sat behind him. "Jace's little brother doesn't look anything like him."

"Neither does Norden."

"There are kids in the corral messing with the horses. I'd better go check." Reba squeezed past Seth in the rocking chair.

Out in the yard, Ursula Younger offered roast beef or peanut butter jelly sandwiches and pop for a donation. Baby Aaric was slung in a backpack. A hand printed sign announced: "Proceeds for Maidie Fortress Bell."

Reba reached the corral as William and Katlyn Runcie tried to saddle one of Pearl's mares. She searched for Tim or Sue Anne as Don rushed over, shooing them away. They sprinted to a gathering of kids who watched one of the Younger boys show off a toy model Navy F-14 Tomcat with missiles and swing wings that changed form in mid-flight, a replica from the recent Gulf War. Abel hung back, but peered around the taller kids with interest.

Reba lent a wary gaze toward Don. He yanked off his cowboy hat. "Dad's not going to pursue the matter. For now." He held out his hand. "Peace?"

So soon? Just like that? *Thank you, Lord.* She grabbed his hand with a grateful smile and reinstalled her Dating Don List.

Tim sprinted by toward his Dodge truck with Buckhead Whitlow.

"Where you going?" Don asked.

"Joe Bosch reported signs of some sort of altercation beyond the corner of Stroud and Runcie Road. Going to investigate."

"I'm coming with you," Don said.

Reba waved to Ginny at the window and rushed for her pickup.

Tim tried to veer out of the driveway, but got hemmed on all sides. Norden hopped on his motorcycle with Abel and led a parade route to the road. Many in the crowd jumped into vehicles and on horses and tried to unscramble the mess to follow them. Reba noticed Jace's silver Volvo among them. Where had he been hiding? At least not with Ginny.

Ginny suddenly appeared, slinging open Reba's passenger door and sliding in. "I'm not sure you want to be here. I'm afraid this is going to turn into a crash derby."

"It's my car that's missing."

"Where's Vincent?"

"Beatrice Mathwig cornered him with talk about Idaho opal mines. Said her late husband had an interest in them. He took her to his hotel room to get some brochures."

"What?"

"She also needed to get back to manage the front desk. He told me we should call him as soon as we hear anything about Pearl. And that he has the necklace under lock and key."

Tim stood on his running board shouting orders as Buckhead steered from the passenger side. Don sat in the back. Reba tried to wave everyone else away as Jace and Tim both turned at the road crossing.

Reba moaned. "They must have guessed we're following a lead on the robbery, but they'll only mess things up, like they've already done."

"Turn right. Now!" Ginny ordered.

Reba sped right at Cahill Crossing.

"Maybe the stragglers will follow."

Reba looked behind. "Yes!" She prayed for safety as she careened down Cahill Crossing and onto Main Street.

"Turn left, quick!"

Reba veered into the alley between the Steak House and Leather Shop, then left again to Runcie-Cahill Cutoff. She paused for the last of the line of rigs to turn on Main and doubled back to Bullfrog Avenue.

"No one behind me. Hope I can catch up with the guys."

Soon they saw Buckhead jump out of Tim's stopped pickup. Jace roared around them and kept going. Reba slowed and Buckhead banged on her window. She rolled it down. "You two get in Tim's truck and hand me your keys. Don and I will get the deputy and try to foil the fire chasers."

They piled out and Buckhead with Don in tow swerved her pickup back to town.

Ginny got in the back before Reba could. She had to hop in the front. She didn't look at Tim but kept her attention on the road ahead.

"Afternoon," Tim said, his head stiff, voice cold. "That was all Buckhead's idea."

He and Reba sat like stones as he tried to catch up with Jace. She hadn't been this close to him since before his wedding. She risked a quick side-glance. Sun-streaked dark hair, black Converse sneakers, and jeans. He'd always been a conflicting combination of sloppy cool and politeness to his elders, tongue-tied with beautiful girls, and sensitive to nerds. Like her. The cool. The cute but not quite pretty.

She tried not to dwell on his shirt sleeves rolled up, revealing a rumple of tanned arm muscles. *Thank God Ginny is here.* A chaperone. A go-between to bridge what might have been and what is. She noticed in the mirror he didn't try to control his lifelong lazy left eye as it fluttered and blinked. Otherwise, he projected control and bravado. She forced her mouth to move. "Your dad says you and Mr. Whitlow want to try some beefalo."

Tim offered a sound close to a growl. "Heifers shouldn't tromp where they don't belong."

Was he talking cows? *Or me and his dad?* "Bulls need watching too," she retorted.

They nearly collided with the silver Volvo parked in the middle of the hole-punched, rain-puddle road. Jace had scrunched branches and sticks next to the tires.

Tim rolled down his window.

Jace made a face like a cat caught in a mouser. "No four-wheel drive."

Tim got out and pulled several boards from his truck bed. He yanked away the sticks and crammed the boards instead. The Volvo peeled out. Then bogged again.

"If you'll leave the boards with me, I'll keep working on it. No need to hold you up," Jace offered.

"You're in our way," Tim said.

Jace backed away and Tim squeezed the Dodge by.

"I'll stay with Jace," Ginny said.

No. Please, Reba mouthed.

But Ginny turned her back and fussed with the boards.

With great reluctance, Reba eased into Tim's truck. *Awkward.* But Tim seemed relaxed, his mood much improved. "Hey, let's call a truce, just for today. Let bygones be bygones." He hummed a catchy tune and beat his fingers against the steering wheel.

Madonna? Elvis? She couldn't figure out which one. "Slow down," she suggested. "Might be other signs along the road."

He offered a quick smile. "Hey, I think you're right."

What? The sudden friendliness. Because Ginny was gone? Or because Jace had trouble? That's it. He's jealous of Jace. Reba felt like humming a tune too.

When she noticed deep ruts that looked recent, they got out to study them.

Tim pointed as he interpreted. "Two vehicles traveled side by side. The tires swerved back and forth like fighting racers."

"Look at the severed branches and shaved bushes too."

They got back in and wound around broken glass, bumper parts, and pieces of tire. They followed the war zone trash scattered across the forest floor. Around a bend a tortured sculpture of mangled red metal in the cottonwoods and tamaracks. "Oh, no! Ginny's Jaguar."

Tim pulled to a stop. "Be careful. There may be someone in there."

Reba pried open her door and crept to the wreck. "Looks empty to me." Blood stained the white leather upholstery of the once sleek convertible.

They searched the crash scene, then waited for the Volvo and any others to appear.

"Hey, Reba Mae, there's something I've been wanting to ask you for a long time."

"Oh?" Every nerve in her body tensed. She had her questions too.

"How come you didn't want to date me anymore? I thought we had a good thing going." He hit his forehead. "How dumb. Of course it doesn't matter now."

"Um, yeah. I think getting engaged and married tends to cut off a relationship. At least, it should. It did. It was you, not me, that broke us up."

"I mean, before that. Sue Anne told me your grandma gave her the go-ahead to ask me out to that dance. I figured you were trying to send a message. You wanted out. It knocked me so bad, I did stupid stuff."

Reba felt like she'd been suddenly doused with an icy shower and flaming fire all at once. Her hands trembled. Numbness began at her feet and started to rise. *Grandma.Did.What?* She couldn't think. She didn't know what to say. Her gut hurt.

"You didn't know?" Tim reached out and touched her shoulder. She felt the old buzz she used to get. She determined not to cry. She wouldn't make a scene. Like throw herself at Tim and beg him to take her back. Or run into the forest and never return.

Calm yourself, girl.

The Volvo roared down the road and joined them. Reba tried to enter into Ginny's dismay over the Jaguar. After her friend's initial shock, she circled around the crunched car. "I'm sure it's totaled."

Tim and Jace agreed.

"You got good insurance?" Jace asked.

"Yes, but what a hassle. Sorry, Reba Mae, looks like you'll be stuck with me longer than I thought." She peered again at her friend's face. "You're white as cow's milk. Why? It's my car that's messed up, not yours."

She took a quick breath. "I'm fine. I just…feel so bad for you, Ginny. It was such a beautiful car." Ginny nodded and turned back to the wreckage. *Thank you, Lord. Thank you, thank you.*

Soon the deputy, Don, and Buckhead arrived. "We took the long route," Buckhead explained. "Had to shake off the Younger boy and his friends, as well as Tucker, and would you believe, the Mathwig Triplets."

Deputy Lomax cut off the side road from intruders and possible traffic and took photos of the crash. "We can determine a match from the blood samples, but it will take time. Now I'll get tracks and evidence. Will also have to call in County Sheriff Ed Goode and some other backups on this one."

Ginny whipped out her camera. "For insurance and posterity."

At Reba's urging, they spread out and searched a wider area, but found no bodies or other vehicles. In particular, not Grandma Pearl's Carryall.

"I wonder if the other rig carried the occupants away?" Tim speculated to the deputy.

Jace joined them. "But the tracks go no farther than the smash-up."

"No one has reported autos coming from this road," said the deputy.

"That's because most everyone's been at our place," Reba reminded him. "And even there, we didn't hear anything at the barn while the robbery took place. Not even the Jaguar driving away."

"We had drama of our own going on," Ginny reminded her.

Reba avoided looking at Don.

"Don, Tim, and Jace. They're all here," Ginny whispered in her ear.

My past. Maybe my present. But of the future?

Tim and Don hurried away and shortly returned with a trailer from the Runcie Ranch. The guys winched the Jaguar on the trailer.

"I'll ride with you," Ginny said to Tim. "I've got to make some calls and find out what to do."

In a quick moment aside, Tim squeezed close to Reba. "Today. It was great. Even though we got kicked out of church."

"You didn't get kicked out." *But I got bumped out of your life. Why?*

"Can I hitch a ride?" Don asked.

"Of course." Reba cheered again at the sudden turn, her and Don doing okay.

As Tim, Ginny, and the Jaguar rocked and rolled down the trail, Reba hiked to her pickup, full of fired up emotions. Riled about Tim and what he revealed. Shaken by the day's emotional ups and downs. Worry about Grandma Pearl. As Don piled in, she turned the key and heard a familiar *putt-putt* and sputter. She crawled out of the cab as Jace looked back from his Volvo.

"What's the matter?" he said.

"Out of gas."

He studied under the hood and below the chassis. "I think you have a leak. You two can go with me. I won't bite."

"Yeah, but will your car run any better?"

"Bad news, it's somewhat of a lemon purchase. It breaks down. Good news, I know how to fix it."

Don got in the back. Reba slid in the front and watched Jace write in a notebook. "Making a report?"

"Sort of. I'm chronicling my adventures in Road's End. How's the back today?"

She tried a stretch. "A little better. Gauze and bandages and pain meds help. I never thanked you properly for the cream. Fortunately, I was wearing one of my sturdy flannel shirts. What do I owe you?"

He looked up with a scowl. "Nothing, of course. Just being a neighbor." He closed the notebook and tossed it on the backseat next to Don. "You ever do anything but work? Like having fun?"

Her freckles felt inflamed. "The kind of work I do is fun."

"Yep, I agree to that," Don said.

He got his crinkly grin back. "I understand. The gun and tackle shop has been the most fun thing I've ever done. Besides the days when I thought I could make a difference in the world."

"Where did Norden and Abel go? I thought they were with you."

"I told Norden to take him home. Safer there." He looked down. She detected something. Maybe a hint of sorrow.

Reba appreciated pulling her thoughts away from Tim's devastating revelation. She tried to focus on Jace, to relax in his presence. The tidy mustache and straight eyebrows contrasted with the curls on top. Four buttons of his yellow cotton shirt undone, she steeled herself against the ripple of attraction. She sure didn't need that. Not now. What a day. She stifled a chuckle. Now Don was the chaperon.

"You and Ginny seem to be friendly." She noted another shadow on his face. His eyes shielded something private.

"She's a great gal. And did you observe green streaks on that Jaguar's red paint?"

"I noticed," Don said.

Grandma's car. Her stomach hurt again. This time with a new twist. Worried over her safety mixed with anxiety in confronting her.

Jace broke the silence. "You're awfully quiet. Tim got your tongue?"

"Of course not. Why would you say that?" Especially in front of Don, of all people. What must he be thinking back there? She closed her eyes. "I'm sorry. I do have a lot on my mind."

"Hey, I understand. All too well."

When they arrived at the Cahill homestead, Jace said, "Get your gas. I'll take you to your pickup. You'll be able to drive it home, but you'd better get that leak fixed."

"Mighty neighborly of you, but Don can do that for me." She hoped she didn't sound too snippy.

Don slipped an arm around her shoulder. "I can fix leaks."

Everyone had returned home. Reba noticed the Model T gone too. She must check on Seth. *Hope he's okay.*

As she pulled up into Don's cab with the gas can, Reba realized something else was missing today. That is, someone. As a rule, Champ would be in the middle of a scene like this. The whole community involved. A chance to be the big leader. An opening to take charge. Yet, he was totally MIA.

Kinda nice.

Now to rescue my pesky pickup. And find Grandma.

Chapter Seven

After retrieving her truck, Reba contacted Deputy Lomax, neighbors, and folks in town. No sign of Grandma Pearl. After she flagged the deputy down for the third time, he didn't try to hide his exasperation. "Go home. Stay by the phone. There's nothing more you can do."

Now alone in the house, waiting and watching, her mind buzzed with what to do next. Exhausted, grimy, lost in a daze, Reba filled the tub with the coolest water she could stand for her enflamed back. She added Epsom salts and after a thorough soak she splurged with almond scented bath beads.

"As close to heaven as you can get," the clerk in Elkville promised her.

She could sure use a touch of heaven. She tried her best to spend a few moments thinking of anything but her earthly real world. She sank into the water, absorbing the sting that stabbed her back. She closed her eyes and imagined swimming in a lake of huge bubbles the size of beach balls that looked like moon-eyed cows. When one popped, the cow disappeared, but up floated huge, juicy hamburgers piled with tomato, sweet red onion, dill pickles, and dripping with steak sauce. Just out of her reach.

I must be hungry.

She had no desire to cook anything, although she'd had nothing but snacks all day. Pizza sounded good. She sat up. *Pizza!* She'd forgotten all about Michael's invitation to her and Ginny. She dropped down with a sigh into the bubbles again.

Sometime later, she jerked up. She must have dozed because the water turned stony cold and bubbles vanished. *Mustn't sleep.* She gasped for breath. Her teeth chattered as she swiped fast with a towel and pulled on cotton pajamas and a robe. *Where's Ginny?* She needed her back cream. *Where's Grandma?* They needed to talk.

She lugged a large down pillow into the living room. When she collapsed on the couch, she tossed and turned, alert to any sound or movement. "Grandma, please stay safe. Come home soon." She dreaded the very mention she might never see her again. Alive. She also feared addressing the news from Tim. Would she have to accuse her grandmother to her face? Or would she keep the fact of learning about the alleged betrayal a secret? In thankfulness for her return. In order to maintain peace between them.

But the inner wound stabbed her again. "Oh, Grandma, how could you?"

She stewed in the dark, eyes wide. Then she sat up. Scraping noises seemed to be coming from outside. She tiptoed to the door, heart thudding. Someone loitered on the porch.

Shadows drifted through the sheer white curtains and onto the wall by the fireplace mantle. Her grandmother's rocker scraped across the boards. Reba pushed against the front door and felt for the lock and bolt. She leaned against the wall and held her breath. *Creak. Creak. Creak.* With a lunge to the far side of the window, she squinted into the moonlight and almost laughed out loud in relief.

She unbolted the lock and whispered to the rocking silhouette, "Don, what are you doing here?"

"I'm not moving, so don't go fussing, girl." The glint of a shotgun slapped across his lap proved he meant to stay.

"I have to admit, I'm glad you're here. Do you know if Tim made it home yet? He and Ginny have sure been gone a long time."

"No. I called Sue Anne and asked about him about an hour ago."

She clicked the door shut and added a fresh entry to the positive side of the Dating Don List. He had her back. He would try to protect her.

Long after midnight, Reba awoke to the sounds of a car and headlights beaming through the front room window. By the time she peered out, the lights switched off. She stuffed her feet into tennies, wrapped her bathrobe tight, grabbed a flashlight, and sprinted out. "Who is it? I thought I saw a door open."

Don was already at the car. She stumbled on the driveway as she bumped into the ribs of a body and heard a groan. She flipped the flashlight down. "Grandma! Are you all right? What happened?" She knelt down and felt a stab of relief to view the dearest person in her life.

"I think I'm okay," Pearl said. "I tripped getting out of the car. My bad knees again. But don't worry about me. Get the dogs. They're scared to death."

"That's not the only thing scared in here," Don reported. "There are two men tied up with mouths taped and quivering like porcupines. They both look a bit battered and bruised too."

Reba helped Pearl get to the house. She put a call in to Deputy Lomax and then to Vincent who drove right over. They both insisted they take Pearl to the emergency room at the Elkville hospital for a checkup, but she refused to go. "I know when I'm hurt. This is nothing. I'll heal up fine."

Reba tried to scold her for taking such a risk.

Vincent took both of Pearl's hands in his. "You scared us to death."

Assured he seemed sincere, Reba resisted thinking about him and Beatrice in his hotel room talking about opal mines.

"I know. I'm sorry. But I had to." Pearl raised sad, weary eyes to Reba. "I've got to pull my weight around this ranch. Can't leave it all to my granddaughter to do."

Reba reached out to hug her as tears threatened. She agonized, torn with love and dismay, the bond of family and the newly suffered stab of distrust.

Pearl rasped out, "I was more determined to fight back than to be frightened. 'Course, now I'm shaking like aspen leaves. I can still taste the blood from the bumps I took. By the one called Wade." She licked the inside of her mouth and pointed to a tall guy with thick, curly black hair. He glared back at her. "He's the leader of those two. He drove the getaway car." She grimaced. "I'm so sorry about Ginny's beautiful Jaguar. I'm afraid that's my fault." She looked around. "Where is she?"

"With Tim. They're hauling her car to some late night garage."

"I stopped at Whitlow's Grocery earlier," Vincent said. "They told me Tim and Ginny took the Jaguar to an Elkville shop."

"They should be back by now," Reba said.

Deputy Lomax arrived with County Sheriff Ed Goode. "It's not your fault, Pearl," they both insisted when she bemoaned Ginny's car.

"I'm afraid it is. If I hadn't gone after them, at least that would have survived."

"If you hadn't, no telling who else might have gotten hurt. They certainly did plenty of violence to your house." The sheriff stood to attention, as though deferring respect to one of Road's End's most beloved citizens.

"I had to do it," she repeated. "They violated my home. I had to prove I can take care of myself and protect my own property, my ranch."

"Grandma, they were armed."

Pearl snickered. "They thought they were, but they didn't know Cole's revolver held blanks. No one but me knew that if they'd pointed the shotgun my way that might have been a different story. And I found out I've still got a hefty roping arm. I knocked the revolver out of Wade's hand like a toy."

"The charges are adding up. They'll have some serious jail time ahead of them," the sheriff said.

"At least they didn't maim or murder me," Pearl replied.

"And we're so incredibly glad of that." Of course Reba was grateful. *I still love her, no matter what she allegedly did.* "What's the other guy's name?" She looked over a short man about her age with premature balding head.

"Pwah-sohn. P-o-i-s-o-n. Go figure."

"Maybe he's French."

"Nothing French about him except the name, far as I could tell. He does spew some salty language. They both do. Better to leave that tape on them." Pearl turned to the sheriff and deputy. "I did learn they consider themselves part of some gang. They were headed to join up with some others and they didn't seem anxious to visit any family members."

The deputy wrote notes. "Gang, eh? Could be some beer buddies or an ex-con reunion."

"I discovered why they picked my place. They hung out at the Picaroon Saloon and found out I'd be at church Sunday morning. They waited for their buddies and when they didn't show, they decided to see what they could steal for the road. They're big into pawn shops and some sort of black market."

"How did you manage to tie them up?" the deputy asked.

They all fixed on Pearl with full attention. "They drove me to that out of the way road stop off Water Wagon Road and Wade shoved me around a bit. Then they tried to tie me up, but Blue and Paunch snapped and growled at them like wolf dogs. Never saw them look so terrifying before. I got the revolver before Wade had a chance to try to shoot them and expose the blanks. Then the dogs put the fear of God in their cowardly hearts as they got circled and corralled. When they tripped over themselves and fell down, they pounced on top of them. They're the real heroes. I think Wade and Poison both might even have a bite or two on them."

Don brought in a couple huge gunnysacks. "Here are their pickings from your place."

Reba searched and found her jewelry box. She decided to start wearing her treasures, at least on Sundays…and maybe going out with Don. She felt an inward groan as she picked up the music box Tim gave her. *Better toss it.* The sadness squeezed tighter. *If only…*

"Well, will you look at this?" Don lifted out some strands of barbed wire from one of the sacks, both Runcie and Cahill varieties.

"That should solve at least one mystery." Reba peered deep into

Don's eyes.

The deputy and sheriff transferred the prisoners to the patrol car.

"I'll call Lisl if there's any more trouble," Reba called out. She felt a touch of villainy in her heart, both on the deputy's behalf and Don's.

Pearl determined to rest on the couch until Ginny arrived and both Vincent and Don stayed. Pearl dozed off and on as Reba took pain pills and watched through the front window for a sign of a vehicle. Vincent and Don discussed Seattle Mariners, Road's End mineral discovery legends, and the price of wheat.

An hour later, headlights pointed toward them. A passenger door opened and a pickup with trailer quickly departed. Ginny entered the house with thick black eyeliner smudged, smelling of ginger and baby powder, curly hair pulled back on one side with a large wooden barrette. "We had to wait for a tow truck to take the Jaguar to Boise. Apparently, all of the drivers were out of town in Elkville. Finally, a guy showed. My insurance carrier works with a dealer in southern Idaho."

Reba detailed the events in her absence.

"Pearl, I'm so glad you're safe," she responded. "I'm sure my insurance will kick in to replace my car. Meanwhile, you're stuck with me without wheels."

Reba stifled a yawn. "Can you endure more time in our rustic village?"

Ginny tossed her head. "It's been fifteen years since I've lived here and nothing significant has changed. But I find I have. Not sure if that's good or bad. Maybe I'll find out."

"Well, I'm delighted to have you here. Can you please lather my back?" Reba stretched and groaned.

"Of course, girlfriend. After that, let's eat. I'm starved."

"Me too. How about you, Grandma?"

"You girls go ahead. Find what you can. But first, please help me get to bed."

Vincent winked. "I take the hint. I'm going home."

"Me, too," Don said.

After Ginny daubed Reba's wound, she prepared her Skillet Mess with sausage and rice, spinach and mushrooms, black olives, dried tomatoes, and cheese smothered in a garlic tomato sauce. "And spoon bread on the side," she announced. "I'd make you some Greek Death but don't have hot chorizo, green peppers, or near enough garlic."

Reba wolfed hers down. "You'd make someone a wonderful wife."

"That's what Paris thought. Boy, was he wrong."

"Maybe you need to cook for him more often. Or have you thought about the mommy track?"

"It's not that simple. I've run away, you know."

"When? Where?"

"Now. From Paris. We have our problems. We haven't been getting along too well."

Reba sat up straight. "But you seem like the perfect couple."

"Ever since I heard the news the ten year fairytale marriage of Prince Charles and Diana is a painful fake, it hit me. Mine is too."

"Oh, Ginny, I am so sorry. I hope and pray you can work it out." This revelation troubled Reba more than she wanted to admit to herself or Ginny. Reba tried to let this news shake out and settle in, to figure what it meant for her. Why did she care so much about finding a husband? Going it alone might be the best way.

Hanna Jo abandoned her lovers or they cast off her. Prince Charles and Diana to divorce. Ginny and Paris seem estranged. Maybe *amour* isn't enough. Love can't be trusted. Or what one thinks is love. It seems people you deeply care about can't be depended on to love you back.

Is there no such thing as true, lasting romance?

She shut her eyes. Thoughts too dismal for so late at night.

With mouth full, Ginny asked, "What do you cook that could steal a man's heart?"

"That's easy. Only three dishes I'm any good at...beef stew, beef veggie soup, and tamale pie. I put lots of basil in the stew, dill in the soup, and pile Grandma's jalapeno cheesy cornbread mix on top the pie."

"Well, it's a start. And all hope is not dead. For example, your grandma sure seems pleased to have Vincent around."

"Of course. They've been friends forever." But what about flirty Beatrice?

"She seems more school-girl excited to me. And so does he, for that matter."

"At their age?"

"What? Your grandma's sixty-nine. A widowed great-aunt of mine remarried at age seventy-five. They're as happy as lovebirds."

"That reminds me, we missed going to Michael's place tonight for pizza. I think he wants me to get better acquainted with his latest blonde."

"She seems nice enough. Say, does Road's End have a dry cleaner's?" She stared into Reba's blank look. "Of course not. Stupid me. I didn't bring anything that can be washed."

"Let's go shopping. We could drive up to Coeur d'Alene or Spokane."

"I can't believe what I'm hearing. What about your ranch work?"

"A couple of the Younger kids can help with chores. They've done it before. Besides, I need a break." *Especially after I talk to Grandma.* "We'll go after we're sure the heifer and Grandma and Seth are all okay."

Ginny chewed some more, dabbed her mouth with a napkin and made eye-to-eye contact with her. "Tim told me about your conversation in the forest before we arrived."

A quickening stab of tears threatened to overwhelm her. She looked across the living room at Pearl's closed bedroom door and shut the kitchen door too. "What did he tell you?"

"That your grandmother practically shoved Sue Anne into Tim's arms. And that it wasn't until today he realized you didn't even know."

"Why? Why did she do it?" Reba broke into sobs.

🐎 🐎 🐎 🐎

Reba slept little but she got up early as usual and before Dr. Olga Whey stopped by to check the heifer with paralysis of the hind legs. "Even though she's still down, she's alert and bright. I'm glad to see she's eating. She should recover with time and therapy. Let me know if her condition changes."

Fire Chief Buckhead Whitlow arrived soon after. "I tried to give

Seth a report on his cabin fire, but he's not home. Or won't answer the apartment door, though the Model T's in the garage."

"I'll check on him," Reba said.

"Looks like it was a gas leak for sure. There was so much gas in that cabin, most any spark could have caused the explosion, especially cooking."

"He wasn't using the stove."

"Smoking?"

"He doesn't do that."

"Even shoe scrapes across a carpet."

"Ahhh. Speaking of gas leaks, I've got to get my pickup looked at."

"Check with Franklin Fraley. He's been doing some mechanic work on the side when the logging's slow. Or else you'll have to go to Elkville."

❦ ❦ ❦ ❦

Reba rode Johnny Poe to Seth's place. On one side of the garage wall hung all sizes and shapes of chisels, knives and hand tools, along with several highchairs Seth built for the town's new babies. On display was a blackboard with a chalked to-do list: "Wash. Shoo the king snake. Spray bedroom. Pull up shades. Weed garden. Whittle at the bench."

She found Seth sitting underneath his own Camperdown Elm, grown from another Grandpa Cahill cutting. "Buck tried to find you."

"I know. I saw him wandering around."

"He says you had a gas leak."

"Don't matter. What happened had to be for a reason."

"So, you have a king snake around?"

"He thinks he owns the outhouse. I have to talk to him loudly whenever I go out there, to tell him he doesn't belong. He usually scoots out of the way."

She noticed a larger than usual alertness in the old man's inky, sunken eyes, though his bent body seemed just as fragile. "How old were you when you moved here?"

"Old enough to know you don't hit women with whips."

What an odd, unexpected reply. He must have Champ on his mind. "It wasn't on purpose. Johnny Poe wasn't where he was supposed to be and I got in the way. Anyway, I came here for two reasons. To make sure you're all right. And to hear more about Maidie and your family's story."

The old man kept whittling.

"You promised to tell me."

A shape formed in the wood. Seth smoothed and sanded with care, taking his time. He turned the block over. The top resembled a helmet over a long stream of hair. "I can show you instead."

When he kept carving, she said, "I don't get it. What does it mean?"

Seth licked his lips and dabbed his mouth with a bandanna. "There's not much time left, but it's not too late. Nothing will be wasted."

"Is that a riddle? What are you talking about?"

He looked at Reba with fiery intensity like she'd never seen before. "I realize how mortal I am. I must die, as Maidie did, as all my family did. Isn't all of life a preparation for the time we leave this earth? If we see a picture of ourselves as a corpse, we take notice."

Alarm bells rang. "Are you ill?" He did seem paler than more recent days when he whittled woodpeckers and owl in the sun on Main Street with his friends.

"I received two letters in the mail last week. One from a Canadian cartel who has decided to do open pit mining near Worthy, Nevada, in part on the property where my mother had her mine. So there is a time factor."

"I'm very confused. Please explain."

He carved out wide, deep eyes in the wood, and the beginning shape of a nose and mouth. "I want to try to rescue my mother and sisters from that cartel's machines."

"Are they buried at your mother's mine?"

"Not exactly buried. I've got to find them first."

"Some of them might be alive?" She attempted a quick assessment of how old they'd be. Older than Seth who was ninety-one.

"No. They're lost. But I think I know where they are. And there's the other letter." He carved and sanded some more.

"Who was it from?"

"Hanna Jo."

An electric bolt sliced through her.

"I've been havin' a dream. Whether it's an actual dream or a vision-like, I can't tell. We're on the mountain trail going up to Worthy to Mama's diggin's. Uriah Runcie gets us to the prospector's camp and they're friendly this time. They offer us a drink. We enjoy their company. We laugh and sing cheerful songs. Then Uriah remembers he forgot Mama's hairbrushes. My heart sinks because it won't do to arrive at the diggin's without Mama's special request. So we jump in the wagon and return to Goldfield."

Reba's chest heaved and she began to breathe normal again. "You said this is a dream? It didn't really happen?"

"Not sure what it is. When we got back with the hairbrushes, we don't stop to visit with the prospectors. I'm startin' to feel a delicious and calmin' kind of contentment that everything's goin' our way. But it gets dark sooner than usual. We can't see so well. So we stop to camp. All night I listen for the gusty wind through the wires, that familiar song, but all I hear is coyotes howlin'. They close in on us, yappin' and callin' for backups. Then we're surrounded. Uriah shoots round after round. One of them…his teeth gnashes my face and I fear he's found dinner. I scream and wake myself up."

"That's a nightmare. You have it often?"

Seth gave a quick nod. "When I go back to sleep, we're at the foot of the mountain again and we're being followed. Uriah loses them before the turnoff. We reach Worthy and there is Mama alive, her skirt blowin' in the breeze. And she's wearing her turquoise necklace. I'm so overcome with joy I can hardly contain myself. The girls are there too and happy. They pick me up and swing me around. Baby Maidie is healthy and cooin' and gigglin'."

"Oh, Seth, how wonderful. Sounds like how it will be in heaven, don't you think?" She wondered if Seth heard about Champ and their confrontation over the squash blossom necklace.

"That's when we climb back to get the goods and Mama says,

'Who are those people?' I look up the hillside and we're surrounded by men with guns who start shootin."

Reba imagined the dread and fear, the doom of imminent, violent death.

"I look around for Uriah to defend us, but he's gone." Seth lifted his carving. A neck, a raised arm and fist. The arm held a weapon.

A sword?

He sanded the edges. "Anybody who ever met my mother never forgot her. The Stroud women were either strong or crazy. One or the other. Mother was the strong one. Invincible. I remember so clear, every detail. The cruel, rude gales poundin' on me. The smell of the walls closin' in. The sound of Molly's heavy breathin'. The touch of my mother's cold, dead skin. It shocked me that fierce."

"So, is this still the dream? Or is this part real? You saw your mother that day. When you rescued Maidie as a baby, your mother was there too?"

"No, it was in the dream, the one I want to forget. The one I want to never relive."

Seth, you're not making sense. He's so full of unforgotten pain. A crackling silence settled between them. Reba noticed a patch of stubble Seth missed when he shaved. *So unlike him.* She patted him there on the cheek. "Did you ever tell Maidie the stories and dreams about Worthy?"

"I told her the happy ones."

So what did you leave out?

He set the carving on the grass and stretched back against the elm tree. "I'll be headin' out as soon as I can," he announced. "To Worthy."

Reba knelt in the grass to look the old man over more closely. A hitch in her heart skipped a beat. "You mean, Nevada?"

Seth nodded. "I've got a fire shut up in my bones. I want to play descants with my fiddle and hear the wire winds once more before I die."

"Why didn't you go when you were younger and stronger? Why wait until now?"

"Because of Maidie. And…other things." He picked up the carving again. "God says, 'go now.'"

Oh, dear. Reba would never want to discourage anyone from do-ing God's will. But it was obvious. This was over and out, beyond a sensible call. "I'll drive you there. Is that what you're wanting? I'd be glad to do it. Maybe Ginny will come with us, if she's not gone by then. I'll get the Younger kids to help out on the ranch for a couple days."

"I'm taking the Model T."

Reba frowned at the frail wisp of a man. "No need for that. I've got to get my truck's gas leak fixed, but that won't take long. It'll be what? A couple days there and a couple days back. Less than a week. I'll get someone to look in on Grandma too. You can't go alone."

"You're right about that. But I'm going in my car."

Reba placed her hands on her hips and gave him her best bossy face. "You can't possibly do that. Do you have any idea how long that will take? You'll be worn to a frazzle. There's no need."

Seth closed one eye and tilted his head. He put his fingers up as if measuring the distance from Road's End to the sun. "Considering a few stops and making allowance for breakdowns and such, Road's End to Goldfield is 740 miles. On long road trips, with an upgrade done by Franklin Fraley, the Model T should make about 140 miles a day. It'll take less than a week."

He'd been planning this for a while. "One way, you mean. Twice that for the round trip. Why drag it out so long?"

"I have my reasons."

"Well, you'd better state them or I'll refuse to let you go. So will Grandma. Besides, I thought you said there was a time factor. The Canadian cartel and all."

"If everything goes right, I'll make it in time."

Reba concentrated on the carving in Seth's hands. Was that ar-mor covering the shoulders and chest?

Seth closed his eyes and bowed his head. Reba walked Johnny Poe to the other side of Seth and started brushing his mane, their backs to the direct sun. Her mind dipped in desperation. She had to talk him out of this. He couldn't survive such a trip. And what about that letter from her mother he mentioned? What did that have to do with this nonsense? Maybe she could bluff him. "You absolutely cannot go alone." *This is a test, Lord, only a test.*

He pulled a pencil and small notebook out of his pocket and made a quick mark. "Yes, I know."

"You know what?"

"I'm not going alone."

"Good. Who is going with you?"

"You are."

Whoa. Better make myself clear real quick. "Oh no, I'm not. Not unless you let me drive you there in my pickup. A quick trip there and back. That's the only way, time-wise, I can be involved."

"That letter from your mother…it was postmarked Silver Peak, Nevada. That's right next to Worthy." He paused like he wanted that to sink in. "That's where she is right now."

Reba clutched a wad of Johnny Poe's hair and wound it around her hand. The horse jerked back and she let go. "What difference does that make? She didn't write to me. She wrote to you."

"She wrote to us both." He reached into his pocket and handed her a slip of paper.

Keep it, Reba was tempted to scream. She wanted nothing to do with her mother. No matter what, she wouldn't change her mind. She refused to take a slow boat to anywhere. Or a snail's pace Model T car trip to the desert. She gaped at the folded note, not much larger than a man's thumb, as though torn from a scratch pad. Whatever the words, they could not begin to make up for years of silence. Of abandonment.

Why bother? Why deepen the wound?

"You don't have to read it for yourself." Seth's eyes narrowed and glazed as though he discerned her every thought. "Read it for me. And for Maidie."

That didn't make sense. What did either of them have to do with what happened between her and her mom? She attempted to distract him. "I wore the necklace to church yesterday."

"I know. It was part of the plan."

What plan? She rubbed her forehead as a headache clamped her skin. She owed Seth something for all his years of kindness. She felt herself weakening. Finally, she gave up. She resigned herself to humor a dear old man who so recently lost his closest family member and only true friend. And probably wasn't in his clearest mind.

Against her inner instincts, her practiced survival and coping skills over the years, she opened the note with delicate care.

> *Dear Reba Mae:*
> *Please Come!*
> *Love, Mom*

She stood there a long moment, trying to hang on to the comfortable rut of habitual resistance and unbelief, yet stunned by the sudden unexpected. Seven words changed everything. She marveled at the inner shift. Like some huge oceanic tectonic plate. She felt herself soften, to dare consider the risk, the gamble, and the great leap over a lifetime crack in her being. To dare to hope.

But she had to drag her heels some.

"Maybe she mailed it from this Silver Peak place and is halfway across the globe by now," Reba said. "So like her, don't you think?"

"Nope. She's there. Trust me on that." The old man's cloudy, gray eyes cleared.

"Even if she is, why doesn't she come here? Why must I leave my job and everything and go there? How is that fair? And how will I find her?"

"That's how it is."

Irritation rumbled in her stomach. The old resentment pounded her forehead. "I'll have to think about it."

Seth nodded. He slammed the carving knife into the ground with a swift, sharp thunk. "She was strong, you know. Strong as Eve. My sweet Maidie never was crazy, until an evil wind blew. With God's help, we must drive it out."

As Reba scrunched the paper in her jeans pocket, another trickle spouted from a crack in the great dam she'd erected. Far across town and over the pasturelands, Reba thought she heard some wind full of bluster, trying to tell her something. She strained to listen, but it was garbled.

She realized with a start she had been wrong. Words did exist to call her out, to force her to consider taking a strange journey. She marveled that such few words could also apply a small drop of salve to her embittered heart.

She patted the horse beside her. "I won't go without Johnny Poe. No way."

Seth's only response was to hold out the female warrior who clutched the outstretched sword. "This is yours. This is for you."

She reached for the carving. Her mind wobbled as she slowly rubbed over all the shape of it, the smooth rounds and the sharp, rough ridges. *What am I doing? What is happening? Where does this lead?*

🐎 🐎 🐎 🐎

Reba and Ginny finally connected with Michael to respond to his invitation.

He roomed in the country outside the village of Poplar, halfway between Road's End and Elkville. His garage studio reeked of rotten grapes and once served as storage for wine barrels and coal tar. To use a bathroom, Michael had a key to enter the owner's back porch room. "I make sure I never stay long enough to need the facility," Reba told Ginny.

Michael met them at the door, barefoot and paint stains on his Idaho Vandals shirt. Then he stretched next to Nina on a dingy white chenille spread that covered a couch-bed combination. He perched two pizza boxes on his chest. "You want double cheese or meat lover's?"

Reba took a slice of the cheese, grateful for the competing aroma. She settled on top a nightstand, after clearing it. Ginny grabbed a piece of meat lover's and ate standing.

They bantered about people they saw at the funeral, while watching a Star Trek rerun.

Reba tried to call his bluff on Nina. "I hear you're taking pre-med classes."

"Yes, I want to be a pediatrician. My mother's one too."

Well, how about that? "Where's your family live? Where are you from?"

"Seattle. There are lots of them. They're mostly scattered all over from Tacoma to Vancouver."

Reba wondered whether she should venture the topic of their own family. She took a deep breath and dove in. "Michael, do you happen to know where our mother is right now?"

"Sure. In the Nevada desert somewhere. It's on the postmark from her last letter."

Reba caught a chill. "She writes to you?" *Often?*

"Two or three times since I left to come here. I even wrote back."

Nina gave him a look. "The guy who rarely returns my phone calls?"

"I know. Don't be shocked. I do have my duty-bound side."

As soon as the show ended, Nina pulled on a sweatshirt over her tank top and announced, "Prep for early class. Chemistry."

Reba walked her to the door. "Sorry you have to leave so soon."

She touched Reba's shoulder. "I'd like to get better acquainted. I think we could be friends." She left in a gust of wind that blew a tall stack of newspapers around the room. Reba scurried to gather them.

"Don't bother," Michael said. "Nina will clean for me."

"She's your housekeeper too?"

"Yes. And no. It's not what you think. She lives in a dorm at the university and needs the money."

"She'll make some doctor a great looking wife some day," Ginny commented.

"Are you saying I ain't her type? She reminds me a lot of Mom."

Reba felt the old hardness across her chest and knotted in her stomach. "Well, I wouldn't know." She took a stab at a question she'd avoided before. "Did you...know your dad?"

"He took off the day after my fifth birthday. Haven't seen him since. Heard he runs a fishing line in northern Alaska somewhere."

"Going to check it out sometime?"

"Maybe."

She frowned. It's not like he had other pressing matters. Why not now? "I'm going to find Mom," she blurted. "She wrote to me too.

From Silver Peak."

"Ah, the wild horses." He rose up and spilled the pizza boxes. "Hey, if you need someone to help out at the ranch while you're gone..." He stopped.

"What about it?"

"I've got some free time."

Chapter Eight

Seth scanned the Model T, trying to see it as others might. Though he vowed to take his journey by this mode of transportation, he determined to improve it as much as possible. "There were newer models with sleeker lines," he admitted. "This one used to glimmer and shine before the dents, scrapes, and rust set in. Can you help me get it in shape for better highway driving?"

Franklin Fraley strolled around the antique car, stooping inside, kicking the tires. "I'll bet it was something in her day. You taking a trip?"

"Yep."

"Which direction?"

"South."

"That all you going to say about it?"

"Yep."

"Well, is your engine strong?"

Seth rubbed his chin whiskers. "Seems to be."

"We could add an electric starter. That would be convenient on a long trip."

Seth mulled that over, prone to keep the crank he was used to. Too much modern and it wouldn't suit him anymore. "Any other way to upgrade it?"

"Well, you've already got the Ruckstell 2-speed axle. That's the best upgrade for performance and I'm sure you'll appreciate it going up a hill. I could probably add a Z head for some extra compression. That would certainly help. It's a simple bolt-on."

"That sounds pretty good. Can you paint it?"

"Nothing wrong with the paint job."

"I want it extra spiffy."

"Well, you can have any color you want, as long as it's black."

Seth smiled at the Henry Ford quote. "Nope. It's got to be purple. That was Maidie's favorite color." And this trip was for Maidie. And her mother and grandmother. "I also need some non-welded safety chain besides the drawbar, just in case it needs towing. Or would my regular tow chains work okay? Never can tell what's needed on a long trip like this."

"Push comes to shove, you'd be better off to trailer it. And strap it down at the wheels, not the axle. Too much pressure will bend it. But you probably knew that."

"Never had to tow it before."

Seth and Franklin drove the Model T a few miles to make sure the fuel tank didn't leak. Seth poured in a full can of gasoline when they got back. "Water cans are a problem, filling them from town to town. Traffic will be a nuisance. Will follow as many dirt roads along power lines as I can. You know, frontage roads and old abandoned highways."

Franklin pulled off his greasy Fraley Logging hat and wiped his forehead. "White Bird Grade is your first challenge."

"I'll take the old grade instead. Less steep." And full of poignant memories. He'd driven it before. Years ago. The first time he and his father and Maidie came to Road's End. And to court Hester Owens now of New Meadows decades later. A sad shadow lurked over his heart.

Franklin agreed to paint the Model T. "I'll take it to my garage. I'll fine tune everything and I should be able to get 'er done within a week or so."

Now that the trip seemed a reality, Seth studied a map the next few nights and fine-tuned a travel schedule. He also resolved to begin selling and giving away everything he and Maidie owned and not destroyed in the fire. Reba and Ginny stopped by to help him cart away boxes of barbershop items, tools, and fishing equipment.

A large box of fishing tackle in her hands, Ginny asked, "Won't you need some of this stuff when you come back?"

"Hardly any of it and I can always start over." He handed Reba a box from the garage of cat design wreaths and assorted feline Christmas ornaments. "Keep anything in there you want."

Ginny snickered as Reba rolled her eyes. " Hey, Grandma has been after me to return funeral dishes. Want to come along?"

"You ask her yet about Sue Anne and Tim?"

Reba wanted to dodge that question, but she couldn't. Not with Ginny. She could pull the truth out of taffy. "Not yet."

"You tell her about Seth's trip, about your promise to go with him?"

Reba crafted the words with care. "She knows about the trip." She dug in mental heels to stall any more prodding. "I'll get to those issues. At the right time." *I know, I know. It better be soon.*

They headed first to the Road's End Hotel run by the Mathwig triplets. They crossed a wooden sidewalk under a lodge pole pine braced overhang. Hummingbird and hollyhock windsocks spun in the breeze. A metal monkey swung from the tin roof. Lights strung around seemed leftover from Christmas.

Beatrice and Charlotta watched a western serial on television. They waved and turned the sound down as they walked in. Adrienne greeted them at the front desk wearing denim overalls and a silver necklace engraved with the words from Isaiah 46:4. "I apologize for my informal attire. I've been repairing the furnace and rewiring the living room to install a chandelier."

"I thought you used to be a doctor, not a handyman," Reba said.

"Dentist," Adrienne corrected. "That skill is not exclusive. Had to use drills and such, you know."

"Last week she installed new windows and fixed the plumbing," Charlotta added. "We watch the TV programs for her, so she doesn't get behind. It's the least we can do."

"What's this 'we' stuff? I just returned from a five-mile hike. Alone." Decked out in bright pink tennies and gray sweats, Beatrice turned to Ginny. "I don't know which body parts will give out first, so I try to exercise them all. I'd rather die of pulmonary embolism than boredom."

Reba handed Adrienne a box of glass casseroles and plates. "There's not a bite of anything left. Such good cooks, all of you."

"Charlotta's the gourmet," Adrienne said.

"Everyone loved her huckleberry pie," Reba agreed.

Adrienne pulled off a denim cap with a wistful turn to her mouth. "I'm going to miss her. In the early days, she was much different, you know. Maidie, I mean. She was smart. She and I made a castle doll-house once from a blueprint she drew. And she was an avid reader. She loved William Faulkner and Flannery O'Conner novels."

"She won county and state flute contests. Drove the other competitive kids bonkers," Charlotta mused. "But she played like an angel."

"She wasn't always a saint though," Beatrice broke in. "She'd dash down the street, raring for a fight, if anyone even hinted at playing bully."

"After her fiancé Zeke died, she holed up in that cabin. Got real withdrawn. She'd scream herself into raging fits," Adrienne said.

"Seth calmed her some when he handed her a hoe and gloves and a set of gardening books and shoved her outside. She spent every fair weather day after that, growing things. She had the most beautiful daffodils, tulips, irises and petunias. I think digging in soil helped rid her of some demons." Charlotta pursed her lips and turned the sound on the TV higher.

"Turn that down," Beatrice ordered.

Charlotta glared and switched the set off. "I brought Maidie gardening books from the library. She raised beds and figured out the best kind of fertilizer. Of course, Seth helped her. He also bossed her around on the order of where to plant what. I told her that didn't matter and to use straw mulch. Works every time. Won't get caught on a frosty August night before you get produce."

"Do you happen to be going to Cicely Bower's place?" Adrienne asked.

"Yes, we are, after we stop by Paddys."

"I glued this broken vase for her. A guest knocked it over and it was one of her favorites. Would you mind returning it?"

The Paddys lived at the trailer park in the manager's cabin with latticework front porch and a crooked TV aerial. A large whiskey bottle nailed to a cross hung from the high point of the roof.

"Is that wishful thinking?" Ginny asked.

"More like a hopeful prayer, I believe," Reba said.

Their sons, Amos and Pico, roamed the countryside to fend for themselves. Meanwhile, Tucker had advice for everyone on parenting. "Let them go. Give them a chance for the good life. Don't hold on so tight."

Ida Paddy cooked on a wood stove and washed clothes on a ridged board. No refrigeration. A small propane freezer for meat. She used a radio to call Whitlow's Grocery if she needed food or household goods.

She once told Pearl, "I know folks don't know why I married him. All my life I felt stupid and untalented. He makes me feel like the smartest woman on earth."

Another time she said, "He's not lazy if he finds a project he can and wants to do."

At the drop of a Budweiser, he could sing one long hymn to the glories of beer. But drunk or sober, he had his serious political side. He bought a polo shirt, slacks, and sandals at the thrift store to wear standing in line for his government disability check. All the while, fed up with Washington. One of his favorite phrases summed up his religion and politics: "Don't you find it interesting there is no such thing as a meaningless coincidence or a truthful politician."

Tucker would do anything for anyone in need. If he wasn't passed out.

Ida tried to guide him or fix him. But after awhile, her caring turned to anger against his addiction and against him. "How much more do you expect me to go to the wall for you?" she'd rant.

Then one day she clamped her mouth in silence if the subject turned to Tucker. Her renewed faith helped her determine to take on the challenge, to see the relationship to the end, that after the boys arrived.

Tucker bore scars of his own, both physical and emotional. There was a night in Vietnam, a roaring fire he tried to quickly beat into glowing embers. He reached his hand to stir the flare on the kindling. Something stung him in the back. A pale, bloodless runner, a messenger, collapsed in front of him. "We're surrounded," he said.

Somehow Tucker survived, but liquor became his painkiller.

Getting off the sauce on behalf of Maidie Fortress for almost a week left him craving to be himself again. He longed to keep the laughter of his sons alive. He needed something significant to do, to keep him occupied until he could go completely dry. Ida didn't need him at the trailer park unless a trailer broke down. Or the plumbing needed repairs. Now he was so desperate to be a free man, he almost cried out to God. *Almost.* That ventured into Ida's territory too.

He peered around at the sound of a knock. Two angels hovered at the cabin screen door. Reba Cahill from the church and her Greek friend. He twitched with alarm. "What are you? Some kind of prayer patrol?"

Reba marched right in and her friend followed. Tucker backed away, ready for a retort at the first judgment. "Returning Ida's dishes from the funeral," Reba said. "We included extra cookies too. Thought Amos and Pico might enjoy them. You and Ida too."

Tucker sweated, nervous like a tick with the ladies in his home. He looked around and wished he'd done more to pick up the clutter and swipe at cobwebs slung across the scatter of rooms. The boys and Ida deserved that much from him. He noticed the young women looking at him and waiting.

"I'm not crocked," he assured them. "I've become the mother of all teetotalers. Green tea. Rooibos red tea. Actually, I'm down to Perrier and apple juice. I need to get my gut right. Did you say you got food in there?"

"Cookies. Chocolate chip and oatmeal raisin." Reba placed several bags on a 1950s vinyl dinette set.

"I know everyone hates me," he blurted out.

Reba looked him square in the eye. "No, they don't."

Her positive frankness startled him. She must not run in the right circles. Come to think of it, he hadn't noticed her running in any circles. Another Road's End loner. Except for Ginny George. And her grandma. And her dancing at the Grange recently with Don Runcie. "You're right. Hate would be preferred to indifference. Or ridicule."

"Don't play the victim role," Reba scolded. "You can make your own choices. If I didn't know better, I'd say that's liquor talking."

He'd never admit to her how he wondered at times why pitiful souls like him were allowed to live. Why God allowed him to stagger under his blue skies and tread His green earth. Depression burrowed deep hellholes. *I should'a died in Nam. Or before I used up one molecule of oxygen. What a waste.*

"Everyone enjoyed your playing at Maidie's funeral," Reba continued. "You did notice that?"

"I think so. I sure enjoyed it." That was stupid. "Even though it was a most solemn occasion," he quickly amended.

Reba patted his arm. "I understand what you meant."

A vision of a silhouette formed in his mind. "You know what? I staggered home one full moon night and I saw Maidie."

"Saw her where?"

Tucker shivered at the memory. "Crouched at the Hanging Tree, howling like a wolf, and singing a haunting lullaby."

"Are you sure it was Maidie? How much did you drink that night?"

Tucker straightened and pulled at his shirt sleeves. "I was drunk, no doubt about it. But it was no hallucination. I remember it so clear.

It sobered me right up at that instant."

"I'm so glad to hear you're holding on right now."

Tucker warmed at the compliment. "You are so much like your grandma. I'll tell you one thing, Pearl Cahill is the best thing that ever happened to Road's End."

"Thank you," Reba said.

"And I'll tell you another. I'm a man who owes no one anything. I pay my own way. And that counts in this world. Or should." He clung to the truth of that statement. A righteous, sober strength pumped him. "Well, shouldn't it?"

"You're right about that." Reba glanced at her watch. "Hey, we've got to go. More stops to make."

Tucker stuffed his hands in his pockets reluctant for them to leave. "So, what's up with Seth? How's he doing since he lost Maidie? I thought I'd drop in, if he's up to company."

"He's working on his Model T. He's planning a trip south."

"What? Is that so? When and where?" Tucker leaned forward, eyes intense, crowned with more than curiosity.

Reba reached out for the doorknob. "Perhaps next week, he says. Maybe you can talk him out of it. I told him he's too frail."

"South, you say?"

"To Nevada, back to Goldfield where his family came from. He's taking Maidie's ashes with him. I don't think he'd mind me telling you, what with you and Seth being friends."

A prickle rose up his spine. He's going for the gold at his mother's mine. After all these years, *he's going for it.* "Yeah. Yeah, we are. Seth's my only real true friend. Besides Ida. How long will he be gone?"

"Not sure. At least two weeks, I'd guess. Talk to him, Tucker."

Oh, I sure will. Excitement rose through his frame and delivered a burst of adrenalin. He mumbled an affirmation.

"Sorry to run off," Reba was saying, "other deliveries to make."

He waved at the young women as they drove off in Reba's pickup and his mind whirled with notions. He'd never been more certain of anything in his life. He had to figure a way to go with Seth. He made some swift calculations, financial and physical. He had a money stash under his side of the mattress, funds he'd otherwise use to drink. If he could stay sober at least another week, Seth might let him partner with him. He had to. That trip's agenda had his name imprinted on it. In gold letters.

He bit into a chocolate chip cookie as he heard the boys bang open the front door.

Maybe he'd find a little color himself. He'd snoop along the way for signs of recent digging. What if he made a strike? Wouldn't that be something? Ida wouldn't have to work so hard at the trailer park. They might retire early.

At the least, the excitement and stimulation of the travel would help him stay off the bottle.

Reba halted the pickup in front of an old two-story clapboard house, newly renovated. The front yard sprawled around the edges with the contrast of clumps of wild pink rose bushes and one of the few verdant, manicured lawns in town. Several firs, some pines and a blue spruce dotted the grounds.

Six weathered steps led up to a large covered porch with wooden benches. Shades up, filmy lace curtains framed the windows. Angels and ivy etched panes topped double front doors. A breeze whipped around them as they eased out of the truck and they inhaled sweet pine scents and stretched stiff legs.

"This is our last stop," Reba announced. "Cicely Bowers' place."

"I met her and her niece Trish at the funeral," Ginny said. "Nice people. Trish sure has a sad story."

Dark clouds began to bunch up, like a flock of dirty sheep peering down.

Ginny looked at a faded "For Sale" sign facing the house and against the fence. "Is Cicely going to move?"

Reba chuckled. "Nah, that's left from when she bought the place. If you'll notice, most people around town display For Sale signs all year round, just in case someone drives through who's interested. Most any house is available in Road's End, if the offer's right. If the sale goes through, they resettle down the street or across town. Or head down the highway."

The door opened before they knocked. The house reeked of pop-corn and hot caramel and chocolate that covered a woodsy smell. Cicely Bowers swept long, thin arms around them, dressed in red silky over-blouse, black tights, barefoot.

She had the quick eyes of a keen mind. When she took the dish-es, her words came fast, like skipped stones. "Girls, please come in. There's a squall coming. It may even snow. So strange this Idaho weather. Can snow any day of the year."

She twirled as though waving a magic wand. "Come to the rec room. I'd love to chat a bit, if you have the time." She fanned her fin-gers at them, nails squared and red, all the exact same long length.

They followed her past a large kitchen. A pot of morel mush-rooms soaked in salt water on the stove, floating like sea anemones. "Just picked them out of the forest."

She led them to a room spilling over with books and games and black velvet ottomans. Egg yolk yellow, blank walls held nails where something should be hanging. A window looked out on a large man-icured backyard with wood and black iron benches, rope swings, and a basketball half court. "The former owner had lots of children," she explained. "It works for my guests. Do you have children, Ginny?"

"No, but plenty of nephews, nieces, and cousins."

Three paintings hung on the wall in front of her, the center one of Cicely's house with white picket fence. On the right, a close-up of the glass over the front doors with etched angels and ivy. The left paint-ing didn't look finished, but was definitely of Cicely's backyard in an impressionist style. Cicely's form was unmistakable on the wooden swing. Shadows ghosted the other shapes. "Look at the signature," she said.

Reba leaned closer. She tried to read the scrawl of the autograph: "Patricia Rebecca Hocking. Is that Trish? The gal who has been stay-ing with you?"

"Yes, isn't she talented? Her mother paints much like that too." She wound her pencil thin legs around a stool. "I went to Missouri for Trish's wedding. She married a nice young man, Davis Stanton. I was so impressed with the church family. The women sewed curtains for the social hall and cushioned the pews in Egan green, Trish's fa-vorite color. The choir director wrote a song for the couple and sang it from the balcony. The town mayor toasted them at the reception."

Reba almost snickered. *Yeah, Champ would do that.*

"We were all so proud. Trish Hocking, unwed mother, finally settling down. Davis Stanton, formerly into drugs and hard living, prepared to be a husband. Becky Hocking, six-years-old, ecstatic to have a father." Cicely studied the painting. "The marriage lasted seven months. A bed of bitter roses. Trish said he didn't know how to treat a woman. And Davis claimed he couldn't keep up with her credit card spending. That was about six years ago."

Ginny snorted. "Ha! A familiar story."

"I've been married three times and the best advice I can give is you shove your shoulders in and listen hard." She grimaced and of-fered them both a cut glass bowl of silver foil wrapped Hershey's Kisses. "Trish announced she was pregnant and took Becky with her to St. Louis. No forwarding address. It was so hard on her parents. Neoma and Hank didn't see Ned until he was three years old. Mean-while, Davis moved to Vegas."

Reba gazed at Ginny. They were each lost in their own thoughts of flawed people and broken relationships. Trish so much like Re-ba's mother, Hanna Jo. Ginny surely related to the runaway, but she hadn't left kids behind. And she did try to talk to Paris most every day.

She sensed Ginny trying to steer the conversation away from broken marriages. "Reba tells me you used to own a hat shop."

"Yes, in Seattle. A woman I worked for asked me to do modeling for a client of ours at a charity fashion show. I didn't know until I arrived I would be modeling hats. Every time I sauntered down the runway, I became a different woman. Maybe it was the real me. I came into my own. I believed I could charge the world.

"The client let me buy any hat I wanted at a discount rate. I bought them all, quit my job, set up my own hat shop, and made more money than I ever wanted."

"But how did you get to Road's End?" Ginny asked.

"One day I packed all my hats and aimed east. I wanted to see new sights. But my car heated up climbing the Winchester grade. I limped into Road's End, saw this house for sale, and never got any further. It's felt like home ever since. Would you like to see my hats, at least what I have left?"

"I sure would," Ginny said.

Reba too, though she wouldn't admit it. She loved seeing Cicely in her many hats. But if it wasn't a cowgirl hat, she had no use for it.

They followed Cicely upstairs to a dormer room, one huge walk-in closet filled with clothes in three colors: black, yellows, and various shades of red. A long wall of rows of hooks hung with flowered hats, ribbon and lace hats, and plain chapeaus. In the middle of the room stood a large mahogany framed mirror.

Cicely placed a large hat on her head. Its brim covered her countenance. "I was there when all three of my husbands left this earth. Lost my daughter too. Leukemia, like her father." She rose up, a spunky look in her eye. "Some folks think I wear these hats to attract a man. They're wrong. I wear them to declare my delight in living, my gumption. It's who I am."

Reba stared at the fully alive woman. *And who am I?* Apart from the ranch, that is. That unnerved her. The ranch defined her. Without it, she floundered.

They stared in wonder at this whimsical woman who resided in this conventional house in this curious, quaint, and rustic village. She hadn't left Seattle. She brought Seattle with her. The culture of class, mystique, and the dance of life.

"Is Trish here now?" Reba had a sudden strong desire to talk to this young woman. To quiz her about what made her run. Maybe she could glimpse some understanding of her mom.

"No, she left this morning. Found a job in Reno, working for a friend of mine. I'm afraid it's partly because we heard her mother and children might be coming by for a visit next week. I sure hope they do." Cicely bowed her head. "Would you mind? Pray with me for Trish, Neoma, Becky and Ned. They have a lot to work out."

Now? After an awkward hesitation, Ginny and Reba closed their eyes as Cicely rattled the gates of heaven for attention on behalf of this estranged family. Reba had no doubt her prayer had been heard. But she wondered how long it had been since she'd prayed for her own.

Lord, help me talk to Grandma.

Chapter Nine

The day after Tucker Paddy found out about Seth's plans, he meandered down Main Street and perked up when he spotted Seth on the whittling bench. He sat down beside him and wasted no time. "You need a companion for your big trip."

Seth leaned back and stretched his arms. "No, I don't."

"But you definitely need me to come along." Tucker pulled clippers out of his pocket and trimmed his nails.

"Why is that?"

"Because I can find all the good side roads. I can scout ahead for danger." He rubbed his nose and scratched his ear with the clippers. "I can keep a good eye out for you, keep you from making wrong turns. You know, many out there in that big world yonder can't tell a trail marker from a crumpled tumbleweed."

Seth bent down, intent on his carving. "I know how to get there."

"How do you know? It's been many decades since you traveled those roads. You could get stuck on paths that go nowhere. The desert is a maze of detours and dead ends to confound the most determined of men."

Seth stretched his back against the bench. "All I have to do is go south on Highway 95 to Winnemucca and turn west, then south again. Hard to get lost with that straight a shot."

Tucker realized he'd better change his tactic or he'd lose his opportunity. "I realize that. You're sure right. But after you get to the desert and need to find your way around, I've got a good sense for, uh, finding treasures and such. Remember those garnets I discovered around Elk River? That's what I mean." Tucker beamed as Seth sat up. Then he sank into silence when he recognized a familiar profile approaching.

Champ marched over to Seth. "You can't take off like that with Maidie fresh buried. It's not proper. It shows a lack of respect for the dead."

Seth eyeballed Champ and his indignation. "She's not buried. I just picked her up. She's right over there." He pointed the stick at the floor of his Model T.

Champ did a gradual pivot to gaze at an urn.

"Is that a shocker for you? You look a bit peaked, Champ." Seth returned to his carving.

"That's ridiculous. I'm no such thing."

"Why, yes," Tucker agreed. "You look downright white in the gills."

Seth shaved a long curl of wood from his stick. "Champ, that squash blossom necklace belonged to my mother, Eve Stroud. What makes you think you own it?"

"You can't prove that."

"Maybe not. But I know it as sure as I live and breathe. That's enough for me." He picked up the long, twisted shaving. "For now."

The McKane brothers including Abel strolled across the street. "Seth, I hear you know where the skeletons are buried," Jace said.

The old man nearly pricked himself with the carving knife as it dropped and he leaned over to pick it up.

"And the gold too," added Norden.

Champ glared at Jace and stomped away without a word.

"What's busting his britches?" Tucker asked.

"I think anger's his lifestyle. You can feel it snap and sizzle when he comes around," Jace said.

"Better watch out," Norden warned. "That man's waiting a chance to vindicate himself against you. That kind doesn't take confrontation lightly. I learned that on the football fields."

Seth blew shavings off his wooden wolf. "Where there's anger, there's a bitter root."

"Maybe so, but try to be a law-abiding citizen and you're liable to get cussed out by his honor the mayor," Tucker replied. "Why does he take his troubles out on everybody else?" Tucker lowered his voice and stared at Norden. "I've seen lots of strange doings in the dead of night and tried to report them. To no avail. I tell ya, things aren't what they seem in this town."

Road's End barber Alfred James joined them. "During Maidie's funeral and all, Champ seemed civil enough. Like the old days. But as soon as the mournin' was through, he got to ragin' again. Look what he done to poor ole Reba. He should have been charged."

"He's got something fierce to prove," Jace remarked. "That makes a man ambitious or dangerous."

"Or both." Seth handed the wolf to Tucker and picked up another piece of wood.

"You giving this to me?" Tucker asked.

"Thought your boys might like it."

"Yes, they would. Thanks. I'd make them toys like this myself, but don't have the knack." He rolled it in the hem of his ragged shirt for protection. "I made a chicken skeleton once as a science project. The teacher wanted to display it in class the rest of the year. Nearly busted my buttons. But I never saw it again. Don't know what happened to it." Tucker mulled that over. "Great teacher though."

Alfred spit out his chew. "One thing I can say for Champ, he's no genteel Sunday farmer. He's a dirt-under-the-nails rancher who eked out a hard living by working the land all his life."

Jake faced them all down. "That's commendable. But how come no one fights him? No one stands up to him?"

Tucker knew why. He learned long ago, some folks naturally lead and others follow. That was in a rulebook somewhere. He'd always been a tagalong. "Because there's no one to make him accountable for anything. He's the king pin and that's all there is to it. Least whiles, for the present."

Reba returned home from chores on the ranch that afternoon to sounds like a herd of wild horses stampeded the roof. A white plague of hailstones banged against the metal and salted the yard. Meanwhile, Reba groaned under the weight of a headache. And the undone task of talking with her grandma.

Ginny plunged into the ranch house with an umbrella. "I can't believe this weather."

"We had a spit of snow several weeks ago. You need to remember, we're in the mountains at four thousand foot elevation. We can have snow or hail most any day of the year." She massaged her scalp. "I've got to check our crop. We planted a few acres of wheat. Hail can beat it down and ruin it."

Before dinner, Ginny changed again, this time into a long caftan dress in shades of blues and mocha with a wooden necklace and bracelets. Bare feet peeked out from the sweeping hem. She shook her arm, jangling the bracelets. "Seth made me these a long time ago."

"I thought you were cold," Reba said.

"No, just wet. Now that I'm dry, I'm comfy."

Reba yawned. "I haven't slept much in days, maybe weeks."

"Is something bothering you?"

"It's Don. And Grandma. And Mom. Seth and his trip. And me. It's so many things, I'm confused."

"I'll tell you one thing about Don. I caught him looking in a mirror to practice his smile."

"What?"

"Says something about a man, don't you think?"

That he smiles in a mirror? "He might have been checking his teeth. Did you think of that?"

"With his mouth closed?"

Poor Don. Am I supposed to put that down as a negative on The Dating Don List? Hardly seems worth it.

"So, are you and Don dating or not? What's the status?"

"We went to a Grange dance and saw Silence of the Lambs in Elkville."

"A serial killer movie? Not very romantic."

"I agree. I kept my eyes closed through much of it. No fireworks yet. And that's fine with me."

"Is he interested in you? Or in your ranch?"

"He's got plenty of land to inherit. He doesn't need mine. Grandma and I are land rich and dollar poor. You should be suspicious of me instead."

Reba found Ginny hunkered underneath Grandpa Cole's Camperdown Elm. "Hi, girlfriend. Remember when we hid under here as kids? I believe the tree was lower to the ground then."

"And we were smaller. Lots more nooks where we could hide. Have you talked to your grandma yet?"

"About Tim and Sue Anne?"

"And about you joining Seth's Model T tour to the desert."

And about her mom. "Haven't found the right time."

"I heard he's going to leave most any day."

"Next Wednesday."

Ginny poked around in the sparse grass and picked up a bookmark. "I might as well go with you too. The Jaguar replacement I want is in Vegas. It'll take them a while to add the features I had before. I thought I might ride with you at least to Reno and rent a car the rest of the way. Or maybe they'll deliver it to a dealer in Reno."

"That's the long, long trail home."

"I'm in no hurry. But tell me again, why are you bringing Johnny Poe?"

"Lots of reasons, including making sure he stays away from Champ because he'll hurt him. And Grandma, because he'll hurt her."

"Your grandma's not going to be happy she was the last to know."

"And I can't ask the Younger boys to help out until she's aware of it at least. But she's with Vincent right now. I don't want to intrude."

"Come on, girl. Time's passing. Just out with it."

But how did she broach the subject? Did she ask about Tim and Sue Anne first? And what if they have some sort of a blowout, what then?

The ranch house door opened and closed. Vincent walked out to his car and started the engine. He rolled past but didn't see them tucked under the sprawl of branches.

"Now. Go!" Ginny said. "I'll read my book until you give me the 'all clear' signal." She held up a copy of *The Burden of Proof* by Scott Turow.

Reba's stomach tensed. Her mouth pinched dry. She must do it, but she dreaded both the initiation and the result. She couldn't recall a confrontation between them since her bout of hiding in the root cellar when she was seven. She felt like that little girl now. Angry and determined, but also caught in a hole with the roof slammed down.

She strolled to the railing, pushed each foot up the steps to the house, and opened the door. "Grandma?" She strained to listen. Someone was crying.

When had she ever witnessed her grandmother weep? She whimpered a bit at Grandpa's funeral. She noticed a few dab of tears at Maidie's service. She hid a face a time or two when Reba questioned her about Hanna Jo. But bawling?

The sound erupted from Grandma Pearl's bedroom. Should she walk out of the house and pretend she hadn't heard? Maybe she hurt herself worse than she admitted with that run-in with the prisoners. Does she need a doctor? Her red-hot anger about Tim and Sue Anne tempered some before they'd ever addressed it. The issue washed cool by unexpected cries. They certainly couldn't face it head-on now. Whatever stirred such intense sobs surely didn't connect with the topics Reba intended to bring up.

She hesitated in the living room, suspended with indecision, torn with what to do. She noticed the boxes they rescued from the exploding cabin now removed. Had she been looking inside those and mourned Maidie's loss anew?

"Reba? Is that you?" Her grandma's voice, shaky with emotion.

Had she made some noise? She should steal out. Let her alone. Give her space. But it was too late. "Yes. It's me. Can I get you something?"

"Is Ginny there too?"

"No, she's outside reading." Under Grandpa's Camperdown Elm safe and sound with no duress. *Why didn't I stay out there?*

"Come here, please. Let's talk." So it begins, ready or not. "But don't turn on the light. I'm a shambles."

Shades down, no lights, but Reba could still see fine with the lighter Colonial colors surrounding her grandmother. Yellow painted walls on one side. Indigo and light blue, yellow, and red flowered wallpaper on the other. White trim. Homespun navy rug woven of Sun, Moon, and Stars pattern. Grandma Pearl slipped off the white linen bed set and sat on a slatted wood chair. Face drawn, eyes puffy, she pulled another chair close for Reba.

Reba eased in, back straight and not touching. Suddenly the welt on her back flared again. She wished she had Jace's cream slathered all over.

Pearl's kind eyes welled into a pool again. "I have a confession to make."

Now she wants to tell me about Tim and Sue Anne? This moment? How bizarre. Maybe someone told her I already know. *Ginny?*

"About Maidie."

Maidie? Didn't see that coming.

"When Seth gave you that squash blossom necklace, I realized Maidie did remember. She knew all along. But somehow her mind... well, I don't know how her mind worked. Guess we never will." Pearl engaged a long pause, attention latched on two cardboard boxes in a corner of the room. The contents seemed undisturbed, the same as Reba stacked them after the robbery, the worn leather journal on top one of them.

Pearl finally turned to her, peered into her face, and smoothed down her hair, a familiar gesture from her youth she hadn't done in a long time. "Reba, Maidie was your grandmother. She was Hanna Jo's mother."

A cold numbness shot through Reba. Dizziness knocked out her full vision. The woman next to her blurred, a photo out of focus. What was she saying? That she isn't my real grandmother? "Why didn't you tell me before? Why now?" Did her mother know?

"Vincent just now scolded me for keeping it from you. He practically stormed out of here in disgust. The thing is..." Pearl stopped to pull out a handkerchief from her sleeve. She blew her nose. She plied an effort to gain control. "I told Hanna Jo when she turned eighteen. She rushed out of the house and I didn't see her again...until she showed up three years later with you. I tried to talk with her about it, but she got very upset. Said some nasty things. And disappeared once more. I didn't want to lose you too." Pearl's eyes begged her to understand. To stay.

Reba stood up. She had to move. To clear her vision. To shake her mind back to some semblance of a normal setting. A stab of bitterness rushed back full force. All the lies, the deceit. She couldn't hold it back any longer. "How come you shoved Sue Anne at my Tim?" Now Reba was sobbing. Why mention that *now?* Reba, you're confusing the issues. She couldn't help it. The dam had burst. "Why did you think you had any business at all telling her to ask my boyfriend to that dance?" Control yourself, girl. Maybe you were wrong. What if Sue Anne lied to Tim about that? Think, think, *think.* Breathe. Listen.

She dabbed her eyes and peered at Pearl, hoping for insight, prying for raw truth. The woman she thought to be her grandmother sat stunned, as if in shock. "How long have you known?" she asked. "All these years you held that in?"

"No. Tim told me recently. The day of the robbery, while we were out looking for you."

"Ah, fresh news. Maybe that's good. But added to this other..." Pearl heaved a heart-wrenching sigh, her face twisted and tortured.

Reba's heart sank. So, it's true? All those years she completely blamed Sue Anne. And Tim. But her grandmother was most at fault.

The elder woman's eyes cleared. "All I can do is ask for your forgiveness. I hope and pray you will forgive me for my part in all the wrong done."

"So, you did push Tim and Sue Anne together? Behind my back?"

"Yes. I encouraged Sue Anne. She seemed crazy about Tim and you seemed so...lukewarm..."

Lukewarm? "He was my life. I loved him." *Maybe I still do.* "He was the rancher husband so perfect for me. Lukewarm?" Reba knew she was shouting. She kept telling herself to grab control. *Come on, girl. Slow it down.* She felt like two people, one set on meltdown, the other talking to Johnny Poe in front of a broken down barbed wire fence, trying to get him to calm down. To step forward. Well, she would do more than that. She would jump right in.

"You didn't want to take a chance of losing this ranch. That's why you're so paranoid about my dating Don. Don't you see we'd add a ranch, not take one away? But no, you couldn't consider that. It's not about my happiness or me at all. It's about you and control. You're worse than Champ Runcie." Okay, she said enough. She slapped her arms together and held so tight her back ached.

Pearl's faced caved into full surrender. She aged before Reba's eyes, a shrunken shell of a woman with no fight left in her. "I plead guilty. Those motives did rear inside me." She held up a hand. "But one more thing. I did believe it was also God's will." She hitched a quick breath as though to say more.

Reba clamped her hands to her ears. She couldn't bear to hear it. "God's will? Was it His will for you to keep the truth about my family from me? If I'd known, I could have done more, been more for Maidie. And was it his will for Sue Anne to entice my boyfriend into her arms? To take my place?" *To bear his children? The kids who could have been mine.* Reba collapsed into a deep fatigue. She longed to be away from here. Far away. Grandpa's Scotland sounded appealing.

Just like the time Reba asked Pearl about her father, who he was. Reba recalled she felt numb, stupid, like the only one in the room who didn't catch the joke. She couldn't understand, couldn't process what this all meant. "You mean, he was a stranger to her? She didn't catch his name or anything?" Reba's stomach churned now like it did then.

"Reba..." Pearl didn't cry visibly. It was more like crying *in.* "Hanna Jo told me...there were too many...she had no idea which one..."

Agony took over, crushed her. All these years her mother had ignored her, dismissed her, but Hanna Jo was someone with a name, a face. She had the potential for turning around. Of coming back. Now Reba realized with a pang of despair she always assumed finding her father would be simply a matter of being told who he was. Find Mother first. Then the father would emerge in the picture. Eyes and hair color, shape of nose and a mouth that said, "I love you. I've missed you. It's been complicated, but now you're here." He was out there and could be found, identified. Hanna Jo was the main link. She would fill in the missing blank. But the truth crushed her.

"I so wanted a peaceful life for you," Pearl was saying. "That's part of why I never told you these things. That, and I had my own hurts to work through."

"But you realized you had to tell me sooner or later?"

"I hoped maybe not. Naive, of course, but it was my prayer. I didn't want you living with the shame."

She remembered the note. Was it still in her jeans pocket? She pulled out the snippet of paper and waved in front of Pearl. "I'm going with Seth on his journey. And I'm going to find Mama."

Pearl nodded, eyes sunk in circles of sorrow. "I guess I've always known someday I would lose you too."

*** *** *** ***

Reba tried to drum up a semblance of enthusiasm as she and Ginny started to pack. After all, this was as close to a vacation as she'd ever experienced. But the emotional rift with Grandma Pearl decimated any attempts of joy or excitement. Dazed, disoriented, she forced herself to plan, to get organized for the venture.

She opened both bedroom doors, so she could commiserate with Ginny. "I can't believe Michael offered to come help on the ranch while I'm gone. Vincent too. With part-time help from the Younger boys, even with their inexperience, Grandma...I mean, Pearl...will have quite a crew to boss around." *For certain, she won't be missing me.* Would she ever want Reba back? Even if she wanted to return? She ought to marry Don and help him run the Runcie Ranch. *That would serve her right.* Of course, that included Champ too in the deal. She hunched in a sigh.

Ginny tugged on black and white beaded earrings and fluffed her dark curls. "Are you sure we're not packing too early? I don't want my clothes to get too wrinkled."

"I've got a clothes bar in the back of my truck. Hang some there." Reba made a mental note to include a tent and camping supplies. They might not hit the towns right for a motel or restaurant every night. Or they might be booked. "Seth insists he's ready to leave Wednesday morning. That's tomorrow. I'm guessing he didn't make reservations along the way, so we may have to rough it some."

"I hear we're camping at a place called New Meadows the first night. Let's see, I've got suntan lotion, hat, sunglasses, and long sleeves. Lots of skin cancer happening these days and we're headed to the desert."

"Make sure you have plenty of film for your camera. You can be our official photographer. Never know. This might be a historic event."

"Got it. Plus, I brought my video camera too. I'll make sure it's charged up and ready to go."

"It's very handy to have a rich friend." If only she wasn't so beautiful too.

"A friend with wealthy family that happens to be generous. These were gifts. Now, if I can figure out how to use them right."

Reba clipped on bronze earrings and put on matching bronze chain and cross around her neck. That's all she needed for jewelry. Simple and matched anything a redhead would wear. She thought about the cigar box and squash blossom necklace stored in the hotel safe. Funny how Champ hadn't brought that up again. She let herself indulge the thought she owned a mini-mine of gold and turquoise. Like a savings account. Or an investment in non-risky stocks and bonds.

At the last, she included the wooden woman warrior in her backpack. Courage infused her as she held it.

She heard a rap at the front door. She opened to Vincent. "Pearl and I took a trip into Elkville. She's unloading supplies in the barn and wouldn't let me help. She wanted me to come right over and give you my report."

"Well, come in. Don't just stand there. And thanks so much for helping out on the ranch while I'm gone."

He pulled off his canvas hat. "Pleased to do it. I explored the bookstore for information on turquoise jewelry and stopped by Severs Jewelers with the squash blossom necklace to get it assessed. He hemmed and hawed at first. Told me turquoise is a strange stone to value. Depends a lot on preference or the region and traditions. Some customers like them green. Others want only blue. There are lots of shades in-between and all the mottled varieties with matrix or spider web markings are popular."

"Did he give you a guesstimate?"

"He confessed that sample was the purest blue he'd ever seen, as well as excellent craftsmanship for a cruder antique. And most turquoise is set in silver. The gold ups the price, of course. Would be almost priceless in any collector's book. An heirloom." He looked up at the ceiling, as though a computing directory hid there. "He told me he'd write you a cashier's check on the spot for $3,000. Not to buy it, mind you, but to lease it for a year. For display. For show to his customers."

"Are you kidding?"

"No, ma'am. What do you say?"

That would certainly pay for the trip with Seth. It wouldn't be near that much, but neither would it be cheap, even with some camping out. She could buy a new trailer for Johnny Poe. Maybe a Featherlite with fiberglass and aluminum. With storage rack and extra stall for a horse companion when they travel. *But still...*

"I need to think about it."

"Reba, what's there to think about?" Ginny intruded. "That kind of deal is a win-win."

"But I don't want to do anything with it until we settle the dispute with Champ."

"I bought a velvet-lined case." Vincent held up his hand at her objection. "Felt it needed something more than a cigar box. A going-away gift. I'm taking it back to the hotel safe right now."

"I want another look at it."

"Me too," Ginny said.

Reba felt startled again by the beauty of the necklace.

"Exquisite." Ginny traced each part and turned it over.

After Vincent left, Pearl walked toward them, a drag to her leg after a long day. Reba started to reach out and hold her arm, but pulled back. Pearl wouldn't want that, plus a wide gulf of anger separated them at the moment.

Reba turned to Ginny, "I'm going to Elkville. Want to ride along?"

"Do they have a manicure place?"

"How about a beauty salon?"

Ginny grabbed her purse. "That'll work, as long as someone can fix and polish a broken nail."

Whenever Reba or her grandmother visited Elkville on Sundays, they attended a growing Community Church. Enoch James, a boy she dated on the rebound after losing Tim had been a member there, as well as a grandson of the Road's End barber. The romance ended with Enoch, but the attachment to the church, the pastor, and his wife remained.

Pastor Kiersey and his wife Iris transplanted from California like most of the newcomers. Elkville now boasted a flower shop, drugstore, and movie theater. The public swimming pool provided lanes for racers. U.S. and Elkville Days flags hung across the street in front of the Hong Fa Chinese Restaurant.

Reba dropped Ginny off at Clip, Snip 'N Curl and parked in front of the Kiersey home.

"Kevin's at the church, but do stay a moment to visit." Iris Kiersey welcomed her into the tidy basement that doubled as a playroom and office. Several Kersey children followed them, but Iris shooed them out.

"That's all right," Reba said. She steered the chat to events in Road's End and the trip with Seth.

"Enoch was asking about you recently."

"Hasn't he gotten married?"

"It's been an on and off engagement. Either him or her. I don't think he's gotten over you." Iris gave her a wistful look. "I'm sorry it didn't work out. You were such a cute couple."

But not enough spark. And he wasn't interested in the ranch.

While the Kiersey brood chased each other in and out, Iris took both her hands and offered a blessing for her trip. Reba left soon after and sighted Pastor Kiersey's battered coupe in the church parking lot.

She followed the sounds of activity in the gym and nearly collided with him as she plunged through the front door. Dark brown hair disheveled, a rip in his knit shirt, smudged shorts and nursing a black eye with ice wrapped in a towel, a typical weekday for this youth-oriented minister of the gospel.

"I see you're busy."

He grimaced. "If you're looking for me, follow the line to my office."

Five teens filed past her, one hopping with two boys holding him. Down the hallway they chugged as Pastor Kiersey pulled out tape and bandages from a closet in his office. They wrapped the boy's bleeding shin while he held the ice.

Reba reached out. "I can hold it for you."

Pastor Kiersey smiled thanks and finished the doctoring.

The boys let out a *whoop* and rushed back to the gym.

Reba let go of the ice. "I can come back later."

"You saved me from more war wounds. It was getting a bit rough for mature types like me. Glad to get a break. What can I do for you?"

Reba told him the revelations about Tim and Sue Anne and Maidie, about the tension between her and Pearl, and about the gift of the necklace. When she got to the part about Vincent and Severs Jewelers, he commented, "I go there sometimes. Special gifts for Iris. I've tried to encourage the owner's son to come to church. Did you know your brother Michael and his friends Greg and Samson played basketball with us last week?"

"No, that surprises me. Were you able to work in a good talk with him?"

"Not yet. Just surface stuff."

"Do you have any advice for me?"

He sighed. "Not really, except I sense you have a strenuous spiritual as well as physical journey ahead of you. Watch and listen. And please don't allow bitterness to dig deeper roots. I can hear it in your voice."

When they bowed their heads to pray, the strain of the past weeks hit her full force. Yet she left the church with a lightness of peace. She felt ready for what loomed ahead.

That evening dark clouds moved in and a torrent of rain fell most of the night. Thunder rolled and rumbled as lightning pealed all around. After a crash that sounded on top of the ranch house, Ginny knocked at Reba's door. "Are we going to get hit? It sounds so close."

"Never been hit yet."

"I've heard of golfers getting killed on flat fairways. And here we are in the mountains, even higher."

"Well, we aren't playing golf. But I do feel like I've been hit by lightning. Come sit with me. I've been thinking."

"About what?"

"My life. My non-life. My I-don't-know-who-I-am life. My love life."

"Aha. Let's hear it."

"I've been considering my options. After I get back, I'm going to get Don to ask me out on real dates. Maybe I'll grow to love him in that kind of way and get my rancher husband after all. Maybe it's God's will."

"Well, that's the most convenient choice. But your grandma will have a fit."

"For no good reason. And she's not my real grandma. She told me so."

"She cooked your meals and tucked you in bed every night since you were three-years-old. That's more than most grandmas do." Ginny emphasized each word. "She and your grandpa adopted Hanna Jo. That makes her your legal grandparent."

"Whatever. Why not be upfront about it from the beginning? If I have to move out, I will. If Don and I get married, of course I'll be on my own."

"I can't believe I'm hearing you talk like this."

"Maybe it's time I think about myself and my future. No one else is." Maybe no one ever has. *Certainly not Grandma.* "If I don't fight for myself, who will?"

"So, why don't you stay here and fight? Why are you running away from Road's End and your ranch? I thought that's what you want."

"I'm not running from anything." *Well, maybe.* "I will never be like my mom. But I am going to find her. And for the very first time ever, I think she wants me to find her. If I don't, I may never know who I really am. And who I need to be."

The lightning stopped, the thunder ceased rolling, and Ginny returned to the guest room.

Chapter Ten

A slate sky framed the early morning after the hail and rain. By the time Reba, Ginny and Johnny Poe reached Main Street, the skies cleared and poured gold sprays over their heads, the basalt ground already dry in places. A rare view of swans and a squadron of Canada geese flew in a tight formation fly-by across the crimson and gold sunrise.

They parked behind Seth and eased out of the packed pickup. Reba wore her favorite tan cowgirl hat and comfiest brown leather boots, a tan button shirt, and her favorite brown Wrangler's.

Ginny donned purple Paloma walking shoes with rhinestone button on the straps, lavender Capri tights and matching spaghetti strap over-blouse. "In honor of Maidie," she explained about her color choice.

Reba perused Seth's well-equipped purple Model T, which rivaled Whitlow's country store. Tongs, portable grill, coffee pot, cast iron skillet and pot, assorted dishes. Flour and crackers, corn meal and rice, beans and jerky, salt and sugar, coffee and tea, vinegar and pickles, smoked meat and lots of dried fruit, as well as canned sardines, tuna, fruits and vegetables. He even had an ample supply of Pearl's granola trail mix, covered and tied down.

"Are you going to be our chuck wagon cook?" Reba asked.

"Not me. I bring the grub and start the fire. You and Ginny can do the cooking."

"Aha, now you tell us." She handed him one of the walkie-talkies. "What is this?"

"So we can communicate on the road. Here. Punch this button and start talking."

He turned it all around. "I need to keep my hands on the wheel. The play in the steering requires both hands. I can't use this."

Tucker showed up with his guitar, a shotgun, and gold panning equipment, like an adventurer on a treasure hunt. His mustache looked like it had been bleached. "I'm Seth's personal bodyguard." He touched the mustache. "Incognito."

Seth handed him the walkie-talkie. "You're also in charge of this."

Tucker poked around and started a dialogue. "I'm just the guy. I hitchhiked one time with a trucker who had a CB. We need handles."

"That's easy. I'll call you Tucker. You call me Reba."

"Oh no, that won't do. Finding a handle is required and it's a science. A name you can remember. A reflection of your true identity. An extension of your inner soul."

Oh, brother. "Tucker, this is for emergencies only, when we need to make contact. You can call me...Reba Mae."

"Nope. Mine is Off The Sauce. You want Carrot Top or Ranch Boss?"

Ginny grabbed the other walkie-talkie from Reba. "You're the driver. I'll be the radio contact from the pickup." She turned it on. "Off The Sauce, Greek Girl here. Any messages for Carrot Top?"

I have created a monster. "I am definitely not Carrot Top."

"Ranch Boss just tuned in," Tucker blasted out. "Off The Sauce and T-Rod over and out. 10-4."

"Who is T-Rod?" Ginny asked.

"Seth, of course."

A shiny silver Volvo pulled in behind the pickup and trailer. Abel bounced on the front leather seat. Jace rambled over to them. "This the pack train to the desert?"

"Are you coming too?" Ginny asked.

He nodded. "If there are no objections." He peered at Reba.

Figures. It's a joy ride to him. His whole life's a playground. "Check with T-Rod." She pointed at Seth and tried to shove aside the bit of inner buzz his joining them generated.

Ginny walked over to talk to Abel and Jace ran over to Seth.

"I thought little brother would like an adventure," Jace explained when he returned. "We'll follow a day or two at least. I'm having a hard time keeping him entertained."

"I see you brought a First Aid kit," Ginny called out.

"Oh, yeah." He walked to the Volvo and held up another white box. "A Body Fluid Clean Up kit too."

Reba almost gagged. "Gross. Sure hope we don't need that."

"That makes a midwife cowgirl like you flinch? I'm shocked. I had one on the shelf at the store. Might come in handy."

"I'm used to cows, not humans."

When a crowd began to form, Tucker traipsed toward the town center.

"What are you doing?" Reba asked.

"Going to make a speech. This is a historic occasion. I'm ready to tell all I know about Seth Stroud."

"Please don't do it through the walkie-talkie."

Jace touched Ginny's. "Great idea. I've got my cellular phone, but it won't do much good in the car pool, since none of you have one."

"I've been thinking about it," Ginny said. "Several cousins who work in our business have been pushing it."

Reba snorted. "Not me. The only electronics I want is my calculator and electric pencil sharpener."

A horn blew as Tucker began his speech. Everyone turned as a horse and rider rode down the street. Champ appeared with U.S. flag and red, white, and blue helium balloons flying.

"Is he going to give Seth the keys of the city?" Ginny said.

"Surely not," Reba replied. "He's on his way out of town."

"I think Elliot Laws is too. Look."

A crew cab dually pickup pulled in behind Jace's Volvo. Thomas Hawk and Elliot rode in the front seat with Reine Laws as driver. Two appaloosas peered out from a back trailer.

Champ presented Seth the balloons and a huge gift basket of smoked salmon and cheese, caviar, canned nuts, large candy bars, dried fruit, summer sausage, hot *habanero* salsa, and a bottle of red wine. He handed him an extra-large bright yellow t-shirt with permanent ink signatures from a multitude of Road's End citizens and a "To Nevada Or Bust" insignia in front. Seth pulled it over the shirt he wore amid cheers.

"He's only going to be gone a few weeks," Reba stated.

Champ glared at her and intoned to Seth, "May the Lord watch between you and us while we're absent from one another."

"That sounds very spiritual," Ginny remarked.

"It was the Mizpah between Jacob and Laban, who didn't trust each other," Reba explained. "Not sure Champ realizes that, but it fits." She strolled over to Seth who battled the balloons. "Let's tamp these down short and tight in the back. Less hazards that way."

His eyes glazed, Seth gladly handed them to her.

Reba walked back to the pickup Reine Laws drove. "Where are you guys headed? Are you coming with us?"

"Seth inspired us. We're on a long overdue pilgrimage," Thomas told her, "Elliot and I are headed to the Nez Perce battleground site near White Bird. We aim to ride horseback on the route of Chief Joseph up near the Canadian border."

"Wow. That's incredible." Reba turned to hurry back to her rig and almost charged into to Pearl. "I had to say goodbye," she said.

Of course she did, but a tight uneasiness gripped Reba's mid-section. A spurt of love-distrust anchored her response. They exchanged a fleeting hug. Reba's emotions tumbled into chaos again. Her mouth wouldn't work. But before she could manage any words of response, Pearl ambled over to Seth. "Give Hester my love."

Ginny and Reba looked at each other. "Who is Hester?" Ginny asked.

Reba shrugged. "Don't ask me. I know nothing about anything."

Pearl stepped back to them and answered their question. "Hester

Owens, Zeke Owen's sister. Maidie's fiancé way back when."

Ah, so maybe my great aunt? "I presume Zeke was the father...and my grandfather."

Pearl lowered her voice. "Seth assumed that too. He's the one who brought the baby girl to me and Cole. He asked me to find a family for her. Maidie was in hysterics after the birth and not taking care of the baby. He worried for the infant's safety. As you know now, we kept her ourselves."

"So, didn't others in Road's End know? That Hanna Jo was adopted and Maidie's child?" Ginny asked.

Pearl sent Reba an offertory smile as though an attempt to do penance. "Truly, no one at the time questioned us about it. The way it happened, with us out in the country and little contact with folks. We introduced Hanna Jo as our baby and everyone accepted that. And with Zeke dying so tragic in a fall off a roof before he and Maidie could be married, in those days a shame for Maidie. I don't think anyone knew about the baby until she was born. Not even Seth."

What a load to carry. No wonder Maidie went bonkers.

Pearl continued. "A man wouldn't pay much attention to signs of pregnancy, especially an uncle. But most any woman would."

Maidie must have started her recluse ways back then.

Ginny frowned at Reba and smiled at Pearl. "I think what you and Mr. Cahill did was pretty noble."

Pearl teared up and mouthed a *thank you.* She held out her arms for another hug and Reba complied, her heart heavy. She felt cold against her, a strange kind of reversal for a woman she'd loved most of her life. *I wonder if she senses it?*

Pearl weaved back to the sidewalk and when they returned to the pickup, Reba burst out, "But why hide it from me?"

"Maybe she said nothing about it to protect Maidie. Did you think of that?" Ginny buckled her seatbelt and motioned for Reba to do the same.

"No, I guess not. I sense I really need this trip with Seth." Revelations? Or further unraveling? "I've got a lot to sort out."

"Hey, so do I."

A hawk circled above them, higher and higher.

Seth stacked the gift basket on top his goods and lifted out green tinted goggles. He handed a set to Tucker and pulled his on.

"I have got to get a picture of that." Ginny snapped some shots as Seth cranked the Model T and moseyed into the seat. The antique car nudged forward down Main Street. Those in the car pool behind him followed. They all waved to a crowd of yells and whistles like in a parade.

Lisl saluted from the front of the post office, flag flying high.

Tim and his family viewed them at the apartments. Kaitlyn rushed over with another drawing. A redhead riding Johnny Poe who rose on hind legs.

Buckhead and Venita Whitlow at the grocery store.

Norden on the sidewalk with his Harley looking like he wanted to join them. He spun a few wheelies and trailed behind them a few blocks.

No one hurrahed in front of the saloons. Perhaps home sleeping it off.

Beatrice and Charlotta wore bathrobes and fuzzy slippers. Adrienne ran in place wearing workout clothes and tennies.

As they approached the Paddy Trailer Park, a 1975 orange Toyota wagon waited there with Ida, Amos, and Pico. "Stay home, Tucker," Ida yelled. "Or I and the boys are coming with you."

The Model T stopped. "Who will take care of the trailer park?" Tucker yelled back.

"Polly and Kam Eng said they'd look after it and we're all packed."

"Then, come on. But you'll have to go to the back of the line." The boys cheered and they all piled into the orange wagon.

The Model T turned left on Water Wagon Road along Road's End Lake shore. Fishermen lined the banks and gave them cursory looks. They tunneled under the overhead footbridge stretched from the lake to the edge of town and passed remnants of a sawmill and logging camp.

Reba edged her pickup to the far side of the road as a wide load farm implement approached. Going thirty mph, they cruised by the old original logging mill, cleared what remained of the pine forest, and neared Highway 95. Seth waited for clearer traffic before engaging the highway full bore to the open high prairie. Variegated patches of wheat fields rippled over green rolling hills, intermixed with goldenrod plots of canola. Two windmills spun, one on each side of an old house, a former one-room school.

Ginny peered in the rearview mirror. "Look at all those people following us."

"They're probably going to trail along for part of the jaunt today."

"Or tag along for the whole journey. What have we gotten ourselves into?"

"Did you notice that woman in the pickup and tent trailer at the back of the line?" Ginny asked.

"Yes, ever since Road's End, but she doesn't look familiar. Perhaps a tourist? Or a camper from the Road's End Lake State Park."

🐎 🐎 🐎 🐎

Neoma Hocking started the van and looked behind at her two grandkids and the tent trailer. She waved at Cicely in red blouse and tights and Franklin in dusty gray coveralls. *Our farewell party.* Her gaze lingered on Franklin. Something about him attracted her.

She drove out the way they and the broken axle pickup had been hauled in by the logging truck two days before. She recalled the woodsman with hardhat and snoose tobacco can mark in his back pocket who found them five miles out of town, stuck on the side of the road. He had cheerily introduced himself.

"I'm Franklin Fraley." He pointed to the Fraley Logging Company sign on the truck. "I can haul you to the nearest garage in Road's End, if you don't mind sitting in my dirty cab."

He looked so much like Hank she kept blinking her eyes. But his voice was lower, deeper. He also appeared younger. Maybe because he was healthier than when she last saw Hank on his final sick bed.

"You must be Cicely's niece from Missouri. She thought you might be coming by."

That surprised Neoma. "I wasn't sure myself if I'd actually come this way. We're on our way to the California coast."

"Uh huh. Looks like it's gonna rain. In fact, it might snow. Won't be the first time here in the middle of May."

"I only meant to stop an hour or two. But it's been such a long drive and my eyes shut a bit. I'm afraid I plowed off the road. Stupid thing to do, especially with the children." Why did she turn right at Winnemucca? *Lord, if you'll help me out of this, I'll never do such a foolish thing again.*

By the time they reached the Road's End turnoff, the sky overcast the landscape in shades of gray. A gas station's Open sign flashed on and off. They wound about a mile down a country road with fields on each side, a forest of pines and slate lake water ripples appeared in the distance.

"Many folks consider Road's End a restful stop on the way to somewhere else," Franklin chatted as they entered town.

Now the Road's End Hotel and the Pick Me Up Saloon came in view on Main Street as Neoma prepared to cross Main Street and head out of town. What was that ahead? An antique car leads some kind of parade. Why were all those people crowded around? Neoma recalled Cicely and Franklin talking about some old man on a trip to the desert with rumors he was going after gold buried by his family years ago.

Why didn't I leave earlier? She knew the answer. As usual, the kids dragged their feet.

Twelve-year-old granddaughter Becky met Neoma's gaze with her habitual glum look. She crossed her eyes in that way of hers that said, "Don't you dare ask what I'm thinking."

Her five-year-old brother Ned strained to see like a caged puppy against the seatbelt. He pulled out the wooden whistle Franklin gave him and blew it. Twice.

"Make him stop," Becky complained.

"Ned, give it to me." She reached back her hand. Should she veer north on Main Street and the east route to the Highway? But she'd have to pass them sooner or later. Might as well straggle in line now and watch for an opening.

Neoma knew Aunt Cicely was right. She should drive straight to Reno to make contact with her estranged daughter, Trish, head to the Pacific Ocean to spread her husband's ashes, and on to Disneyland, her concession to the kids.

The longer she sat there, waiting for the end of the procession, the more she considered the symbolism of the old man's pursuit and how in some ways it mirrored her husband's story.

The Hocking family's migration west ended abruptly, far short of the goal. Two thousand miles of prairie, mountain, and desert to cross. Gold seekers did it. So did droves of cattle and wagon trains loaded with pioneer families and dreams. But the Hocking ancestors hunkered down instead at St. Joseph, Missouri to run a boarding house.

"I'm headed west," her husband Hank told her two months before he retired from his engineering firm. "I'm going to be the first direct descendent of Theodore Hocking to stick my bare feet in the Pacific."

Hank packed Theodore's gold panning supplies in the tent trailer while Neoma imagined long visits with her college chum in Utah, a side trip to Aunt Cee's in Idaho, long novels to read, and lazy evenings of pulling out new sable brushes and an old easel on a California beach. Her husband's weak heart dictated otherwise.

Her vision cleared from the past to the present one in the mirror where she stared. No sable brushes for her. No easel on a beach. She admired again the hat Cicely gave her, with a satin floral jacquard brim and sisal crown. She could almost smell the fragrance of the gardenia blossom trim. The grosgrain band felt soft and firm against her head.

It would do for a stylish model in a Renoir painting. Instead it adorned a grungy grandma with large Band-Aid on her forehead. She peeked in the mirror. She wondered what difference hair highlights and a bit of makeup would make. But what for? No one left in her life to impress.

She peered at the grandkids, Becky in the front seat, Ned in the back. Becky wore a perky panama with chinstrap. Ned had a cotton-ducking cap with coffee-colored long bill. Gifts from Cicely. Ned pranced around like a cocky young Hemingway in his.

She noticed a break and eased onto Main Street, turning right to follow the caravan that kept to the pace of the Model T. Five miles later, she spied a stretch of road to zoom free of the slow moving line of traffic. Perhaps it was a reluctance to get to Reno too soon. To put off facing Trish. Or the certainty Hank would have participated in this trek, if he had been here. A token of doing an Old West pioneer adventure. Neoma crept in line, though she didn't know a soul on this peculiar tour.

A small yellow bi-plane crop duster buzzed overhead. Bicyclers with helmets and packs sprawled along the highway. Undulating hills and rocky cliffs plastered with vetch and lupine purple wildflowers. Reba drank it all in.

"Pass them," Ginny urged. "Quick. There's no oncoming traffic. I need some road pictures of Seth."

Reba shot around Seth then pulled in front as Ginny snapped shots. She veered to the right side and pulled back in line when the caravan passed. She gunned another pass as Ginny waved to everyone and squeezed back in their slot in-between the Model T and Volvo.

Jace blared his horn and waved his fist.

"Oh my, road rage," Ginny opined. "Even in peaceful Idaho."

"Well, let's don't try that trick again. Go for safe and sane picture taking from now on." Soon, oncoming cars and trucks splattered tiny rocks and splashes on Reba's pickup. "It's a good thing Seth and Tucker have those bug-eye goggles. Their windshield won't help that much."

"And Tucker insists on a helmet."

The Model T rumbled slow but steady through the road lined with a mix of pines, cedars, firs and spruce. Seth tried to stay at the edge of the pavement for easier passing and aimed for frontage and gravel side roads when possible.

"He might as well stay on the highway," Ginny said. "As long as he's visible, drivers will steer clear of him. And we're a brigade of protection behind him. Besides, we'll never get out of the state at this rate."

"I am so used to speeding through here. It's nice to ease the pace, to see patches and designs of nature. To pay closer attention to the hard-working farmers and study their crops. Try to guess what they are." Life in slower motion.

"Yeah, stare each bug in the eye before it splats against the windshield."

"Oh, Ginny. Where's your romance?" But Reba couldn't help but chuckle.

Ginny pointed at old barns dotted across the wheat and gold-yellow canola fields. "Those don't look in use. In fact, they're ready to tumble."

"Nobody tears down barns around here. Farm machines work around them."

"Laziness? Or sentimental?"

"Yep, and stubbornness. Or they want barn mulch."

"The extra slow way. Just like Seth and this trip."

A grove of cottonwoods edged a creek bank. Random clumps of pines made pockets of forests here and there in the wheat fields. Billows of pillow-shaped cumulus clouds piled high above dark green prairie grass.

"Ginny, look quick. There's our one view of the Seven Devils Mountains in the distance. The rugged ones with snow on top. You can count them. At sixty-five mph, they quickly disappear. Most people miss them. Today we've got a clear day and full shot."

"Speaking of which..." Ginny rolled down her window and stuck the camera out. She kept the window down a few inches until she held her nose. "What's that awful odor? Smells like cat pee."

"It's those bushes with the yellow tips."

Ginny closed her window. "Special. Getting a bit too close to nature."

They tried to take in the sights. A helicopter with red lights flashing whirled above a small horse pen, broken, bent, and untended. Three vapor trails from jets crossed each other in the sky between a large splat of clouds spread in wisps and swirls. Dark soil ground had been plowed under, left fallow.

Seth made a hand signal to turn right off the highway and onto the Cutoff Road to bypass Elkville.

As they followed, Ginny asked, "By the way, where's the nearest latté?"

"Maybe Reno?"

Ginny groaned. "I'm in full cold turkey remission."

An hour later, Reba gazed at the winding Noxell Ranch driveway, close to the head of White Bird Grade. Mixed breeds and colors of cattle lounged in the pastures. Mule deer with large ears and black-tipped tails hopped away to a pine forest.

"Why is Seth turning in here already? We've only been on the road an hour."

"Potty stop? Looks like they have a portable outhouse."

The Model T halted in front of a barbecue pit and some picnic tables. Reba parked alongside and got out to release Johnny Poe from the trailer. Thomas Hawk and Elliot rode their appaloosas with dark spots over white hindquarters around the grounds.

Seth announced to everyone he was hungry. "I've been up a long time already. And no one lives in the house anymore. I know the caretaker/ranch hand. Make yourself at home."

Jace and Abel joined Reba and Ginny with a woman in her fifties with two children. "This is Neoma Hocking and her grandkids, Becky and Ned. She's on her way to Reno, got stuck in our caravan, and wants to get acquainted."

"I've been following you since Road's End," Neoma said.

"Do you happen to be Cicely Bower's niece?" Reba asked.

"I am. She told me about the elderly man's trek. I found it fascinating. I'm on a similar one of my own. Mind if I join you a while?"

"Of course not. We're headed to New Meadows this evening."

Becky stared at Ginny and reached out to touch her silver Omega watch.

"She's been wanting a watch of her own," Neoma explained. "I'm sure that is pretty spendy."

And she has three more like it. Reba noticed the girl's young, clear face, just a couple years and a touch of cosmetics shy of pretty.

A gale of wind hit hard. They bundled up, gazed at the country-side prairie and shared provisions for lunch.

"Like a church potluck." Reba helped spread out red checkered tablecloths covered with elk jerky, fried chicken, corn on the cob, three-bean salad, potato salad, and Pearl's leftover jalapeno cheddar cheese corn muffins and rhubarb-apple pie. Reine Laws added fry bread and beans.

"Like a royal buffet, without the sushi," Ginny added. "And high on carbs."

Becky picked at her meal. She pulled her knees up, clutched them, and hid her face. She perked up at Neoma's mention of hot fudge sundaes. "Sounds so good. I've been hungry for one ever since someone mentioned Dairy Queen."

"That may be a while, at the rate we're going."

"Will make it all the more pleasurable," Neoma said.

"I want to see Mama," Becky whined.

Neoma sighed. "Me too, I think."

"Did you enjoy your stay with Cicely?" Reba asked.

"Yes, we did. Aunt Cee is my father's youngest sister and prominent guest at all family funerals and weddings. She's a colorful memory in my otherwise gray world. 'If Aunt Cicely comes, it's party time,' my daughter Trish would say. Aunt Cee lost a daughter to leukemia and widowed three times. I knew she'd understand what I'm going through."

After they ate, Seth on fiddle and Reba and Tucker on guitar, they sang as many verses as they could recall of folk songs such as "Blowin' in the Wind."

The Paddy boys, Neoma Hocking's grandkids, and Abel and Jace played a game of Hearts. Reba noticed a toy model Navy F-14 beside Abel. A lazy Noxell Ranch dog watched thrown sticks and Frisbees with amusement, but made no move for them.

"Would you believe he was once a vicious brute who annihilated rabbits and chipmunks?" said Yarbo, introduced by Seth as the caretaker.

"What's his name?" Abel called from the game.

"Compromise," Yarbo replied. "We call him C.P. for short."

"Good name." Jace dropped his cards and wiggled his hands.

"The key to any valuable and lasting relationship." Ginny held up her book.

"I agree. Listing pros and cons are good for any debate," Reba concluded.

Jace cocked his head. "Oh? You debate? I thought it was your way or no way."

Reba stuck her tongue out at Jace. *Why did I do that? Stupid.*

A six-passenger pickup truck gunned down the driveway. A man in hardhat and Run For The Health Of It t-shirt got out.

"Hey, Franklin, good to see you," several yelled.

"You missed lunch, but we still have some pie," Neoma said, a blush in her cheeks.

Franklin dug out two pieces of apple pie from a tin plate. "I wish I was going with you all the way, but somebody has to stay in town. It seemed deserted all of a sudden."

Ginny wound an emerald scarf around her head and snuggled into her emerald hooded windbreaker.

Reba admired the scarf. "Hey, that's a good idea. It's hard to keep a hairdo in this breeze. At least we're all in the same condition."

Tucker tugged at his wife and they danced an Irish jig around the unlit campfire ring while Seth fiddled and the others clapped in rhythm.

A gale began again and overhanging branches threatened to rip off. A brief downpour drenched them.

"Are we having fun yet?" Jace yelled.

"Yep. This is livin'," Seth replied.

When the weather cleared, debate ensued about going down steep White Bird Grade with the Model T.

"I already figured that in," Seth told them. "I'm going down the Old Grade. You all can take the highway if you like."

"And the Old Grade goes right by the trail head to the Nez Perce war," Thomas Hawk commented. The elder man's weather-lined face and hands added to his bent posture, looking more cowboy than Indian with his dusty jeans, boots and black bandana tied around his neck.

Elliot rolled a cigarette from a plastic bag of tobacco. "Grandpa, you need to get your horse shod."

"I'll do it myself. The last time I ran into a smart-mouthed farrier who didn't like Indians or long hairs. Then when I left him, I'm sure he beat her around the kidneys with a tool. The horse developed a kidney infection."

Elliot hit his saddle with his fist. The horse shied forward and whinnied. "One thing I liked about the military. Once we headed to the Gulf and faced battle, we had each other's backs, no matter who we were or where we came from."

"Maybe if we had a few more wars, we'd be kinder to each other."

"I can't believe you said that. War is hell and you know it."

"Yes, much of our tribe's sad history happened near here, the great battle at White Bird."

"What started it?" Jace asked.

"Gold discovered around the reservation. One shot rang out. That's the short version," Elliot said.

Thomas sprawled on the wet grass with a blanket. "But the longer version is that the government reduced the promised reservation's size. The young bucks wished to fight, but Chief Joseph forbade them. Soon altercations gave them more reasons for vengeance. It became impossible to hold them back. So, Chief Joseph led many men, women, and children from the Oregon reservation to supposed freedom. They managed to elude five thousand Army troops as they fled through Idaho.

"There was much confusion, controversy, and quarrels among our tribe members and with the government. Wrong was done on all sides. My family abided by the government's treaty, such as it was. Yet I believe Chief Joseph and his non-treaty band were disposed to live peaceably, as we all were. We didn't travel his path, but we have his blood."

"Often the government offered half-truths," Thomas continued. "Sometimes humans are unaware of the enormity of their own deceit and the consequences."

"Yes, a fascinating psychological phenomenon," Elliot added.

Reba squirmed as this truth hit home. She knew the same thing happened to otherwise good people. *Lord, help keep me honest and true.* Reba scanned the valley and mountain ridges around them, imagining soldiers and Native Americans lurking there, avenging ancient grudges.

"Elliot and I, we are going to travel in their moccasins, to see what they saw," Thomas said. "We will start at White Bird Canyon, and finish forty miles short of the Canadian border at the forced surrender near Bear Paw Mountain in Montana."

Jace walked over to Elliot and shook his hand. "We thank you for your service to our country."

"Thank you." Elliot gripped him back with both hands.

"Should have taken out that evil Hussein guy, though," Tucker said.

"I did everything they told me to do," Elliot replied. "When you're in the army, they own you. We were plenty ready to kick butt, but never got the okay."

"It must be hard to take the uniform of a country's leaders who didn't always treat your own people fair and just," Jace commented.

Reba had been thinking the same thing.

"Perhaps, but there are good and bad people, no matter what race or tribe. There are misfits in every group. It's important to sort them out. I've learned to pow wow with the good ones and deal best you can with the bad."

As the children played hide-and-seek with playful shrieks, the rest sat silent, each lost in their own thoughts. Reba stole glances at Jace, marveling at her new views of him.

He looked back at her and then asked, "Elliot, who would you peg a hero from this last war?"

"Any one of my buddies, the guys in my troop. They'd die for me and I would for them. Also, Stormin' Norman Schwarzkopf, a great warrior."

"Well said."

Seth got up and walked to his Model T. "I'm headin' out," he announced.

Everyone scrambled to prepare to get back on the road.

Reba listened to Seth explain his car to Yarbo. "Gas on right, spark on left, have to crank it..."

Ginny leaned close and whispered to Reba, "I've heard rumors

Abel is really Jace's son."

Reba froze. "Who told you that?"

"It's been buzzed all around. On this trip. In Road's End. I'm going to find out one way or another before this trip's over."

Reba peered at Jace once more as he packed Abel's toys in the Volvo. Could it be? *It seems I'm surrounded by deceit.* Just when she thought she might make peace with this irritating man, her view of him soured again.

Chapter Eleven

Seth drove out on the highway behind a huge logging truck piled with forty-foot poles. Debris blew all over them and the road. Ginny began sneezing. She shut her window tight and Reba turned off the air vent.

The trucks crept ahead of them as the road ascended to the top of the White Bird Grade. The Model T in Ruckstell high and with added Z head horsepower maintained about twenty-five mph. At the top they reached 4,245-foot elevation. Plenty of turnouts and truck ramps lined the highway with forest on both sides and high rock cliffs.

Reba and Ginny along with the Nez Perce family in their pickup turned left across the highway to accompany the Model T along the Old Grade road with lesser decline. Jace and the others headed down the steep highway and agreed to meet them in the town of White Bird at the city park.

A sign stated: White Bird Battlefield 7.5 miles. After a quarter mile trek, Seth stopped the Model T. He got out and began to pick up fallen rocks in the road. Reba, Elliot and Tucker jumped out and braced against the wind to help him. They journeyed on with steep drop-offs to the left of them. Yellow, white, and purple wildflowers seemed to grow out of the rock to their right. No Trespassing signs marked barbed wire and broken down fencing.

When the cliff hanging drop-offs alternated to the right side, Ginny shut her eyes and began to whimper. "Why didn't you warn me, buddy?"

"Stay low. Hold tight. This too will pass."

"Just hold on to that steering wheel and stop talking."

Around the bend and past the deepest drop-offs, a red motorcycle and rider had stopped along the roadside. As the rigs passed, he pulled in behind them.

Ginny tried to read the graffiti on the guardrails around the curves. "Whoever had the nerve to risk their lives to splash words on a place like that?"

"You have your eyes open? That's an advancement."

"Barely. I'm squinting."

They rounded a few curves with no guardrails and crossed several bumpy cattle guards that rattled their rig. A stretch of loose gravel ended the paved road.

"They sure do need to fix their fences," Ginny muttered.

Reba's mind flashed to Michael and Vincent doing fence duty at the Cahill Ranch. For the first time, it seemed right to her. *Just miss me a little, okay?*

An old, rusty tractor and other ancient implements sprawled near a swampy pond. Except for the telephone poles, the landscape mirrored the Old West. Another sign: White Bird Battlefield 1 Mile Ahead. They came to cattle holding pens and an upright fence. Near a knoll of trees a herd of horses clumped together. They reached the Trailhead of the Battlefield.

The Model T parked on the left side of the road beside a long driveway entrance to a private residence. Reba and Reine parked their pickups and trailers in the turnout at the trailhead. From there to the highway beyond stretched a valley of dips and hills. A closed gate blocked the trail.

The Harley-Davidson biker pulled alongside Reba. The driver wore a bandana skullcap on his head and black leather vest and pants. He pulled out a map. "Who was fighting here?"

Reba pointed to Thomas and Elliot. "They'll tell you all about it."

Ginny got out. "I want to know more about that biker." She pulled out her camera and followed him to where Thomas and Elliot stood with their appaloosas.

Seth and Tucker watched Reba guide Johnny Poe out of his trailer. Tucker reached out to pet him and almost got bit. Then Johnny Poe nuzzled against Seth.

"Well, I know who's liked around here." Tucker went over and opened the gate. He read aloud a sign. "Things to remember. Please stay on the marked trail. Poison ivy, rattlesnakes, uneven terrain and high cliffs pose potential hazards. Summer temps can reach over 100 degrees. Bring plenty of water. There are no restrooms."

"It's the possibility of danger that makes a place interesting," Elliot remarked.

"We're headed to that cleft in the hump of the hill." Thomas handed Reba his binoculars. "You can see some of the rest of your party up there at the Nez Perce Historical Site."

Reba adjusted the binoculars to her eyesight and panned the landscape until she found the highway site. With a little more change of the setting, she spied Neoma and Ida leaning over a railing. The kids chased around, in and out of sculptured walls. In the parking lot Jace and Abel tossed an object back and forth near the Paddy's orange Toyota.

Ginny grabbed the binoculars and handed them back to Thomas when she scanned through them. "That's so cool."

"We will be gone at least as long as you," Thomas said. "I have traveled the trail from Oregon to Idaho already and have wanted to do this for many years. Seth's persistence at his age to do his own journey nudged me to go now. I am so glad my grandson agreed to go with me." His eyes glistened.

"I need to clear my mind of the fog of war," Elliot said. "Strange that I try to do that by reliving another war."

"Be safe," Seth said.

"I'm bringing this with me. I've already started reading it." Elliot held up a book: *Chief Yellow Wolf: His Own Story.*

"I thought Chief Joseph was the main man," Reba said.

"He was. Young warrior Yellow Wolf accompanied him on the flight, before he was a chief. This is his personal eye-witness account, recorded by a writer named McWhorter."

Thomas touched Seth's forehead and began a blessing. "You hold the key, but have little strength. You are faithful and your enemies will fall at your feet. Endure patiently and you will be kept from the hour of terrible trial. *Godki pewakunyu hanaka.*"

Thomas sang the chorus of "God Be With You" in Nez Perce and they all tried to join in, one by one. Even the biker.

Above them an overcast sky shed sprinkles as they pulled away from the trailhead. The two men on their spotted rump appaloosas with saddlebags and packs waved until they were out of sight. Reba grappled with a rush of melancholy. She considered jumping on Johnny Poe and galloping after Thomas and Elliot but decided against it. That was their trail, not hers. Realizing that confirmed to her she did belong with Seth and his migration to the desert.

Reine Laws followed their rigs into White Bird on the Old Grade before she headed back to the highway and north to Road's End.

"I should be reading a book," Ginny remarked. "I brought three with me. A Dean Koontz mystery. A John Grisham thriller. And a Danielle Steele romance."

"Which one will you choose first?"

She rummaged through her bag. "Aha, I actually have four. I think I'll finish reading *You Just Don't Understand* by Deborah Tannen. It's about the different languages men and women speak."

"You've got all those books in there? You're going to ruin your back carrying that much weight around. And I didn't know that speaking a different language was a gender thing."

"This author says women and men live in different worlds as far as their words go. They can walk away from the same conversation with completely different impressions of what was said."

"If that's true, how does any couple ever communicate? Or get along?"

"Well, I know at least one couple who doesn't. Cruel, rude winds are against us."

"Is that Shakespeare?"

"No, I think it's from the Bible. That's another one I need to read."

🐎 🐎 🐎 🐎

White Bird had its charms, a rustic town with western storefronts mainly catering to the saloon crowd. A skull and crossbones flag flew next to a Fresh Eggs sign. A billboard advertised Hell's Canyon jet boat trips. For Sale signs flourished everywhere.

"We need to do the western fronts for the stores in Road's End," Reba commented.

"Well, suggest it to the mayor."

"That would make a good campaign slogan, don't you think? For anyone who ran against the mayor."

"What? Road's End Needs False Fronts?"

Reba snickered. "Maybe not."

They arrived at the city park. Empty. The biker waved and drove on through town toward the highway.

"I never even asked his name," Reba said.

"I'll tell you anything you want to know. Name: Ransom. Hometown: Idaho Falls. Destination: headed home after traveling the Pacific Northwest. Occupation: Harley-Davidson shop manager."

"But is he married?"

"Nope. And doesn't want to be. Been there, done that."

Reba chuckled. "And you got plenty of pictures."

"That I did. He took mine too."

Soon the rest of the gang arrived at the city park.

"We got derailed at the White Bird Bridge. Russian truck drivers from Spokane dumped a load of apples. We all picked up some."

"Hey, what's that?" Pico said.

Ginny looked up and discovered a snake intertwined in a branch of one of the trees where she and Reba had been sitting. She shrieked and scooted across the yard.

Tucker coaxed it off its branch and handed it to Pico. Both he and Amos held and fondled it. Abel took a turn too and threatened to throw it at Becky. "Go ahead," she taunted. He did and she caught it and ran after Ned.

"Those kind don't bite, you know," Becky told Ginny. "Grandpa Hank told me all about them."

They quickly got on the road again. Down Billy Goat Lane, across the bridge to Pittsburgh Landing, back on the highway along the Salmon River, and to a pit stop at some outhouses. Across the river a roadside table and sandy beach crammed with people.

"Another stop?" Ginny complained.

"Someone has a going problem, I guess."

Ginny plucked some wild apricots and crabapples.

"Better be careful. You'll get a tummy ache if you eat too many."

A bald eagle perched high on a tree top branch as an osprey soared.

"You know what?" Ginny said between bites.

"What?"

"I've never been more scared in my life. And never had so much fun."

"And it's only our first day."

Down the road and over a bridge at Riggins, they turned left to follow Seth along the Salmon River and drove several miles up a canyon. They stopped at a wide rocky beach with a grassy knoll and set out a picnic of snacks, water, and sodas. Tourists with Illinois plates stopped near them to take a picture of a moose standing in the river, then they aimed their camera at the Model T.

While the men attempted to fish for trout, the ladies looked for berries to pick.

Tucker tracked a critter that invaded their cache of trout and dumped everything out of the tackle box. He persisted after the animal until it plunged into the river. Tucker and his sons watched it swim away.

"Looks like a beaver," Pico suggested.

"He sure was a fat one," Amos said.

"I think it was pregnant and a she," Tucker replied.

When Tucker complained about how many bugs he swallowed

and that every pothole and rock in the road bumped and slammed him against the Model T seat, Ida offered to give him a ride with them in the orange Toyota. He backpedaled. "It ain't so bad."

The caravan veered back on the highway and they quickly developed a routine. About once an hour Reba stopped to exercise Johnny Poe. The others kept going, cooled off engines, or got gas. A rare glut of traffic threatened a potential collision. Reba and Jace stopped along the road and tried to slow down those coming from behind.

When she plopped in the pickup, Reba rolled her window down a few inches.

"Brrr, put that back up," Ginny complained, as they set off again.

Overcast with a downpour earlier that morning, it cleared again by afternoon with arches of bilious white clouds. An hour later their next break they took turns at a solitary unisex porta-potty rest stop with handicapped reserved parking sign next to the small building.

"Is the toilet only for handicap use?" Ginny inquired.

"Arrest me. I'm going in," Reba retorted.

When she came out, Ginny finished reading aloud a passage out of her *You Just Don't Understand* book. "So, this author thinks it's crucial to look at a person when you're talking to them. Paris rarely looks at me anymore. Not really. Not into my eyes. He's got his mind in a project, or glued to the TV, or looking around to see what else is going on. From a male perspective, what do you think?"

Jace responded, "Whoa, I'm no relationship counselor, even though I earned two simultaneous master's in strategic intelligence and international relations. Worthless degrees that way."

Ginny closed the book. "But you give me the impression of a man who knows what he's about. And you do look at me when you talk to me."

"Thank you. I believe that's a compliment. A professor once told us if we wanted to learn more about ourselves, we should travel alone. The more foreign the place, the better. So I walked through the hills of Ireland, poked through the flea markets in Barcelona, and rode elephants in Africa."

"And now you're in Road's End. What have you learned so far?"

He laughed. "That I don't enjoy traveling alone. Sharing a chocolate chip malted Blizzard at Dairy Queen with a friend is way more fun."

"But there are no Dairy Queens in Road's End. Come on. You must have discovered a deeper insight than that."

"I think I know more than I want to know. Some things are difficult to accept." He stopped smiling and twisted a cup in his hand as Abel tugged at his sleeve. He tossed the cup in the air and Able ran to catch it.

"A business question. What do you think about the Internet?" Ginny asked. "We're starting to get a taste of it with the George Marketplace Delis."

"It's a forum for commerce, including stocks. But I foresee all kinds of difficulties, including potential for fraud. I have a passion to provide good, clean business practices."

"You didn't answer my question."

"I'm afraid it will become a necessary evil."

"I hate to interrupt this fascinating conversation," Reba said, "but I have a word for you. Next!" She pointed to the potty room.

When Ginny entered, Reba asked, "How long will Abel be visiting?"

"I'm afraid it's not just a visit. I may be raising him."

"That's an unusual thing for a bachelor brother to do."

"It's called compassion, I think. Or doing one's duty."

"But there's such a thing as compassion fatigue."

"Is that why you're sitting at a separate picnic table?"

"Is that an invitation?" Reba moved over.

Abel rushed to them and Jace tousled his hair. "How about you, Reba? Is this trip your attempt to get out of Road's End and see the world?"

"It's not too complicated. I'm here for Seth, but I'm also looking for my mother. In Silver Peak."

A man in a BMW pulled into the lot. Cocky grin on his face, he blurted out, "They're late."

Reba looked him over. Wrinkled t-shirt. Oily pants and cap. Probably an Idaho millionaire.

"They're late," the man said louder. A cigarette spewed fumes around his mustache and beard.

"Who you looking for?" Jace asked.

"Mickey and Donald from New Jersey. We have a transfer to make. You seen them?"

"Don't believe so."

"Well, I can see you have the personality of an olive." He stubbed out his cigarette with his shoes. "I don't believe they're coming after all." He got in the BMW and drove away.

They looked at each other and Reba got the giggles. After a couple less than feminine snorts, she said, "Boy, was he wrong. You brim with personality."

"I think that's the first positive statement you've ever made about me."

She tried to scowl, but couldn't control the chortles. When she gained control, she said, "Don't get a big head. Brimming with personality isn't always a plus in my book."

Before they got back on the highway, they waited for a Volkswagen to pass. On the back, a painted sign: "Just Married Again."

Winding along the Little Salmon River, they rode around a string of six bicyclists with helmets and packs. A hotshot driver passed them all right before a curve.

"That one's testing his karma," Ginny said. "Makes me so nervous. I don't want their karma messing with mine."

Up ahead, a semi slid off the road into a ditch and the speeding driver ran into it while it was being pulled out. They had to stop while they cleared the road. A flagger visited with each of them.

Ginny asked about the speedster. "All I know is he was cited for inattentive driving and failure to provide proof of liability insurance."

"What's Jace doing?" Reba asked Ginny.

"He's talking to a couple guys. I think they're hitchhikers."

"They're getting into his Volvo."

"Maybe he knows them?"

Reba got out of the pickup and walked back to Jace's car. He got out to meet her. Two males piled out too.

"Reba, meet Irving and Quigley. They're going to join us for a while."

"Where you from?" Reba quizzed.

"New York," blond Irving said with a distinct accent. He towered over six feet, tan as Jace, and wore tattered khakis with a knit shirt two sizes too short and tight.

Thin, dark-skinned Quigley with gold rings on each of his fingers and left ear lobe replied, "That's my business."

Reba frowned at Jace with a this- one's- got- an- attitude look. "You got family somewhere?"

"Two brothers in Vegas and six nieces and nephews," Irving said.

Quigley's glance darted around. "Haven't seen them since I left home at fifteen."

Taking Jace aside, Reba asked, "What's going on?" She tried not to show her irritation.

Jace shrugged. "They're hitchhiking to Winnemucca. To enter a golf tournament."

"Oh, yeah? Where are their golf clubs?"

"I stowed a bag that could be clubs in the trunk."

"Where is Irving really from?"

"He said his last name is Antipova, so I'm guessing he's Russian."

"Was he part of dumping a load of apples on the White Bird Bridge?" Reba poked Jace in the ribs until he headed with her to Johnny Poe's trailer. She attempted to sound stern. "You do realize that you are so taking a risk on Abel's behalf, as well as the rest of us, don't you? What if they're criminals? Or worse."

"Perhaps I should have done this different," he admitted. "I'm used to being my own boss. Making my own decisions."

"Done what different?"

"Having them tag along."

"What do you know about them?"

"They asked about where I'm going and got caught up in the adventure. I couldn't see the harm. I've picked up plenty of hitchhikers and never had a problem."

"You should have asked the rest of us first."

Jace's jaw hardened. He slumped into his crowded Volvo and slammed the door. "If they cause any trouble at all, I'll kick them out, or drop out of the caravan. How's that?"

After that, Reba kept her attention on Irving and Quigley when she could. When they took another brief break, she noticed they stayed close to Jace and away from her. Except when a tourist joined them. When Irving found out he could speak Russian, they jabbered with great animation. Reba understood a few words, such as Gorbachev, *glasnost* and *perestroika*.

"I can't tell if they are for it or against it," she said to Ginny.

"Are we traveling with a communist? My father and grandfather would have a living fit."

Along the Little Salmon River, a mild sun and gentle south wind cleared the skies. However, they ran into a swarm of insects. Seth and Tucker wrapped bandannas over their noses and mouths, but they still had to swat to keep them away. Eventually they got past the barrage.

Ginny put down her book. "I figured out true love is a lot like murder."

"Really?"

"Think about it. You've got to have motive, timing, and opportunity."

"Okay."

"No murder is an accident. Nor is love."

"Well, it will have to be for me. I know a lot about birthing calves, fixing fences, and training horses but little about men. Or any relationships, for that matter." Like Grandma Pearl. My mother. Jace. *Whoa, why did I think of Jace?* Why not Don instead? Out of sight, out of mind?

"You need to go to Australia. Maybe you'll be romanced by a cowboy like Crocodile Dundee."

"Only in my dreams."

"Seriously, what do you want?"

"I want a man I can love who will be willing and able to partner with me on the Cahill Ranch. I'm waiting for the right guy to be attracted to me who has the proper job description."

Ginny chuckled. "You kill me, girl."

Depression snagged her like the whip of a calf roper. She did want a life companion, but of course he must be the right one. Someone especially suited for her. Perhaps such a guy didn't exist. She tried to shake her mood by gazing into a field of blue lupine mixed with golden yellow balsamroot, purple asters, and wild dandelions. Such random beauty in a messed up world.

Ginny leaned into her window. "Hey, look at that huge deer with the big horns. Stop and let me get a picture."

Reba looked across the field to a small clearing in the trees. A huge, majestic animal with antlers posed majestic and stately. She signaled and pulled to the side. "It's an elk. A four by five non-typical and he knows it's not hunting season."

"What? You would shoot him?" She aimed the camera and clicked.

"Any fall. The meat's good and the antlers very valuable." Reba pulled back on the road behind all the rest of their group while watching for a chance to pass. She flipped on the wipers when a sudden spray of rainfall splattered across the windshield. She managed to smear the crushed bugs.

"Oh, yuck. What I'd give for a bucket of hot, soapy water right now."

🐎 🐎 🐎 🐎

The cold sunset like a dream burst into layered hues of purple and mauve.

"Wonder if that's due to volcanic ash?" Ginny mentioned. "It can circle the globe and cause sensational skyscapes."

"We always have wonderful sunsets." Reba scanned the horizon. "But that is extra special."

The Model T steered down a dirt roadway outside the town of New Meadows. Reba noticed behind her Jace let the hitchhikers out before turning. They waved and trekked down Highway 95.

A woman in flannel shirt and jeans, bandanna tucked around her neck, leaned against a post on the porch of a large ranch house. 1940s style. Single story with long, low roofline. Two-car garage with one side empty, the other crammed with an over-sized pickup.

Seth eased out of the Model T and held out his arms. She strolled forward, beaming. She touched his hand and he grabbed her in a long bear hug. He held her hand as they walked around the Model T.

"Been so long since I've seen this. And you. Different color though. Pretty snazzy purple." She directed the rest of them to park around a stand of aspens.

"I'm Hester Vaughn. Used to be Owens. That's my maiden name," she said to Reba. "We met once when you were a little girl, right after your mother ... "

"Abandoned me?"

She offered an apology. "You have your mother's eyes though your hair is deeper auburn than her dark blonde. The last time I saw her, that is."

"And you are Zeke Owens sister?"

"Yes, that's right." She replied with no hint of a smile.

Reba noticed Seth shot her a warning look. What was that all about?

A Border Terrier about twenty pounds with coarse, wiry double coat, dark lively eyes, and short muzzle, bounced out the front door. "And here's Killer. He'll be so glad to have company."

The Paddy boys and Abel circled around him as he jumped and barked, nuzzling his black nose into them.

"He's great on a hunt," Hester said. "He squeezes through anything and can run on any kind of terrain."

Ginny laughed as she tried to pet the quick dog. "So that's why you call him Killer."

Hester invited them inside a large two-room cabin where she cooked on a wood stove. Reba could see no refrigeration except a small propane freezer.

"She flies a helicopter," Seth remarked.

"I drop supplies and medicine when back roads are impassable," she explained. "You caught me just in time. I'm about to walk my cattle to the summer range. I'm getting tired of hand feeding them."

Seth's smile took a dip. "I hoped you could join us."

"Oh, Seth." Those two words reeked with longing.

While dinner was being prepared, everyone took a notion to want a ride in the Model T while there was still some visibility.

"That'll use up all my gas," Seth said.

"I've got plenty of backup for you," Hester assured him.

When it was Reba's turn, she talked Seth into going a bit further on a country road.

"I'm surprised at how noisy it is," Reba remarked. "And how windy. It feels like we're going faster than the speedometer says. You and Tucker are going to be battered by the end of this journey."

"Not me. I'm going to feel alive. The more weather, the better."

Back in Hester's house, full of Formica and paneling, Reba noticed a journal tossed upside down on the counter by a kerosene lamp. She thought of the old leather one of Maidie's in a cardboard box in Grandma Pearl's bedroom. "You keep a diary?" Reba asked.

"I record morning, noon, and evening--temperatures, my chores, and any thoughts I've gathered that day. Keeps me from being a bit more than an aging speck of humanity." She scrubbed Seth's grimy socks and stained white t-shirt on a washboard. "You got anything else that needs laundering?"

He shook his head.

"You too bashful to have a woman clean your undies?"

"I wouldn't even let Maidie do it."

Hester sighed. "I'm so sorry I missed her funeral. Couldn't get away. But you know my heart was with you. And her."

His eyes misted like morning dew.

Hester answered a rap at the door. In walked a tall man in his thirties with strong, sun-bronzed face holding a string of fresh trout and a rabbit. At first sight, Reba flashed a thought that she'd seen him before. Or maybe dreamed about him. *Weird.*

"Come meet my friends," Hester said. "This is Soren Patrick who lives down the draw and runs a horse ranch for an absentee corporation landlord. He's also my helicopter partner and backup. Looks like he brought more dinner."

"Or breakfast." He spread out his catch and hunt and pulled off his dusty tan cowboy hat.

Reba rushed to a quick judgment. Determined eyes. Sturdy body. He looked like a man who longed for one full ride on a championship bull. Long, thin fingers. Muscled arms. Dark brown hair almost black but in direct light, peppered with gray. He matched the definition of hale and hearty. Her heart skittered. *And a rancher.*

"Reba runs her own ranch," Ginny countered.

She's reading my thoughts.

Soren looked Reba square in the eye and seemed to ignore Ginny. "What kind of ranch?"

Reba tried not to stutter. "Actually, it's Grandma's. We, you know, when we can, seed and harvest hay. We tend miles of fence for twelve hundred acres. We've got cows. And horses. A little hay." Her mouth felt parched. *What's wrong with me? This sounds so stupid. Of course we have cows.* She licked her lips. "To be exact, we have sixty head of cattle in forest and pasture land. We also pack elk hunters on weekends in the autumn." *There. That's a bit better.*

"Show him Johnny Poe," Ginny urged. "She broke him when she was sixteen-years-old and hardly anyone else can ride him but her."

What's she trying to do? This man won't be impressed with that.

"You show him your horse," Hester urged. "I'll fry some of that fish."

On the way to the corrals Soren said, "I think we almost met one time."

Reba looked his face over, tried to memorize it. "Oh? When was that?"

"At a jewelry store in Elkville. You and a guy were looking at rings."

Enoch James. The boy she met at Pastor Kiersey's church. The grandson of Road's End barber, Alfred James. Her memory jogged. "You were there with a woman with long, straight brunette hair." She hesitated. "Neither of you seemed very happy."

"That's the moment she realized she couldn't go through with it. She couldn't marry me. She left the next day and I haven't seen her since."

"That's too funny."

"It wasn't at the time."

"No. What I mean, in the jewelry store looking at rings...that's when I broke up with my boyfriend, Enoch. He wasn't..." *A ranch-er.* A nice guy, but she finally realized he didn't fit her criteria. "We agreed to..." *Actually, I insisted.*

"You turned around and we bumped. Tears flowed down your face and I wiped them with my shirtsleeve. I got a real good look at you."

"Yes. Your shirt. I remember it being soft." And silky. And powdery blue. "But we never saw each other again."

"Until now."

Whoa, was this a sign or something? Soren Patrick, the rancher. But in New Meadows, not Road's End. How would that work?

Soren did a study of Johnny Poe's eyes, teeth, legs and form. Reba was relieved he stayed calm, showing his best manners. Perhaps the mares on either side helped. But he kicked up a typical fit when they left.

Reba expected some sort of comment, an analysis. Instead, Soren excused himself to wash up for dinner. "Even I detect the fishy smell."

As soon as he was gone, Tucker scooted from behind a huge white-flowered bush and motioned Reba over.

"Why are you hiding here?"

"I've got something to say to somebody and I figured it should be you." Tucker puckered his lips and touched them with a finger. "I'm worried about Seth."

"Why? What's wrong?"

"Oh, he's doing fine physically and all. Better than me sometimes. But," he whispered so low Reba had to ask him to repeat it. "He's got a huge wad of bills he carries in his sleeping bag. I think it's everything he owns. Thousands of dollars. He could get ripped off and be destitute."

Reba studied the man Road's End considered its town drunk and peered into an honest soul. "Thanks for telling me. You could have kept it a secret and stolen it yourself."

"I struggle with many things, but I'm no thief. What do you think we ought to do? You know, to protect him?"

"He should have kept it in the bank."

"Some folks don't trust them."

Reba peered at Soren waiting down the trail for her. She wasn't sure how he could help. She didn't know him well enough yet. Maybe Ginny had a solution. Or Jace. "I'll think of something. And thanks so much for confiding in me."

"Oh. And here." He handed her a bottle of wine. "Could you hide this somewhere? It's starting to get to me."

"Where did you get this?"

"It was in the basket Champ gave Seth."

Chapter Twelve

After a dinner of crusted trout, steak, and grilled rabbit, Soren invited them all to his place for homemade ice cream. "I've got vanilla or strawberry."

Hester and Seth declined.

So did Tucker and Ida. "Sorry, we're way too full and we have some catching up to do."

"Do you have hot fudge sundae sauce?" Becky asked.

"No, I'm sorry. I like it plain."

"Well, I have my championship to defend." She went outside with the other kids to play another round of Hearts with lantern light on a spread of blankets.

Neoma retired to her tent after borrowing a bucket to sponge bathe.

Ginny tugged on Reba. "We'll follow you to your place."

Jace pulled on a cap. "Me too."

After a mile walk through the woods that opened to acres of pasture, they entered a ranch house with pine and oak furniture and casual clutter.

After Soren filled all their bowls, Ginny said, "That's the creamiest, richest ice cream I've ever tasted."

"It's an old family recipe," Soren replied.

"That you won't share?" Reba prompted.

"Only with family."

Reba blushed at his intense stare.

Jace heaped more scoops of ice cream. "Where do you keep your cows?"

"Several years ago I phased out the cow side of the business to focus on breeding. We breed mares and sell the weanlings and yearlings."

"Race horses?"

"Some are used that way, if they show promise."

"I'd be very interested in seeing what you have."

Reba gawked at Jace in surprise until she recalled he had owned racehorses before. Maybe still did.

He took them to a pasture and showed them a palomino gelding, thoroughbred stallion, blue roan, and bay roan. "They're cow horses with balance, conformation, color, and athletics. They also do well in the performance arena. We breed them that way."

"You prefer pasture to stalls?" Reba noted.

"Yep."

"What did you think of Johnny Poe?" Ginny asked.

"Hard feet, sound legs, tough and self-reliant. Nice medium horse, strong build. Looks like he's got jump and drive in his legs."

Reba leaned against the corral fence. "He was vicious to break but became my best saddle horse and he's got cow sense."

"He has his head put on right, good rib spring, and he could fill a square."

"He likes to lay down on his back and let you scratch it," Ginny said.

Reba blushed. *Oh, Ginny.* He didn't need to hear that.

Soren leaned close to Reba. "But what about attitude? I like animals with a good mind and disposition."

Reba wriggled her nose. "That definitely leaves out Johnny Poe."

Ginny inclined against the split rail gate. "Does your wife work with you?"

Soren pulled at his cowboy hat. "To be honest, I lived with a woman for seven years. I'm not proud of it, at least not now." He gave Reba a hard-to-read look. "When I converted from making it all about me to being a follower of Jesus, I asked her to marry me. We even went to the jewelry store to look at rings. She balked big time right there and moved out instead. I regret it. Wish I could have made the relationship work."

"I can relate," Jace said.

Me too. Reba reached over and petted the palomino. Was Jace offering a hint about Abel? Did she want to know his history too? *I'll bet it's messier than Soren's.*

While walking back to their tents at Hester's property, Reba divulged to Ginny and Jace what Tucker told her about Seth's money stash.

"At home I hide mad money in empty cosmetic containers or cookie jars," Ginny said. "On the road, I tuck it in ... well, you can guess where."

"He's been wearing his beat-up boots lately. He needs a boot clip," Jace said. "With his pants over his boots, no one can suspect a thing. Or get to it without taking him too."

"I do that too." But not that much money, of course. "That's a great idea. First chance we get, we'll buy him one. Meanwhile, what do we do?"

Ginny spoke low, looking all around. They could hear the children play spotlight with a flashlight. "One of us needs to get that money and store it somewhere safe. That Model T is too open. No way to lock it."

"We can't do that," Reba sputtered. "That's criminal. As long as we know about it, we can keep an eye out. It's been okay so far."

"I agree," Jace said.

Reba volunteered a grateful smile.

In the dark of night with assorted lights, they seemed like a mini-village. With a start, they discovered strangers squeezed in on them, not realizing this was private property not a public campsite. The couple and their two kids were welcomed and Ginny passed around vinegar to drink. "It will repel the mosquitoes," she claimed.

The children chased Hester's dogs while Seth whittled wooden chains and links for the children. The rest gazed at the wide expanse of stars and planets.

"Just think," Jace said. "The Hubble telescope is up there right now hoping to bring the origins of the universe into focus."

Ginny yawned. "Yep, all that money. All those blurry pictures."

"I'm sure they'll get it fixed."

In their tent Ginny tucked into her borrowed sleeping bag. "Quite a full day, don't you think?"

"I'd sure like to ask Hester about her brother."

"How come?"

"He was Maidie's fiancé who died in a tragic accident. He most likely is a relative of mine. Maybe my grandfather. So she would be related too."

"I'm much more interested in what you think of Soren Patrick."

Reba's emotions tore between irritations about changing the subject. An important one to her. And the racy skip she felt at the mention of the cowboy's name. "He seems like a decent guy."

"What else?"

"I don't know enough to say more than that." *Liar.*

"Sure you do. He's good looking. He runs a ranch. He seemed to be loyal to his love interest. And he's available. Doesn't that fit your profile of the perfect match?"

"I suppose on the surface it does." *And deeper.*

"Fess up. You're thinking serious thoughts about him."

"I don't want to talk about it, thank you." *What's the point?* They may never see each other again.

"Okay, I'll change the subject. I wonder how your grandma's doing with her crew."

"I'm sure they're getting along fine. It's obvious she doesn't need me."

"I noticed Hester has a phone. You could call her."

"I suppose I could." Reba turned over in her Coleman bag. But why? If everything's hunky-dory, that's good for her and bad for me. If it isn't, that's bad for her and tempts me to gloat. It's a lose-lose situation right now. Besides, it's only been one day. What could there be to know?

Within minutes, Ginny snored in a perfect pattern of *hkh-sssss-hkh-sssss-hkh-hkh-sssss*. Like a cat with nasal problems. She was out for the night.

Reba played the usual tricks to shut off her mind. She scrunched her pillow and tucked her head in different positions. She imagined bubbles and candlelight surrounded her. She let her mind wander in *what if* fantasies. First, it was Soren. Then Jace. Even Don. Maybe a glass of warm milk.

She noticed a light still on at Hester's place. *Should I?* She'd just take a little stroll and check things out. She eased out of the sleeping bag, slipped on her bathrobe, and stole out of the tent. When she got to the door, she hesitated. Maybe Hester had already gone to bed and left a night-light.

She bolstered her nerve and tendered a *tap, tap, tap.*

The door swung open. Hester's wide smile tamped down to a polite welcome. Was she expecting someone else? Seth? Reba got that third wheel sense she often conceived around couples. Now what? Out with it. "I had trouble sleeping. Could I get some milk? Warmed up, that is."

"Of course. Come in, Reba Mae. I'm delighted."

Reba Mae? How did she come up with that? Well, I won't stay long. She can still have her other company.

Hester led to the kitchen and poured milk in a saucepan. "You have such a large home," Reba remarked. "Do you have children?"

"Oh, yes, five of them. They're all scattered now."

"None of them wanted to stay on the homestead?"

"No, but that's okay. I encouraged them to find their own lives. Maybe if we had a son. They're all girls."

So, they didn't get boot camped into the cowgirl thing, like Reba did. She pondered whether to broach the subject. But it was now or never. "About Maidie..."

Hester turned sharply in her direction.

"I only very recently discovered that she's my real grandmother." There, she said it. And it still seemed strange. Another thought dawned... "But maybe you didn't know?"

"Oh, I knew. Like everyone else, after the fact. Seth and I...we were close in those days."

"Who else knew?"

"Besides Maidie, Seth, and me...only Pearl and Cole. And perhaps the father."

The father. Could that be Zeke, her brother? "Zeke...he had a terrible accident. He died before...my mother was born."

"Yes. Fell off a roof. But it wasn't an accident." Hester handed her a bright yellow mug with hot, scalded milk.

Reba clutched the mug to ward off the ribbing of frost inside. "What do you mean?"

"We...Seth and I...couldn't prove criminal intent to the satisfaction of the sheriff. But the roof had been oiled. Zeke had oil on the bottom of his shoes and the backside and sleeves of his shirt. He slid off that roof slick as scum."

"But who would purposely do such a thing?"

"I have my suspicions." She covered her face. "It's been so long since I've gone through all of this. Seth and you being here...it brings the good and the bad."

"I'm so sorry. We don't have to talk about it."

"Yes, we do. The time has come." She heaved her sorrows and steadied herself. "Zeke might have committed suicide. I have to face that possibility."

"But why? He and Maidie were engaged." And he had a baby on the way. Did he know that?

"I don't know. Maybe Maidie already showed signs of her craziness. Perhaps memories of his war duty. What happens on the battlefield doesn't remain there. It lives on in soldiers' nightmares. I've pondered it over and over."

Reba waited as Hester gathered courage to delve into the pain.

"I realize you loved Maidie, even before you found out she was your grandma." Hester poured the rest of the milk in another mug and stuck the pan in the sink. "Sometimes she helped Zeke do his roofing jobs. I have wondered if she slathered the oil herself."

Oh dear God. Please, not that. Why in the world would Maidie want Zeke dead? But didn't Grandma Pearl mention she went into hysterics after my mother was born? What was her state of mind during her pregnancy?

"There is another option. And I realize none of these theories is pleasant. Or provable. However, the roof from which Zeke fell...it was a bunkhouse. On the Runcie Ranch. Champ hired him to do the job. And he insisted he work day and night to get the job done immediately. The first day, he did fine. But when he returned that night, with poor visibility, oil had been added. Whether he did it, Maidie did it, or Champ did it...he was on the ground with a broken back and found dead the next morning."

"Who found him?"

"Champ."

But what really happened? And why? Who had something to gain by Zeke's death? And what did Hester mean, 'the time has come'?

As Reba pondered these questions, she thought of Seth. His money. "By any chance, do you have a boot money clip we could borrow?"

"I sure do. My husband owned several."

"It's for Seth."

"That's even better."

Back in the tent, sleep still competed with restlessness. She kept jostling in the sleeping bag as a storm moved in and grumbled all around. As she finally nodded into semi-consciousness, she wondered what Grandma Pearl was doing.

The cardboard boxes sat in the corner of the bedroom where Pearl stacked them. However, the contents scattered over her bed and a cedar chest against the wall. Embroidered linens. Sets of floral china. A family Bible with a family tree included. Sheets of flute music. Tarnished silverware. Sterling silver candlesticks. A christening gown. Knitted blankets and crocheted baby booties. A yellowed wedding dress. Maidie's? Or her mother's?

A stack of letters addressed to Maidie Fortress from Ezekiel Owens dated in the 1940s during WWII. And a leather-bound, hand tooled journal wrapped with a leather strap.

Pearl expected assorted knick-knacks and other trivia. This store of prizes could easily ruin. Why weren't they kept in a more protected place? How amazing they survived at all. Maybe Seth pulled them out of a chest. But why?

She picked up the letters and started to read. Too heartbreaking. *Oh, Maidie, I'm so sorry for your great loss.* She never had a chance for a full life. A husband. Children. Well, she did have a child, but that one was taken from her.

Oh, Hanna Jo, where are you? How are you doing?

At the bottom of one of the boxes, stuck under a corrugated divider, she discovered a woman's picture. She looked familiar. For one thing, she had Seth's eyes. And Maidie's. *This must be Eve, his mother.* Pearl gently rubbed the photo and peered closer. She wore the squash blossom necklace Seth had given Reba.

A thought warmed her and heated to a searing point. She shuddered with a fresh sense of power, like she held the winning card for a big pot. And no one else yet realized it. "Why couldn't this hold up in a court of law?" She tucked the photo in a folder inside a dresser drawer. "There, Champ Runcie, take that. For future reference."

Her spirits lifted at the unexpected find, in spite of the grief she endured about Reba and their estrangement. Hanna Jo's too. *No wonder the Lord never gave me kids of my own.* She couldn't parent well the single one she'd adopted.

She touched the journal and caressed it. Dare she pry into this? Or would it be as painful as peering into those letters from Zeke. Perhaps she should put them all away or dispose of them. Keep them forever Maidie's un-tampered, private world.

She clutched the journal and headed for the boxes. Then stopped. No. Seth specifically stated he wanted her to keep these. Caught in a vortex of sensations foreign to her usual common sense approach, she sat down and weighed spiritual guidelines. Guard each one's dignity. Bring light to darkness. The truth will set you free. Love covers a multitude of sins.

Would opening this journal threaten Maidie's dignity as a person? Or would it only reveal darkness? Could truth bring release? Or would it only chronicle sin and bring shame?

There was only one way to find out.

She carefully untied the narrow strap and lifted the leather binding. Several empty loose pages covered the top. She pulled them away and began to read.

Several hours later, Pearl packed some canvas bags, including the leather journal, and tossed them in her red Jeep. She careened down the driveway and stopped to call out to Vincent coming the other way. He pulled the old ranch pickup next to her.

"I'll be gone a few days. Maybe more. I'll call you tonight. Please tell Michael he can use my kitchen, if he wants, since I won't be here to fix meals. Key is in the windowsill flower box. Got some very important business to tend to."

Vincent's concern showed in his eyes and his arm stretched out toward her. "Why the hurry?"

"I've got to talk to Reba. In person. Now."

"Can't you wait for a phone call?"

"No. This has to be face-to-face."

"I'll come with you."

"No, I need you here." *Should I share the news with him?*

"What else can I do for you, besides direct Michael, and do ranch chores?"

"Pray. I sense spiritual warfare." Another thought came to her. "Come with me to the hotel. I want to take the turquoise necklace with me. It may be useful. And I promise I'll be very careful with it."

His brow furrowed, his full face a frown. "Are you sure about that? You'll set yourself up for robbery. Or worse." He rubbed his forehead. "And Champ will be furious if he finds out."

"He won't know. And if he does, I can take care of him."

"I don't like the sounds of this. This is no time to be stubborn. Please let me come with you."

Her mind fought against her heart. *Yes, please come. Be my strength. My companion.* "Vincent, I know you'd do anything for me, but this I have to handle myself, with God's help. And I truly do need you here."

His face twisted in doubt. "Okay, but I beg you to be careful." He reached across and touched her shoulder. "Call me. Often."

She clutched his hand. "I will. I just hope I'm not too late."

"I'll follow you to the hotel."

The next morning Soren Patrick arrived at the campsite with a saddlebag initialed S.P. full of jerky, sardines, a loaf of sourdough bread, and sharp white cheddar cheese. He handed it to Reba. "May come in handy on the road. You can return it the next time we meet." He tipped his hat. "And you're all welcome to stop again when you come back through."

Ginny poked Reba in the back.

Reba blushed crimson.

Hester brought Seth a gift basket wrapped in cellophane. "I shrink wrapped with my hair dryer," she said. "At least this will be protected from the bugs."

Ginny clicked shots of them all as they prepared for the next stage of their journey. She nudged Soren and Reba together for a photo. "Come on, smile. Don't look so awk-ward." Then she paired Hester and Seth who showed no shyness in a cozy coupling.

Seth and Tucker put on the bug-eyed, alien looking green glass goggles.

Soren asked about the Model T's mileage and took an admiring walk around. Seth warmed up like he was a car salesman. A new customer to brag to. "Gas headlights. Brass generator. Ruckstell rear end. Rocky Mountain brakes. And I just had a Z head installed."

"And cracked leather seats," Tucker added.

Seth continued. "Fuel tank is under the seat. Measured with this here stick. Ten gallon tank and extra gas can."

"We're all carrying extra for him, too," Jace called out.

Seth nodded. "I can travel fifteen miles per gallon. And also have water and oil cans on the running board. And this touring model has more luggage space than any others its age, in the back seat and floorboard." And as he said many times before, pointing to the steering wheel, "Gas on the right, spark on the left, and have to twist its tail, of course."

"I can do it now," Tucker insisted. "No reason for you to wear yourself out."

Seth's forehead wrinkled with doubt. "Okay, you just go right ahead."

"I'm good for kick-startin' it too." Tucker kicked the left tire. His sons kicked the other three.

Everyone gathered around to watch Tucker do the routine. A few taunted him but most urged him on.

"I've got my stop watch," Jace said. "Can you beat Seth's time? Go!"

"I'm not in a race," Tucker insisted. "This is a work of art."

He bowed and strolled to the front of the Model T. He leaned over and pulled the choke with his left hand while pushing in the crank with his right. He primed the intake with a couple slow spins. He climbed inside and pulled the handbrake back, turned the switch to the battery, pushed the spark lever up, He set the throttle a few inches down and sauntered again to the front. He turned the crank to the eight o'clock position, pushed it in, and with his left hand wrapped his fingers aligned with his thumb around the handle. With a swift motion, he pulled the crank up to twelve o'clock. The engine rattled on. The Model T purred. And Tucker beamed.

He turned to Seth and ushered him to the driver's seat. Then he grabbed Ida and sang at the top of his lungs, "He was dying to cuddle his squeeze."

Everyone cheered and headed for their rigs.

After a stop for lunch, Seth reported, "There must be a leak in the fuel line. I may need a tow into the next town."

"We can push it," Jace suggested.

"We can't pull it all the way to Jordan Valley."

"Sure we can or we can keep filling it until we get there," Jace insisted.

The man they saw at the Nez Perce battle trailhead, the one on the red Harley, stopped next to them.

"Hey, Ransom," Ginny called out.

He high-fived her. "You guys know where the hot springs are?" He pulled a paper from his vest pocket. "Three Forks Hot Springs."

Jace looked at his map. "Looks like you go east about thirty miles from Burns Junction. Past the tiny community of Rome."

"Yeah, I think I went right by the sign. Not very visible. You need some help here?"

"We're trying to limp into Jordan Valley."

Another motorcyclist southbound with silver helmet on silver BMW stopped. Reba stared at the white paint or paste on his face. "Did you happen to notice a late model black and white Chevelle? May have been speeding."

"No, we didn't. What's the problem?"

"He scammed a friend of mine. It's payback time."

"We'll keep an eye out."

"I'm looking for the Three Forks Hot Springs. You see it on your route?" Ransom quizzed.

"Just come from there. Come on, I'll show you." The two bikers sped away together.

A mile out of Jordan Valley, Oregon the Model T chugged and jerked and slowed down. Tucker put his hands on the dash to keep from sliding forward. He shot a quick look at Seth who furiously worked the throttle and spark. "No gas?" Tucker ventured.

Seth gave up and pushed the left pedal halfway down in neutral. As the engine sputtered to a halt, Seth shrugged. "It's downhill. We'll just coast in."

The car rolled along gaining speed. About halfway down the incline, Seth hit the brakes with his right foot. Nothing. The car continued to accelerate. Seth tried the handbrake, but that didn't work either.

"We're too loaded down," Tucker yelled. "Can you put it back in gear?"

"We're going too fast."

As they sped into town, Tucker waved his arms in an attempt to warn those behind and ahead while Seth gripped the wheel, knuckles white. They swerved around cars and the tires squealed.

As the car sailed, Tucker's hat blew out. "Oh, God, we're going to die." His head sank to his chest. "And I never drank a drop the whole trip."

"Pray we don't hit anything or anybody," Seth shouted. "Hold on. We've got to make that curve." Before they negotiated the turn, the road began to rise and they could feel the car slowing.

"You've got to turn into that service station and stop."

The road ascended. The car decelerated but not fast enough. Seth swerved as wide as he could and turned the wheel with all his might toward the service station. The Model T's tires squealed and the back end swung around a full circle. They still moved forward but at a slower pace. As they approached the gas station building, Seth stomped on both the brake and left side gear pedals. The car lurched into gear pitching both men forward. The car heaved a couple times before halting a few inches from the shop wall.

"Grab something to block the tires," Seth hollered.

Tucker leaped out and grabbed a couple boards on the ground and shoved them under each side of the front passenger tire. He rubbed his bruised knees. "Whooee, I'll bet we were going over fifty miles an hour."

Seth gasped a few breaths of relief. "Nah, I don't think so."

"It sure felt like it."

"Thank God we could stop. I hope we can get a mechanic to fix the brakes without sending to Timbuktu for parts."

Tucker opened the hood. "I wonder if the motor's busted. If the engine's been run hot and the block is cracked, it will be quite inoperable, you know."

Their fellow travelers surrounded the Model T.

"Thanks for that cheery news. All it needs is some water and the brakes fixed. And Franklin Fraley."

"Well, he's not here. But don't worry. With a rebuilt engine, it could be a real hummer. I know. I forgot to mention I used to own a 1904 Oldsmobile Curved Dash."

A policeman greeted them. "I've got you clocked as speeding, reckless driving, passing on the crest of a grade or a curve, and disturbing the peace. Now, get out so I can inspect whether you're driving under the influence."

"I never drink," Seth said as the rest of their caravan gathered around. "My brakes quit on me."

"Show me your license and proof of insurance."

"They were stolen."

"Oh no, Seth, when did that happen?" Reba cried.

"I don't know. Maybe a year ago."

He meant to drive all this way to Nevada without a license or insurance card?

Seth sat dazed on the running board. Tucker pulled a wrench out of the toolbox and dove under the Model T. Two denim-covered legs and worn brown boots poked out one side.

"What are you doing?" Ida shouted at him.

Tucker scooted out. "While Seth is in the pokey, I'm going to fix the brakes."

"Ginny, you look awful pale. You okay?" Jace asked.

"You saw her. Reba came close to plunging us over the cliff edge trying to keep up with Seth."

🐎 🐎 🐎 🐎

Later Jace reported, "Seth has to pay a fine and get his license and insurance before he can keep driving. That may take a couple days."

They all groaned.

"But I think Ginny got us reservations at the local motel." Reba turned to her friend. "Didn't you?"

"I tried to. But they're all booked. However, the manager gave me directions to a couple campgrounds and ranches where we can set up our tents and gear."

"I'll help Seth best I can," Jace continued. "I've got some resources. Each of you decide whether you want to keep going or wait for him. I'm staying here." He looked at Reba. "That old man's the total reason I came on this trip. No reason for me to leave without him."

Reba turned to Ginny. "You're the one with a schedule. What do you want me to do? I'll drive you on, if you want. That's quite a slow-down for you."

"I'll think about it."

"I'm staying at least tonight," Neoma said. "I'm too fatigued to drive on."

"I'm with Tucker," said Ida. "And he's intent on fixing the Model T."

"But what is there to do?" wailed Becky. "This town is smaller than Road's End."

"For one thing, you'd better watch out for the turkey vultures," Tucker said. "They come to this place every year."

"Stop scaring the kids," Ida scolded.

"But it's true."

Ginny interrupted. "I saw a poster at the café. A two-day rodeo starts tomorrow at 1:30 p.m. That's why the motel's not available. We can cowboy and cowgirl up."

Becky looked dubious, but all the boys whooped and hollered. "What are you going to wear?" Becky asked Ginny.

"Let's go try to buy some jeans like Reba's. Surely they have some around here. Only with some bling."

Becky ran to ask her grandma. "I'll pay for it," Ginny shouted. "Me and Becky are buds."

When they returned from shopping, Ginny announced, "Well, we didn't find bling, but we did discover some distressed jeans. In red."

"And Ginny bought me jewelry too." Becky showed off her red boot earrings and matching necklace.

They found a plot of ground with no facilities that a farmer rent-ed to them. Neoma pulled a small portable table and lawn chairs from her tent trailer. Ginny overpaid for more from the local businesses and a few residents. They soon established a community picnic ground in the desolate space. The tents set up, Johnny Poe fed and watered and brushed, two sheep escaped from a nearby pasture ambled toward them. The Basque shepherd called out and uttered a long monologue in his mouth-puckering, tongue-trilling language and lots of body motions.

Reba nodded a lot at him.

"Did you understand him?" Ginny asked.

"I went with Vincent one time to a Basque Center in Boise. To some kind of festival. Plenty of music and dancing. I remember flashes of black, red and white costumes. We ate some ham stew. Very tasty. Had a kind of custard for dessert. But no, I didn't understand much, except maybe his name."

"Okay, what's his name?"

"Can't say."

"You don't know?"

"I can't pronounce it. Closest I come to is Gara-Ka-Beachia. And I can tell he seems madder than a bull in bumblebees. Best I can make out, someone rolled boulders from that yonder hill on his camp."

"I sure hope he doesn't think it was us."

🐎 🐎 🐎 🐎

Ginny and Reba set up camp next to Neoma after Reba got Johnny Poe settled.

"I think it's wonderful you're taking care of your grandkids," Reba ventured as they watched the children practice roping fence posts and run barrel ride figure eights around chairs.

"Yeah, but you know what? The older generation needs a break."

"It's getting to you?" Ginny said.

Neoma raised her legs on a boulder. "Some kids take a long time to grow up. Trish was sixteen when Becky was born. That doesn't excuse her choices, but she did feel trapped. Much like I do now."

"And with you losing your husband too," Reba noted.

"There's been no time to grieve Hank's loss. No place alone to bawl. No solitude in which to scream. Not with the constant duty to care for the children and their needs." Neoma rubbed her forehead. "Trish disappointed and humiliated me. She abandoned her marriage and her children. And she abandoned me. She left me when I needed her most. She assumed I'd care for her kids and had no needs, no life of my own."

Was that how Grandma Pearl felt? "But you're going to see her in Reno?"

"If she'll let us. I want to know what she has to say. I want to listen to her. But at this point, I don't expect anything from her. I just wish she would understand that I'm still grieving the loss of my husband and it feels like I've lost her too. I can't relax and be the kids' grandma. I've got to try to be both mother and father instead. I know I could have coped better with Hank's help, but that wasn't meant to be. Somehow I've lost my way." She offered a half grin. "I used to paint years ago."

"What kind of painting? Like your daughter?"

"Not as good as hers, the ones she did at Aunt Cee's. But I've done oils and watercolors. I've got a dozen canvasses locked up in a storage shed in St. Joseph. Bowls of waxy fruit. Sprays of brambly roses. I did one of Trish riding a horse. My favorite."

"Maybe you can do that again."

"Perhaps. I'm not sure."

Chapter Thirteen

The day started dark and overcast as the kids chased each other around the cars. Jace tried to clean his gritty windshield. Reba backed Johnny Poe out of the trailer. And Tucker threw boxes from the Model T onto the temporary campsite as he shooed mangy mongrels away.

"What are you doing?" Reba asked Tucker as she fed the black horse flakes of hay.

"Getting rid of some of this cargo. It's loading us down. We should be able to travel faster now."

"Put them in the back of my pickup. You'll incur Seth's wrath and be arrested for littering."

"Don't need another jailbird on this team, that's for sure."

Jake stopped and looked over. "Seth's not in jail. He was feeling pretty weak. They kept him overnight for observation at the hospital and then he has to go to the county seat to do some paperwork."

Two males with backpacks stalked toward them. "Hey, guys," Jace greeted. "Irving and Quigley. You haven't made it very far."

Irving dropped his pack. "We hit a dry spell in the hitchhiking. Any chance we could bum another ride? We're still headed to Winnemucca."

Some guys in a black Jeep Cherokee jumped us. We had to lie low for a few days," Quigley said.

"Was that a random act or did they have a reason?"

"Um, we did have a run-in once with them in Boise."

Ida strolled over and patted Irving on the shoulder. "Howdy, boys." She turned to greet Quigley but he jerked away.

"Don't touch me, lady."

Ida studied him. "You're awfully mad about something."

Quigley glared at her. "Lots of things in this world to be angry about." He spit out tobacco chew.

Ida dug deeper. "But you've got a tick in your bur that appears awful personal."

He picked tobacco remnants from his teeth.

"Maybe if you guys looked for a job, things would improve you," Ginny suggested.

"Oh, but we have a job," Irving insisted.

Quigley gave him a warning shot and he said no more.

Amos and Pico ran over to them. Pico jumped up and down and pointed. "Those are the guys who messed around with Seth's Model T that night at the lady's house."

Reba stared at the boys. "Are you sure? That's a very serious charge."

"Are you talking about at Hester's place? Jace left them out on the highway about then."

Amos hung his head. "They snuck in there. We saw them and heard them talking. Somebody paid them money to do it."

Jace grabbed both men by their collars. "Is that right? Did you sabotage the Model T?"

"No, man." Irving squirmed to get away and Quigley tried to bolt, breaking Jace's hold.

Tucker rammed his shoulder into Quigley and spun the smaller man around.

Jace kicked Irving hard in the back of the knees, knocking him to the ground.

Quigley whirled back around, away from Tucker, pulled out a knife, and grabbed Reba around the neck. "Back off or she gets slit."

Jace straightened, held up his hands in front of him, and slowly circled. "Hey now, calm down. No need to do anything stupid."

Quigley spouted orders. "Everybody pay attention. Or she gets hurt. Against that fence. Now!"

The village of travelers gathered at the fence, helpless and horrified.

Irving lifted from the ground, his eyes wild and desperate, and motioned the group to move. They all took a few steps back. Becky whimpered. The boys crowded behind the adults. Tucker looked like he was going to spring at Quigley and Jace got his attention and shook his head.

Irving stepped toward Quigley. "Release her and let's get out of here."

"She's on our list too. Let's take her with us. She might be worth some bucks."

What list? As Reba scrambled to figure a way to get free, she heard a familiar snort and clomp of hooves from behind.

"Not worth it. Not like this," Irving negotiated.

Johnny Poe ambled to a few feet in back of Quigley and Reba.

"What's that noise?" Quigley turned to Irving. "What's going on?"

Before Irving could reply, Jace shouted, "Watch out. Look behind you!"

Quigley wheeled around and the knife barely missed Reba's neck. Reba bent over and kicked hard toward Quigley's knee. Her foot collided against him with full force and he dropped in agony. She lost her balance and fell on her back, hitting a hard rock square in the ribs. She cried out as she lost air. Ginny rushed to her with sobs.

Quigley rolled the wrong way under a rearing Johnny Poe. Hooves crashed down...once, twice. At first Quigley yelled curses at the horse and attempted to wave him away. But he soon squeezed into as tight a fetal position as he could manage as Johnny Poe reared again. Hooves hit flesh and Quigley yelped in pain.

Jace had already gotten in front of Johnny Poe. "Down, boy. Whoa!" he ordered.

Johnny Poe stopped, stock-still and eyed the man who dared command him. Jace stared him down without a flinch and grabbed hold of his rein. Ida ran over and grabbed the knife lying in the dirt.

"That's a good boy," Jace said quietly. "You did great. You saved Reba." Jace pointed at Quigley. "Somebody better watch him."

Tucker rushed over with his shotgun. "I'm on it."

"And we've got to get him a doctor," Ida announced.

Quigley moaned on cue.

Jace walked the horse to the trailer and tied him to a hook on the side of the trailer. He patted Johnny Poe. "Well done. You and Reba make a great team."

In the mêlée, Irving escaped. As Tucker guarded the wounded Quigley, Ginny tried to help Reba up. Ida and Neoma corralled the kids to the tents and tried to reassure them they were safe. Then Neoma drove to town to contact the police.

Reba cried out in pain when she tried to take a deep breath. "I think some ribs might be cracked."

Jace ran to his car and brought Ginny some wide ace bandages. "Wrap these tight around her."

"I'll need...Jace's...cream too," Reba wheezed. She was just aware enough to notice the look in Jace's face. Alarm? Certainly concern. The glimpse quickly disappeared in the need for action.

"Did anyone notice the direction Irving ran?" Jace questioned.

"He's in the horse trailer," Becky replied.

"Are you sure?"

"Yes. He slipped in there when Johnny Poe attacked Quigley."

"Okay, stay back, all of you," Jace warned.

"Be careful," Ginny whispered. "He might be armed too."

Jace crept toward the trailer and slammed the back door shut. Johnny Poe jumped and a shout of protest from inside confirmed Irving's presence. "Hey, guys, I don't have any weapons and don't aim to hurt anyone. That's all Quigley's doing."

"Then come out there," Jace ordered.

Irving cowered inside.

They heard a police siren. The patrol car parked near them, lights flashing, and Neoma pulled up behind. The same policeman who accosted Seth earlier listened to the full report. "Okay, keep that horse calm," he demanded.

Jace held firm to Johnny Poe as the cop approached the trailer, gun drawn. "Irving, out of the trailer, hands high." A chastened Irving pushed the door open and stepped out, hands up. He was handcuffed and pushed into the back of the patrol car.

Then he cuffed Quigley. "The EMT is on the way." After he questioned everyone else, he approached Quigley, still lying on the ground and hunched in pain.

He refused to reply to the policeman. "I need a hospital. And you should arrest that horse. He's crazy."

The policeman and Jace picked a screaming Quigley up by the shoulders and dragged him to the patrol car.

While they waited for medical assistance, and after Ginny doctored Reba, she interrogated Irving. "What list am I on? Who put you up to this?"

Quigley glared at her. "Irving, don't tell her nothin'." He whispered, "I'm not through with you, girl. Or your horse." His face mirrored pure venom.

After the ambulance arrived and they strapped Quigley to a gurney and loaded him up, both flashing light vehicles drove away. Reba refused medical attention over Ginny's objections. The kids had calmed down and were now thrilled with the commotion.

"He won't return and get us?" Amos prodded Tucker.

"We'll take care of you."

Jace and Tucker took turns on guard duty with the shotgun.

Ginny aided Reba in getting to their tent. "How you doing?"

"I hurt. But I found a position that's not too bad. How about you?"

She heard a sniffle and cough. "Oh, Reba, I was so scared. Why would those men want to hurt you? When I think about what might have happened..."

"It was just Quigley, not both of them. I don't think Irving is a bad guy. And God took care of us."

"Yes, He did. But Quigley threatened to come back."

"The police have him."

"But for how long? And what of this list he mentioned? What's that about?"

"I don't know." Reba twisted, aching, maneuvering for relief.

Ginny grinned at her. "You handled yourself pretty well. Got a solid kick in. His leg has to hurt as least as bad as your back."

Reba winced and nodded. "Hope so."

"Should be fair warning to Jace or any man not to cross you."

Reba let out a laugh then her face contorted. "Stop it!"

Ginny winked. "Love you, friend."

"Love you too."

Reba tried to sleep but the safe haven of oblivion eluded her. Quigley haunted her. She doubted he'd made an idle threat. She watched the silhouettes of the two men who watched over them, especially the one who controlled Johnny Poe when it was needed most. The one who bared a hint of feelings in an unguarded look.

The next day, Jace left early. "I went by the sheriff's office," he said when he returned. "Seth will be released from the hospital in the morning. Be prepared to head out again."

"Will he have his driver's license?" Reba asked.

"With picture and all. He even passed the written test."

That afternoon they all attended the Jordan Valley Big Loop rodeo at the arena across from the cemetery. The events included saddle bronc riding, team roping, and bull riding.

"The bulls were the best," the Paddy boys agreed.

"I liked the barrel racing better," Becky said. "So did Ginny."

"That's because they were all girls," Pico scowled.

Ned spread his lips wide in a mimic. "The clown was the coolest."

Abel put on his pout face. "I wish Jace would let me enter the Junior Steer Riding. I could of done better than those other boys. None of them stayed on."

"But you've never done it before," Amos said.

"Don't matter. I could tell by watching how easy it was. Irving told me he did calf roping before. At a rodeo near Houston."

"He's either a fibber or he sure gets around," Jace said.

"I hope he's safe," Abel replied. "He was always sneaking me candy bars and then Quigley stole them away."

The next morning they cheered as Jace arrived with Seth. They lined up and after a crank by Tucker, Seth led them out on the road. Tumbleweed stretched along roller-coaster asphalt. Salt flats stirred with the dance of whirling dust devils. Sage looked like an oily skid, a wet mirage.

Two youths in a 1991 Ram Jet Camaro honked their horn a dozen times before speeding past the long caravan. They barely missed an oncoming semi as they made an obscene gesture at Seth in his Model T.

"Makes me mad when drivers like that risk all our lives to get nowhere in a huge hurry," Reba said. She pulled up her sunglasses and craned her neck for a wider view in the outside truck mirror. "Have you noticed that black and white Chevelle at the end of our line before?"

Ginny craned around to look. "Not really. Why?"

"He never passes except when we stop somewhere. Then somehow I see him behind us again. Happened yesterday. And now today again."

"Maybe he wants to join our caravan. Or likes Model Ts. Or could be coincidence."

During a roadwork delay, Reba watched a machine slice through a mountainside. Hundreds of swallows flew in and out, trying to re-establish their homes.

After more than an hour back on the road, Ginny shouted, "Stop!"

Reba pulled to the side. "Why?" She didn't look at Jace and the others as they passed by. Especially Jace.

"What are those people doing back there?"

Reba looked beyond a side dirt road and some Joshua trees that looked like cruel old men, all bent up and contorted, shaking twisted fists. Beside a large white and burgundy Ford van with matching trailer a man, woman, and boy seemed to be cutting a fence. "Working their ranch, I suppose."

"They have a Minnesota license plate."

"Let's find out. We need to stretch our legs anyway." She flipped the pickup around easy enough not to unsettle Johnny Poe.

Reba got out and headed to the trailer to get her horse out, her senses full of a sweet and sickly sage scent. Though they heard a forecast of a hundred degrees in the shade, with a little breeze and no humidity, the atmosphere proved comfortable enough, even pleasant.

"You need some help?" sociable Ginny called out.

"Howdy," the man greeted. "Thanks, but we're just collecting samples."

"We're getting us some Necktie," the boy said.

"Ah, the wire," Reba replied. "I've heard of that kind."

"We have permission from the rancher," the man said. "We always get that first. Unlike some folks. There are guys on the road who give us all a bad name. They never ask permission. They just cut and take."

Ginny laughed. "Barbed wire bandits."

"Do you know much about barbed wire?" the boy asked.

Reba replied, "Oh, sure. I work with it most every day on my ranch. I know they have prongs and points and they prick. And they establish boundary lines to mostly keep critters where they're supposed to be."

"There are more than five hundred varieties. We're collectors," the boy said. "It's our hobby."

"This far away from home?" Ginny said.

"Anywhere we find it. Usually it's rolled up and abandoned. Or piled in corners of fields. Or hung in trees or on posts," the man explained.

"Sometimes the best ones are thrown in junk piles," the boy said.

"Or cast into rain-washed gullies and deserted fence-rows," the woman added.

"In the small Idaho town where I'm from," Reba explained. "We use only the old heavy, ornamental kind of wire."

"It's everywhere, if you know where to look. So far we've seen mostly the modern kind. We prefer the Old West sort like yours." The man held out his leather-gloved hand. "We're the Thornbirds. I'm Yale. This is my wife, Xena, and our son, Zach."

Ginny shook hands first. "Cute--X, Y, and Z. We're with the Model T that passed by not long ago."

"An old man driving?" Yale said.

"Yep. We're with him." Ginny looked at the boy. "We've been chewing nothing but cactus and lizards for days."

The boy gave her admiring look. "What does it taste like?"

"Barbed wire and chicken." She winked at him.

"I think I like scorpions better," he shot back. "Especially the tough, hairy ones."

Ginny faked a gagging sound.

Xena popped him on the bottom. "Don't mind our son. I think he's been in the desert too long."

Ginny chuckled. "So have we, although it's only been a couple days. I thought he was talking about the Scorpions music group." She started whistling "Wind of Change."

When the tune stopped, the boy pulled a piece of red licorice from his pocket. "I met a collector who didn't even know the difference between Scutt and Buckhorn wire. Anybody knows that."

"Not me. How do you tell the difference?" Ginny said.

"The number of strands. And how it's twisted. Also, the number of points and how far apart."

"How many different kinds are there?"

"Hundreds, maybe bazillions."

"I'm a doctor in real life," said the father. "Radiology. Xena's a fourth grade teacher. We sell wire pieces to display in cafes, filling stations, and even barbershops. We collect it, trade it, sell it, and exhibit it."

"There's a huge display of barbed wire in Delbert's Diner at Road's End, with stories attached," Reba said. "And I think we had some of those bandits you talked about in our town recently. We caught them though." Reba watched Johnny Poe shy as far from the barbed wire as he could.

"You better watch out for two really bad guys stealing wire on this road," the boy revealed.

"Oh? Can you describe them?" Ginny prompted.

"One is real tall with curly black hair. The other one is short and almost bald."

Surely it couldn't be. "Do you know their names?" Reba asked.

Yale replied, "One of the ranchers told us they're escaped convicts. Don't know anything else. But we're staying on the alert. We were told not to approach them, only report."

Reba shot Ginny a glance. Her eyebrows lifted as she shrugged.

The boy piped in. "What are the four inventions that most influenced the settlement of the West?"

"Uh, I'm not sure. How about you, Reba?"

"I'll bet barbed wire's on the list."

"Yep," the boy crowed, very pleased with himself. "Plus the revolver, the repeating rifle, and the windmill."

"I wouldn't have guessed that last one." Ginny said. "But I'll have you know, I'm a collector too. I collect shoes."

Zach frowned. "How come?"

"Because I can. And because I like them."

"You speak with barbed tongue." He snickered at his own pun.

"You have a point there."

Zach high-fived Ginny.

"Come on, we better go," Reba prodded.

"See you on down the road." The boy shook out his leather gloves.

The next morning, a sand-soaked lash of wind hit them whenever they stopped. The sandstorm stung eyes, pitted skin, clogged noses, especially for Seth and Tucker in the Model T. In spite of that, when they approached a field of old abandoned cars, Reba noticed Jace turned in and stopped.

She pulled up beside the Volvo. "What's there to see in a trash yard?"

"One man's junk is another man's treasure. I want to investigate that burned-out shell of a former 1985 blue Dodge. I used to own one just like it."

"How could you tell from the highway?"

"I couldn't. Abel also had a need to stop and there are no trees."

"Oh. Goodbye, then." Reba veered back on the highway.

A 1969 two-tone blue station wagon way ahead of them slammed into a black cow on a stretch of the highway. The force of the collision turned the cow into a half-ton projectile that bounced off the hood and shattered the windshield.

"My face feels numb," the driver said. Her arm muscles were so weak she couldn't pick up her purse.

A roadster stopped and promised to contact some help. They urged Seth to keep going as the rest of them waited for an ambulance to arrive. The man in the black and white Chevelle stopped to chat with the woman and handed her a business card.

"Ambulance chaser," Jace commented.

"Hey, we have reason to suspect that Wade and Poison, the guys who vandalized our house, might be out and roaming around," Reba said.

"I thought they got locked back up."

"That's what we thought. Just a possibility. Thought you should know."

That evening they stopped at a wide spot along the road between Orovada and Winnemucca. With a couple portable grills, they prepared a feast of barbecued steaks and potato fries while watching a display of red, orange and gold streaks in the sky. Reba leaned back in a lawn chair and listened to clusters of conversations, mesmerized by the glints of receding sunlight.

Tucker twirled a half circle back and forth around a bottle. "Do you ever get the willies thinkin' we're all being watched? Like we're in bottles?"

"Why are you so fixated on that particular bottle?" Seth goaded. "You bring it out every night. Aren't you afraid it'll get you sucked back into drinking?"

"Not if it's empty." He displayed it upside down. "Not a blinkin' drop."

Ida interrupted with, "I hear Elizabeth Taylor's getting married again."

"What is it? Her twentieth?" Reba asked.

"No, this is her eighth wedding," Ginny told them. "Another proof of how patient God is."

"Why is that proof?" Ida asked.

"He doesn't zap people who mess up multiple times."

Ida peered at Tucker. "That's for sure."

Becky looked up from a book and blurted out, "How cool. I just learned this is a palindrome year."

"No, it ain't," Amos said, "It's the Year of the Sheep. Polly Eng told us."

"You don't even know what a palindrome is," Becky retorted. "And there's another one coming up in eleven years." She looked around the group.

Neoma asked the obvious question. "Why don't you explain palindrome for us?"

Becky straightened her shoulders and put on a prissy grin. "This is 1991. In eleven years it will be 2002. What do those two years have in common?"

Everyone pondered until Jace broke the silence. "It's not a leap year."

"No," Becky replied.

"It will be next year." Pico popped a big gum bubble.

"Well," Jace continued. "It could be that in those two years you get to go on a road trip with a great guy like me."

Becky rolled her eyes.

"Or the years are the same whether read forward or backward."

Pico and Amos squinted their eyes, deep in thought.

"Cool," said Abel.

"Reba, get your guitar," Ginny said. "Let's sing some camp songs."

They began with "Tie A Yellow Ribbon Round The Ole Oak Tree" and Jace led next with "Leaving On A Jet Plane." Then Seth pulled out his fiddle and rasped the words to "King of the Road." Becky huddled up next to Ginny as two cars passed, honking their horns. All the kids jumped up and ran behind Reba's trailer.

Jace called them back.

"We thought it was Quigley and Irving," Becky said.

Neoma held a wet rag against her head.

"Are you feeling okay?" Reba called to her.

"Not really. The closer we get to Reno, the harder my head pounds."

"Make Ned sleep with you tonight, Nana. It's too crowded. I can hardly breathe." Becky kicked dirt devils, hair stringy over a sullen face full of freckles.

Ned jumped up and down on his sneakers and looked for a desert rat to chase as Becky ran over to Abel and the Paddy boys playing marbles.

Neoma let out a groan. "Becky looks so much like Trish at that age. And just as prickly."

"I've got some pain meds," Ginny offered.

"Only Tylenol® works for me."

"Got that too." She brought some pills and water.

Ned rammed Matchbox cars down dirt lanes with his arms and legs caked with grime and fell over on his back.

Ginny scooted over to him. "Why are you laying in the dirt?"

"Looking for lost clouds. My mom used to do that with me."

Reba listened to the other kids as she tried to prepare for the trip to Reno the next day. Ginny and Neoma would be leaving the caravan. She'd miss them more than she realized. Especially Ginny.

Nearby, the kids discussed finding a new game.

"Let's play, who is telling the biggest lie?" Amos suggested.

"You guys play. I'll be the judge," Becky said.

"I am a spy for the F.B.I.," Abel said.

"I can turn the desert into a rain forest," Pico said.

"I am a thousand years old," Amos said.

Abel kept going. "Green is really red."

Amos looked to his mom for inspiration. She shrugged. He looked into the sky. "The sun is frozen."

"Ha! I can catch and eat a wild stallion raw," Pico concluded.

"Abel wins," announced Becky.

Pico stomped his feet. "That's not fair."

"Okay, you win. That's the biggest lie."

Ned strolled over to them. "Let's play cowboys and astronauts. You guys try to fly away and I'll shoot you."

"What a dumb game." Becky pulled out a deck of cards.

"Not Hearts again," Pico wailed. "You always win."

"Don't be a baby," Becky scolded and dealt out the cards to the boys.

Neoma leaned into the women. "I'm so glad the kids have had this time. They are doing so much better."

"I think the lying game could be a teaching moment." Ginny said. "My grandpa would most definitely give a sermon."

"Is he a preacher?"

Ginny laughed. "No, an honest businessman with a high sense of morals."

"A lost art. Lies are so easy to tell and such hard work to maintain," Neoma said.

"They take lots of practice getting them just right and keeping them straight, that's for sure," Ida said.

"And they're addicting," Neoma replied.

"You still nervous about meeting with Trish?" Reba asked.

"Yes." She closed her eyes and gently rubbed them. "I haven't told you the whole story. The day of my late husband Hank's funeral, Trish divulged to one of the church elders she owed a score of debts. She said she wanted a fresh break for her and the kids. The elder had some means and he was caught up in the emotion of losing his good friend. He also was mindful of the Scriptures that say, 'give to those who ask.' If he had come to me, I would have warned him."

Neoma seemed to shrink in the chair. She grimaced as though

pain shot through her. "He bailed her out. And I don't blame him. But she took the money and pawned a ring of her father's in St. Louis. The kids received cards from her at Christmas postmarked New York City. We haven't heard from her since."

"Now that she has a regular job, maybe she can pay him back," Ginny counseled.

"He's already been paid. I sold the St. Joseph house to reimburse him. I had to. My conscience wouldn't let me do otherwise. Soon after Trish left, our friend's wife got cancer and the bills ate up their savings."

"It's so hard to forgive something like that," Ida said. "I know. I've had my chore of forgivin' to do. I'm still in the forgivin' department every day of my life."

"At least the rage is no longer there. I feel that's progress," Neoma added.

"Forgiving won't *undo* anything in the past. That's for sure." Neoma's story revived an acid stirring within Reba. Her mother abandoning her. Tim and Sue Anne and Grandma Pearl's part in the betrayal. Learning too late about her Grandma Maidie. There, that's the first time she said that. *Grandma Maidie.*

"But it might help you get on with your life." Ginny stood up and started dancing. "Come on, this may be our last evening together. Reba, get your guitar. Seth, pull out your fiddle. We need to dance."

Becky put down her cards and joined her. Soon, so did Amos and Pico as Ned crouched in the sand with his cars. Neoma grabbed Becky's hands and swung her around.

After the entertainment, Becky crept close to Ginny. "I told the biggest lie of all when I said I had the worst family in the world, the grouchiest grandma, and the most irritating bratty brother." She shyly peered at Neoma. "I'm sorry."

Ginny winked at Reba. "I think we've had our teaching moment."

🐎 🐎 🐎 🐎

Later Ginny talked Reba into driving all the way to Winnemucca for a motel. "I need a bed and shower." Ginny gazed at the landscape.

"The desert reminds me of the ocean. The great expanse. The sloping horizon. Makes me feel so small and vulnerable."

"As I recall, the ocean is much wetter and a whole lot noisier."

Reba got low on gas a few miles out and stayed in the car while Ginny knocked at the door of a mobile home. She talked through a slit of an opening and ran back flailing her arms.

Reba started the engine in alarm. "I've never seen you run that fast before. In fact, I don't remember ever seeing you run."

"Hush and roll up all the windows. There are tons of giant mosquitoes out there." She slapped her arms. "There's a gas stop two miles away. Can we get that far?"

Reba slowly edged back on the highway and rolled into the station as the putt-putts became jerks.

Ginny whistled. "That's sure expensive."

"At this point, I'm glad to pay it."

"Not so fast. It's my turn. I've got it."

The best Winnemucca motels announced No Vacancy, so they settled for a sleazy looking discounter. The thin drapes and smudged windows could be seen through better closed than opened. A shaky pressed-board dresser with filmy mirror. Headboard nailed to the wall. Reba tossed cracker-sized, threadbare, yellowed towels on the floor to cover the grimy surface. The TV featured static snow on every station except local news.

They took turns making phone calls from an unkempt motel office. Reba pulled the tan phone from under a spill over stack of bills and letters. She kept punching buttons and redial to check with Grandma Pearl, but got the annoying *boh, boh, boh* busy signal. In disgust, she handed it over to Ginny. Later, she came out of the office with puffy eyes and a sniffle. Reba didn't pry, but she whispered a prayer.

In their room, Ginny said, "To make peace, I think Paris and I have got to meet face to face. Phone calls aren't doing it." She scrubbed off face makeup with cleansing cream. "But that could also make it so…final."

The next morning at a Winnemucca restaurant, the waitress with glum face dawdled at empty tables, moving salt and pepper shakers and condiments around, and loitered at a Lotto machine. She finally acknowledged their presence by tossing down a can opener and single serving cans of orange juice with dirty tops. Ginny refused to drink from it. Reba stuck a napkin in a glass of water and attempted to wash hers.

A man from the kitchen yelled out, "What's he in for?"

"I don't know," the waitress shot back.

"I think I'll kill him."

"His seventeen-year-old son," she explained to Reba and Ginny. "He and his buddies got busted last night. Again. Our breakfast special is ham and eggs or eggs and ham. Or you can try the breakfast bar. It's got cold cereal and oatmeal. Or all of the above. What'll you have?"

"Coffee and two of those Danish rolls." Ginny pointed to the counter.

"Two fried eggs over medium," Reba said. "And the cereal."

"Do you have any Almond Apple Muesli or Peanut Butter Crunch?" Ginny asked.

"Um, don't think so." The waitress scratched her head with the pen.

"Then I'm staying with the Danish."

An elderly woman with short gray hair tight and kinky against her head walked in with a cane. "I don't want none of your sass today," she told the waitress and plopped down to light a cigarette in the non-smoking section.

"Not to worry. I'm all sassed out." The waitress turned back to them. "We lost another waitress and I had a knock down fight with my roommate last night and moved out. I'm plumb tuckered."

In the breakfast bar line, a uniformed gentleman nudged Reba ahead of him. "Deputy commander for the Cadet Squadron of Civil Air Patrol, at your service." Bulldog frame, baritone voice, his breath stronger than a bear's, the steel-rimmed tinted glasses and dark, thin eyebrows seemed out of place.

"I make jewelry, do sculpture, and paint," a towering thin man with earring, cropped honey-colored hair with dark roots, sideburns, and nail polish responded, as though everyone was expected to relate a bio.

Reba smiled at them both and filled two bowls, one with Raisin Bran and the other hot cereal with butter, brown sugar and cream. She waited as a woman slinked by her in black nylon stockings and leather sandals, full smocked dress with long sleeves, white bonnet over hair pulled back in a bun. Either River Brethren or Amish.

Jace and Abel strolled in and sat at the table beside them. "I saw the pickup and trailer. Not sure where the others are. We left earlier."

"You seem determined to sit at separate tables," Reba remarked.

"Seems safer that way. Where's your friend?"

"She'll be right back. She's calling her husband. I presumed she wanted a private conversation."

"I'm sure she did. Johnny Poe is sure kicking up a fuss out there."

"I've got to let him run soon. He's getting trailer sour again. He's as bullheaded as me."

"Where did you get your bullheadedness? Not from your grandma. She has the kindest eyes."

Oh, but she can be quite bullish. Reba stared in astonishment at the familiar form of the woman who walked into the restaurant. "Not at the moment, I'm afraid. There's fire in them. And she's headed this way."

Pearl stomped across the dining hall to Reba's table. "I'm so glad to find you. Where is Champ?"

"Champ? What do you mean? He's not with us. We haven't seen him the whole trip. Why are you here?"

"I need to talk to Champ. Don says he left home right after all of you got out of town." Pearl plunked down at Reba's table and tried to catch her breath.

Chapter Fourteen

Reba couldn't get over the shock of seeing Pearl here. Like an invasion. An intrusion on her privacy. She'd so gotten used to their road travel routine. Without her grandmother.

As though reading her thoughts, Pearl blurted, "Wade and Poison...those two guys who vandalized my house. They escaped from the county jail. The sheriff suspects help on the outside, since they couldn't have done it themselves."

"You know what? We already heard that. I think they're stealing barbed wire along the highway out here somewhere and who knows what else? Is that why you're here"

Pearl signaled the waitress and ordered coffee. "No. I've got other things on my mind."

Like what? "I tried to call you this morning. Your phone's busy."

"Oh, dear. I either left it off the hook or Michael's using it. I'll check with Vincent."

Ginny arrived, exclaimed at sight of Pearl, and gave her a big hug. She sat down, munched a Danish, took a sip of coffee, and frowned.

"It's cold and bitter."

"Mine's not. Let's trade," Pearl said. "I don't mind cold and bitter today."

When Seth and Tucker arrived, Pearl greeted them both with a quick squeeze. "Seth, did you read in the newspaper that the Canadian cartel has closed their deal on Worthy Mountain?"

"No, I sure didn't. That changes things some. A bit tighter deadline than I figured." He seemed to stew about it as Jace and Abel strolled in. He calmed down to repeat the road protocol. "I've already told Ida and the boys. If we get separated, meet at the Fernley mall. And remember our survival tips as we get further into the desert. Drink lots of water. Don't get dehydrated. And don't stay in the sun too long. And definitely don't look straight at it."

"I read about getting water from a cactus by stabbing it with a knife," Abel noted.

"That's good to know," Seth agreed.

"We need waterskins too," Abel said.

"Canteens work fine. Ice chest, ice chips, and ice or soaked gel bandannas come in handy too."

Jace scooted his chair back. "I think Abel and I will go on ahead of the rest of you. It's a straight and fairly safe stretch of road for the Model T and we'll hang out in Fernley until you arrive."

Ginny made eye contact with Reba. "I think we'll go on ahead and hang out in Fernley until you arrive. I want to stretch out my time with Reba. We might even go to a movie. Maybe they're playing *Thelma and Louise*. It's about two best friends on a road trip. Like us."

"I've heard about it. But is it out yet?" Reba looked at Pearl, reluctant to call her grandma. "How about you? Would you be interested in a movie?"

"You know what? I think I'll tag along with the Model T. The rest of you go your own pace."

Reba hid her relief as she and Ginny paid their tabs. "Aren't you going to eat something?" Reba asked Pearl.

"I'm fine. I pulled into a diner at McDermitt."

Reba waved goodbye to Pearl, Seth and Tucker as she and Ginny headed for the pickup and trailer. "Looks like your grandma brought the Jeep," Ginny remarked.

"But why is she here at all? I don't get it."

"She looks like a determined woman on a mission."

What mission? How much worse can she mess up my life?

Pearl reviewed the three challenges she faced in the next few days as she cruised behind the Model T. Find Champ Runcie. If possible, protect Seth from Champ. And show Maidie's journal to Reba. The timing was crucial. Reba endured so much already, she had to be prepared for this revelation. *Lord, help me. Guide me.*

She almost collided with the old Ford cranker when Seth slowed to pull into a gas station at the edge of Winnemucca. He and Tucker got out and looked around the car.

"The tires got punctured through to the tubes," Seth reported. "It was something thin and pointed so they'd leak slowly."

Pearl parked and joined the inspection. "Do you have any idea who did it or why?"

"No, but they were in a hurry. Looks like one poke per tire and they missed the spare."

"What can you do? Can you fix them?" Pearl asked.

"We've got the spare and one extra tube. And I brought patches and rubber cement. We should be fine. It'll just take some time."

"But don't you need a mechanic or tire store?"

"Not when I've got Tucker."

"Anybody got a grudge against you?" Tucker inquired.

"Not that I know of. How about you?"

"The same. Could be random vandalism."

Or it could have something to do with Champ. "Report it to the police. At least it'll be on file in case this escalates," Pearl said.

A dapper man in tan sports coat and khaki pants pulled up to the gas tank in his 1971 white bottom, black top Chevelle. "Hey," he called out. "You got trouble?"

Seth sauntered over. "Tires got slashed. You know anything about it?"

"Nope. But I might be able to help you." He held out his hand. "The name's Dalton. I'm in insurance. Be glad to do business with you. Anytime. My specialty's claims on car accidents. That would include slashed tires. Be sure to give me a call. I'll make you an extra good deal." He handed him a card.

"Haven't we seen you before?" Tucker asked.

"I've been on the road, same as you."

Pearl's curiosity piqued, she walked nearer for a closer look at the man. Especially since she happened to be on heightened alert concerning Seth's safety. The man opened his Chevelle and rummaged around. Pearl noticed a handgun on the floorboard. She tugged her black leather shoulder strap purse and reached inside the concealed compartment to feel the cold steel of Cole's revolver. This time without blanks. He handed Pearl a card too. *Dax Dalton, Insurance Claims. Boise, Idaho.* "You're some miles from your office," she noted.

"Seemed like an interesting time to be out on the road. That's where I pick up some of my business." He turned to Seth. "Nice Model T you're driving. Never saw a purple one before." He got up close to Seth's face and plastered his smile. "Got to watch out. It's a long stretch between towns out here."

Seth moved away with a wave and he and Tucker began loosening all the bolts from the split rim wheels. Pearl realized there were a few more steps to repairing a flat on a Model T compared to a modern car. Split rims, tubes, etc. She watched for a while but when she noticed Dalton swerve out of the gas station, she honed in on the Chevelle. Should she stay with Seth or trail suspicious stranger? Something about him...

"I'll be back," she called out. She wheeled to the highway and turned west to track the Chevelle. She stayed far enough behind to attempt not to be noticed yet keep him in view. He suddenly made an illegal U-turn back toward town. She waited for an off-ramp to make the direction reversal, staying on the surface street to sight him again. She hoped he'd gotten back off the highway quickly. And he had. She spotted him as he crept past the gas station where Seth and Tucker doctored the tires. Then he sped up and kept going straight down the main street of Winnemucca.

He made a right, a left and another right on Mizpah Street then stopped at a golf course. She meant to pass on by and head back to Seth but on a hunch she parked a half block away. Dalton entered the clubhouse and about ten minutes later a 1960s beat up jalopy drove into the parking lot next to the Chevelle. When two familiar men piled out, Pearl ducked down. She didn't want another face-to-face confrontation with twice-escaped prisoners, Wade and Poison.

She waited until she witnessed them join Dalton on the driving range. She got her Jeep in gear and eased out to Mizpah Street to look for the nearest phone booth. When she spied one several blocks away, she hopped out and dialed the number for the local police department listed in the chained phone book. "They may be armed," she warned.

She also called back home to Bitterroot County Sheriff Ed Goode. With her sightings reports given, she motored back to Seth and Tucker. When she noticed three police cars with lights flashing race by she commented, "Wonder where they're going?"

"Looks like Dalton missed an accident," Seth replied.

Pearl chuckled to herself. *No, he didn't.*

Although a long haul for the Model T after the late start out of Winnemucca, the whole caravan stayed in Fernley that night. A number of them bowled at the local alley. Ginny and Reba enjoyed Tom Hanks and Meg Ryan in the romantic comedy *Joe Versus the Volcano*.

The next morning they discussed who would take the side trip to Reno, before heading south, realizing it would add about seventy miles more round trip. The women wanted to be with Ginny and Neoma for that last jag, a time to see them off. Tucker wanted to try his luck at a bigger casino, so he rode with Ida and the boys in the orange wagon. They left before Seth did.

Reba encouraged him to purchase new tires.

"Don't have time. Don't want to spend the money. I'm already behind the ball. Think I'll head down Highway 50 now."

Reba wondered if he still had the money clip in his boots. She got her answer when he hiked his pants leg to pay for his motel room. "You'll really be sorry if you have trouble out in the middle of nowhere."

The others agreed, including Pearl. "If you want to get all the way to Goldfield in the Ford, you'd better take care of the tires."

Though with great reluctance, they finally convinced him a Reno stop was a smart choice. Jace, Abel, and Pearl followed him to the big city.

Reba and Ginny arrived at Reno first, the rustic metropolis surrounded by desert, "The Biggest Little City in the World." After circling a wide berth around the town on McCarran Boulevard, along with stretch limos, racy cars with stripes, weaving motorcycles, and bicycles in lanes and on sidewalks, they crossed the Truckee River in the middle of downtown where they spotted a kingfisher, heron, and assorted ducks.

"It's definitely a smaller version of Vegas," Ginny commented. "But with its own personality. The flashing lights, the shows, plenty of entertainment and media, and under the shadow of a huge cross at the city entrance."

"Is the cross because of Christ? Or superstition?"

"I'm sure it depends on who you ask." They passed Carson City, Virginia City, and Lake Tahoe highway signs. "We're so near Lake Tahoe, it sure is tempting to take a side trip there. But I think I'd rather go there with Paris sometime."

"You think that will ever happen?"

Ginny shrugged and studied the inner city sights. "Where are the gift shops? It's my mom's birthday next week. She'd love something from Reno. Let's stop and look around."

"I can't park this pickup and trailer just anywhere downtown."

"Then head to McCarran or the first mall with a parking lot."

"I think I saw something like that on Virginia Street."

"Well, take us there."

Reba followed Ginny into a shop smelling of a mix of cinnamon, sage, and lemon. Candles of all colors and holders of various shapes lined several rows of shelves. A few clothing racks displayed Middle Eastern long dresses and skirts. Wreaths, silk flower bouquets, and paintings filled the walls.

"I always get Mom an angel. I've done that for years."

"I've seen the display in your dining room," Reba replied. "Is there an angel she doesn't already possess?"

Ginny scooted to the aisle full of figurines. Reba studied a wall of paintings. She considered her plain bedroom wall. *It needs something.* She stared at an ocean scene with greenish waters, sea gulls, and waves bursting against a cliff side. Far out on the horizon, a ship sailed. Amber sunset beams infused clouds and whitecaps that whipped and splayed the seascape. She thought of Grandpa Cahill. Not her real grandpa, as it turned out, but the one who raised her, the only one she knew. And he loved the sea, part of his Scottish roots. And the ocean reminded her of more pleasant days in college and fun times with Ginny on the beach.

Ginny bumped her elbow. "Hey, which one do you like best?" She held up an ivory angel with huge multi-feathered wings, flowers in her hair and on the dress hemline, holding a basket bouquet. The other wore a chain mail armor protective vest of dusty blue and carried a scroll like a herald.

"I like the male one, but he still doesn't look like a fierce, protecting warrior. Why do they always make feminine angels who look more like they're in the heavenly choir rather than ready for battle?"

"Aha, I'll get the other one."

She returned with an ivory angel carrying shield and sword and in full battle uniform. Reba remembered the woman warrior Seth carved for her, packed in her suitcase. "I've always gotten the sweet ones before. Here's Archangel Michael. I'm getting Archangel Gabriel too."

"And I'm buying this." Reba pulled down the ocean scene.

"Ah, that makes me homesick after all this dry, hot sand for umpteen miles and no beach."

"And Paris? Are you homesick for him?"

"That's more complicated. But, yes, I do miss him. But does he miss me?"

They paid for their purchases and strolled to Reba's pickup. "So, have you found out about Jace and Abel yet? Their relationship?"

"Not for sure," Ginny said. "But I'm eighty percent positive Abel is Jace's brother."

"Why so?"

"Because Jace insists it's true and he's never lied to me. Yet. That I know of. The twenty percent has to do with his father, wondering how far the rotten fruit falls from the branch."

They drove to the Ford dealer who temporarily housed the special order Jaguar, a two-door white convertible, saddle tan leather seats, twelve-cylinder engine, and automatic transmission. Ginny and Reba got in for a ride across town and again around the loop.

"Comfy," Reba said. "I feel like I'm Marilyn Monroe in *The Misfits*."

"Where's your cowboy?"

"Marilyn had aging Clark Gable. I have Don Runcie."

Neoma stopped at the first gas station on the way into Reno to fill up and use the phone booth. She called the number Cicely had given her. "Trish?"

"No, but I'll get her. Just a moment."

Neoma listened hard for any sounds to discern her daughter's present background. Soft music played. Instrumental. Big band sound from the 1940s.

"Hello?"

"Trish? It's Mom. We're here in Reno. Did Aunt Cee tell you we were coming?"

"Yes, she did. I've been waiting a long time. I thought you'd be here sooner." No hesitation. A touch of anticipation.

"Well, we did take our time. Can we see you?"

"Where are you? I'll meet you there now. It's easier than explaining directions." Her voice so familiar, like they'd only talked yesterday. But she felt the chasm that still separated them.

Neoma and the children waited at the gas station as she paced in front of the convenience store. Becky and Ned punched each other and begged for Jolly Ranchers and Necco® Wafers. This wasn't how she pictured it. Such a public, noisy, and busy place. No privacy for hashing things out, to begin to try to make things right. If only...

Then Trish was there, running to her, hugging her and the kids. Everyone cried and nobody cared who saw, who stopped to stare. The kids forgot about candy. And nothing more needed to be said. Not then.

🐎 🐎 🐎 🐎

That night Becky called out through the wispy darkness of the motel room. "I asked Mom to go to the beach and to Disneyland with us, since we've got lots of room."

"What did she say?" Neoma held her breath.

"She said she'd have to talk it over with you. Please, Nana, we could have so much fun."

Neoma was glad Becky couldn't see her face. Tears rose from a deep well within her, a cleansing, healing flood. *Lord, help me.* They still had so many issues. So much to talk through. She didn't know how they'd handle it all. *But Lord, I'm going to trust you.* They'd figure it out a step at a time, along the way. On their own trail of adventure, discovery, and perhaps healing.

Becky whispered something else.

"Honey, I didn't hear you."

"I wish Ginny could come too. I think Mom would really like her."

Neoma smiled, thankful for Ginny's brief influence in Becky's life. She fell asleep dreaming of flying in the wind on a horse she had as a teen, plowing through Missouri cornfields and trampling soybean plants, circles of meshed tangles of oak, cottonwood and hickory trees everywhere. Then she was at her favorite park overlooking the Missouri River. Boats cruised below and pockets of fishermen here and there crouched on the tree-lined beach. In the distance, storm clouds clashed over the Kansas-Missouri border. A triple

~ 233 ~

burst of vertical lightening shot across the Kansas horizon. She knew a heavy downpour would pelt her at any moment, but she didn't care. She never felt more free.

The next morning, after a call to Trish, the kids piled into the back of the truck wearing their Cicely hats. Neoma made room in the trailer for one more occupant's belongings.

Trish Hocking with black beret, crimson hair down to her waist and clear brown eyes, slipped into the passenger seat. "Mom, after we've had Dad's service at the ocean, and after we've gone to Disneyland... " She turned back to throw a kiss at the kids. "Can we go to Vegas? To see Davis. I know it's too late for us," she added quickly. "It's for Ned and Becky."

Neoma touched Trish's shoulder, so grateful she thought she'd burst. "Sure, we can do that. But first, before we leave town, I need to say goodbye to some friends I made on the road. From Road's End."

When they arrived in front of the casino, Becky rushed out to hug Ginny and tugged her toward the car, to introduce her mom.

Tucker was hyped. "I'm more than feeling lucky. It's a slam-dunk. I've been reading some inside information. I've got the system figured out. A mathematician and computer expert wrote this book I've been reading. Don't get much better than that. It won't take long before I'll be right back." He scooted through revolving glass doors.

Meanwhile, Seth fumed as he waited in the Model T outside the casino. He felt the pressure to get to Worthy, especially since they were getting so close. *This is a test, only a test.* A persevere and endure test.

Worn down by the long days of travel and grueling desert, Seth tired of trail food and the constant noise and intrusion of company. He craved solitude and real home cooking. Maidie's. Or Pearl's. He grinned to himself. *Or Hester's.* Sweet Hester. The one he let get away. At least, she had a good life. Actually, they both did. Seth had few regrets.

"Excuse me, sir, aren't you the guy on a mission?"

Seth turned around and gazed at a young man with boyish face and microphone standing next to a KRNV TV van. "What did you say?"

"I'm Halburt Halstead from KRNV TV. I've been hearing about a caravan led by an old man in a purple Model T. You fit the bill. Thought I'd check it out. Are you him?"

"My name is Seth Stroud. I'm from Road's End, Idaho, and I'm just passing through your fair city."

"Well, I'll be. Road's End, that's it. You are the story. Mind if I ask a few questions?"

Uh oh. What did he get himself into? "If you make it quick. As soon as my partner arrives, we're on our way."

"On your way to where?"

"Goldfield."

"But that's a ghost town."

"I'm taking my niece's ashes to be buried with the rest of her family." He looked behind him on the floorboard to make sure the urn was still there.

Ginny rode up in her new Jaguar with Reba in the pickup and trailer behind her. "Seth, how come you're still here?" She stared at the TV van. "You stirring up attention?"

"You part of this man's entourage?" the reporter asked.

Ginny got out of the Jaguar and peeled off her sunglasses. "Are you filming this?" she asked the reporter.

"Yep. For full disclosure, my camera guy's in the van."

Reba scooted back to the trailer where Johnny Poe kicked the walls.

Halburt switched back and forth between Seth and Reba. "Who's the redhead?" He meant Reba but shoved the microphone toward Ginny.

"She's a cowgirl. Herds and brands cattle, builds fences, births calves, and loads hay, and that's all before lunch."

"Great. I do features on small towns and ranch life of the west." He followed Reba to the horse trailer. "Can I do an interview with you on your ranch sometime?"

"It's my grandmother's ranch." Reba slid into the pickup.

"That's even better. I'll include her too. I could never live that kind of life, but I'm fascinated by those who do."

Ginny snapped a picture of him. "I'm fascinated by reporters. Hope you don't mind."

The young reporter struck a pose, mic at his mouth, head held high. He tossed her a printed biography. "I grew up in Montana. My father's a Harvard-educated horseman. My master's degree is in English Lit. I was inspired to be a journalist by Bob Simon, the CBS correspondent captured with his crew by Iraqis for forty days. Last year I moved to Reno and took this job. Long story. Short love affair." He chuckled and relaxed. "The love affair--the reason for Reno."

"All very interesting. But I'm not doing an interview. I'm just a friend of theirs."

"Oh, I thought you might be undercover for NBC or CBS." He looked her and the car over. "That's why the résumé. I always want to be prepared."

Ginny slipped the camera back in her bag. "Isn't that the Boy Scout motto?"

"I get first dibs on an interview with the cowgirl and her grandmother." He turned to Reba. "Isn't that right, Miss?" He handed her a business card. "Call me as soon as you get back home and I'll set it up on location."

Ginny and Reba burst out laughing after the reporter left. Soon after, Neoma joined them, along with Jace and Abel.

Tucker bounced out of the casino with Ida. The boys followed, tossing down yo-yos.

"How'd you do, Tucker?" Jace asked.

"I made fifty dollars more than I went in with." He took a victory lap around his wife.

"Oh dear, the demon has been released."

"Nope. I'm quittin' while I'm ahead." He looked around at their dubious faces. "Really. I'm a disciplined kind of guy when I set my mind to it."

Ida spoke up. "I think it helps I threatened the boys I will go right back home if he gambles again on this trip."

Neoma got out and hugged everyone.

Jace walked over to the passenger side of Neoma's car. The door opened and Trish eased out. "Hi, Jace. Didn't expect to see you again." She leaned into his chest and he wrapped his arms around her.

Reba looked away and tried to hide a sudden rush of discomfort. Jace and Trish? What's that all about? She tried to remember if she'd seen them together while Trish was in town. Not even at the funeral. It was just Jace and Ginny.

Jace leaned over to the open back window. "I sure have enjoyed getting to know these two."

"You know my mom?" Becky asked.

"Yep. She sure talked a lot about you."

Soon they all waved goodbye to Neoma now aimed west on Highway 80. Seth cranked his Model T and crawled in with Tucker. Ida rolled out behind them in the Toyota. Antsy to get going, Seth left before Reba who stayed in Reno to be with Ginny as long as possible. The silver Volvo sat empty nearby. "Where are Jace and Abel?"

"Not sure. You know, it's your turn to come visit me." Ginny switched on the new Jaguar engine. "If things stay tense between you and your grandma, I can even offer you a job."

"Oh, sure. As a deli chef?"

Ginny tossed her head with a swish of curls. "No, as my assistant. I need someone to pal around with while I do nothing of importance. We're both good at that."

Reba snickered. "You got that right."

"Seriously. I do need a helper. I remember that public relations class we took. You had a knack for ideas. I think we could make a good team. Even on this trip, we've inspired a few people. Maybe not earth-shattering, but crucial to our small world."

"I appreciate the offer. I really do. And I miss you already. It's going to be awfully quiet in that pickup in those long hours left on the road."

"Maybe Tucker will talk to you on the walkie-talkie."

"Oh! I forgot to give it to him. They're both in my truck."

"You'll have to find someone else to share with." She winked. "I'm sure you'll think of someone. I thought about heading your same direction to go home, but with two cars we wouldn't be able to visit. So, what's the point?"

"See there? We could radio each other. Come on, Ginny."

"Well, for one thing, I promised Becky I'd meet them at the beach."

"Yeah. I forgot. Becky sure looks up to you. You're her hero." She hated to be the first to say goodbye.

"Well..."

For Pete's sake, don't cry, Reba. We'll see each other again. We're both grown women. "I feel like that day you drove off when your family moved to California."

"But we're much more mature now."

She couldn't help it. The tears gushed. "No, I'm a kid again... whose best friend...is leaving."

Ginny flung herself at Reba. "Thank you for being there for me. I so needed this time." They swung back and forth together and finally Ginny pulled away, entered the car, slammed the door, and drove down the road without looking back. Except in the rear view mirror.

Intent on the disappearing Jaguar, she jumped when someone tapped her shoulder.

"Where's Pearl?" Jace asked.

Reba wiped her cheeks as Jace handed her a tissue. Where did he get that? Didn't matter. She sure needed it. "I don't know. She wouldn't tell me why she's here and claimed she's looking for Champ. The next time I turned around, she vanished. No trace anywhere."

"So not like her. You still going to Goldfield?"

Reba fought back weariness after all that emotion. "Yep. How about you?"

"Oh yeah. Me and Abel we're panning for gold. Aren't we, buddy?" Standing forlorn on the sidewalk in front of a Reno casino, Reba almost imagined a future with a guy like Jace that included a boy like Abel. Her *what if* created a full screen scene. Country girl learning to settle in the city. Driving Abel to school. Attending PTA meetings. Hostess of business cocktail parties. Because, of course, Jace would never stay in Road's End.

She settled herself into reality. This moment. This place. The road trip left ahead of them. What if this was all they ever experienced together? She marveled at the quickening current of contentment. How come she felt more relaxed with him than ever before? And something else. "You seem different," she pointed out. "That is, since when we started."

"Really, Reba Mae?"

For the first time, she didn't resent his using that intimate name reserved for a few. But she hesitated before she blurted out, "What's up with you and Trish?"

"She and I had some long talks," he admitted.

"Like you and Ginny?"

"I count them both as friends. Can't you and I be friends too?"

"Isn't one redhead enough to handle?"

Jace stuck his hands in his pockets and looked around at the sights of Reno. "It's been my experience that every redhead is miserable in her own interesting way. Trying to figure them out is like taking on white water rapids in your mind."

So that's why he kept her at a distance. Prejudice against the color of her hair.

Johnny Poe kicked against the trailer. "I'm going to have to ride my horse somewhere out on the road. So, if I pull over, don't worry about me. Oh, and you can have this if you want." She held up a walkie-talkie.

He grinned and grabbed it. "Watch out for hitchhikers," he said with a wink.

Chapter Fifteen

Reba and Jace backtracked east to Fernley, with Jace leading the way. The walkie-talkie squawked and Jace blurted out, "Ranch Boss, Abel wants to know how you learned to play guitar. You teach yourself?"

Abel wants to know? "I can't talk to you without a handle. What's yours?"

"Give me one, Ranch Boss."

Mystery Man? Hitchhiker? Makes Me Crazy? "How about Big Beaver?"

"Big Beaver! That's the best you can do? Don't I inspire anything better than that?"

Wise Guy? Smart Aleck? Pain In The Drain? She gazed out at the desert landscape. "How about Critter or Tumbleweed?"

"Nah. Abel says his is Tomcat."

"I'm not sure that's a good idea. It has other connotations. Abel, how about Desert Eagle?"

"Ranch Boss, that one's a winner. So, should I be City Kid?"

"Or Country Club?"

"Country Club? Is that what you think of me? No, I'm Computer Guy all the way. That captures my essence. Now, Ranch Boss, how did you learn to play guitar?"

"Computer Guy, Seth taught me. It seemed to calm Maidie. When she was riled and he couldn't play for her, I'd do it."

"Desert Eagle asks if Ranch Boss's red hair is natural?"

What? "This is a strange conversation, don't you think?"

"Hey, inquiring minds and all that."

"I don't put any color on it, if that's what you mean." *And if it's any of your business. Or Abel's.*

"Ranch Boss, it's been my experience, you can tell a lot about a woman by what she does to her hair."

"Oh? What has that to do with Abel?"

"You mean Desert Eagle? Actually, he's dozed off. Did anyone ever tell you your eyes are a disturbing shade of green?"

He's flirting with me. "Disturbing?"

"Very. Ranch Boss, how old are you?"

"Is this a game of Twenty-One Questions? If you must know, I'm twenty-five." *Going on thirty. Fast.* "And how old are you?"

"Thirty-two. And pee-yew. Your horse just messed the road. Again."

She relaxed against the seat and pressed the plastic box close to her lips. "Computer Guy, that's what horses do who are cooped up in a trailer for long periods of time."

"I've always considered horses stupid and unpredictable. Except for Johnny Poe, of course."

"Are you teasing me?"

"Yeah. And it feels good."

Yeah. Real good.

They turned south on Highway 50 to Fallon. Traveling at sixty-five mph, they eventually caught up with the Model T and Ida and the boys. A scorching wind dulled daylight to a dome of steel. Sand the color of honey flurried over the pallid desert in vertical tunnels. Soon dark clouds scudded over them.

Reba mused at the sight of a truck pulling a flatbed trailer with one huge rock tied down in back as she watched for mile markers and open ground to release Johnny Poe from his trailer fever and give him room to run.

A truck with a Please Drive Carefully sign on back zipped back and forth between them. They passed a rider with two horses tied together carrying heavy bundles on their backs.

Finally, she noticed a wide enough stopping place to let him out. She pulled over and so did Jace and Able. Jace rolled down his window. "Hey, I'll stay here with you. It's awfully deserted looking out here."

"No reason to. Please don't. I won't be long or go far."

"Okay, Ranch Boss. I've got a stop to make of my own just a few miles down the road." They waved as he drove on by. "Be careful, Ranch Boss," he garbled from the walkie-talkie.

She backed Johnny Poe out and rubbed him down. "Sorry, boy. I've been neglecting you." She noticed tiny wildflowers of white and yellow scattered on the desert floor. They seemed like a private giggle, a divine laugh, a minute treasure in such a harsh terrain. Invisible to the traveler on speedy wheels.

She rose up in the saddle she set. The black horse strained against the reins as a sudden blast pierced the barren landscape. Then another.

Oh, no! Lightning? She couldn't hold back her untrusting steed. She was at one with him as he flew through the air. She soared with the might and strength of the beast under her. Johnny Poe devoured yards of ground with such fierceness Reba wondered how she'd ever make him stop before he collapsed.

The horse raced west around the base of a mountain, past clusters of old, weather worn wooden building foundations. A chunk of rock wall, a stone cabin and some adobe dwellings whizzed by as Reba tried to halt the runaway. They veered north along a narrow chasm, a dry arroyo of some sort. After what seemed like miles, she forced Johnny Poe to slow to a trot. "Good boy. I know this is a weird place to you. Unfamiliar smells and the foreign feel of sand kicking up." She calmed him enough to get him to stop. "Well, you did get a run."

Reba peered around at sagebrush stretched out in endless rows, as though planted that way by pioneer sage farmers. She recalled Thomas Hawk telling her the bleak desert landscape rewarded stillness. Attention that darted too quickly missed millions of pinpoints of tiny blooms. Or a coiled rattler. Whether speeding down the highway on wheels or plowing through the sage on horseback. She took advantage of the solitary quiet to get bearings on her surroundings, her life.

She leaned tight against the horse's sweaty flanks, concerned that one small movement or sound might stir him again. His black hide contrasted with brown summer grass and brush, a parched piece of the world under a darkening overcast sky. Gusts of gritty wind stung her face.

Reba heard a low rumble. Thunder snarled angry threats in the distance, charging the air with nervous energy. She tugged the reins northward into the wind and kicked her heels. Some aged gray fencepost sported rusty barbed wire that marked the range boundary from the steep arroyo beyond. She slid out of the saddle and attempted to lead Johnny Poe over the wire. Rain splattered her face like the first splashes from a pot about to boil over on the stove. Obstacles like boulders, brush, and terrain forced her on one path toward the arroyo as a violent spray burst over her. She urged the horse to the edge of the arroyo. The rain battered them as though fired from a skyward shotgun.

Not a great time to forget her slicker like a numbskull greenhorn.

A deep male voice pierced the noise of the downpour. "Get away from that bank."

She jerked around and saw an Indian. His dark and flowing hair pulled back ponytail style, he grabbed the reins, leaped on Johnny Poe, and whipped him north.

"Hey!" Reba shouted.

But that's all she said before a violent wind blew her back, snapping the stampeded string of her hat to her neck. She tripped and stumbled down into the arroyo already alive with rushing water that climbed higher toward the bank. She kept sliding down in wet sand as she tried to get footing to climb out. She turned at the sound of hoof beats. Flying black locks and black mane rushed toward her. The Indian on Johnny Poe.

Reba screamed. "Get off my horse!"

He halted the horse, slid off, and shouted, "Get out of there." He kept a hand on the reins and held the other arm out to her as he leaned over the embankment.

Reba hesitated.

"Come on," he ordered.

She grabbed his arm and he pulled her up hard. Too hard. She landed face first, the breath knocked out of her. Her already bruised ribs racked with pain. She sank into the gritty mud.

"Keep moving." The Indian remounted and sped away.

A wall of brackish desert stew the full width and height of the arroyo pushed boulders, tree trunks and varmints in its wake a few feet away from her, crushing any object that offered resistance. The noise was deafening. She sprang to her feet and ran toward higher ground as water in the middle of the flash flood rose higher than the bank. The ground where she stood moments before tumbled into the torrent.

Hailstones rocketed to the ground again mixed with rain and stuck to the caked and gritty mud. They slapped her and slashed across her back and hands as she plunged forward, her arms on top her head. She tried to roll into a ball. Soon the hail subsided and the rain softened. Cool drops soothed her sores.

The instant river still roared as she slogged through the mud in the direction of Johnny Poe. The pounding of stony hoof beats on the hard desert floor emerged from stillness. Johnny Poe? The long, low rumble echoed louder, clearly more than one horse. Growing bright in the dimness, the white lead horse loomed first, followed by ten others. Their reckless running filled the evening shadows with pulsing clatter, a whiplash of speed. The din and racket made her heart beat in her head like the sound of Pentecost's rushing wind.

Then abruptly, the leader caught the whiff of a strange horse. He uttered a sharp, loud blowing breath through his nostrils, a neigh like a distress call. The band halted. The stallion left the herd and trotted close like a friend wanting its nose rubbed. He let out a soft nicker with a rattle. He cocked his ears. A swish of the tail, a twitch of the lips and nose, every nerve taut and alert, he held his head high and his tail arched like a pluming banner.

That's when Reba noticed Johnny Poe without rider walking in the path of the stallion. From behind, the Indian stole up to Reba. "Don't get near him," he warned low but intense.

Johnny Poe sniffed the air like trying to sense a mean streak as the stallion moved closer. Then he exploded and lunged. He towered over Johnny Poe with hooves and a gaping mouth as though to swallow him. Johnny Poe yanked away from the gnashing teeth.

"No!" Reba tried to rise up.

"Stay away," the Indian repeated.

The wild stallion at first edged out of sight, then leaped from behind a boulder to rush Johnny Poe. Then abruptly stopped. He loped forward and nuzzled close, like a loner who wanted company. Johnny Poe grunted. The wild horse let out another nicker and moved closer, as though to offer a greeting. But suddenly he sniffed the air and whipped away.

The harem of mares and colts circled as the spirited stallion dashed around and let out a scream. He gnashed and pawed with lightning quick hooves and gleaming teeth. He kicked powerful, muscled hind legs as he circled Johnny Poe. Eyes wide, ears pricked, nostrils flared, he sniffed again as Johnny Poe backed away in a careful, slow retreat.

The stallion snorted and shoved a mare with his neck. He lowered his head in a menacing manner, his ears flat against his head, and rushed toward the mares. He raised his long neck and head and slowed the band. They halted when he thrust his head higher. A dominant mare led the band, but seemed very aware of the stallion's commands.

They made a rapid single-file exodus with the aid of the mare as the stallion brought up the rear. He directed the band from behind by various turns. Several times he stopped to look back, as though being followed by an unwelcome intruder. The mares kept going when the stallion abandoned the band to escape further up the canyon. He ran free, mane and tail flowing in the wind, muscles rippling with grace and power.

Now that Johnny Poe was safe, Reba resisted the impulse to clap her hands in a standing ovation.

The Indian attempted an apology. "I'm sorry. I had to act quickly. That band was headed for disaster. And so were you."

Reba sprinted to Johnny Poe and the Indian followed. "Who are you?"

"I'm Egan Toms. A lawyer from Phoenix. But I vacation here sometimes. My place is that cluster of buildings and stone cabin you stumbled by on your runaway horse. It belongs to my family. Has for decades. You seemed to be having trouble staying in control and I knew a flood was coming. I tried to help out."

"You're not Nez Perce, are you?"

"Of course not. I'm Paiute."

"Well, now that I've been totally surprised, soaked, robbed, and humiliated, could you please lead me back to the highway?"

"You're welcome."

"What kind of response is that?"

"I'm sure you meant to thank me for saving your life."

Reba hated the creeping flush of crimson that threatened to betray the rise of fierce emotions. Her demoralized pride paralyzed gratitude. "Where's your horse?"

"She joined that band again. I'll get her back. Follow me." He bolted away around the steep-sided gulch now swollen with rainwater.

Reba eased up on Johnny Poe, every muscle afire, and followed the Paiute. The return trip seemed much shorter, even with the slower, steadier gait. Two donkeys stood tethered beside the rundown cabin where he halted.

"I don't want it to look too inviting," he explained.

She could see her pickup and trailer in the distance. Also, another car parked near it. Jace? Perhaps he sensed her danger. She got down from Johnny Poe. "I don't suppose you'd have a drink of water for me and my horse?"

"Most certainly." He entered the hovel and brought her a glass full and a bucket filled for the horse. She looked closer. He wore two rings, one on each hand. The gold and turquoise in a design reminiscent of the squash blossom necklace gave her a start.

"Do you mind me asking where you got those rings?"

"Not at all." He pulled one of them off. "Would you like to purchase one like it? My grandfather Blue Moon Toms makes them and sells them."

"They remind me so much of a necklace I was given recently. Gold and turquoise. A squash blossom, I was told."

Egan Toms studied her so intently she felt he bored a hole into her. "You remind me of someone. But she handles her horses much better than you do."

"Oh? And who might that be?"

"We call her Wild Horse Hanna. And she helps my grandfather make gold and turquoise jewelry. Like these rings."

Hanna? Like Hanna Jo? Surely not... "Where does she live?"

"In Silver Peak. That is, she used to until recently."

Reba was as stunned as if she'd hit into a geode with a pickax. "But she's not there now?"

"I don't believe so. My grandfather would know. He lives in Silver Peak. Did you want some of the jewelry?"

"Not exactly. I'm looking for my mother who I haven't seen in over twenty years. Her name is Hanna Jo Cahill and I'm headed to Silver Peak on a hunch she's there."

Egan Toms put on a pensive face. "I see. I'll be right back." He entered the stone cabin and returned with a pen and notepad. "Here's my grandfather's name and where he lives. Perhaps he can help you."

Reba took the note and stuffed it in her pocket, next to her mother's note. "Why did you call this woman Wild Horse Hanna?"

"That's my grandfather's name for her. He worked as a cowboy most of his life on ranches in Nye and Esmeralda Counties. He still rides horses. He loves wild horses best but doesn't own any. Wild Horse Hannah drove him crazy because he wanted what he considered his horses, wild horses, left alone. She often tried to ride them. 'This valley is not big enough for the two of us,' he insisted. He often said she rode them scary near the cliff."

"Then he might not be too friendly about my asking about her."

"Oh, he'll be gruff about it. But if he thinks you're family, he'll cooperate all he can. After all, they came to terms enough to make jewelry together."

"Well, it's been nice bumping into you." She tried not to smile. "And thank you. I believe this was a divine appointment. Of a most unusual sort."

"Yes. I believe so too." He peered into her eyes, her soul. "You are welcome. May you find what you're looking for."

She rode Johnny Poe toward the highway and realized the extra vehicle was a red Willys Jeep. Grandma Pearl? She gave her a quick hug and cared for her horse and got him in the trailer. As she imparted the information she received from Egan Toms, she followed Pearl's stare across the field. A man rode a donkey across the sandy surface toward them like a mirage. Until she recognized Egan.

"I wanted to make sure you were okay," he announced, as he stepped down.

Reba introduced him to Pearl. "Show her your rings."

Pearl stole a look at the glove compartment in her rig. "I brought the necklace with me."

"Why on earth did you do that?" Reba scolded. "Out here in the desert? It could be stolen. Or lost. Or you could get mugged or worse."

"No one knows it's there." She paused. "Except you two."

"I would like to see it," Egan said. "Please trust me, even if I am a lawyer."

"That's providence. I have something else to show you." She drew out the necklace and the photo.

Reba gasped. "Who is that wearing the necklace?"

"Eva Stroud, Seth's mother."

Egan took hold of the necklace. "Amazing. This had to come from the Worthy Mine. It's so like my grandfather's work."

Pearl explained the necklace controversy to Egan. "Would a picture like this hold up in court?"

"If you could prove the date and identity, it sure could. Actually, showing evidence like that to a contester might be enough to avoid a lawsuit."

They watched their legal counsel ride away to his humble abode on his donkey.

"You're making me nervous," Reba said. "Put the necklace and picture away."

She tucked them back in. "It seemed like the right thing to do when I started out."

"I don't understand. Where have you been? And why did you come out here in the first place?"

Pearl clamped her mouth shut after saying, "There's much more to be revealed." However, her face softened as she tapped Reba's arm and whirled around to the Jeep.

After tending to Johnny Poe, they drove away and picked up speed to catch up with the others. They passed Walker River Paiute Reservation and Walker River and approached what Reba considered a huge junkyard. Reba slowed, signaled and pulled in when she recognized Jace's silver Volvo. Pearl followed.

Jace and Abel headed toward her with shiny faces and a twinkle in their eyes. "Hey, guess what cool thing Jace just bought?"

Reba looked around at all the assorted wrecked cars and rusty parts scattered in a field. Before she could venture any sort of snappy answer, Jace prompted, "Come here, I'll show you."

Reba and Pearl followed him to a warehouse building with an Oliver's Fire Sales & Salvage signature overhead. Inside shelves and floor displays crammed with assorted antiques. Furniture. Metal signs. Toys. Carnival novelties. Jace proudly ushered them to a car. "A '55 Chevy Belair. Pristine condition. White convertible top. Glacier Blue body. Red interior. Only needs a few repairs."

"Why?" Reba sputtered.

"Why what?" He stared at her in complete confusion.

"Why would you make such a purchase right now?"

"Because it's here and if I don't buy it, someone else will."

"But what are you going to do with it?"

"I just started a new hobby. The ideal would be to tow or trailer it. But since I can't do that with my inadequate Volvo, the owner's going to store it for me. I'll come back and retrieve my treasure sometime after our trip."

"I still don't get it."

"Well, Ranch Boss, you've got your horse and trailer, I've got my car."

As if that was in any way similar.

As Oliver the owner hovered nearby, the women politely looked over the engine and interior while Jace and Abel chattered with much enthusiasm about the car's other details. Then they headed outside and got in their rigs.

Out on the road Reba's walkie-talkie squealed. "Rancher Boss, and how have you been?"

"Computer Guy, I nearly drowned, got trampled by wild horses, and was attacked by an Indian."

"You're kidding, of course."

"Tell you more later. 10-4."

As they neared Hawthorne honeycombed, dirt covered air vents and thick concrete warehouses covered with dirt appeared. Strong crosswinds across the high desert sagebrush ruffled up sand drifts.

"Computer Guy, what are those?" Reba crackled into the walkie-talkie static.

"Rancher Boss, ammunition bunkers."

"Really. And so close to a nice burg. Lodge and casino, twenty-four hour restaurant, McDonald's fast food, a Safeway grocery."

"And unexploded bombs."

"What?"

"So I've been told."

"Rancher Boss, this is Desert Eagle. I forgot to tell you I got a miniature toy car at that man's place exactly like Jace's 1955 Chevy. Can't wait to show it to Amos and Pico."

"Wow, that's neat."

"Yeah. I bought it with my own allowance. Over and out."

In the distance, Reba peered at homemade one or two man mining operations and a man on horseback up one ridge and down the other. Not a good place to stop to camp. Not much burning materials for fire, except for a few twigs and dead sagebrush.

They caught up with Seth when he stopped near the skeleton of a busted double highway sign marked Coaldale. Once again they were surrounded by buckskin, tan, and gold sand and soil spread across the mostly barren desert floor.

Pearl and Reba joined Seth, Tucker, Ida and sons, Jace and Able as they set up camp outside the Coaldale area.

"Looks like an abandoned ghost town," Reba remarked.

"That's because it is," Seth replied. "A former coal mine community."

Tucker helped Seth set up his tent and he collapsed on his bedroll. Every so often Reba checked on him.

"Either Seth is the unluckiest guy alive or..." Pearl began.

"Or what?"

"Somebody's trying to sabotage him." Pearl offered her opinion after a rundown by Reba and Jace of the journey so far. "Add the brakes going out and tires slashed as well as the cabin explosion."

"You think they're connected events?" Reba asked.

"Hasn't the possibility crossed your mind?"

"No, not at all. I guess I attributed each one to life hassles, which we all have." Reba hated to admit she'd been thinking only of herself, not Seth and his troubles. And though she still had no idea why her grandmother had come, she appreciated the company with Ginny gone. *Even if I can't forgive her yet.*

Pearl looked up and down the nearby road and all around.

"You expecting company?" Reba asked.

"Maybe."

That evening the desert seemed to hold its breath, immune from the drug of continuous noise and racket of the road travel. A deafening silence descended and settled heavy there. Reba breathed in the cadence and nuances of the desert twilight.

Somebody stirred. Seth crept out of his tent with a lantern. "Can't sleep. It's too noisy."

Jace told about purchasing his '55 Chevy.

"Most all models of cars made in '55, '56, and '57 have great designs," Tucker mentioned.

"And next I'll need to find a '56 and '57 Chevy," Jace concluded. "To complete my set."

Reba recounted the flash flood and wild horses.

Jace sat horrified. "Are you saying that's all true?"

"Yep."

"I met Egan Toms the Pauite," Pearl affirmed.

"I'll never let you go it alone again," Jace asserted.

"I made it through just fine, thank you." Reba tried to stare him down but had to pull away. His declaration didn't bother her as much as she felt it should.

"I had a horse once tangle in a stallion fight," Seth said. "A vice grip of teeth ripped his hide. And nearly every rib broken."

Jace's face flickered shadows in the reflection of the campfire. "I've been around horses who can get wild at times."

"I chased wild horses once or twice," Seth pondered. "When we lived in Goldfield. The sensation's like trying to catch the wind. No, it's like trying to capture a storm and the stars all at once. The pursuit. The risk. The danger."

Reba stared at the old man and imagined joining him in the chase. Then she tried to calm the fever of the day's over-excitement by tuning into the rhythm of crickets and critters on the prowl. She devoured chili beans. As she sprawled on her sleeping bag in the dirt, her stomach clenched. She wanted to retch.

She groaned and asked Jace and Abel to water Johnny Poe.

"Can I pet him?" Abel asked.

"Sure, but be careful. He's not a kid horse."

To prove her wrong, Johnny Poe followed Abel, willing to please, wanting to play. "I bet I could teach Johnny Poe to count," Abel said. "I saw it on a movie once."

Please, I don't want a trick pony. Reba's pangs grew worse. She moaned in her sleeping bag. "I don't feel good. What did you put in the beans?"

"It's just a gastro problem. You aren't used to hot chili peppers," Pearl said.

"Well, if I die, insist on an autopsy. I think I've been poisoned." She considered again Pearl's assertion of someone trying to harm them and pondered how a person would contaminate chili beans. But everyone except the boys ate the beans and she was the solitary sick one. Was Pearl trying to do her in? Was that her mission after twenty-five years of raising her? Follow her into the Nevada desert and watch her die a slow, painful, gaseous death?

She giggled despite the agony. Pearl gave her an odd look and offered her pills. "Antacid," she claimed.

In her unstable frame of mind, Reba wondered again. She studied the woman's face for any hint of evil intent. Dare she trust her? One way to find out: she'd either survive or not. She chewed the pills, waited with growing apprehension, and soon felt blessed relief.

🐎 🐎 🐎 🐎

By early morning, Reba's ribs ached, her back itched, but her stomach felt fully recovered. A constant, driving dust storm swirled down on their heads and blurred the view of stones on the ledges of far away mountains and the sides of craggy hills.

Seth rambled about Worthy, perhaps because his final destination loomed so close. One moment it was 1912 again. The next it was 1991, all mixed in a blend of coffee, biscuits, fried apples and wood smoke smells.

"Mama's place was beautiful. Half mountains, half desert, with pines overlappin' the sage. Tucked in the hills like a fold, it boasted an underground stream and a rich strike. So Mama claimed. She should have called it Veridian."

"Why?" Reba asked.

"That's the shade of green sandwiched in there. I saw it on an artist's palette one time."

"It's also the color of that snake." Reba watched a two-foot long lentil-green reptile shake its tail and slither into a crack like a tongue between teeth.

"Look at the color of the wind, whether it's friendly or evil," Seth said. But he didn't explain what different colors a dust storm could be. All of it was evil, as far as Reba was concerned. The wind cried loud and long.

And so did Tucker. "There was a rattlesnake curled up by my bedroll when I woke up," Tucker claimed. "And I heard wild horses running by our tent all night."

"Pettifogger," Seth said.

"What did you say?" Reba asked.

"I said he shouldn't pettifog."

"I'll have to look that one up in the dictionary," Jace whispered.
Reba snickered. "Must be an Old West term."

"I know the world's longest joke about being lost in the desert,"
Tucker said. "But I'm saving it for when we're really bored."

"Yes, do save it," Seth said.

"In that case, I'll show you the rattlesnake eggs I stole." Tucker
pulled out an envelope with a desert graphics scene of a cactus, sun
going down and a curled up snake. "Any of you want to see them?"

The boys gathered close.

"The problem is, I was supposed to keep these in a cool place to
prevent hatching. Caution when opening. Anyone want to try?"

Abel carefully opened the flap. Amos tried to peer inside. Pico
marched over and opened the envelope to a loud rattle and shake.
They all shrieked. Pico began to cry.

"Hey, it's okay. Look." Tucker showed the boy a thin wind up
mechanism inside.

"Why do you think God created so much desert on this earth?"
Ida asked.

"To remind us he can refresh parched souls?" Pearl suggested.
"Or maybe so we'll understand the concept of thirsting after righ-
teousness."

"Or experience being sunburned to death." Jace slathered his and
Abel's arms with sunscreen.

"Those mountains around the desert remind me of a promise of
escape," Seth remarked. "Some people say that's why we need wilderness, whether or not we ever set foot in it. We need the possibility of
escape as surely as we need hope."

"Are you sure *you* aren't being a pettifogger?" Tucker danced a jig
and plopped down by Ida.

"Well, for me, this particular moment is pure pleasure." Ida
reached for Tucker's hand as she watched Amos, Pico, and Abel dig
roads in the sand with their Matchbox cars.

Chapter Sixteen

Jace finished wiping a layer of sand and grit off his Volvo and walked over to Seth. "Today, if all goes well, we finally arrive in Goldfield and you'll be on your way to Worthy, your mother's place. What are you expecting there?"

The old man poured himself a cup of coffee from the campfire pot. "I don't know how it will end. I only know I must go. At the least, I'll get Maidie back to her Mama. That's important."

"And to her grandma and aunties," Reba said. *Isn't that right?*

They all turned around as they heard a car motor on the road. A long, black stretch Lincoln limousine appeared and parked along the pavement. A back door opened and out stepped an older woman with curly red bouffant hair that looked like a wig or at least dyed. Crimson lips and nails matched. "Somebody call for a taxi?" she asked.

"Aggie!" Abel squealed. He raced to the woman, then turned around and dug his '55 Chevy and Tomcat miniature toys out of the sand, and rushed toward her again.

Jace sauntered over as the rest gawked. "Mom, what's going on?"

Mom? Reba couldn't begin to guess what a vehicle like that would cost. And how strange that Abel would rush to her. Wasn't the boy's mother one of her ex-husband's other wives? A strange family.

"You are." The woman looked around and settled on Seth. "That man was in the paper and on TV. Since I was in the area, I wanted to find out what the fuss was all about. And how come you got involved?"

"In the area?"

"McKane Enterprise. We bought Worthy Mountain as an investment. Your father is part owner now. We're part of the Canadian cartel. The owners, the shareholders. One of the shareholders is from Canada. But you surely knew that. I was sent as a representative to check it out and sign the final papers." She smiled at Jace. "Don't look so surprised. You know I kept my position in the company as part of the divorce settlement."

He peered at Seth, then Reba. "But I didn't know about Worthy Mountain."

"Why not? I've been leaving messages on your phone."

Reba studied Jace. So that's why he came on this adventure? Was he trying to slow Seth down because he was suspicious about what he'd take from the mine before his father took over? Was he part of the sabotage? What's going on here?

"But I haven't used it for days," Jace replied. "I keep forgetting to charge it up."

Sure. Good excuse. Seth is going to be too late after all. *And I had Jace pegged right from the beginning.*

Jace introduced his mother as Agatha Finley McKane Hempthorn of Casa Tierra, California.

"Isn't that close to Santa Dominga?" Reba asked.

"It sure is." Agatha looked her over with a quick glance Reba interpreted as a dismissal.

Before Reba could ask if she knew Ginny or her family, she raised her head to investigate the drone of a whirring sound. The noise hammered louder. A rush of wind and a bulging form appeared and soon hovered above them. A helicopter with huge double propellers and the wail of rotors circled once and the belly underside swept over. Abel raised his hands over his head to try to reach it. The copter looped toward an open area of fairly flat ground and landed amid a swirl of dirt and sand almost as bad as the earlier storm.

Doors opened and two males stepped out from either side. Soren and Irving the Russian hitchhiker. Reba was glad to see one of them. She watched the cowboy's long legs lunge over the desert expanse in a very few steps. He kept his eyes on her the whole way. She resisted the urge to bound toward him with hugs.

"A limousine and now a helicopter. To what do we owe this unexpected visit?" she asked.

"On my way to Vegas. I've got horses to look at. Thought we'd drop in if we spotted you along the way." He peered at Irving. "Actually, I had to let him out. He keeps tipping the chopper."

"How in the world did you happen to connect with him?" Jace asked.

"He told a truck driver to drop him off at our place. One thing led to another. I think he wants to make amends with you all. I do believe he's sincere."

Irving pulled Jace and Seth aside in an intense private conversation. Moments later they hiked over to Soren. "Tell me again, what do you think of this guy?" Jace asked.

"I think I can't carry more than 2,700 pounds total," he quipped. "If you get me over that weight, I can't get 'er up. I'm off balance. I've got to let him off here, whatever you decide."

"How come everyone's looking at me?" Irving said. "I've lost pounds on this trip."

That raised an icebreaker chuckle.

Jace looked at Reba. "Irving says he and Quigley were hired to hamper Seth and the road trip, so we'd all return to Road's End. Irving needed the money, so he agreed. But he drew the line at threats of violence."

"By who?" Reba sputtered.

"A guy named Dalton."

"But why?"

"I don't know. He's got lots of explaining to do, after we get Seth safely to his destination." He turned to Pearl. "What do you think? Is this guy the real deal? Is this a true confession?"

She looked him over. "He didn't have to come back and face everyone. That's one sign of repentance."

"Well then, he can ride with me and Abel. He says he's headed for Vegas. Has some family there." Jace peered again at Reba. "That is, if everyone agrees."

"We're following the Model T. What do you think, Seth?"

Seth swatted his arm. "He's Jace's responsibility. He'll keep a close watch."

"What did I hear about threats of violence?" Agatha said.

"Quigley tried to hurt Reba with a knife," Abel told her.

"Quigley's in jail now." Reba wanted to assure everyone, including herself, but recall of the man's hate-filled glare shattered the allusion.

Agatha turned to Jace. "So, you're still picking up hitchhikers? You haven't learned your lesson from San Francisco?"

"What happened in San Francisco?" Reba prodded.

"A girl he picked up robbed him at gunpoint. Took everything, including his car."

Reba glared at Jace who grimaced. "She was a redhead too. And bopped me over the head with the revolver." He touched a spot on his skull.

Ah, he's got lots of reasons to be conflicted about auburn haired women.

Seth straightened his back best he could and reported, "Next stop Goldfield and Worthy."

"And Silver Peak," Pearl added.

"Glad we caught you when we did." Soren's glance lingered on Reba.

She gave him a practiced polite smile, trying to keep it casual as she thought, *So am I, cowboy.* She had to admit at least to herself she enjoyed the horse breeder's attention in front of Jace, as well as everyone else. Felt good. *Real good.*

After a round of emptying the coffee pot and chitchat about horses to buy, mysteries to uncover, and a mother to find, Soren sauntered to the chopper. The rotors beat again, whipped the air and sand, and soared over them.

"I need to be going," Agatha announced. "I'll be staying at the Mizpah Hotel for a few days."

"You know Seth traveled all this way to visit the Worthy Mine one last time before you take over," Jace explained. "It used to belong to his mother."

"Well, he can't remove any minerals."

Seth reached out his hand to her. "I'll be sure to check with you if there's anything I want to take out of there."

"Mother, why don't you ride along with us?"

She smirked. "Not quite my style. Abel, mind your Uncle Jace." She gave the boy a quick squeeze then slid back into the long stretch limousine and the chauffeur drove her toward Tonopah.

Reba stared at Jace again, determined to figure out his motives.

He stared right back. "I swear I knew nothing about this."

"No need to swear." But did she believe him? "Abel seemed to know your mother well."

"She's the one who sent him to me and Norden."

So many things didn't add up with Jace and his family. *At least as dysfunctional as mine.*

Before they left the campsite, Reba overheard Pearl grill Irving about the man named Dalton who hired him. "Was his first name Dax?"

Irving nodded.

"And does he drive a black and white Chevelle?"

"Yep. That's the guy."

"Well, I don't think we need to be worried about him anymore."

"Now, how could you possibly know that?" Reba butted in.

Pearl offered one of her irritating, stubborn wouldn't-you-like-to-know smiles.

Irving added this tidbit. "I do know Dalton himself was hired by another guy. Somebody from Road's End."

"Who?" A chorus of voices surrounded him.

"Don't know. Won't help even if you torture me. Dalton never told us any name."

"I think I can guess." That's all Pearl would say.

"But what possible reason could there be to hijack Seth's trip?" Reba prodded.

Pearl tromped to her Jeep and slammed the door shut.

When they arrived in Tonopah, Jace provided a guided tour on the walkie-talkie. "Rancher Boss, this frontier town attracted gold seekers, soul savers, bartenders, and teachers. It's called 'The Queen of Nevada Silver Camps.' An estimated hundred miles of mine tunnels were discovered under the city by a man named Jim Butler and his mule."

"Computer Guy. Another boom and bust town."

"10-4."

They passed a guy who rode a bicycle made from tin cans. A green tinted cross perched on the hill behind casinos. A man ranted something incoherent with a megaphone up and down the streets. Hills in the background belched up gold and silver as their craggy tops and outcroppings still cried out for discovery.

A bright green building seemed out of place with blends of brown, soft gold, and beige decor all around. Houses crammed in dirt yards beside scores of empty stores on unleveled lots. Buildings jutted out in streets. Backyards included mine shafts. Nice homes cozied next to shacks and mobile homes toppled on tailings.

No sign of building codes.

They all stopped near the Nye County Courthouse when Seth pulled over next to some stands to buy Death Valley Gazette, Tonopah Times-Bonanza, and the Reno Gazette. In one a picture of Seth next to his purple Model T, and "Idaho Man On Model T Sentimental Journey." The others headlined "Purple Model T Leads Road Adventure" and "91-Year-Old Searches For Missing Family."

"A slow news day," Jace remarked.

Reba and Pearl headed for the Mizpah Hotel which flanked a winding Main Street. They got out for a brief tour and noticed Agatha's limousine in the back. The lobby flashed slot machines through cut glass doors. A classic painting of an elderly woman with scarf-covered head praying over a bowl of soup hung on a second story wall. They peered into an open room behind a black wooden door numbered 306. Red velvet flowered paper lined the walls, red carpeting on the floor. Out in the hall they admired a wooden coffee table with marbled top beside a green velvet settee with matching chair. Overhead hung crystal chandeliers. Posters advertised live entertainment, video poker, and a country western dance hall.

Reba grabbed matchbook covers. "For souvenirs."

"Jack Dempsey, one-time heavy-weight champion, was a bartender and bouncer here," Pearl mentioned. Then she choked a kind of gasp.

"What's the matter?"

"I thought I saw someone I recognized in the reflection of that huge mirror over the bar."

"You sure have been jumpy. I wish you'd tell me why."

"All in good time."

Whose time? Hers? Or mine? Reba remembered her brief time with the Kierseys and tried to pull in the peace she felt with them. Patience. Not her strong suit.

On the way out of Tonopah, they viewed snow-capped Sierra Nevadas and clumps of cottonwoods and juniper trees in the desert. Reba spotted a summit marker of 6,200 feet. Higher than their own mountain top home.

From Tonopah to one of several dirt road turnoffs to Silver Peak, a panorama of multiple layered mountain ranges spread like ridges on a washboard. Mining shafts, potholes and digs spread everywhere at the bottom. Dirt roads wound to the top. Clouds of dust from occasional desert riders could be seen in the distance. Black cows roamed around trailers, shacks, and scruffy sagebrush barely high enough to hide a desert rat. Reba spotted a small herd of camels next to burros.

One of the attendants at the Mizpah told them, "When this place was humming the whole mountain range vibrated." The only thing that vibrated now was the crackle of the walkie-talkie that startled her.

"Ranch Boss, aren't you glad that a six-hour stagecoach drive is now only a half-hour by car or truck?"

"Yes, Computer Guy, that's unless you're following a Model T."

"Which we are to the bitter-sweet end. Not much longer now. Excited?"

"I think so."

"So are we. 10-4."

The road-weary band, sunburned and feeling scruffy, peered at an empty desert valley and a sign that read Goldfield, 5 miles. Tossed bottles and broken glass littered the side of the highway. Four hundred in population, the same as Road's End, kept this historically registered ghost town alive.

They turned a corner and stared at a sign stretched across the street: "Welcome Seth Stroud and Friends." The town's citizens prepared a grand entrance for him. Past a bar and a grocery store into Goldfield, a five-piece band played for a dozen singers. They heard "Alexander's Ragtime Band" and then "He Played It On His Fid, Fid, Fiddle-dee-dee."

Seth jumped out of the Model T with his fiddle and joined in. The spectators dressed in period clothing loved it. They ran up to him to wave or slap his back. Several media personnel held out microphones to Seth. When he ignored them and kept fiddling, they turned to Tucker. Ida ran interference and answered most their questions. Their boys and Abel and kids from the town chased chickens.

"Hey, Seth," hailed a man in wheelchair tattooed with scars with patches of white hair on his otherwise baldhead. "Play 'Hitchy-Koo' for us." Whiffs of smoke from his pipe encircled him.

Seth played the tune and folks danced in the street and on the sidewalk.

A motel and saloon owner announced he'd saved rooms for them all. Jace and Abel, Reba and Pearl, Tucker, Ida, and the boys took him up on it.

"Seth, you can stay with me," the Hitchy-Koo wheelchair man offered. They punched each other's shoulders, howled, and chattered.

After the celebration quieted down and they cleared the street for through traffic, Reba and Pearl peeked in the windows of the U-shape four-story Goldfield Hotel. Across the street from the courthouse, it was now boarded and closed. A large, ornate four-story edifice remained well preserved in the dry desert air. Made of red brick and gray granite, black wrought iron balconies bordered many windows. White post railings and huge brick columns fashioned the front portico and double doors. They peered inside a lobby with grand piano, leather settees, and velvet chairs. The dining room filled with leather-backed chairs, tables spread with linen covers, silverware, glasses, and even sugar bowl with heavy mantle of dust. A setting petrified in time. All dressed up with no people to serve.

Reba rubbed another circle of clean on a dirty window. "The last owner didn't take everything with them. I've heard this place is still active though."

"Still active? It's closed down."

"It's haunted. They claim ghosts live here."

"Don't know about that. It's certainly not neglected. The folks still in Goldfield seem to take care of things here."

But Reba suddenly dreaded spending the night. Despite the cheery greeting they received, the town had a mood, an atmosphere. Perhaps a reminder of an unhappy time in Seth's life.

"You know, there's a scent of a story in any old dwelling or town like this," Pearl commented. "A discerning person can get a whiff of it. I'll bet a really nosy person could sort it out."

"Well, I'm discerning there's more than a whiff of a story you're not telling me." Reba stuffed hands on her hips in her best scolding manner.

Pearl turned to her with woeful eyes. "You'll know everything soon enough."

Meanwhile I'm left hanging. Out of the loop. Did everyone know something important except her?

Seth joined them with a welcome interruption. "So much is coming back to me. Right here in this place Papa met the fight promoter Tex Rickard and the famed Stuart Brannon and introduced me too.

Quite an honor."

"Who's the friend you're going to stay with?" Pearl asked.

"Cal Tiggers. He studies bones. Used to be a kid same as me in Goldfield back in the old days. He went home to get ready for company."

"How in the world did you recognize each other after all these years?" Reba inquired.

"He read the newspaper article. And he was wearing a name badge. All the old-timers here are. Some local gal got it organized. They're sponsoring a dinner and dance for us tonight. A kind of Goldfield Heydays Reunion. You want to see the place I used to call home?"

He led them to a modest dwelling still standing. Someone had recently given it some tender love and care. Reba and Pearl investigated the place as Seth touched the front door and walls.

"I remember one time we finished the chores outside and scurried to the house for the next chore. My sisters had to hold the door because it was loose from its frame. I was holding a bowl of slop. The next thing I knew the bowl was yanked from my arms and I was shoved out in the yard. Mother came shrieking at me, her arms flailing, face full of hell's wrath."

So, Seth's mother wasn't the saint Reba imagined, even with the passing of gentled years.

"She beat on me with a heavy wooden spoon," he continued. "And called me names I never heard before. Then she told me, 'Get out.'"

"Get out where?" I said.

"Get out of this house and out of my life."

"She had been stone quiet for some days so I was double stunned. I rolled over on my stomach and lay real still until she tired of beating me. I hurt too bad to cry. Mother had never ill-treated me before. Nor any of my sisters. Her method of discipline was a sharp rebuke and denial of dinner. One less mouth to feed."

Mesmerized by the revelation, Reba reached out to trace a tear on the old man's face.

"Sister Molly, Maidie's mother, lay down beside me for a long time. Finally I said, 'Go away.' I did not have to say it twice. She jumped up and took off. I lay there until it got dark. When I pushed myself up, I was so bruised I could not think what to do. My two other shirts, one for church and one for school, and some underclothes were rolled in a bundle and tossed at my feet.

"I sat in the dirt all night, waiting for someone to come out and tell me to get back in the house. When no one did, a bit before daylight I grabbed my bundle, walked out the rickety gate and down the road. An hour later, I passed a shack. Mrs. Grundy saw me from her window and coaxed me to stay with them.

'I will,' I said, 'until mother tells me she is sorry and begs me to come back.' But she never did. I found out later Papa hid at the barbershop. We both stayed there until we got ourselves a shack. Soon after, Mama left for her mining operation. Papa and I moved back into this house."

Pearl and Reba, and Jace and Abel followed Seth to Cal Tiggers rough-cut, unpainted, weathered gray house that leaned windward. The trash-strewn property scattered with old car parts, rusty metal tools, glass jars of nails and screws, and wooden boxes full of mystery items. Seth's old home seemed in much better repair.

"I'd say it was pretty unusual anyone staying here all those years," Pearl remarked when they arrived.

"He didn't. Told me he moved back a decade or so ago. Goldfield never knew if it was coming or going. Most folks claim plans to move on even if they've lived here many years."

Tiggers met them at the door and wheeled outside. Red plaid shirt under overalls, two lower teeth missing, index finger gone at the knuckle. He peered around as though seeing it for the first time. "Gotta stop going to auctions. The place is gettin' filled up."

A middle-aged woman, barefoot and in pigtails, crept out the door and swept the front porch.

"Is that your daughter?" Reba asked.

"Nah. My daughter's fat and ugly. She ran off with her Mama."

A housekeeper? Or more? At his age? She searched for a new subject. "So, you study bones?"

He shot her an appreciative glance. "Yep. Bones tell us a lot. Like how someone died. They're like jigsaw puzzle pieces."

"Do you solve crimes?" inquired Pearl.

"Not much anymore. I'm retired. My job was part archaeology, part criminal science. I'm still going to make my fortune here, but I spent my investment money. These people moving out, they don't believe anymore." He warmed up to the conversation, looked almost animated.

"Is there still gold around?" Abel asked.

"I'm in a mining dispute right now. One piece of advice: keep it quiet when you find something valuable or some company will claim it's theirs. The Golden Rule around here: the one with the gold makes the rules."

Reba did a quick study of Jace. What must he be thinking with his parents soon taking over the Worthy Mine?

"You have a mine?" Reba asked.

"The wife got tired of waiting. She went to Broken Arrow, Oklahoma to be with her sister. She sends me a card at Christmas and my birthday, in care of my attorney here in Goldfield."

Reba wondered if the pipe smoke and a thick crop of hair in his ears affected his hearing. "But you own a mine?" she repeated.

"Three hundred ounces of gold per ton of dirt and rock on my property. Some dig every day, sunup to sundown. Hard physical work but they make enough to pay groceries." It was obvious he couldn't manage that anymore.

"What do you do here?" Reba asked.

"Three things. Gamble, play at mining, and go to Doomsday Society meetings. And listen to the cactus grow."

"That's four," Abel said.

He reached out and tousled the boy's head. "Smart kid." He turned to Seth. "I'd sure like to go with you to the Worthy Mine, but the legs don't work anymore. I'd get stuck and in the way. How do you keep so limber?"

"Driving that Model T."

"Never seen a purple one before."

Seth headed for the Model T. "I'm going to drive around town some. You can follow along or go it alone."

Reba and Pearl hopped in their rigs and chased after Seth. He drove two blocks away from Cal's to a large white house with recent white picket fence and upstairs balcony.

Seth reminisced some more. "That day Mama disappeared in the heat of mid-summer, Papa saddled his horse and nearly died searching for her. Meanwhile Mama returned as cool as brass and filed a claim at the assay office. She showed the clerk pure yellow gold. Papa returned to the barber shop. Some ladies threatened to send me to school, so I decided to take some time off from selling papers and visit Mama again. I hitched with Uriah Runcie and his guard on the water wagon. Riders followed us on horseback. Uriah turned the team to scale the Montezumas and they still kept coming. Uriah stopped the wagon and told us to get off. I and Ben Oates, the guard, stood behind the wagon while he confronted the riders. Ben said it was Uriah's boss, his lawyer and a detective.

'You're under arrest, Uriah,' I heard someone shout.

'What for?' Uriah hollered back.

'High grading my ore.'

"Ben Oates cocked his rifle. I hid under the wagon when the bullets flew. Uriah held up a white shirt and walked over and opened the back of the wagon. Inside was waste mixed with ore. No water. We climbed back on the wagon and the men followed us to Goldfield.

'Why didn't you fight them?' I asked Uriah.

'No reason to do that. We'll be out of jail quick as a desert rat and your Mama's place is protected and still hidden.' He slapped my back. 'And we're all alive.'

"That's the first I heard Mama didn't mine the gold herself. She and Uriah stole it."

Reba hugged his sagging shoulders. "It must be hard in some ways to come back here."

"I got a sense of what it was like for Rip Van Winkle. It's like coming back a hundred years after a fairy enchantment and finding most your friends and family gone. Nothing's the same as I imagined it.

The Runcie place here, for instance." He pointed at the white house in front of them. "Seemed like a mansion when I was a boy. Always thought of them as rich folks. Now, it's just a fairly ordinary house. But the Runcies left Goldfield with plenty of gold."

Reba, Jace, and Abel went to a local shop for supplies. Reba looked for engine oil, a spare fan belt, and radiator hose for her truck. While Jace looked at tools, Tucker stole up behind. "Do you think Seth has a secret mine stash out there?"

"Don't know," Jace said. "Abel and I aim to search for our own. You and the boys want to join us?"

"I hear there's gold out here all over the place."

"Maybe so. Mostly small flakes, I suppose."

"Large nuggets too," Abel claimed.

"Me and Seth have been partners all along the road, you know. Don't think he'd hold out on me, do you?"

"Guess you'll have to gamble which way to go." He plopped down hundreds of dollars for equipment, pans and buckets he stacked on the store counter.

"What is all that for?" Reba asked.

"We might have to dig ourselves out."

"That's sure an awful lot of digging," Reba said.

"We're coming with you for sure." Tucker brought over a metal detector and dry wash series of blowers, tubes, and racks of steel. "How much to buy in?"

"You help us keep our cars running and you'll earn your keep," Jace said.

"You know how to use that stuff?' Reba asked Tucker.

"I'll ask Abel. He's read up on it." He ruffled the boy's hair.

"The best locations are already claimed. We'll have to go pretty far out," Abel said.

"Carry plenty of water," the clerk advised.

They filled up large canteens and hauled a big tank full in the back of Reba's pickup. They stuffed extra ice in a chest alongside a new gas stove.

"We need folding chairs too," Jace added.

The clerk offered a half-off discount. Abel pleaded for a trail bike and Jace chained it to the back of his Volvo.

"Abel read a book that claims gold deposited by ancient hot springs still percolates up thru fissures here," Jace said. "I guess he's getting the fever. I'm also going to look into an experimental new process for extracting gold. High temp chlorine where gold attaches to the chlorine, condenses to liquid and goes over rosin beads like marbles and extracts it. I might be interested in investing in something like that."

Reba whistled. "I imagine it'll take big bucks to get machinery to do that."

"As long as there is one soul left, there will be opportunity to buy stock in gold mine and gold prospecting schemes. From the first glory days, wheeling and dealing, and it's still going on. Gully washers expose new beds of gold."

Jace and Abel left for their adventures in the packed tight Volvo.

"What's your plan?" Reba asked Seth.

"Today to the Worthy mine. Tomorrow the cemetery."

"I would think you'd do it the other way around. Don't you want to see your family's graves?"

His brows creased. "I told you before. They are lost. Only Molly's there."

"I don't get it. You brought Maidie's ashes all this way to be buried only with her mama. But why not keep her in Road's End? With you? And all of us?"

"Because I mean to find them. Bury them all there."

Reba stared at the old man, his rumpled clothes and wrinkled skin. His fevered memories. Had they been following a crazy man? None of this made sense. She caught herself before she made another retort. At least she still might contact her own mom. That would make it worthwhile. Maybe.

"There's still lots of daylight hours left. If we run into problems, we can go back tomorrow." He piled into Reba's pickup with Pearl, the trailer and Johnny Poe still attached.

Sage, sand and hills swelled as far as they could see. After a few miles of pavement the road turned to gravel and faded to dirt. Potholes bumped them along. Reba feared the hitch on her trailer would break, so she slowed down.

The sky swirled with clouds as dust fogged around. Reba stopped to check on Johnny Poe, his eyes looked wild as he kicked against the trailer. "It can't be too much farther, boy. The map shows about thirty miles to Worthy. Seth, are you sure this horse won't be too much for you?"

Seth insisted on going alone to the mine. "The best way to get there is by horse or mountain bike. The site will be missed by truck or car."

"Do you think you can ride Johnny Poe?" Reba repeated.

"If he'll let me. And you don't mind."

"He'll be honored, I'm sure." Reba drove through a canyon with alkali, scattered Joshuas, and volcanic outcroppings with sage. Remnants of bathtub-sized ponds and mineral springs remained. A dugout cellar against a hill. An old corral and well. Several four-wheelers skidded on large sand dunes. And in the Montezuma Range that peaked over 8,000 feet, a flat-topped range of mesas like bald monk heads, hidden mountain springs.

"Stop here," Seth ordered.

Reba helped him back Johnny Poe out of the trailer. Seth talked to the horse while he saddled him and packed on saddlebags, one from the back of the pickup with the initials S.P.

"We'll go on to Silver Peak from here and check with you later." Reba studied the old man. The pursed lips, the gnarled skin, the eyes like Maidie's, yet his face relaxed so much the wrinkles softened into shallow crevices and his mouth the semblance of a permanent smile.

"I truly expected to see Champ show by now," Pearl commented.

"Maybe he won't."

"Oh, he will. I don't feel right about letting Seth go off like that on his own."

"But that's what he wants. This first time, anyway." She yelled out as he rode away, "Don't forget. We'll be back at this spot in two hours."

Without a backward glance, Seth raised his hand in response and Johnny Poe trotted to an ancient trail, visible only to discerning eyes.

Dipped into a small creviced canyon after climbing some rises, Seth found the twisted descent. He didn't expect to see any of the recognizable barbed wire fencing left from so many years ago. But some stuck out like last-stand rebels in the drifts. Another sign. A familiar ape's head shaped rock glinted in the sunlight.

Crumbling adobe walls, even palm trees, and hints of a garden long ago disappeared. A few half-buried rocks still marked the walk-way path. Holes and a shaft remained among a few creosote covered timbers and a lone saguaro.

He relished the sweet smell of remnants of an early morning shower. Angry cactus wrens scolded a five-foot-long bull snake. In the distance, crimson dirt. Seth slowed Johnny Poe and slipped off his back. He slumped full length to the ground as his legs gave way. He rested prone until the hot grit burned too bad. He rose up and thought he viewed an apparition, a blurred vision of a man on a horse.

He got closer and more focused. "Hi, Champ. I was expecting you."

Chapter Seventeen

The un-maintained dirt road to Silver Peak from Goldfield crossed marsh flats marked "Drive at your own risk." Miles of beer bottles stretched before them, whole and broken. Reba drove the pickup across the chaparral country clumped with junipers, cottonwoods, and scrubby pinion pines scattered near houses dug into the mountain.

On each side of them straight dirt roads of nothing seemed to lead to nowhere.

A senior couple with a tent trailer and satellite dish receiver waved. Reba stopped to greet them, travelers briefly bonded by a shared out-of-the-way meeting.

"We're looking for rocks," the woman said, "before the squall hits. We heard in town there may be a heavy downpour around Silver Peak."

They pulled away and a half-mile later, they hiked on spongy sand as Pearl wrestled with a charley horse in her left calf and toes. A pair of long-eared jackrabbits hopped through bleached cattle bones.

Reba gazed at a multi-colored rust red and black tailing the size of a mountain.

A man on horse with bedroll in back, tarp in front waved at them and then they gazed at young and middle-aged hotrodders in battered pickups stirring up dry storms on a large sand dune area. Outside town a flat-topped dark cinder cone resembled a huge, decaying beast.

From the north hill they viewed all of town. Trailers replaced tents, but they could still pick up and leave in a hurry at the first opportunity. Alkali dirt covered everything and swept in great piles against the mountains. Remains of former mills still visible.

A sign welcomed them to Silver Peak: "A Virtual Paradise."

Pearl chuckled. "Well, at least one resident has a sense of humor."

They passed the Vinegarroon Saloon, a former schoolhouse, the present K-8 elementary school, and a children's park and play area. They stopped at the post office to ask about Blue Moon Toms. The original one room post office stood next to a modern replacement, a single-wide mobile home. Four mules tied and tethered and loaded with bundles lounged in the front. Inside, empty pigeon hole openings banked one wall next to a small oak desk with swivel chair, and a cot in the corner.

No one answered their "Yoo-hoo" calls.

With the pickup covered with thick white dust fog, like most every other vehicle in sight, Reba stopped in front of a rock shop to wipe the windshield clearer with an old t-shirt. They entered the shop.

A teen girl greeted them with frizzy blond hair, too much make-up, and blood red acrylic nails. She looked Latino with Asian eyes. After their inquiry, she apologized. "Can't tell you a thing. I'm new in town. Visiting my Aunt Jackie for the summer. This is her shop. Just got here from Kansas. Can you believe this place?"

Pearl studied a collection of mineral specimens amid displays of silver and beaded jewelry.

"This is cavansite," the young clerk said. "This one's rhodochrosite. Here's hemimorphite. And, of course, you recognize the gold."

"You sure know rocks, especially being so new."

The girl beamed. "I've been studying every night. You're some of my first customers." She looked outside. "There's Aunt Jackie now. I work in here while she delivers the mail route."

Jackie's age lines on her face and arms contrasted with long blond hair in schoolgirl braids. A deep tan covered arm bruises and scabs from some chronic ailment. "Sorry I'm late, Cheech. The job description includes knowledge of repairing and welding the mail truck, if needed, and no fear of snakes. I had to make full use of all that today."

"They're looking for a man named Blue Moon Toms," Cheech said.

She gave them a quick study. "You buying jewelry?"

"No, we're looking for someone we think he knows," Reba explained.

"If you let me go home first, I'll take you to him. Better yet, follow me to my house. Won't take me long to change my greasy clothes."

They pursued Jackie's mail truck to a shack with screen doors, screens on the windows, and a swamp cooler. Paint bleached off. Patched shingles and blue plastic tarps with old tires to hold them down on the roof.

A teen boy drove up in a decrepit pickup just as they arrived. After introductions as Jackie's son, he offered a pitch. "The pickup belongs to my dad. I deliver ore to the mill. I also know how to operate a cat, if you know someone who needs a driver."

"Cat?" Reba said.

"Caterpillar tractor."

Jackie's mother, Genevieve, greeted them rocking in a chair on the front porch. "Come in and have some brownies and watch the Price Is Right."

They entered into a pine scent like room spray or scented cleaner. Jackie and her mother took them to a room with jewelry making items organized in clear plastic boxes of all sizes. "Can't grow anything," Jackie said. "The ground's like cracked skin. So, we decided to make jewelry. I sell it at the rock shop. It's local silver."

"Silver Peak still has a silver mine," Genevieve told them. "But we hear it's going to close down. The lithium mine is still working and some platinum."

When Jackie returned in fresh white Capri pants, canvas shoes, and yellow and white striped blouse, they followed her to an overgrown school baseball field. Jackie left an ice chest with sodas for some ball players, two of them another son and a daughter. Down the street they observed a desert dream that died. Half-built resort with dance hall, bowling alley and staked-out streets. A red brick and bright white wooden gate leading nowhere.

A couple wild dogs yapped at them. A Book Mobile passed by.

Back on the road they spotted a prospector working a claim near broken-down, abandoned cars. Mining gear parts piled around mounds of dirt and systematic potholes.

"Not good country to run through at night," Pearl commented.

Reba spotted a snake curled under a house. "That one found a cool place to hide."

Tiny shacks with sheet metal patched roofing and brick houses neighbored next to each other with scattered lots. Jackie took a quick right without signaling and wound down a curvy dirt road. Blue Moon lived in a tidy trailer next to a tepee and a couple rusted cars and old refrigerator in the yard. An open door exposed a loft room with mattress, pillows, TV, and portable camp toilet.

Pearl tugged out the squash blossom necklace from the glove compartment and she and Reba sauntered toward Jackie as she tapped at the door.

"Go away. Leave me alone," a male growled.

She raised her voice. "It's Jackie from the rock shop. Some nice ladies are here to talk to you."

He slid the door a crack. Charcoal gray eyes pierced them with suspicion, one eye glazed as though diseased or partially blind. Finally, he opened the door wide. The black felt cowboy hat covered Blue Moon Toms' hair. He wore a navy scarf and cotton, bright colored print shirt. A gold and turquoise ring could be seen as he clamped an empty pipe in his teeth. "My biggest challenge is tourists crowding me."

Inside his trailer they marveled at the turquoise samples spread on tables. Various shades of blue, blue-green, green-blue, and green.

Also bright mint, apple, and neon yellow green. One stone was sol-id colored, almost clear. Others ranged from spider webbed with brown, black, and red to golden.

"I have many sources." He spoke slow, deliberate, practiced through experience as though not to waste precious breath. "Tur-quoise depends on the whims of nature. Not a lot of it available. It is petrified water, you know. Magic."

Reba recalled reading in a college English Literature class of the sky as "a turquoise-vaulted dome." "Do you get some of the turquoise from around here?"

"Yes, a little, but it's almost gone. Mainly a labor of love."

"Do you mind us asking where?" Pearl ventured.

"Ah, that is an old family secret."

"Of course. But we aren't here for the turquoise. Not exactly, that is. But I would like to show you this." She pulled the velvet-lined case from her purse and tugged out the necklace.

"Where did you get that?" He tossed down the pipe and his face gnarled like an angry gnome.

"A relative died and I inherited it," Reba explained. "What do you know about it?"

He recoiled against a wall. "It came from my turquoise mine many years ago. There is one other almost like it, the same design, but with much less gold. One of my former wives has it. That's why I live alone. She and her sister fought over it constantly. Drove me over the cliff. My mistake was to marry them both."

"Where did you get it?"

"It has been in my family many years. There was a battle on Wor-thy Mountain. When it was over, my great-uncle found the necklace lying on the ground. Later, he found the mine. But it has always been haunted with spirits so no one cared about the turquoise until I start-ed to mine it. I leave the spirits alone, so they don't bother me." He breathed hard, out of breath.

Reba got concerned. "Please do sit down. We didn't mean to up-set you."

He sat on the floor, knees up. "I deserve some peace and quiet, time to prepare for the life to come. When I die, no trace of me will remain except through stories. My spirit will whoop with the wild horses, forever away from my wives."

Reba squatted too, trying to connect the best she could with him. "Worthy Mountain...is that where your mine is?"

He frowned. "I tell no one."

"Well, about wild horses...I'm looking for a woman named Hanna Jo Cahill. She's my mother."

He studied her face and screwed up his mouth. "Yes, she is in you. I am sorry she became sick."

"Are you talking about Wild Horse Hannah?"

"Yes. I accomplished my ambition. I outlasted her. But it has not made me happy." He tapped the stem of his pipe against his cheek. "She did not leave me to die in the flash flood."

Reba smiled. "Neither did your grandson Egan. He saved me from a flood too."

"Then we are even."

"Where is my mother now? Do you know?"

"I hope she is one with the wild horses. I refuse to ever be broke again. To run free as the wild horse is the great joy of any man. Or woman."

Fear shot trembles through her. Was she dead? Had she come this far but too late? There was no turning back. She had to know. "But where is she?"

Reba helped him as he tried to rise up. He limped across the orange carpet to a small roll-top desk. He pulled down the top and reached into a drawer. "A woman called me. Hanna gave them my name as a contact. Kind of like her next of kin." He peered at Reba. "Which I'm not, of course." He sorted through some scraps of paper. "Here it is. I wrote down the phone number." He handed it to her.

"Phone number for what?"

"Some clinic. An institution. That's where Hanna is. Or was. It's a Reno number."

"Can I use your phone?"

"It will be long distance."

"I'll pay you."

"Give me the necklace."

"You're kidding. Right?"

Blue Moon sucked on his pipe and eyed the necklace with longing. "Sure. I'm kidding.

Make your call."

Reba reached a mental health institute that refused to confirm the identity of any of its patients. But the woman who answered provided the address. "On McCarran Boulevard," she told Pearl. Why was her mother in such a place?

Blue Moon provided a partial answer. "She tried peyote for joint pain. I think only once. But it set her off real bad. She started seeing nightmares in the daytime. The police hauled her off."

"We'll go see if she's still there as soon as we can. First, we've got to check on a friend. He was on his way to the Worthy Mine."

Blue Moon's eyes squinted. "Why?"

"His mother used to run it. A long time ago. It's got a lot of memories for him."

"What's his name?"

"Seth Stroud. His mother was Eve Stroud."

Blue Moon bolted straight up. "She's one of the spirits. I'm coming with you." He rushed to the door and looked out. "Where's your horse?"

"Seth took it."

"I'll get another for your trailer and bring mine too."

Chapter Eighteen

"Where's the mine?" Champ asked.

Seth scooted back on Johnny Poe. "Why do you want to know?"

"My father often talked about it."

"What did he say?"

Without warning, Champ slammed his horse into Seth's. Seth heeled Johnny Poe ahead of Champ and careened away from a cliff's edge. Champ trailed close behind. The two riders pushed their steeds ahead and sprinted about a half-mile. They slowed as a battered Worthy Mine marker came into view.

Seth turned Johnny Poe around to face Champ who still charged toward him, breathing fire like a red dragon. Seth could almost smell the smoke and sulfur. He sweated a mood like he'd wreak havoc on anything that moved. All those years he bullied his family and fellow citizens into service he'd perfected a country gentleman's tyranny. It was as if he spent years preparing a strategy for when this day might come. Champ pulled up his horse at the last moment, spraying sand and dust on Seth and Johnny Poe.

Seth knew he must wait for the best timing for combat, so first some bait. "The necklace...you meant it for a bribe." A statement, not a question. "Where did you get it?"

Seth lowered himself from the saddle.

"It was mine. I got it from my father, fair and square. It was meant for Blair."

"Then you gave it to Maidie. Why?"

"You can't prove that. She stole it from me, when she worked as our nanny."

"Why did your father have it?"

Champ slid off his horse, avoiding Seth's eyes. "I don't know."

"It was my mother's." Seth prepared himself to firmly express what he'd suspected since discovering the necklace in Maidie's attic. "The one who murdered her took it."

A jolt hit Champ's face. His mouth wrenched out of joint like a man with a stroke. Seth realized Champ didn't know the connection to Eve Stroud's death. Champ straightened and tried to recover. "It wasn't me. I was just a toddler at the time."

"I know that."

"There could be more than one of them."

"Perhaps, but unlikely, and Mama's was missing. After your father had it made for her, I never saw her without it on. Except that day... Someone either stole it while she was alive or right after..."

The two men stalked each other, getting closer.

"Your sisters. They were there. Any one of them could have killed her."

"But that doesn't explain how your father got the necklace."

Champ stood stone silent, his eyes now fully focused and piercing Seth's. Moths and flies flew around them and the horses. Several scorpions skittered across the sand. "Are you sayin' my father's a murderer?"

Seth riveted his attention to the ground and uttered a quick prayer. *Jesus, open the truth.*

"He had no reason. No reason at all." He kicked sand with his boot. "Of course, we heard rumors over the years."

Seth kept quiet, tried not to move.

"We heard rumors your ma was a thief and an adulteress."

Seth slowly looked up, his heart heavy. But he didn't take the bait.

Champ jabbed again. "I guess your ma and my father were about even in the sin category."

Seth repeated his question. "Why did you give the necklace to Maidie?"

The move was so sudden Seth had no time to get out of the way. Champ lunged forward, threw him to the ground, and held him down. Seth surrendered to the hot sands and Champ's wrenching arm hold. He peered deep into Champ's eyes and discerned hate as hard as cold gunmetal. He turned his head aside to try to breathe, Champ's knee in his gut. He felt depleted, weakened by age, the long trip, and the harsh desert.

Champ grabbed a large rock. Seth prepared for the blow. He stiffened and waited, then relaxed. He braced for death. Loud whinnies, clomping hooves on hard rock, and the sounds of a bolting horse broke the silence. The rock swung down and crashed inches from Seth's head. As the weight of Champ's body lifted, Seth rolled and struggled onto his hands and knees. He opened his eyes and saw Champ rush after a retreating Johnny Poe, grabbing his reins. The other horse was gone. Johnny Poe bucked and pulled as the rancher fought for control.

Champ and the black stallion wound around each other in a sweaty struggle of wills. Seth struggled to rise, falling back to his knees. A flash in his mind of a defiant youth, strong enough to last the night outside his own house, humiliated, sprawled in the dirt, drove him to his feet. He called to the horse, talked him down, and Johnny Poe halted.

"I could have killed you," Champ said.

"I've had my time. I'm living on surplus. Sometimes I feel I've lived too long. I've seen and heard too much."

"Hey, wait a minute. It's not my fault what my father did. It's not my fault Maidie got herself pregnant. I'll bet she and Zeke got together and decided to blame it on me."

"In that case, there was no need..."

"No need to what?"

"To kill him."

"He fell off my roof. An accident. That wasn't my fault either."

Seth stared long and hard into his eyes. "When I saw Zeke on the ground and dead, he had oil on the bottom of his shoes, on the back of his pants and shirt. Like he slid off an oil slick. Why was there oil on that roof? The one you hired Zeke to fix? With Zeke dead, you could better hide something. Something you did. And blame it on him."

Champ glared back. "It was an accident. Besides, my father hired him, not me." A hint of dawning shined in Champ's face then vanished. "Look, old man, Road's End couldn't exist without my help, my backing. How about those fires and mill shutdowns? What did the church do? Pray? While you were like pansy planters on your knees, who got the people back on their feet? Me. I had the foresight and tenacity." He gleamed with satisfaction.

Now Seth peered deep in his eyes searching for a glint of his soul. "Why did you come here?"

"What?"

"Champ, why are you right here, right now, under this blazing sun near Goldfield and Worthy Mine?"

"Because I wanted to see what you were up to."

"So, you left your ranch work and family and all your town projects to come visit me here in the blasting heat of this desolate desert. You couldn't wait until after I got back to chat at the whittling bench about the good old days and hear of the adventures of my trip?"

"I have a duty to the town of Road's End to know what's going on with the citizens."

Seth grunted his skepticism. "Sounds pretty weak." He went for the jugular. "Do you believe in God?"

He ogled him in surprise. "What does He have to do with this?"

"I think you answered my question. And you're wrong about the reason you're here. I prayed you'd come."

Champ's face got so stony for so long, Seth feared he truly had gotten a stroke. Finally, Champ spit the words out. "Why would you possibly bother the Almighty with such a trivial request?"

"So we could settle things once and for all, in the place where it all started." Seth looked into the beady, black and deranged eyes and felt Champ's mind murdering him.

"What is it you want, old man?"

"The years have piled up and no justice has been dealt."

Champ rambled in a rant. The words scrambled together, indiscernible. His face twitched in desperation. He seemed beaten but didn't know how to back down. "What is, is," he concluded.

Seth felt dizzy, dehydrated, and spent, but also full of a strange, deep, absolute peace. *I trust you, Lord.*

Champ screamed, "Maidie was nuts and you know it. Can't believe a word she said."

"She wasn't crazy until evil was done to her." Seth's fists clenched tight at his side. "Maidie gave me much joy in my youth and in my old age. She cooked and cleaned for me and filled her house with sweet talk and wonderful music. She took care of me the best she could when her addled brain made her useless to everyone else."

Champ breathed hard. "I don't get it. There you are, a crippled old man with nothing to show for your life but a mess of carvings, a dead niece, and a rusty old Model T. Yet the whole town of Road's End reveres you. The whole world beats a path to you and listens to any drivel you spew from your mouth." He reared back as though to slam full force into Seth. "I could destroy you in a second, anytime I want." His chest ballooned with victory, sure he had gotten the last word in. "One of us has got to go."

"Pearl knows." Seth's voice rang strong and steady as though he rehearsed those two words all his life for this one fateful moment, even though the sun beat him dry and parched.

"Knows what?"

"About Zeke. About Maidie. About everything."

"How could she?"

"Maidie wrote about it in a journal. I gave it to Pearl. Maidie might have been crazy, but she was never dumb."

Champ struggled for breath, for control. "My father wasn't to blame for your mother's death. There's no proof of that. He led an exemplary life."

"Except for theft and adultery. Why not murder too?"

"Everything you claim about my father could be said of your mother."

"Yes, we are all the children of Eve in that kind of way. We have all sinned. But as far as I know, she never murdered anyone."

Champ pulled out a handkerchief and wiped his wet forehead. "I'm not proud of what happened."

"Is that an admission?"

"If you only knew the humiliations I have suffered."

"There's humiliation enough to go around for everyone. Life itself. Growing old. Failures. Dying. It comes to us all."

"I'm a good man who's done a few things wrong. Everyone has. Strike those out and I've done good with my life." His higher pitch added sharpness. Spaces of indrawn breaths revealed he knew he ventured into risky territory. "It was all Maidie's fault."

"If anyone was a saint, it was Maidie."

Champ had a wild look. He picked up another rock and Seth braced for the hit, but Champ tossed it away. "I don't need you on my conscience. You're not worth it."

"I'm thrilled to know you have one."

He whirled around and headed for Johnny Poe.

"Stop! Don't do it. Don't go near him," Seth warned.

Champ seemed more determined than ever. He tried to mount the agitated black horse. After a couple failed attempts and muttered curses, he finally sat in the saddle. The horse took a few steps forward, lunged his head to the ground, bucked high, and circled. Champ rode like a rodeo professional, laid back, arm swinging, anticipating the rebel horse's erratic moves.

Then Johnny Poe halted. He stepped in place as though in total submission. Champ beamed at Seth with a smirk. "I'll let Reba know I found her horse wandering around. By the time they find you, if they do, you'll be cooked." He pulled the water canteen out of the satchel and waved it at the old man as he spurred Johnny Poe toward the markers. The horse galloped south, his head high, his rider hanging on.

Champ reined the horse but he rushed past the markers and over the boulders. He made a high lunging leap over the embankment, but too far right and too near the cliff. Seth heard the results and could guess what it meant. After a loud rumble and tumble of rocks, horse and rider crashed somewhere below.

Seth waited in the electric aftermath, sun beating down like a celestial spotlight. He felt ancient. As decrepit as he'd ever felt. He knew he only had enough energy to go one direction or the other. He finally shuffled along the burning sand, his mouth raw and gritty, his tongue shriveled. He dragged his gaunt, swollen limbs toward Eve Stroud's former garden in the desert, now filled with millions of white, yellow, and pink pinhead wildflowers. In their midst a rattler's skeleton coils.

A few rocks marked the path of a former walkway. A pile of crumbled rocks near a hidden hole in the mountain. The sweating stopped. He felt dizzy. A cramp in his hamstring began as an annoyance and rose to an aching crescendo.

He dropped to the desert floor and heard high and tinny music. Like Indians chanting. Or angels singing. The music grew louder and much sweeter than the earthly warbling of wires. So, this was the end. He would die here. The silhouette of a hawk circled across his face.

Chapter Nineteen

Blue Moon led Pearl and Reba to the Worthy Mine hidden in a cleft of the mountain against the foot of a butte. Brush, weeds, multi-sized pebbles and sagebrush covered the holed out entrance. The ape's head rock jutted from the hill. Scruffy shadows like a day old beard where mountain and desert met further obstructed the view.

They saw Seth collapsed at the entrance.

Pearl slid off the horse and scooted over to him. "Is he dead?"

Blue Moon checked his pulse. "No, but he's very weak and dehydrated."

They revived him with wet cloths and sips of water. When he regained full consciousness, Blue Moon explained, "My family and I have been guarding this place for years. We were convinced some day family members would return."

Seth gulped some breaths and more water.

"We've got to get you medical help," Pearl said.

"No! Find Champ."

"Champ?" Reba looked around. "What are you talking about?"

"Over the cliff." He pointed up the hill. "But don't let Reba go."

A thought stabbed her. "Johnny Poe. Where's Johnny Poe?"

Tears puddled his eyes. "I'm so sorry. I tried to save him. Something went wrong. Terribly wrong."

Pearl stayed with Seth as Blue Moon and Reba tracked horse prints in the sand. They scoured the cliff edges for sight of horse or man. Blue Moon discovered Johnny Poe down the cliff, crashed against a boulder, body bent.

Reba screamed as she slid down, ripping against cactus and sharp, chipped rocks. "Nooo!" She cradled the lifeless head and wept. A few minutes later she felt an insistent tap on the shoulder.

"There's a man barely alive down there."

She pulled up from her awkward position, stomped a sleeping leg, and peered further below. Champ's body awkwardly straddled jagged rocks. She barely heard pitiful cries of "Help!" She wiped her tears and pried herself to alertness. "What should we do?"

"He's in a lot of pain with a number of injuries. As a rule, he shouldn't be moved in that condition, but we can't leave him here in the heat and elements. I have some Desert Juniper herbs for pain that might help. Meanwhile, I'll figure out a travois of some sort."

Reba's mouth so dry she couldn't swallow, she grappled to speak. "I can help. Not sure about Grandma and Seth."

When they returned to the mine entrance, Pearl and Seth were gone, but some timbers removed left space enough to squeeze through. "They must have gone inside." Blue Moon peered in and yelled.

Pearl called back and a lantern light appeared. "Here we are. I'm trying to keep Seth from going too far and getting lost."

Seth stumbled forward and while everyone sipped water, Blue Moon said, "We need to push against the wall."

"Where?" Reba asked.

Blue Moon grabbed a shovel from his saddlebag and banged against a hardened edifice inside the entrance. As the wall began to disintegrate, Pearl said, "Seth, are you sure you're ready for what you might find?"

"That's why I came. What is, is." He punched the wall with a rusty pick. Every hit renewed his vigor. The years peeled away from his face and whole body, as he penetrated a possible solving a nearly eighty-year cold case mystery. Then his pick clattered metal on metal.

"Is that a steel door?" Pearl felt around the dirt caked shelf.

Blue Moon and Seth cleared away the rest of the debris.

"You hit a door knocker," Reba said. Underneath wood she noticed a brass mail slot.

They pounded until layers of crusted dirt broke away.

Seth turned the doorknob. "Locked."

The thick blonde wood with white faded patina more than six feet tall fell back as they all shoved. Seth handed the lantern to Pearl and turned on a flashlight. So did Blue Moon.

They began to pass through one at a time. Reba bumped into a kind of workbench stored with pottery bowls and dishes. She scanned other objects. A couple rusty open buckets and some with lids, oil wick lamps, a pickaxe, and sledge hammer. The light also illuminated two Winchester rifles next to a barrow.

"It's a cave. Is this where your mother lived?" Reba asked Seth.

"I never saw this place before. She lived out front, outside the mine."

"Maybe to throw off suspicion," Blue Moon said. "Look at the rough stone rocky wall and the floor full of tailings with blue and green tints."

"What is it?" Reba inquired.

"Turquoise," Blue Moon said.

"Like the gem, you mean?"

"Of course. I knew this mine was here. My family has known for years. I've been picking out turquoise from the other route for decades."

"But I thought this was a gold mine," Reba said.

Seth held the cool rag against his forehead. "I've been ashamed to admit it, but Mama didn't have an actual mine. That is, I didn't know about the turquoise. Didn't realize that part of the necklace came from her mine. I did discover she took gold Uriah Runcie brought her from other mines and recycled it as her own. And though the law was against her, most folks in Goldfield thought highly of this practice. 'God put gold in the dirt and it belongs to him or her who digs it out,' they said. Those who disagreed felt they owned the mines outright and what was brought out of them."

A sweep of the lantern revealed something else. "It's also a grave."

"Yes, I knew that too," Blue Moon said. "I heard the spirits call."

Reba wanted to check on Seth and his response to this grisly unearthing but she couldn't help gawk as she counted four skeletons. One lay prone on top a cave shelf like a catacomb. Another kneeled and stretched over this one as though grieving the loss. Two others sat at the foot, heads lurched forward, guards to the end.

"It wasn't deadfall," Blue Moon commented.

Reba stepped closer. "This one has a hole in the head."

"Could be a bullet." Pearl turned to Seth. "Oh, I'm so sorry."

"It's okay. That very well could be my mother."

"But why is she here? Why couldn't you find her when you came back?"

"I don't know. Somebody had to move her."

Reba placed the lantern on a shelf. "What are these wooden molds and equipment for? And over here looks like a safe and vault, like the remains of an old bank." She tried to open it. Pearl and Blue Moon pulled too. Out spilled hundreds of twenty-dollar pieces.

"Don't get too excited," Seth warned. "I'm pretty sure it's counterfeit. Mama minted bogus five, ten, and twenty gold pieces and circulated them at big occasions like Tex Rickard boxing events. The more visitors from far away places, the better. Mama and Papa spoke harsh words about it. He told her to stop, but she persisted."

"Your mother ran quite an operation from this site," Pearl observed.

"She was a smart business woman. But, I'm sad to say, not an honest one. She took advantage of the seclusion of the Worthy Mine."

Reba eased by the safe and inched out of the cave room full of skeletons. She couldn't endure the sight anymore. Her changing impressions of Eve Stroud colored her former sympathy. No wonder bad things happened to this woman, who apparently was her great-great grandmother. She opened herself and her family to all sorts of vices and evils.

Yet, Seth still loved her through the years, part of the God-given bond of a child for a parent. She fought an immersion into gloom. A bond she'd never experienced. And now she'd even lost Johnny Poe. She tried to stifle a sob.

Seth covered his eyes as he exited the room. "I knew coming back might expose my mother's wrongdoing. That's one reason I never returned with Maidie. It would be too much for her." Family skeletons in a closet cave. "At least I know now where they are. And I can bury them. Next to Molly and Maidie."

Reba refused to leave Johnny Poe when they decided to take Champ away. And despite her fierce objections, Pearl insisted on staying too. Seth and Blue Moon fashioned a crude travois from rope and cactus tree branches for poles. After some Desert Juniper, Champ cursed them and the universe with every as-gentle-as-possible move to get him settled and down the hill.

Blue Moon promised to return with more shovels to bury Johnny Poe deep enough to keep him from carnivorous critters. "I'll get hold of emergency services, the first chance we get," Blue Moon said. "As soon as they arrive for your friend, we'll return."

"He's no friend of ours," Reba insisted. "You have a phone?"

"I'll send a smoke signal." She couldn't tell if he was kidding or not.

Seth picked one of Blue Moon's mares to ride. The mare with the S.P. saddlebag stayed with the women. Blue Moon pulled the travois.

Reba tried to feel empathy for Champ's howls of agony. But all she could think of was her beloved dead horse. Because of him. And Maidie's shame and despair. Because of him. She tried to drum up a smidgeon of something positive out of this horrific scene. "At least I didn't have to put Johnny Poe out of his misery. That would have unhinged me."

Reba and Pearl poured water from the canteens to drench bandanas for their necks and heads and slurped the rest. The last of the sun blocker cream skimmed over exposed skin, they hunched under the sparse shade of a Joshua tree. Large, erect, evergreen arms aloft and spread wide, waving like the biblical Joshua. They guarded Johnny Poe as the men disappeared from view.

Alone together here in the desert not far away from skeletons of her newly found family members, Reba blurted out, "I want to see her."

"Who? You mean, Hanna Jo?"

Reba nodded.

"It won't be easy."

"I still want to go."

Pearl moaned either from the insufferable heat or pangs from the exploits of her errant adopted daughter. "So do I."

Sweat streamed from Reba's pores and drenched her clothes. "I thought you didn't care for her anymore. You never talk about her."

"I love her very much, as much as I love you." Reba peered at the woman who looked every bit the age of her sixty-nine years. "The agreement Seth and I made...I could adopt Hanna Jo if I never revealed who her mother or her father was, which I assumed was Zeke."

Reba tried to absorb every respite of coolness from the stingy shade she could by sitting still and quiet. Yet she shook. A kind of nervous tremor. Grief over Johnny Poe. For Seth. Fury against Champ.

Pearl sighed. "I admit it. I wanted to keep the Cahill Ranch from the Runcies, for a number of reasons. All the run-ins over the years. So many situations. I also wanted to protect you. There's bad blood in that family. And I certainly did not want to spend family holidays with Champ if you married Tim." She hesitated. "Or Don."

Flashes of scenes of Thanksgiving and Christmas, just her and Grandma Pearl, came to mind. She added Grandpa Cole's vibrant presence years earlier. And on occasion, the addition of Vincent. A righteous anger vented through her veins again. "But was it right for you to make that decision for me?"

Pearl rose up, unsteady on her feet.

"Where are you going? You need to stay here."

"Over to the mare. I'll be right back." She staggered a bit and opened the saddlebag with the initials S.P. and slid out a leather wrapped, hand tooled journal. She hugged it to her chest and scooted down beside Reba. "I've been praying about the right time to show you this. For some bizarre reason, it seems the right time now." She shuffled through the pages and stretched it out to Reba. "This is Maidie's diary from decades ago. You can scan over the rest later. I marked the entries to read now."

Reba reached out for the journal with her sweaty hands. Another tremor. This time of apprehension. She tried hard to brace herself for the contents. What was so traumatic that caused Pearl to tremble? Was this what impelled her to drive from Road's End all the way to the desert? "Why don't you read it out loud to me?"

"Sorry. I can't."

Reba grasped the leather. She cradled it on her arms and gently tapped the page to keep it open. With a quick scan, she noticed a gap in time between the entries. Full of trepidation, she began to read.

May 15, 1944 ... I've been taking care of little Donnie Runcie while Blair works the mill office. His father Champ came by to pick him up today. I'd never seen him so roaring drunk before. He asked if Seth had returned home from the barbershop and I said No. He went off with Donnie then returned an hour later alone and with a rope. He grabbed me and tied my hands behind my back before I had mind enough to know what he was doing. He was real strong and I kept saying No, No, No. He said it was the pants and perfume I was wearing that made him do it.

October 12, 1944 ... I told Champ about what I feared and asked him what he was going to do about it. He told me Zeke did it. I told him Zeke never did any such thing and never would.

November 22, 1944 ... It is the day before Thanksgiving and Zeke fell off the Runcie roof. I can't stop crying. I want to stay in my room and never come out.

February 23, 1945 ... A baby boy was born first and real quiet. Could not get him to breathe or cry. A baby girl arrived soon after and she bawled and bawled no matter what I did, a high piercing wail, and I cried hard too until Seth took her away. Finally I got some sleep. I woke up when Champ came to my room and grabbed the good little boy who never made a sound. I yelled for him to bring him back but he stole my baby, the quiet one. I wish he could take the awful pounding in my head away too. And bring back my Zeke.

A tense, awkward silence burned the seconds, more scorched than the desert sun. In the distance storm clouds clashed. Humidity threatened to smother them. Then a smatter of sizzling rain. Reba willed her glazed eyes to focus, to read the entries again, more slowly, prodding the words to make sense. What did this have to do with her? Somehow she knew it did, but her mind rebelled. She tried to connect the dots and they scrambled into noisy static.

"Why did Champ come here?" she finally said.

"Guilt. He determined his and his father's sins never be exposed. And I wonder…"

"Wonder what?"

"If Zeke's fall had anything to do with Champ attempting to hide what he'd done. With Zeke alive, he could profess his innocence for Maidie's pregnancy. With him dead, others would presume…"

What was Pearl saying? What did the journal reveal? She couldn't think clear. Then the truth slammed her. *Champ raped Maidie.* Her mother was the result of that rape. And a baby boy. Champ's my… grandfather. That makes Don…an uncle. And Tim my first cousin. She tried to speak. "That morning…after Maidie's funeral…I saw Champ at a tombstone…near Coyote Canyon. It was marked David Daniel, February 23, 1945."

"So that's what he did with the twin." Pearl pressed her lips together and clutched her hands against them.

"Why be so sentimental toward the lost son and so hard against us?"

"I'm pretty sure he doesn't know the connection. And most every man has some spark of humanity. Even evildoers."

"Did he hire the Dalton gang to try to stop Seth from coming here? Did they also blow up Seth's house? And what about the vandalism of ours too? None of it makes any sense."

"It doesn't have to. Tormented men do crazy things. Plus the fact some of that gang adlibbed along the way. And Champ has not been known for having a whole lot of logic in his actions."

They waded through their thoughts until Blue Moon and Seth returned with four wheelers and two men. When they brought out the large shovels, Reba shuddered with fresh sobs. *Lord, this is too much.* She had to turn away. Pearl stood silently with her as her shoulders shook. They removed saddle, blanket, harness and finally buried Johnny Poe. Reba managed a few words about her horse and then composed herself after the makeshift funeral.

They maneuvered the wall and door back in place to protect the skeletons from predators.

Seth distributed to each of them a handful of counterfeit gold coins. "I'll ask Cal Tiggers to study the bones. We also need to bring soil and plant samples from around the scene. Although it may not make much difference, whatever he finds. But I need to know for sure these are my family members. Then the past is past."

"What about justice?" Reba wondered aloud.

Seth leaned against her. "All will be rectified some day by the One whose judgment is just and final."

"And full of mercy," Pearl added.

Reba's head throbbed. "But it's obvious someone moved Eve's body after Seth found her. And it's possible he or she or they coaxed the girls into that room somehow or they ran in to be with her and refused to come out and then were locked in."

"It's too horrible to consider," Pearl replied.

"Do you think Champ suspected any of this?"

"That would explain why he wanted to hide it all. Perhaps he heard his father say something."

His father. My great-grandfather. The one who probably murdered Seth's mother. *Who was my...* Reba had to shut her mind down.

🐎 🐎 🐎 🐎

After the return to Goldfield, they found out Champ had been life-flighted by helicopter to Tonopah and then to Spokane, Washington where specialists in spinal injuries could treat him.

"Whatever his condition, I think he has some charges to face," Jace said.

"His condition is part of the sentencing," Pearl added.

Jace informed his mother of the skeletons at the mine and the need to transport them to a coroner, a friend of Cal Tigger's.

"We'll wait with you for the results, then follow you back to Road's End," Pearl told Seth.

Seth looked Reba straight in the eyes. "I'm not leaving," he announced.

Pearl and Reba stood dumbfounded. Questions and objections clouded their faces.

"The house we lived in here is for sale for a not bad price and I'm going to buy it. I need to stay down here a while and finish taking care of Maidie. And Mama. And my sisters."

They tried to protest. What more could he do? But he insisted.

"There are still questions in my mind I need to sort out. Right here. I want to spend more time at the mine, if the McKanes will allow, and dig for answers around town."

"We'll miss you terribly. You know that, don't you?" Reba replied.

"I'll miss you too. I have very little family left alive. But I knew from the beginning this would likely be a one-way ticket."

Reba again started to argue with him, but he cut her off. "Tell the guys at the whittling bench goodbye for me. And you can use the garage and apartment and garden however you want. Or sell them. They really belong to you now anyway. And to Hanna Jo."

"We're going to go find her." Reba felt fully confident of that.

"I believe you will. Give her a kiss for me." Seth hugged Pearl as though he wouldn't let go.

"Seth…" Reba began. The words froze in her throat.

Seth hugged her tight and whispered, "Thank you. Thank you for making this final journey with me."

The old man seemed settled, at peace, resigned to his fate for his last days.

Before Pearl and Reba left Goldfield they said farewell to Tucker and his family who headed back to Road's End before them.

"Don't spend too much time in the casinos," Reba cautioned.

"Not to worry. Been there, done that." Tucker waved and scooted into the driver's seat of the orange Toyota wagon. Tucker beamed. So did Ida.

Thank you, Lord.

Ida and the boys pulled on their ice bandanas as they drove away.

Reba and Pearl paused at the Goldfield Cemetery in front of five plain white temporary cross markers with no names next to the Molly Stroud Fortress' flat gravestone. One each for Eve, Lucina, Radene, Valmy. And Maidie. White decorative rock scattered through a pile of broken pieces of purple and turquoise glass around them.

Jace drove over to them. Abel showed off gold flakes he panned and proudly displayed a mustang adoption kit. "It includes registration card, a list of horses, a bumper sticker, a certificate, and they'll mail me letters."

Reba couldn't help giving hugs and kisses for them both on their cheeks. It seemed fitting and proper after the adventures they'd shared. She wasn't sure if she wanted more from Jace or not. Too much in her life to assimilate right now.

"I'm so sorry about Johnny Poe," Jace whispered in Reba's ear. "I know there will never be another horse like him for you."

His words brought more comfort than she believed possible. But she couldn't express it. Not at that moment. She simply nodded instead.

Irving piled out of the Volvo from the back seat. "Hey, where's my hug?"

Reba and Pearl stretched their arms in tandem to reach around the huge young man. "Jace promised to take me all the way to Vegas. I think that's where I belong."

"Our prayers will be with you," Pearl said.

"See you in Road's End," Jace continued. "Eventually. We'll visit with mother first. Then we're going home by way of Vegas and Casa Tierra. Abel and I have family to see too." He fist bumped Irving.

"Thanks for interceding for Seth about the Worthy Mine situation."

"Yeah. Like divine providence." He gave her a wink.

They waved until the Volvo was out of sight.

When they reached Desert City Mental Health Institution near Reno, Reba put on the squash blossom necklace at Pearl's insistence. "Maybe it will jog something for Hanna Jo. I don't know for sure. But then, we have no idea what kind of condition she'll be in."

Reba felt the cool, smooth stones. "I hope it doesn't make it worse for her."

The institution's main entrance was way in the back. A narrow, cobbled path led to the front doors. Men of all ages played basketball in a fully fenced cement court. Dreary brick outside walls had high window slots.

Inside, linoleum floors shined. Office girls smiled while filing papers in long, endless drawers.

A woman with Dr. Joyce Castleberry nametag approached them. Not a big woman, her over-sized movements emphasized her intenseness and importance. "The prosecuting attorney represented the state. Hanna Jo was appointed a defense attorney. Neither of them had contact with her before the trial. But they allowed an unusual procedure: voluntary commitment. If she ever tried to leave before the designated time, they'd change the order to involuntary commitment. She thought it would look better on her record."

Dr. Castleberry introduced them to Thelma, a black woman with hair dyed in gold tones and tied in long cornrows who worked at the institution. "Hanna Jo called in the middle of the night and said the police were taking her here. She was my next-door neighbor. I was allowed into the restricted hearing. They seemed to treat her fair enough, but she felt like they were sending her to prison." She looked around. "Not too far from it. You'll see."

Reba felt a throb and catch in her heart as they followed Thelma down a corridor. Cold strips from ceiling fluorescent bulbs lighted the room and tiles on the floor alternated dark green, light green as her boot heels clomped down the hall that reeked of some sort of acrid chemical. Blank faces of slumped figures in a misfit of castaway chairs turned their way. Reba did a quick study on each of them, prying for recognition of her mother.

She held onto a doorjamb, trying to gain comfort from the cold metal, and leaned forward into what appeared to be the TV room.

Sadness and grief haunted this place, but Reba tried to gather a warm bundle in her heart.

She fixated on someone in a recliner. The hair's not right. Too straight and stringy. Not red enough. The eyes too dull. The face too full and bloated. This can't be Hanna Jo. "Mom?" Reba said.

The woman didn't move.

"Hello, Mom. I'm Reba. Reba Mae. Your daughter." What name did she call me? She couldn't remember. Should she talk louder?

The woman lifted her head, hair flat, frayed, faded. Glazed eyes seemed to try to pierce through a fog. For a moment, a glint of recognition, the length of a camera flash. Then the shutter closed.

Pearl touched Reba's arm. "We can come again. Perhaps in time..."

Reba shook her head and sat down at the edge of the recliner. An air conditioner hummed. A door down the hall slammed. A gentle air draft made her shiver. She looked around the room.

A woman rocked back and forth in a straight back chair eating from a bag of cheesy puffs.

Another woman fussed at a man who switched TV channels back and forth from a children's program to a soap opera. She smiled when she caught Reba's eye. "Howard is our organizer of events."

Howard had his legs crossed, one swinging like a pendulum, his eyes consumed with the screen. His mouth jerked when the woman beside him tapped his shoulder. "See our rooms, then you'll know it's not a party in here." His left arm limped to the side. "Take her in your car and let her see the ducks and flowers. All we see in here is cement." Then he turned the volume up.

Pearl nudged Hanna Jo and motioned toward the hallway. She shook her head.

Howard stood up and jaunted to the bathroom. Another man bee-lined to the TV when the bathroom door closed and messed up the channels.

"He always does that this time every day." Howard's couch companion squinted at the clock.

Howard returned and glared at the man. "Hey, black beard, who told you to live?"

"He's okay," the woman said. "He's just pretend. He's not real."

A deep male voice intoned over the intercom: "Third and fourth floors meet at the door for smoking and outside break."

Hanna Jo got up, held Pearl's arm, and walked to the hall with Reba behind. An attendant led them to a private room.

Hanna Jo collapsed into a chair. Her hands and face shook. Her voice slurred. "My roommate's always sleeping. That's all she ever does, but she's real nice. Her name is Betty Nielson. I call her Bumper." She opened her eyes and stared hard at Reba and at the necklace. "That's mine." She reached out to grab it.

Reba held her hand as she clutched it. "You recognize it?"

"Maidie. She gave it to me."

Reba looked at Pearl. "But Maidie gave it to me too. Did you give it back?"

She pulled away her arm and sat back. "Yes, I did. My father gave it to her."

Reba stood very still. She sensed another possible unmasking or affirmation. She didn't try to look at Pearl. "Your father? You mean, Cole Cahill?"

She smiled and rocked back and forth. "A very nice man. Much nicer than my father."

Reba grasped at another detour. "You mean Zeke? Zeke Owens?"

"Zeke? No, that's not him. They call him Champ. After the name of an airplane. When am I going to get out of here?"

So she knew. *But how?*

Pearl tried to explain to Hanna Jo. "The doctor told us you're on seven day observation. After that, they prescribe a program and set a tentative release date, if you cooperate and show signs of improvement."

Reba noticed a Band-Aid on Hanna Jo's wrist. She gently pulled it back to reveal splotches of deep scratches and dark red stains. "What is this?"

Hanna Jo attempted a laugh. "I stole some toothpicks at the courthouse kitchen."

Reba's stomach churned. No signs of improvement there.

Hanna stabbed Reba with her finger. "Your daddy. How is he doing?"

My daddy? The one from a host of lovers she couldn't identify?

She tried to think of a calm, non-combative response. "I don't know. I never met him. Did I?"

She leaned forward, a wisp of conspiracy in her eye. "Oh, yes. Michael says you know him. He lives right there in Road's End. His name is Don. Don Runcie. Isn't that a kick?" All hint of sparkle faded. Her lids half-closed. She rubbed the Band-Aid on her wrist. "Don't you see? That's why I had to run away. I didn't know about Maidie and Champ and all of it until after I was already pregnant. Don't you see?" Her eyes begged for understanding.

The convulsion of shock paralyzed Reba. She forced herself to overcome, to find control. She leaned toward Pearl. "Did you know that too?" She parsed and stomped on each word in a forced whisper.

Pearl shook her head. "No, I didn't. But I should have guessed. She must have gone right to Maidie's after I talked with her that day she turned eighteen." She opened her arms wide and reached out to Hanna Jo. "Oh, my sweet girl. May God heal you of all you've endured. May he restore you."

Hanna Jo's head lifted, her own arms outstretched. Then they fell and her eye lens shuttered closed again. She stared past them, as though into another world. Pearl held her until an attendant ushered them out.

When they left, Reba asked the attendant about the toothpick incident.

"An oversight. We're so sorry. Whatever you see or hear from the patients, you can be sure that we are careful. We offer everything we've got in order to give them the best care. In a place like this, paranoia can be a rational coping mechanism. What they believe is true usually is not."

Reba pondered those last words as they left Desert City Mental Health Institution. Perhaps what Hanna Jo revealed in a seeming lucid moment might not be fact. But why would she say such a thing? Reba sighed in total exhaustion, weary of the stream of revelations about her family. That infected her. This last one Hanna Jo alluded to could be the worst of all.

Pearl cut through her thoughts. "Don't you see how much God has been protecting you through the years?"

All the way home to Road's End, Reba conversed with the God who seemed to not protect her mother and grandmother. And great-great Grandma Eve.

Chapter Twenty

The morning after, Reba straightened and cleaned the living room from an evening of dinner and games with Pearl and Vincent, Michael and Nina. And Reba who tried not to feel like a fifth wheel. She tossed in a box a handful of random puzzle pieces from a collage of wild horses. Her mind wandered in an array of bits and pieces. She thought about runaway mothers, abandoned kids, and warped childhoods. And Don. Would she ever tell Don...or Tim... or Champ about their true relationship? Certainly not right away. Maybe never. She trembled to think of it. She meant to avoid Don as much as she could. But that couldn't last forever without some sort of explanation.

Meanwhile, Champ still recovered in the Spokane hospital. No one knew whether his spinal injuries were permanent or not. For now, he would be wheelchair bound. And the ranch was not the same without Johnny Poe. And Michael and Vincent showed interest in staying on to work the ranch, at least for now.

Reba hung the sea painting on her bedroom wall and studied it so long she thought she could hear the waves pound the beach and smell the salty air. She tossed the contents of a backpack on her bed and the wooden warrior Seth carved tumbled out.

What was that all about? *I'm no warrior. Far from it.*

Reba stole out of the house and started hiking with a backpack stuffed with water and trail snacks she'd learned to carry in the desert. She didn't know where she was headed, but she had to get away. She'd tramp clear to the ocean or the Canadian border, if she had to. Maybe meet up with Thomas and Elliot, if they still rode the Nez Perce trail.

She tried to sort out the reasons for her malaise. So many doors slammed tight against her. Working the ranch. Living in Road's End. Everything upside down. She missed Seth. And Ginny. And especially Johnny Poe.

A jag of sobs erupted. Words she'd heard all her life teased and tormented her. Have faith. Don't give up. In every storm there's a rainbow. Pastor Keirsey preached a sermon one time on the theme that every time God closed a door, He opened a window. In her case, the tiniest slit would be a huge improvement. Maybe she should hide in the cellar again as she did as a child and never come out. She quivered a sigh. Like Maidie did. Like her mother too.

Maidie and Hanna Joe aligned with her genes, her very being. They belonged to her.

In her random wandering around the corral and across the pasture, she circled back near the barn, a makeshift church on Sundays, and her own personal sanctuary. She peered in. On one side, hay to the rafters. A small tractor parked near a lift and pitchforks. She scanned the building and noticed a shining sliver of light in the corner. She looked up at the loft, wide open, catching some rays.

She entered the barn and scanned the multi-purpose building, sometimes set apart as sacred, other times full of cows and calves and rank odors. She knelt, knees hard pressed on the portable platform and poured out her soul. "What now, Lord? Where do I go from here? Am I destined to be another Maidie? Or a Hanna Jo? What hope can I dare have for my own future?"

Reba Mae, trust me.

She stiffened and wheeled around. "Who said that?" The barn bristled with a presence, but she saw no one. Again she heard, but this time deep and centered within. *Trust me.*

She peered at the rafters, around the stalls, and across the hay bales. *Is God speaking to me?*

She knelt down again, expectant, alert. She waited for another message. All she heard was the buzz of a horse fly, the moos of a cow. She sensed a waiting. Like it was her turn. The tears flowed. "It's one big huge mess. I'm sure you know that." She swallowed and pulled some tissue from her backpack.

After dabbing her eyes and nose, she heaved her chest. "Okay, Lord, I will try to trust you."

She quivered at the gravity of those simple words. She shook all over as a fresh resolve cratered inside her soul. The light from the loft scattered over her. Emotionally spent, she crept up the ladder, across the floor, and crouched at the ledge.

She sat down in the hay loft opening, her legs dangled. Now what?

She gazed out on her fairy tale of a secure world of spreading pastures, scattered trees, lounging red cows, and barbed wire fences. She caught a glimpse of Michael running a horse in one of the corrals, blonde Nina perched on a fence rail cheering him on. She scanned the full panorama of Cahill Ranch land. First, the present. Then her past. Now her future. Her presumed future, that is.

She thought of Road's End. A straggle of scattered dwellings. The narrow-gauge railway line that once wound its way up to the place. The quirky people like none other, each who settled here for reasons all their own. She felt a bit like the hero Will Kane in High Noon who rode back to town to face down the brutes. Except she left town to find and confront them, only to realize they were part of her home.

At least Champ was. Crippled, crankier than ever, and still very much in control as he shouted orders from his hospital bed. And the worst of it, her grandfather. Though he had no idea. Yet.

Maybe someday she would ride out again to the gravestone marked David Daniel and place purple flowers on it. For Maidie's sake. And Hanna Jo's.

She reached for her backpack and pulled out the wooden warrior Seth carved for her. A regal woman ready to do battle. Equipped to win wars. Certainly not her. She didn't even know who she was anymore. Or who she could become.

She brooded on the growing reality she could no longer live in Road's End. Or stay on the ranch. How could she ever overcome the shame of the choices made by people in her past? She hummed a melancholy tune and began a story, much like her Grandpa Cole used to when she was a child. "Do you see that Aspen tree? Did I ever tell you how Aspen got its name? Well, there was a hardened old miner in Colorado named Jedediah…Jedediah Aspen…" She laughed and cried sentimental tears as she recalled simpler, more innocent times.

She tossed down the warrior, blew her nose, wiped her face, and started a new story. "Do you see that girl on the ranch in Road's End? The redhead named Reba Mae? She found it hard to believe in herself and commit to love. She didn't know why until she realized her mother never wanted her and her father never knew her."

Her father. Don. *Of all choices, why Don?* She laughed. "At least I know who he is."

A sound rustled out on the landscape before her. A foggy vision swirled out on the walkway between the house and barn. She blinked hard and looked again. A black horse cantered in the distance, head high, long mane flying, head on right.

Her heart leaped. Johnny Poe?

No. Johnny Poe is gone. However, isn't this the time for the cowboy to ride in, to save her, to sweep her off her feet, so they can ride the wild wind together across the wide prairie? That's how it happens in the movies.

She thought about Soren all the rest of the way home when they missed him in between Vegas trips. After their stop in New Meadows. She kept his saddlebag rather than drop it on his doorstep.

Would Jace come to her rescue?

"They're still in California having a grand time on the beach," Ginny reported in a phone call a few days ago.

Or perhaps an eligible new stranger in town?

Then she recognized the rider.

She swallowed her disappointment as Pearl stopped her blazed black quarter horse underneath the loft. "I brought your mail."

Reba picked up the warrior, tucked it back in her pack, slid the loft door across and bolted it. She scooted down the steps from her perch, and strolled out of the barn. Pearl handed her two letters and a package. One of the letters and package from Ginny. The other from Hanna Jo.

She ripped into Ginny's letter first. She chatted with her grandma about Ginny's adventures with the Hocking family and the family's preparations for her grandpa's big seventy-fifth birthday bash. However, she left out the part she invited Reba again to come visit and the offer to be her administrative assistant. "It's nice to get a follow-up on the Hockings," Reba mentioned. "I wonder how Thomas and Elliot are doing on their trek?"

"Reine Laws told Vincent at the post office a dozen other tribal folks have joined them. Reine's going to spend a few days with them, with some other family members too. After they reach the Bear Paw Mountains and commemorate the surrender, there's a group who will pick them up and take them all the way back to Wallowa Lake in eastern Oregon, where the whole Nez Perce battle story began. There's a pow wow planned for when they arrive."

"Seth's journey sparked so many stories and events. I sure hope Thomas and Elliot have had some great bonding experiences together."

She ripped open the package. A stack of glossy photos from the trip. She flipped through them. Ginny had a gift for candids of the people. Nice framing of landscapes and wildlife. Fun captions on the backs. A montage of memories. And an extra special treasure: some of Johnny Poe too.

She handed the pictures to Pearl and opened the other letter. Her mother's note, the second she'd ever received, as pithy as the first one.

Reba: I can leave now. Come get me please. Love, Mom

She read the words over and over to herself, then aloud to her grandmother. Pearl didn't hesitate. "Well, there it is. Couldn't be clearer. Your next summons."

She slipped an arm around Pearl and flashed the note in front of her. "There's more. There's a P.S. on the bottom. She writes, *My Mom too.*"

Pearl took the paper, scanned it several times and shut her eyes as she held it against her chest. Reba felt the tremor between them. "Well, Grandma, are you up to another trip back to Reno? A quicker one this time. You drive. I'll watch out for the bad guys."

And the good ones too.

~~ the end ~~

About the Author

Born in Visalia, California, Janet Chester Bly received her Bachelor of Science degree from Lewis-Clark State College in Literature & Languages and Fine & Performing Arts. She is a city girl with a country heart who doesn't corral horses, wrangle cows, or even mow her own lawn. "I'm not a womba woman," she says. But she followed her late husband, award-winning western author Stephen Bly, to the country to write books and minister to a small village church. When she lost him, she stayed. In the small town of Winchester, Idaho, she manages Bly Books online and through the mail. She also rakes lots of Ponderosa pine needles and cones and survives the long winters, one snowstorm at a time.

Check out her blog for more info on the writing of this story: http://www.blybooks.com/blog/

Reading Group Discussion Questions

1. Have you ever owned, ridden in, or driven a Model T? What's the most unusual or entertaining mode of transportation you've used for a trip?

2. Which character in the story did you relate to most? And least?

3. Provide a physical and personality description of at least one character of your choice. Which character did you relate to most and why?

4. What is your favorite clothing style? Describe the differences between Reba and Ginny. Why do you think their friendship works? Pick out three things opposite between you and a friend? Do you appreciate most how your friend is like you or opposite of you?

5. What part of fictional Road's End reminds you of a real town you've lived in or visited? What did you like or dislike about the small town lifestyle?

6. Do you think Reba has realistic ideals about a possible future mate? What does she neglect? What would you suggest to adjust her goals for romance?

7. Seth Stroud determined to go on his journey and to drive himself in his Model T, despite his age and the limits of the antique car. What risks was he taking? Why do you think it was so important to him, in spite of it all? What did he hope to accomplish? To make right? What about his odyssey inspires you?

8. What is the most memorable road trip you have ever taken? Why did you go? What were the highlights? Any life lessons learned?

9. How did each of the caravan travelers aid in bringing some sort of insight, inspiration, or comfort to the others on the journey?

10. Both Seth and Reba hear God's audible voice. Why might they find it hard to trust God? When do you find it hard to trust Him? Or other people? How come? Have you ever heard God speak? If so, where were you and what did he say? What was your response?

11. Seth Stroud and Pearl Cahill allude to doing God's will in very different situations. What was the outcome? Have you ever sensed doing what God wants, even when it seemed strange to other people? What was the result?

12. Reba's mother and grandmother struggled with mental issues and she worries those tendencies may be passed on to her. What has been your knowledge of mental illness? Do you relate in any way to Reba's concerns? What would you suggest Reba do?

13. What do you think the flash flood scene in the desert might symbolize for Reba? What image came to your mind in the appearance of Egan Toms?

14. Was it wrong for Seth and Pearl to keep secrets from Reba? Why or why not? When have you kept a secret from someone? What was your motive? Do you need to talk about it with God?

15. In what way do you relate to Reba's conflicted feelings about her mom? What word best describes Reba? Lonely? Desperate? Confused? Or something else? What word best describes you as you are right now?

16. Reba faces dismay and devastation as her family lineage unfolds. How would you have handled such revelations yourself? If you were her close friend, what advice would you give Reba about her relationship with the Runcies? With Grandma Pearl? With her mother Hanna Jo? About continuing to live in Road's End?

17. What character in the story adds the most value to Reba's life? In what way? Who has brought her the most harm?

18. The turquoise and gold squash blossom necklace was a kind of inheritance for Reba. Do you think it proved to be a blessing or curse for her? What would you have done with such a gift?

19. How many 'touches of romance' did you find in this story? Which one did you consider most appealing?

20. Which characters best exemplify the themes: a) deceit and lies lead to brokenness, b) Confession and truth lead to healing?

21. In what part of the story did Reba act as the warrior Seth's carving foreshadowed? Were there any other warriors in the story? Explain.

22. Did you recognize any moments of spiritual warfare in this story? Who was involved and how did they handle it? Have you ever had to deal with spiritual warfare yourself? What did you do about it?

23. Would you have changed the ending? If so, how? And why?

24. What was the strongest message take-away for you in this story?

Notes

Notes

If You Enjoyed This Story...

Tweet about it. Share on Facebook or Goodreads or any of your social media go-to spots.

You're invited to provide a review on your favorite online bookstore site...such as Amazon, Barnes & Noble, or your personal blog. If you do, let Janet know and she'll make a note or link on one of her social medias or blogs. Email her at janet@blybooks.com ...

If you liked this story, you will also appreciate The Horse Dreams Series: *Memories of a Dirt Road Town*, *The Mustang Breaker*, and *Wish I'd Known You Tears Ago*. You can find these books here: http://www.blybooks.com/product_category/contemporary-fiction/

Other Bly Books novels as well as nonfiction for adults and kids available at the online bookstore here: http://www.blybooks.com/

Or access website at QR Code:

Three books are planned for this series with release of Book #2 of the Trails of Reba Cahill sometime Fall 2015. Sign up for the Almost Monthly Bly Books Newsletter for details, as well as to learn of other new Bly Books releases scheduled in the coming months, free chapters, giveaways, and devotionals by both Stephen Bly and Janet. Subscribe for the newsletter at:
http://www.blybooks.com/contact/stephen-bly-books-newsletter/ or access this QR Code:

 Receive monthly devotionals and book updates from authors

Stephen Bly & Janet Chester Bly

You may contact Janet Chester Bly at:

Bly Books
P.O. Box 157
Winchester, ID 83555
janet@blybooks.com

Other Bly books online sites:

Free stuff, blog & store: http://BlyBooks.com

On A Western Trail Blog: http://BlyBooks.blogspot.com

Kindle Bly Books: http://amzn.to/VFM4r0

Ebooks & Estories: http://bit.ly/TD9wqo

Audio Books: http://www.blybooks.com/audio-book/

Personal Facebook pages: https://www.facebook.com/janetchesterbly or https://www.facebook.com/stephenbly

'Like' Bly Books: https://www.facebook.com/BlyBooks

Twitter: @blybooks Janet Chester Bly

Pinterest: http://www.pinterest.com/janetcbly/

Goodreads: https://www.goodreads.com/author/show/269265.Janet_Chester_Bly

LinkedIn: www.linkedin.com/pub/janet-chester-bly/51/3a2/163/

37187018R00182

Made in the USA
Charleston, SC
30 December 2014